GW00580090

W.I.S.H.

Revelations

W.I.S.H.
Revelations

By

Kayla Grosse

the
hodge podge house
publishers

Published by The Hodge Podge House Publishers, LLC
Los Angeles, CA

Printed in the United States of America.

ISBN: 978-0-9972864-4-1 (hardcover)
ISBN: 978-0-9972864-5-8 (paperback)
ISBN: 978-0-9972864-6-5 (ebook)
Library of Congress Control Number: 2019917399

First U.S. Edition: November 2019
First International Edition: November 2019

For the people who believe in me
For the people who fight for me
You make me believe in magic
I love you

CHAPTER 1

I never believed the—*I woke up on the wrong side of the bed*—theory until I turned 22.

On that particular birthday, I realized I no longer had any milestones to attain. After 21, you're just on your way to death as far as I'm concerned. Morbid I know, but the one thing I had to look forward to now was the day I started menopause. There are many negatives to that as well, like your lady parts drying up like the Sahara Desert, sporadic hot flashes and night sweats. Yep—fun times lay ahead in my future.

"Sophia?" a low and sweet voice calls out. "Can you shelve these books for me?"

I shake off my pessimistic musings and I look up at my 75-year-old boss, Mary, with the best fake smile I can muster. She grins back at me, the corners of her wrinkled mouth revealing her yellowing teeth, before she tucks her short grey hair behind her ears. She waits patiently as I fight the urge to groan. It's been one of the longest days of my life. I'm beginning to think I'll never get home. All I want to do is curl up on my porch swing with a good book, a glass of cheap wine, and my Husky, Laker, by my side. That sounds like heaven.

"Sure, Mary," I answer back as warmly as I can. "Non-fiction?"

"Yes. Thank you, dear!"

I stand up from my place at the front desk and resign myself to the fact I'll be stuck here for a few more hours. Mary gives me a look like she knows what I'm thinking as I take the ancient cart from her and make my way through the shelves. When I reach rows X-Y I let out a breath and temper my annoyance. One-by-one I slowly start shelving the books.

My thoughts drift and I begin to wonder how my life became this ho-hum and boring. I certainly never pictured myself as a 24-year-old library assistant. Not that the job was terrible, but it was a reminder of how my day-to-day was almost always the exact same. Wake-up, work, go home, read, sleep, repeat. However, I was jarred this morning because my usual pattern was thrown off.

From the moment my eyes opened I was in a bad mood. My attitude was so awful I swear my dog even rolled his eyes at me. When I discovered I slept through my alarm, all I could do was feed Laker and fly out the door. I didn't even have time to stop and get my regular morning coffee, which definitely didn't help to improve my sour mood.

To make matters worse, I realized I didn't have my iPod, leaving me without music to distract me from the monotony. The final nail in the coffin was finding out I forgot my lunch. I was running low on cash already, and I didn't want to ask Mary to share her meager meal with me. My car recently needed a new starter, putting me out a good $400.00. The last thing I wanted to do was buy lunch after that massive expense.

I hoped as the day went on that my mood would lift. But the library ended up being full of complaining customers and obnoxious high school kids who had nothing better to do than annoy the crap out of me. Apparently, they don't teach children how to read the Dewey Decimal System anymore, making my life unnecessarily difficult. One kid even asked me if we had kindle books instead of *annoying paper* books. I fear for the future of this world on a daily basis at my job.

Needless to say, I can't wait for this day to be over and done with.

As I continue to shelve, I come across a book called,

You Have Nothing to Lose. Damn self-help books and their stupid ideas about dreams and goals. I used to have those once upon a time. Being in the real world for a couple of years makes you think differently. After I moved back to my hometown, Iron Lake, I feared I'd become bitter about life. My mom, Marilyn, continuously asks me why I came back—but that is a difficult question for me to answer.

Maybe I simply missed the quaint way of life—the ease of everything. Other times I think it's because after I graduated, I had no direction or passion for anything in particular. I didn't want to go to graduate school—nor did I have the money—meaning I didn't have many options with only an undergrad degree in women's studies. I let go of a breath, my shoulders tense. *I'm lying to myself.*

I'd like to think those are the reasons I returned, but deep down I don't understand it. I had a gut feeling. One that I had no idea what to make of. It was as if I *had to* come home. As if my inner compass was pulling me back or something.

A shiver runs up my spine and I shake it off.

"Screw you, non-fiction X through Y," I say under my breath. I glare at the cart and wish the books to go away. I swear my eyes are going to burn a hole in the dreaded

4

thing. The faster they're shelved, the faster I can leave.

I think again about my porch swing, the view overlooking the lake and the emerald leaves of the trees swaying in the sweetness of the night breeze. One of the best things about Wisconsin in the early summer is the mosquitoes have yet to aggressively hatch, and it isn't dreadfully humid yet. The middle of the summer though, it is an entirely different story. I sigh dramatically. If only I can go and enjoy this perfect night.

I reach blindly to get another book. When I grab at air several times, I laugh at myself for not being coordinated enough to grab an object without looking. When I turn to the cart, I gape at what I see. The books are gone. Not one is left! Only an empty, sad, old cart.

"Very funny, Mary!" I yell as I peek my head from around the shelf.

Mary turns from where she's standing at the check-out counter, almost half-way across the library. She shushes me with the whole, *be quiet, we're in a library*, look. Confused, I search the rows near me thinking maybe my best friend, Ana, is playing a trick on me. When I find no one there, I make my way back to my row. I gape at the empty cart before turning to where I had been placing the books. I skim my hand along the spines only to find that previously unfilled gaps were now filled with books I didn't shelve.

Impossible. There was at least an hour, if not two, of work on that cart. Then, a vision clouds my mind. It's as if a curtain is being pulled back to reveal a hazy memory. I abruptly recollect an incident when I was only 5. I had blocked it out—made myself believe it wasn't real.

I remember sitting in my room, playing with my hand-me-down Barbies. I know they're secondhand because the blonde hair is disgusting and matted from the prior owner's fingers. I can see this girl in my kindergarten class with a beautiful, brand-new Barbie—I want one just like hers. I wish *super hard* that I can have one too. The next thing I know, one of my worn Barbies turns into a brand-new Malibu Barbie. My mom freaks out. She thinks I have somehow stolen it and grounds me, taking my new Barbie away.

"Sophie dear, are you okay?"

I snap out my daze to find Mary standing next to me.

"Oh, um, yeah, I'm fine. Just hallucinating I think."

Mary's boney, age-spotted hand comes up to scratch her head, looking at me like I've lost my mind. Just as she's about to say something, her eyes catch the empty cart.

"Did you put those books back in the check-in slot so

you wouldn't have to do them?" she asks, an amused smile gracing her thin lips.

"No actually. I finished them already."

Mary begins to laugh in her cute old lady chuckle, the apples of her cheeks turning a rosy pink. When I don't laugh with her, she stops, scratching her head again in disbelief.

I gesture to the shelves, giving her a smug smile in spite of myself. She carefully examines the shelves through her bifocals, pushing them up the bridge of her nose to get a closer look.

"I can't believe you did that so quickly, dear."

I can't believe it either. I'm still as confused as ever by what just happened, but I'm eager to leave anyway. I don't want to think about it anymore. Especially after that bizarre memory.

"Hey, Mary? Do you think that maybe I could—"

"Yes dear, you can go now."

I try to hide my excitement but fail miserably. I always wear my emotions on my sleeve—or so my mom tells me.

"Thank you, Mary! I'll see you tomorrow."

I wave goodbye grabbing my things out of my small cubby. I practically skip through the parking lot to my beat-up 1995 Oldsmobile. It's tan and dented from a hailstorm last summer, but it's my car and I love him. I affectionately named him NIC-NAC after my license plate, but Ana and I call him NAC for short.

Driving through town toward my cabin, my thoughts gravitate back to what happened at the library. There's no explanation for the books magically shelving themselves. I wonder if maybe there weren't as many books as I had initially counted, or perhaps I zoned out from too much thinking and subconsciously re-stocked them all. Then again, the Barbie vision-memory thing is off-putting.

I had put that day behind me a long time ago— convinced myself over the years that it was a strange dream that felt like a memory. I try to dismiss my thoughts, and decide I'm just overtired from the day; of course nothing makes sense right now. I roll down my windows, hoping the fresh evening breeze will help.

The road opens up slightly, the wind getting stronger as it passes through my open window and over the back of my neck, causing my whole body to tremor and convulse ungracefully. I have to chuckle when I pass the pristinely painted town sign sporting, *Iron Lake—You'll Never Want to Leave.* That sign never fails to crack me up. Don't get me wrong our town is beautiful; the perfect quaint resort town. We have an eccentric downtown with many mom & pop shops and restaurants. Then of course, there's the lake itself—*Seven Miles of Heaven!*—as it says on our town's website.

All-in-all Iron Lake is a nice and safe place. It's a very picturesque area that presents exactly like a vacation postcard. During the summer and fall—*my favorite seasons*—the town is full of tourists from all over the country. We have plenty of water-ski shows, cruises on the lake with slot machines, and of course, wine festivals—*another favorite of mine*. However, that's about where the excitement ends. Wisconsin winters are horrible and last months on end. They are cold beyond belief, icy, and snowy. The worst is being stuck in my small cabin for weeks with nothing to do because of the weather. Let's just say I can 100% understand Jack Nicholson's character in *The Shining*.

I feel my shoulders relax as I approach my gravel driveway, happy to finally be home. After winding up the short road, I pull up to what I refer to as my safe house. My cabin is exactly what you picture when someone says cabin. It's little and made of wooden logs, with a porch and a chimney, nestled not too far from the lake. I notice Ana's green Toyota parked in what she calls *her spot*. I park next to it, grabbing my stuff and slamming the door shut. At the sound, I hear my Laker barking excitedly. Ana must have let him out, because he bounds toward me, greeting me by practically attacking my face and body with his fluffy paws and slobbery tongue.

"Hey you big beast! Did you miss momma?"

He whines happily in response. I ruffle his fur and play with him for a moment before making my way inside. When I cross the threshold, I take a deep breath, inhaling the smell of cedar and fresh chocolate chip cookies. The sound of whatever Ana is watching—most likely trashy reality TV—permeates the small space.

My cabin means a lot to me, and I love it more than I have ever loved anything—besides Laker and my loved ones, of course. It had once been my dad's family's summer cabin but became his permanent residence after my parents split when I was ten. When he passed away suddenly, I found out he had left it to me in his will along with a fund to pay for its property taxes. It was only logical that when I returned to Iron Lake, this would be where I would live. It's like a studio apartment—an ample space where a queen bed sits—a chair, couch and television fill the rest of the room. There's also a space for a modest dining area and a kitchen. Everything is very rustic and feels homey. My dad liked darker colors, so when I moved in, I tried to brighten it up with whites and light greens. It isn't much, but it's perfect for me.

I hang up my purse on the coat rack and go farther into the living room area. Ana's blonde, straight hair is hanging over the end of the couch, her feet dangling off the other end. She has her hand buried in a plate full of cookies as she watches a Spanish telenovela. She's so enthralled that she doesn't even look up to greet me. On the television, one scantily-clad, over-make-up'd woman is having a catfight with another woman. They're yelling at each other in words neither Ana nor I understand.

"Just make yourself at home Ana, I don't mind," I call to her.

"Shhh, it's getting good!" she exclaims, her hand digging into the cookies and her eyes still glued to the screen. I shake my head at her antics. I always wonder how she manages to stay so skinny when she eats so much junk food. Nothing gets in the way of that girl and a chocolate-chip cookie.

I plop down in my worn seafoam green recliner, propping my feet up and grabbing a cookie from the plate on Ana's stomach.

"I don't know how you watch this stuff; you don't even speak Spanish."

"You don't have to speak Spanish to understand it, Soph! Listen to the emotion in their voices! Watch their actions!"

"It's two women fighting, *how exciting*."

"SHH!!!"

I roll my eyes at her and grab another cookie, humming in satisfaction at its gooey goodness. Laker jumps up next to me, his massive form cuddling into my side, his fluffy head lying on my lap. I relax, closing my eyes and willing for sleep to take me.

"HEY!" Ana yells, snapping her fingers in front of my face. I fling my eyes open, glaring at her in a playful manner. Her blue eyes are sparkling with a mixture of laughter and annoyance, her perfect lips in a pout to rival any teenage girl.

"Who said you could come annoy me tonight?" I ask her.

"You have to get up! We have places to go, people to see!"

"Ha! I'm not leaving my house tonight, I'm beat."

"*Come on*, Soph! The annual summer kick-off is

tonight. We always go to the bonfire!"

I roll my eyes. The annual summer kick-off is not something I enjoy doing but did every year for Ana's benefit. I completely forgot that it's tonight.

"You forgot, didn't you?" she glowers.

"It's been a long day. I kind of just wanted to curl up on my porch and read a book."

"God, you *are* pathetic! You work around books ALLLLL day! Not to mention you always curl up on your porch and read a book. You need to go out every once and awhile. You know, socialize!"

I groan, rubbing my hands over my face. Ana's giving me the most pathetic puppy dog face known to man. She's even starting to fake cry a little. After a few moments I can't take it anymore.

"Fine," I surrender.

"I knew you would say yes! It's tradition. Not to mention there's a new boy in town, or should I say a new *man.*"

I roll my eyes again. The last thing I need is to try and make friends with the new guy, especially tonight of all nights.

"He's probably 55 and balding," I tell her.

"I actually heard he's really cute. Supposedly he's the

person who bought the Cooper's place."

My mouth drops open. The Coopers had lived in Iron Lake forever. They were the wealthiest family in town and owned a huge house about a mile from where I live. It's practically in the middle of the forest, hidden by the trees. Nobody in town knows why the Coopers left. It was all quite sudden. The house had been for sale for months. Too expensive for any person in their right mind to buy. Apparently not for this new man. I wonder if he's a drug dealer or something. I laugh at my absurd thoughts.

"He has to be balding, old and rich if he bought the Cooper's place," I reiterate.

"Well, we'll never actually know unless we go to the bonfire!" Ana whines.

"You don't have to be pushy, I already said I would go."

"Come on! We have to get you ready. I want us to look extra cute tonight in case the new guy is actually attractive. Lord knows this town needs some fresh meat."

"What about, Chris? I thought you had the hots for him again."

Ana rolls her eyes at me this time before stuffing another cookie into her mouth and talking through her bites.

"I don't want to talk about that asshole right now. He

14

can rot wherever he is."

"*Ooookay* then. Duly noted."

Chris is Ana's on and off again boyfriend. She always claims to hate him, but then the next minute I'll find them making out in the linen closet. I think she likes the fiery nature of their relationship. Even though it's unhealthy, I can tell they both thrive on fighting. I try not to get involved unless I absolutely have to. Too messy for my taste.

"You should wear that new sundress I bought you," Ana says, interrupting my thoughts.

"You want me to wear a sundress? To a bonfire?"

"Why not? You'll be standing in front of giant flames."

"You're crazy, you know that?"

Ana just smiles smugly at me before I reluctantly get up from my chair. Laker jumps to the floor, whining for his nightly meal. As I walk to the kitchen area, Ana follows me with her plate of cookies, sitting at the dining table, staring at me.

"What are you looking at me like that for?"

"*Your clothes*—you could be even more beautiful if you put in some effort."

Ouch. I look down at my simple jeans and favorite vintage t-shirt with a comic image of Superman scrawled across the front. My mousy-brown hair is slightly curled from the light humidity in the air. I have to admit it's a bit unruly since I didn't have time to shower this morning from waking up late. I'm not a supermodel—but I think I look fine.

"What's wrong with the way I dress?"

"What isn't wrong with it? You dress like a geek! I mean Superman, Sophie? *Really?*"

"I like Superman," I pout, sticking my lower lip out. "He saves the world from Lex Luthor."

"Hasn't anyone ever told you that Lex Luthor doesn't exist?" Ana teases, getting up to tweak my cheek playfully.

I smack her hand away, laughing at how ridiculous we sound.

"I think you should wear green," she says. "Your eyes are such a bright green; you should really try and bring them out more. If you don't catch the eye of the new guy, maybe you'll at least get a good lay from a tourist boy."

"Just what I need, a 19-year-old frat boy," I say sarcastically, setting Laker's food down on the floor. He gobbles it up happily as I scratch behind his ear lovingly.

"If you treated men the way you treat your dog, you'd be married by now," she teases.

"Shut up! I love my dog," I coo, kissing the top of

Laker's head.

Ana laughs before she drags me toward my closet, prattling on about colors and hair options. She pulls items out while I sit on my bed—my mind veering back to this afternoon unintentionally. I know better than to tell Ana what happened with the books. She's a black and white kind of person, she's not even superstitious. If I tell her that the books I was re-stocking magically made their way back on the shelves, she would laugh her ass off and tell me to stop smoking so much weed.

"Hello! Earth to Sophie! Are you even listening to me?"

I snap my eyes back up to her, my look a little sheepish. "Sorry, I was just thinking."

"Listen!" she gripes. I urge her on. "As I was saying, since you don't want to wear the sundress, I think you should wear these dark jeans with this emerald silk top. It's one of the most feminine things you have! We need to take a trip down to Chicago soon to buy you some new clothes."

Typical Ana. I just look at her, not responding to her suggestion. A shopping trip is not something I see for the near future. It's not an activity I like doing and neither is spending money. Ana shoves the clothes into my hands.

"Shower and get dressed," she orders. "I have to run

home and change. Meet me at the park at 9?"

"I'll be there."

She hugs me enthusiastically before hopping out the door. I look at the clothes in my hands, walking over to the floor-length mirror next to my bed. I hold the jeans and top up to my body I guess Ana's right. My eyes really do look greener if I wear a similar color. It's pretty. I laugh, rolling my eyes at my own musings. I sound too much like Ana.

"What's wrong with me?" I ask Laker, who just gives me a goofy dog grin.

I turn back to the mirror, gazing thoughtfully at my reflection. I've never cared about the way I look before, and I sure as hell don't want to start now. I stare longingly at my porch swing, then to the rumpled clothes. I know I don't have a choice but to go tonight. Ana would kill me if I didn't show up. I start to strip, walking to the bathroom begrudgingly. It's going to be a *long* night.

CHAPTER 2

If there is *one* thing I'm good at—it's being *exactly* on time. I have the uncanny ability to show up precisely when I mean to, no matter what time I leave my house. That's why I was incredibly irked I was late to work earlier today. Tonight, however, I arrive at the park exactly at 9:00 p.m. I park NAC and make my way through crowds of tourists grilling and throwing footballs. I wave and smile at the few people I know from town, not wanting to make too much eye contact; otherwise they'll drag me into a long conversation I don't feel like having.

I turn my attention back to the ground as I walk. Another skill I have is the aptitude to trip over thin air. I have no idea where I get it from. My mom is a former ballet dancer, and my dad had the ability to look like a Greek statue most of the time. Because of this, I tend to look at my feet more than at what is going on around me. Being so focused on the ground, I don't notice the tall, hard, rock-like wall in front of me until I slam into it. I fall onto my ass, landing on the not-so-soft grass with a hard thud.

"Shit!" I grunt.

"I am so sorry, are you all right?" a raspy, deep voice asks me from above.

The hard rock wall I hit isn't a hard rock wall at all—unless walls can suddenly talk. But with the day I'm having, I think it would have made sense that inanimate objects could speak.

When I look up to the said wall, a pair of the most interesting eyes I have ever seen meet mine. In the dark—with just the fire and a few park lights to brighten the area—they seem almost *violet*. I'm so entranced by the color I forget myself for a time.

"Excuse me, Miss. Are you okay?" The Wall asks again.

Warm, strong hands encase my upper arms and shake me gently, effectively breaking me from my trance. I realize The Wall—who is a man—has crouched down to my level. He is looking at me with great concern in his eyes.

"Yes, yes, I'm fine," I stammer.

I try to stand up a little too quickly. Since he's still holding my arms—attempting to help guide me upwards with him—I'm thrown off balance and the low heel of my

20

shoe catches in a clump of dirt, causing me to topple again. Mystery rock-hard wall man is, of course, there to catch me from falling again.

"Are you sure you are all right?" I can hear the slight distress in his voice, yet there's also amusement. Given our current position it's probably quite obvious I'm a klutz.

"I'm fine," I lie under my breath, not looking at him. My butt is throbbing in pain, and I feel extremely off-balance and frazzled. With a deep breath I'm able to get my bearings and begin a full analysis of *The Wall*.

My eyes travel upward from his black leather oxford shoes to his dark-wash tailored jeans—*my, his hips are narrow*. I feel myself becoming flushed as I continue my wanton appraisal. He's wearing a loose white shirt with a few small buttons open at the neck, revealing a tantalizing section of tanned skin. Over that he has a black leather jacket, worn down enough to make it looked a little loved, but not overly so. His outfit is as expensive as my entire wardrobe, if not more.

Finally, I look at his mouth. I know I'm drooling like a grown woman at a Jonas Brothers concert, but honestly, I don't care. His carefully crafted crooked smile divulges a gentle sparkle of brilliant white teeth. His top lip is slightly thinner than his bottom lip, and they're filled in by a soft shade of baby pink. They're somewhat chapped from the dry air of the bonfire, which makes me want to reach out and wet them for him. I lick my lips, feeling my own personal fire blooming slightly in my lower stomach. Normally I would be embarrassed by my reaction, but I feel compelled to study him like a book.

As I take in the rest of his utterly masculine face, I can tell he's trying to hold back laughter and might be a bit bashful. My eyes latch on to his dusky brown hair, which reminds me of the color of wet sand. Bits of blonde are highlighted by the flicker of fire, and I have the urge to push my hands through it to see the layers of color within the strands. His hair is styled to look disheveled on purpose, like he's been running his hands through it every chance he got. *Sex hair* is what Ana would call it.

After a few more seconds of staring, his tilted smile transforms into a full-blown toothy grin, creating one lone dimple on his left cheek. As soon as this happens, I can't stop my lips from turning up into a smile to rival his own. I mean, how many people have you seen with only one dimple?

At long last, I connect with the dark amethyst of his eyes, and I remember where I am, and that this man is a complete stranger that I've been blatantly eye-fucking for several minutes. His hands are still on my outer arms, the warmth from his large palms radiating through the thin silk material of my blouse. I can't help but quiver as my body takes in this new evidence.

My gaze returns to his amused face, and the next thing I know the warmth of his hands leave my body, and a single finger reaches towards my lips. Before I can ask what he's doing, he places his index finger under my chin and pushes it up, effectively closing my mouth.

"I am afraid if you keep your mouth open any longer you will begin to catch bugs," he says, his voice full of mirth. I tremble at the sound; it's deep, but not too deep, and it causes vibrations to ring through every nerve of my being. His voice holds a slight rasp to it, which makes him even sexier. Finally remembering myself, I clear my throat, wondering how I'm going to explain my overt female gaze.

"Oh, um, I, well, you see, I just…" I babble, unable to find my words. Which is hilarious given I was definitely able to allow my imagination to run wild only moments ago.

He quirks one eyebrow up at me, stirring that flame in my stomach again.

"Are you sure you did not hit your head when you fell?" he asks.

I step away from him, noting that I'm a little too close for comfort. Clearing my throat, I smile through the red-hot blush I feel spreading on my cheeks like wildfire.

"Just my ass I'm afraid. I don't have too much to land on in that area," I laugh awkwardly.

His eyes quickly flash to my derriere. Normally I would have made a comment at his ogling but given I had just spent God knows how long examining him, the least I could do was let him catch a glance at my behind.

He swallows, his Adam's apple bobbing. "I am terribly sorry I ran into you. I was not looking where I was going. You see, I thought I saw someone I knew and had my attention focused elsewhere."

I almost laugh out loud at how proper he sounds. For a moment I wonder if he's going to start speaking with a British accent, but I can't detect any inkling of one.

"Don't worry about it," I assure him. "I was looking at my feet. I'm a huge klutz, and normally looking at the ground stops me from hurting myself, but apparently not others."

He looks at me with a hefty amount of intensity. When I start to fidget under his gaze, he breaks out another charmingly crooked smile—*his teeth are so white!* I almost ask him if they're natural. I'm glad I still have some sort of self-control right now. I don't want him to think I'm *that* crazy.

"I am Ethan by the way. Ethan Moore. I just moved into the Cooper house," he says, extending his hand out for me to shake.

My mouth drops open again. Ana was right. New Boy is definitely not a boy or a balding old man. The word man doesn't quite do him justice either. God, maybe? Okay, so I'm probably over-exaggerating a little bit—*perhaps a lot.* But this *man*…well, he had no semblance of *boy* in him.

I blink back my shock before placing my hand into his much larger one. His hand is so large in fact, that it smothers my small one easily as he shakes it firmly—almost a bit too firmly. I wonder if he came from the planet Krypton and went by the name of Clark Kent—maybe Ana was right again in saying I was a bit too much of a nerd. What can I say? Superman just does it for me. Not to mention, not all men look bad in tights. I think Ethan Moore could definitely pull off a pair.

My eyes have a mind of their own and begin to wander again. Somehow, I'm able to snap out of it when I remember I'm *still* shaking his hand. I quickly release it, folding my hands behind my back so I can't do anything stupid again.

25

"Do I get to know the name of the fair lady I hit?" he asks.

"*Shit*, I'm so sorry! Today has just been one of those days, you know?"

He flashes his smile at me again, his eyes twinkling with laughter and a bit of surprise, most likely because I just swore, *again*. I'm really not good at manners, something my mom continually likes to remind me of.

"I'm Sophia," I finally tell him, not sure why I didn't give him my nickname instead.

"*Sophia*," he repeats back to me, saying my name like he's savoring the sound of it. "It was good to meet you. I am sorry it had to end with you on your *as—tush.*"

I have to stop myself from chortling in a very un-ladylike manner. Not that I care, but did he really just say *tush?*

"Although," he adds, "I do have to say this is probably one of the most memorable introductions I have ever had."

My cheeks burn. "*Again*, I'm sorry I ran into you like that."

"I have to say, Sophia—I do not think I am sorry—but I will accept your apology," he grins.

Not many people have the ability to render me speechless, especially so many times in such a short period.

This Ethan guy seems to have a talent for it, and I'm starting to question my mental health around him. I find my curiosity piqued that a man as young as him, and as handsome, is living in the old Cooper mansion in a place like Iron Lake, Wisconsin. I'm completely baffled and want to know more.

"I have to be going," he says, breaking me from my constantly running thoughts, "but I am sure I will be seeing you again soon." His lips turn up adoringly at me, his eyes reflecting the licks of flame from the now roaring bonfire. When he flashes his one dimpled cheek, my insides melt like a marshmallow on a stick. He walks away then, and I immediately feel like something is missing from my body.

I quickly brush it away, calling after him. "It was nice meeting you, too!"

He glances back, flaunting that smile of his one more time before he's gone among the hoard of people. Once I'm sure he's completely out of sight, I hit my head repeatedly with the palm of my hand.

Stupid, stupid, stupid—I silently berate myself—hoping to pound some of the crazy out.

"Stop hitting yourself!" a voice hollers from beside me.

Soon there's a hand on my wrist, more feminine this time. It forcibly takes my hand and begins smacking me in the face with it. I look up to find Ana, grinning like an idiot.

"Don't do that!" I scold her, pulling my wrist from her grasp.

"Well, I saw you smacking yourself in the head and I thought you needed some help," she says seriously.

"I just did something really stupid," I groan, leaning my face into her shoulder for support. She pats my back in contrived sympathy.

"I know."

"You saw?" I look up.

"Oh boy, did I ever see that. I think half the population might have seen your little eye-fuck fest."

I slap Ana's arm playfully while she cackles at me. I stomp off closer toward the bonfire, Ana quickly catching up beside me.

"So that's the new boy, huh?" she asks.

"The one and only. Though he's definitely not a boy."

Ana grins, "Told you people said he was hot."

I don't want to satisfy her with a response, but I can't help but flush at the memory of his body.

"Man, that was so funny! You should have seen the way he was looking at you though, *oooh baby!* It was kind of like you were a pirate seeking his buried treasure or something. Trust me, he would have let you."

"ANA!" I chide playfully. "Do you have to say things like that?"

"Seriously though, he totally wanted to take you up against a tree right then and there."

"You're so crude."

"Puh-lease! Like you aren't? I seem to remember your mom yelling at you just the other day for swearing like a sailor."

I bite my tongue, changing the subject. "He must be loaded. I mean he's living in the Cooper house for goodness sake."

"You hit the jackpot my friend!" She pats my back in pride. "I'm lucky if I get a guy to fall for me who makes more than minimum wage at Burger King."

"Chris makes good enough money on the cruise line."

"Chris who?" Ana snarls.

Oh boy...here we go again. "Where is he anyway?"

"So, the new guy," she says, ignoring my question. "Besides the obvious hot factor, was he nice?"

I know she isn't going to talk about Chris unless she wants too, so I decide to let her get away with changing the subject.

"Yeah, I guess. He was a little bit strange. His eyes are

violet."

"Violet? You mean like purple?"

"Sort of... they were *interesting*."

"Well at least he didn't have an eye-patch or something, even though I know you have a weirdo thing for Captain Hook."

"I do not! Captain Jack Sparrow maybe, but not Captain Hook!"

"You're such a nerd, Soph. You need to take classes on how to be cool. You're almost twenty-five for crying out loud."

I grumble at being reminded of my impending birthday in less than two weeks. Twenty-five is a quarter of a century— I don't like that! When you have nothing to show for living that long it's depressing to think about.

"Thanks for reminding me."

"Get over it already! Twenty-five is not *that* old," she smirks.

"Thanks, best friend. You're so sweet to me," I tease.

"Alright, I want to know more! What's his name? What did he say?"

"His name is Ethan Moore. Like I said, he was nice and a little odd. He talked all proper like those British tourists, but without an accent. You can tell he comes from a lot of money or high society."

"Hmmm…I'm sure by tomorrow they'll be plenty of stories about him. Not to mention you'll probably be dating him in the gossip circles. He did have his hands on you for an awfully long time."

I push Ana playfully.

"God, the last thing I need is for the town gossip to be about me. I'd like to stay out of the local limelight, thanks."

"Yeah, you better be careful, or you'll end up on Iron Lake's front page, *Hometown Hottie: Gold Digger or The Real Deal?* I'd buy it."

"I hate you," I tell her.

"You love me. Now come on, let's go get s'mores before they're all gone!"

Ana skips the rest of the way to the bonfire gleefully. Put a chocolate buffet in front of that woman and she'll be entertained for hours. Her adolescent behavior is something I love about her though, and it doesn't take me long to join in on the yummy goodness.

After Ana and I have our fill of s'mores, we sit around the bonfire talking to some of our friends from town, all people we've known since preschool. As they tell old stories and make fun of a few unique tourists, I keep replaying my encounter with Ethan.

I wonder if he was wearing contacts that made his eyes look that purple color. Every time I find myself blinking, I see them—looking at me with a hard intensity. It causes my whole body to thrum with anxious energy. I notice that I'm holding my arms around myself so that my hands are placed over the area where Ethan's had been only a few hours before. The almost unnatural warmth I felt when he touched me both baffles me and ignites my curiosity.

I look at my watch, seeing it's exactly 11:59 p.m. *Finally.* I heave a grateful sigh of relief. One more minute to go until this bizarre long day is over. I shuffle through the strange events one final time, wanting to laugh—*or cry*—at the fact that this is probably the most compelling day I've had since moving back to Iron Lake. The big hand on my watch clicks to midnight and I feel my body ease at the sight.

I glance down at Ana who has fallen asleep on my shoulder. Her cell phone is loosely hanging from her hand—about to fall onto the grass from her poor grip. On the screen is a half-typed text message to Chris that reads, *I'm sorry.* I shake my head, before gently pressing the send button, knowing she'll thank me in the morning.

I peer into the crackling bonfire, hot blue flames dancing in the early summer wind. I close my eyes only to have images of Ethan's amethyst stare, blonde-haired Barbies, and magical moving books dance behind my lids. The wind shifts and the breeze turns ice cold—only for a moment. Gooseflesh fans out over my arms and another shudder runs violently through me from head to toe. Ana is still fast asleep and the other remaining bonfire goers seem not to notice the change in the air.

Either I'm getting sick, or something is happening in Iron Lake.

CHAPTER 3

The next morning I arrive at my local coffee shop, *Java Joe's,* precisely at 6:30 a.m. Joey, the owner, greets me with a warm, familiar smile.

"Morning, Sophie."

"Morning, Joey!" I reply happily. "I'll have the usual."

"One non-fat mocha coming right up."

I return his infectious smile while sitting down at the small counter next to the espresso machine. Joey is one of my favorite people to see in the morning. He's always happy no matter the time of day. Maybe he puts me in a good mood more than my daily coffee does. Though I do love my coffee—*a lot.*

"We missed you yesterday morning," Joey says, catching my attention. "Did you decide to sleep in for once?"

"Actually, I was running late yesterday," I say with a wince.

"You? Running late? What has the world come too?"

I give him my signature eye-roll before grabbing my coffee from his outstretched hand and taking a sip. I moan happily, letting the warm, sweet, caffeinated nectar glide down my throat and settle in my stomach.

"You are a man of miracles, Joey!"

"I'm happy to make you happy," he grins.

I try to hand him money, but he waves me off.

"It's on the house today."

I put my hand over my heart in a teasing gesture. "Be still my heart. You are a true angel."

"Yeah, yeah. Get out of here so you're not late to work again."

"Thanks again, Joey. I'll see you tomorrow," I call to him as I walk out, the bell tinkling as the door closes behind me.

I stop on the street for a moment, taking in the fresh morning air. It's surprisingly chilly. I shiver, snuggling my hands around my coffee to absorb its warmth. It is brisk out, but not enough for a chill. I wonder if I really am getting sick, but as the hairs on the back of my neck stand up on end, I get the uncanny feeling I'm being watched. I look around the downtown area dimly lit by the morning sun. Only a few old people are milling about the street this early in the day. I scan behind me and around me one more time. I don't see anyone or anything suspicious, so I brush off the weird feeling. Clearly, I'm still in a mood after yesterday's strange events.

Once I get back into my car—coffee in hand—I take my time, arriving to work a smidge early at 6:55 a.m. I unlock the front doors and flip on a few lights. The library slowly lights-up with its dreary fluorescent lighting. We don't open to the public until eight o'clock, so I have over an hour to myself. It's my favorite time of the morning. I sip my coffee again, humming. Finally, back in my routine, I feel like today is going to go much better than yesterday. I collect books that were returned overnight and start shelving them. A little while later, I hear the door open and close, the front buzzer going off to alert me someone is here. Thinking it's Mary coming in for the morning, I continue going about my business.

I glance at the cover of one of the books, smiling goofily at it. It's some sort of vampire romance novel. I snort imagining Ethan as a vampire. His eyes are a strange color and he is *awfully* tall and strong—he's definitely not cold or made of stone—unless you count those rock-hard pecs and abs I ran into last night. I scoff at my imagination. Ana has been forcing me to watch too many re-runs of

Buffy the Vampire Slayer lately. I shelve the book and take another one, not rushing like I usually would. Today feels like a good day to take things slowly—it is a Friday after all.

I read another book jacket, this one about a warlock and some weird time travel adventure he's on. It reminds me of yesterday and my *magical* book incident. I look at the cart which only holds a few books compared to yesterday's many. I grip the book in my hands tighter, staring at the cart with a new-found determination. I try to remember what I had been thinking about when it happened, and I will the books to be gone. I narrow my eyes and clench my fists—I believe the vein in my forehead starts pulsating.

I'm concentrating so hard that when I feel a large hand grab my shoulder I scream—not just a girly squeak—but a full out, ear-bleeding scream. I turn around to attack my assailant but end up losing my balance. I stumble backwards into the bookshelves before falling ungracefully onto my ass. A few books fall to the ground from the impact of my body, one deciding to hit me squarely on the noggin.

"Fuck!" I yell, rubbing the now throbbing spot on my head.

"Are you okay?" a worried voice asks me from above.

I remember why I'm on the ground. A person is in the library and we're closed. I'm about to freak out and start running and screaming when I look up at the perpetrator. Concern-filled violet eyes meet mine.

"Ethan?"

He nods, offering me his hand just as he had the night before. When I take it, I can't ignore the pleasant sensation that rushes through my body.

"I am sorry I scared you," he says as we come almost face-to-face. "In the short time we have known each other, I have managed to knock you off your feet—*twice*."

He half-smiles like some kind of Prince Charming, and all I can do is open and close my mouth several times like a fish. I'm trying to say something—*anything*—but no words form. Ethan seems to notice my dilemma and helps me out.

"I really did not mean to scare you. I thought you heard me come in."

I clear my throat. "I heard someone come in, but I thought it was my boss, Mary. We don't open for another twenty minutes or so."

"Oh...," he trails off, his smile quirking up crookedly again, the one dimple on his left cheek appearing.

"It's okay. I did leave the door unlocked," I say, rubbing my sore head once more. He apologizes again but I wave him off. "I'm fine, really. So, what can I do for you?"

"I can come back in twenty minutes if you would like."

"It's fine," I repeat. "What is it that brought you to the library this early?"

"Well… books," he smiles again. I hold back a playful eye-roll, taking a second to analyze the way he's dressed. He's a bit more casual today. The light jeans he's wearing have a few holes by the knees, and on his feet are a pair of dark gray Converse. I smirk to myself at his choice of shoes, looking down to see my beat-up red ones. He finished his ensemble with a black and gray plaid button-up shirt. I look at my plaid shirt and snort.

"What?" he asks.

"We match."

Ethan looks down at himself, and then his eyes drift up my body. I suddenly feel like I'm on fire.

"I thought I would try the whole small-town look," he quips.

"You kind of pulled it off—but I still don't think you quite fit in with the locals."

"And why is that?" he asks playfully.

I think for a moment as I look at him. One, he has strange colored eyes, and two, he looks regal. If I were to walk down the street and see him, I would know he doesn't belong in a town with less than 8,000 people.

"You don't seem like the type to live here is all."

He thinks about my words for a moment before chuckling like he's told himself some sort of inside joke and looks at me cheekily. After a few seconds I break the awkward silence.

"*Sooo*, do you really need a book, or did you just come here because you enjoy knocking me on my *tush*," I smirk, hoping he notices my choice of words.

"I do." He grins back, flushing a little. "I do need a book, I mean."

"Alright then, you came to the right place. What can I do for ya?"

"I am looking for an unusual book actually. One that I was hoping to find here of all places—but I am beginning to lose hope."

"And that book would be?"

"*Cooking 101*," he smiles.

I chuckle a bit. I have to admit, he's a *little* funny.

"Let's see if our modest library has a copy then, shall we?"

He bobs his head in agreement as I wave for him to follow me to our cookbook section. When we stop in front of them, I make a sweeping hand gesture like Vanna White.

"I don't know if we have a book with that exact title, but we have many, many books on cooking. Whatever you

40

fancy," I say, trying to reflect his manner of speaking.

He makes a humming noise as he runs his hands over the spines of the books. He then closes his eyes for a moment, releasing a breath. When his hand stops on a random book and his eyes open, he pulls it out and looks at the cover.

"Perfect," he muses, showing me the cover.

"Romantic Cooking for the Romantic Fool?" I laugh slightly.

"What can I say—I need a few tips," he says, his eyes boring into me.

My stomach knots at this new information. Why does he need to cook a romantic meal? Does he already have a wife or a girlfriend? Ana didn't mention he moved here with anyone else. When I take notice of my rampant thoughts, I check myself. This is not like me. I don't fawn over men like this—it's just not something I do—*ever.* Something must be really wrong with me, or maybe it's the lack of sleep. When I become aware that I'm ogling again, I try not to flush with embarrassment for the millionth time around this man I barely know.

"I'm sure whoever you cook for will be very happy," I say stiffly, attempting to make my voice sound even. *Good lord.* I really need to learn how to keep my mouth shut. As

41

I turn to walk away from him toward the front desk, he stops me by gently grabbing my arm. I turn back to face him, discovering his face lit with both amusement and surprise.

"Actually," he says, "I was quite hoping that you would be the one to join me for dinner."

"M-me?" I jabber stupidly, the urge to slap my hand over my mouth very strong.

"Yes, you," he smiles fully this time, flashing his dimple and pearly whites.

"Well—I—we just met."

Ethan takes a large step toward me, his smile turning wolfish.

"It would be a harmless dinner." His voice is smooth and convincing. "I only know one other person in this town and he is not very good at socializing—and we, *Sophia*—for some reason, keep running into each other."

"Literally," I mutter under my breath, causing him to let out a short laugh.

"As well, I was hoping that you would consider showing me the ropes here. You seem to be the person around Iron Lake that everyone trusts."

I cross my arms over my chest. "And how would you know that?"

"Small town. People talk," he shrugs.

"I think that's an understatement," I snort.

He holds up the book, tapping its cover.

"*Sophia*," he says, emphasizing my name, "Will you come over for my first ever home-cooked meal?"

"First ever?" I ask—astonished—to which he only nods. "Do you promise not to poison me?" I smirk.

"Cross my heart," he confirms, making the motion over his chest.

Our eyes lock. I think about the pros and cons of going to his house for dinner. The major con is that the whole town would know about our dinner within hours of it happening. We would automatically be linked romantically. In fact, I'm sure my mom already knows about our previous encounter at the bonfire. I bet money by the time I leave work there will be several demanding messages on my cell phone from her, asking about the new man in my life and why I didn't tell her about him immediately.

The pros are obvious to any person with functioning eyes. He's gorgeous, polite, and seemingly intelligent; and for some reason when I'm around him I feel like a moth to the flame. I've never felt that before or been this much of a flushing, bumbling idiot in front of a person. It's freaking me out the more I'm around him.

"Yes," I finally blurt out. My raging hormones win this time. His face breaks out into a brilliant smile, and I think my womanly parts melt. *Geez Louise*—I need help.

"Perfect," he exhales. "Do you know where I live?"

I nod. "Normally it would be creepy that I know, but given you moved into the Cooper mansion, yes, I do. We're practically neighbors."

"Right, you must live in that log cabin?"

"The one and only."

"I promise I am not a stalker either," he adds nervously, "Small town, as you say."

I grin despite myself. "Just know if you try anything funny, I'll aim for the jugular."

Ethan laughs nervously. "Noted. Does eight o'clock in the evening on Sunday work for you?"

"Sure, sounds good," I say, a slight bounce to my voice.

"Well then, I guess I will just take this book and be on my way."

He follows close behind me to the check-out counter where I sign him up for a library card. I hand him his cookbook as Mary walks in looking slightly frazzled—her glasses crooked and hair not nearly as perfect as it usually is. Having lost track of time, my eyes glance at my watch. She's 15-minutes late. Just like me she's always on time or

44

early, so this is very odd.

When Mary calms down a bit and notices Ethan standing at the counter, her mouth drops open in surprise. I imagine it's similar to how mine had been the night before when I first set my eyes on him. Ethan smiles politely at her, visibly melting her old lady heart.

"Mary, are you okay?" I joke, hoping to embarrass her a little.

She completely ignores me as Ethan sticks out his hand to her.

"Hello, I am Ethan."

"My, you're cute," Mary answers, shaking his hand delicately. "Good work Sophie," she quips, giving me a thumbs-up before walking to the back room.

So much for embarrassing her—she had just embarrassed me! I hear Ethan's faint rumble of laughter through the roaring of blood in my ears. When will I not be completely mortified around this guy?

"This lovely town just keeps getting more interesting," Ethan comments. "Thanks again for the book. I will see you Sunday." Then he's gone, the door closing with a thud behind him. I look at my watch again, praying that time had suddenly moved faster, but it's only 8:20 a.m. It was going to be *another* long day.

By the time five o'clock rolls around I am bored to tears and ready to have a date with my porch swing and a glass of wine. I spent most of my work hours organizing books and mulling over my interactions with Ethan. When it's time to close, I'm out of the library and in my car before Mary can finish saying goodbye. I pull my cell phone from my purse, seeing that I had been right about my nosey mom. The screen reads five missed calls and ten unread messages—though some are from Ana. I decide not to listen to my mom's voicemails, thinking it's better to have this conversation in person, so I make my way over to her house.

She lives a short distance from the library, making it less than ten minutes before I pull into the driveway of my childhood home. It's a modest-sized white house with blue shutters—nothing special or grand—simply home. If you look closely you can see the white paint peeling off the side panels. Mom keeps pestering me to come over and help her paint it, but I keep insisting she hire someone who knows what they're doing.

Before my car's even in park, the front screen door is

thrown wide open and she comes running out—her brow creased in reprimand and dark brunette hair flying behind her like a tornado. I brace myself for the natural disaster that's about to happen and open the car door to receive her.

"Sophia Marilyn Black!" she scolds. "You need to learn how to pick up your phone!"

I hug her—despite her crazy antics—before stepping back to look at her. "Hello to you, too, *mom*."

She blinks rapidly at me with her hazel eyes and gives me an eye-roll that rivals my own. She's on the tall side and still thin from her years of dancing. You can tell by looking at her she is graceful—unlike me. Her hair frames her face in wilted curls, and her small delicate hands are planted firmly on her hips. When her lips press in a tight thin line, I know she's waiting for an explanation.

"I'm sorry, I've been busy!"

"I've heard," she says, a hint of mirth tinting her voice.

It's my turn to roll my eyes. If my mother is acting like this, that means the entire town already has married me off to Ethan. She pushes me—not gently I might add—toward the door of the house before we end up in the kitchen. The entire time mom's chattering away, but I'm not paying attention.

"Are you even listening to me, Sophie?" she finally asks,

exasperated.

I bob my head, knowing she doesn't believe me for a second, and go grab a Diet Coke from the refrigerator. She continues her story.

"I said I was at the grocery store today picking out some apples when April Walsh comes up to me. You remember April, don't you?"

"Yes, mom, we went to school together."

"Yes, yes. Anyway, April comes over to me and asks me straight away about you and this Ethan fellow. She asked me how long you'd been dating, and I told her I didn't even know you were dating anyone—let alone the new person in town! Why didn't you tell me?"

"There is nothing to tell."

"But April said—"

"I haven't spoken to April in months. She knows nothing about my life."

"Then what's all this talk about that Ethan fellow?"

"We ran into each other, we talked for a moment. That was it."

"You're lying to me, Sophia."

I try to hide the guilty look that crosses my face by drinking my pop. As she continues to ramble, my stomach grumbles. I'm hungry, tired, and now all I want to do is eat a giant slice of cheese pizza—maybe a pint of Ben & Jerry's. I picture it in my head. There are literal ice cream pints dancing in my imagination. I can taste the melted, greasy cheese, and delicious tomato sauce on my tongue. My mouth starts to water and I drool a little.

When the doorbell rings out of the blue, it knocks me from my food daydream. My mother mumbles something incoherent before going to answer it. I'm glad for the saved-by-the-bell distraction. I don't need her to know anything about Ethan and me, especially since we haven't even been on one date yet. The last thing I want is her meddling more than she already does in my life. I know she means well, and I don't hate her for it—I just don't need or want it.

When she returns a few minutes later, she's carrying a pizza box. The smell assaults my senses in the best possible way—what a coincidence.

"That was the strangest thing," she says as she sets the pizza on the counter.

"I didn't know you were ordering pizza."

She looks baffled. "That's what I mean. I didn't order this pizza."

"Then who did?" I ask, familiar nervous energy returning to my stomach.

"The boy said I did. I tried to tell him he was mistaken but he insisted it was mine. He even had my name. You didn't order it?"

"No. I did want pizza though—"

I open the box and stare at the fresh cheese pizza—the one that had been dancing in my mind for the past few minutes. I throw the weird feeling away—my hunger taking over—as I grab a slice against my better judgment. I try to brush it off as happenstance. It has to be the only explanation.

"Someone must be playing a prank or something, but it was paid for," Mom adds, scratching her head.

I shrug my shoulders while chewing. I rewind to the few seconds before the pizza came and remember I was also thinking about ice cream. Hit with a knowing feeling, I jump up from my chair, throwing the slice of pizza back in the box. When I open the freezer—*I'm stunned.* There— sitting like it's waiting to be eaten by me—is a pint of Ben & Jerry's chocolate chip cookie dough. I slam the door closed, mom staring at me like I've gone cuckoo.

I jump up, grabbing my purse and jacket. "I have to go."

"What? Why?" she asks, trying to block me from leaving. "Are you meeting that boy?"

50

I don't answer her, just walk around her and to the door.

"Wait, honey! At least take this pizza with you."

"It's okay, Mom," I say. "I just remembered I have to be somewhere. I'll call you later!"

If she said something more, I don't hear her. I'm already in my car and reversing down the driveway. Whatever is happening is all kinds of screwed up. I'm now thoroughly convinced I'm going insane. I want to tell someone what is happening, try to find some comfort. But what would I say?

Hey Ana, guess what? I think I have magical powers!

Ha! Yeah right.

The more I think over it on my drive home, the more I try to convince myself I just need a good night's sleep. Magic does not exist. What is happening to me is just not possible. There has to be a logical explanation for what's going on. The pizza was just a fluke. The ice cream was just a coincidence. The books were my imagination, as was the Malibu Barbie. I have to keep telling myself nothing is out of the ordinary—I just have to.

CHAPTER 4

The rest of my Friday and Saturday go by uneventfully—much to my relief. I stay locked in my cabin, only venturing outside to my porch or to take Laker for a walk in the woods nearby. I read, drink wine, watch bad reality TV, and do my best to avoid any thoughts of the past few days.

Sunday morning comes and goes quickly in a haze of sleep, which means my dinner with Ethan is fast approaching. I managed to avoid Ana all of Friday night and Saturday—which is a feat in itself. If she had gotten a hold of me, she would have been able to tell I was on edge, and I'm just not ready to talk about anything yet. Also, I want to keep my plans with Ethan under wraps. I want to hold that aspect of my life right now close to my chest. For all I know tonight's dinner could go horribly wrong. Ethan could end up never speaking to me again—or we could have an amazing one-night stand—I'm not opposed to it. I can't be sure what kind of guy he is with our limited interactions, and I don't want to risk the gossip. He's definitely mysterious and the way I feel around him intrigues me the more I think about him.

At seven o'clock I take a shower and get dressed. Though I can see Ana cringing at my choice, I wear plain black Converse and a pair of black skinny jeans. I settle for a dressier blue top made from a soft material and minimal make-up. By the time I'm done I think I look decent and like myself. My hair is a little frizzy but straightening it would only involve a lot of effort and it would be back to wavy within an hour anyway. I grab my favorite, over-loved black leather jacket and make my way out for the evening with a farewell scratch to Laker.

Driving the short distance to the old Cooper mansion is a bit scary. There's a long, curvy cement driveway covered in thick woods I have to navigate in the fading light of the day. I have my windows down and notice it's eerily quiet outside—a now familiar vibration cascades down my spine. As I approach the large iron gate, it automatically opens, like it's been waiting for me to arrive. When I finally get a good look at the house—I audibly gasp. In all the years I've lived in Iron Lake, I've never actually seen the Cooper house in person. Nobody ever had the balls to drive up here and snoop around. Ana tried once when we were kids but got scared halfway there and turned back.

The mansion is much bigger than I ever expected. It's made of dark wood and what looks like granite, with huge glass windows at weird angles giving it a very new and modern feel. Stone walkways and a huge wrap-around porch frame the house into the side of a hill. I wonder if it's always looked this way or if Ethan had it remodeled—I can't believe he lives in this place by himself! I bet at least 15 people could live here. When I get closer, I see a separate six-car garage with a Porsche convertible parked outside. I plunk my beater next to it, cringing at how old it looks next to this beautiful, well-crafted machine. Upon further inspection I discover it's a deep red color, and definitely brand-spanking-new.

Exiting my car, I begin my ascent up the steep stone stairs, continuing to look at the house in awe. When I get to the ornate glass door, I ring the doorbell which chimes a short tune. Ethan is at the door in a flash, his perfect one dimpled smile greeting me warmly.

"Hi," I say awkwardly.

"Hi," he says back, stepping aside so I can come in. Once the door is closed, he eyes me up and down appreciatively, "I like your jacket."

I look down at it, smiling a little. The jacket was a gift from my dad on my 21st birthday. I wear it whenever I get the chance.

"Thanks."

"Can I take it for you?" he asks after a few moments of clumsy silence.

"Oh yeah—sure."

He steps toward me, gently helping me to remove it before placing it in his coat closet—which I notice is full of different colored leather jackets and outerwear. When he turns back to me I can't help but admire him. His sandy hair is perfectly disheveled again like he spent the day at the beach. He's wearing a slate gray long-sleeved Henley shirt, showing off the muscles in his arms and well-toned chest. His black slacks fit him to a T and flaunt all the right places. When I meet his eyes—which are framed by thick lashes and dark eyebrows—I notice they're less violet this time. The gray of his shirt makes them appear to be more charcoal-blue.

"Do you approve of my outfit?" he smirks at me, his eyebrow quirked to match his crooked smile.

"You look hot," I blurt out, wanting to slap a hand over my mouth and run out the door. My cheeks flush, my face hot with embarrassment. He clears his throat so that I'll look at him, his eyes filled with laughter and amusement.

"I like your honesty," he declares, "and you look *hot* yourself. I hope you do not mind me saying."

"Um, thanks—it's only fair," I say back, dying to change the subject.

"Would you like something to drink?" he asks, like he read my mind.

"Yes, please."

He motions to follow him, and I comply, admiring the house as we walk. It's beautiful to say the least, but that word doesn't do it justice. I notice the walls are already filled with paintings—I stop immediately when I see a particular print.

When Ethan notices he comes to stand next to me.

"Are you a Warhol fan?" he inquires, hopeful.

"Is this real?" I say with wonder, reaching out to touch it. Before I can, Ethan snatches my hand away, pulling it back rather quickly.

"Yes, actually. It is."

I stare at the painting in awe. It must have been worth at least one or two million dollars, if not more.

"This is amazing!"

"Warhol is one of my favorites," he says thoughtfully.

When I finish inspecting the painting, I look down at our hands. Ethan's still holding mine gently, his engulfing mine. Now that my attention is on them, I feel the heat flowing through our fingers. When I look up to see him staring at me intently, I tug my hand back, suddenly feeling self-conscious. I swear I see him flinch at the action but brush it off quickly.

"Come on," he says. "Let me get you that drink."

In the kitchen, he gestures to several bottles sitting on the counter.

"I have white wine, red wine, beer, cider, gin, whiskey—whatever you would like," he grins.

"Oh, um—white's fine," I smile back, seating myself on a chair at the breakfast nook. As he pours a glass for me, I study the kitchen. It's enormous and pristine, like a top-of-the-line chef's kitchen, and full of brand-new appliances. When I breathe in, my nose is assaulted by the smell of burnt food.

"Did you burn dinner?" I ask before taking a sip of my wine.

He blushes, looking sheepish.

"I may have had a slight mishap with my *buns.*"

At that exact moment I'm taking a sip of wine—I almost spray it all over the counter but somehow manage to choke it down. I can't help but laugh and he chuckles along with me.

"Your *buns,* huh?"

"I am just hoping the rest of the meal turns out better than they did."

"I hope so, too," I tease.

Smiling to himself, he pours his own glass of wine before grabbing a small controller from a counter nearby and clicking a button. Classical music begins to fill my ears, the notes floating through the house. He turns back to me, offering his hand. I hesitate for a moment, before standing and placing it in his. He leads us to the living room over to a very large black leather couch. We sit almost on opposite ends. I'm not sure if I'm happy for the space or wishing he'd move closer.

"So, Sophia, tell me about yourself," he states.

"Really? Haven't you heard all about me from our overly friendly townspeople?"

He gives me a gentle look. "I have heard small, meaningless things, but I want to know the real you," he says sincerely, leaning his body toward the middle of the couch.

58

I think about what to tell him. Immediately all the strange things come to mind, but I can't tell him about those. We've just met—he'll run for the hills.

"Just start with the basics," he adds, seeing that I'm struggling on where to start.

"Umm—*well*—I'm almost twenty-five. I was born and raised here in Iron Lake with my mom and dad. I went to college in Madison and then moved back when I finished with my undergrad. Now I live in my dad's old cabin down the road and spend my days working at the library," I finish, letting silence fall between us. After a few moments, he looks at me patiently, as if he's waiting to hear more.

"That's really it. It sounds quite pathetic when I say my life story out loud," I mumble.

"I do not think it sounds pathetic at all. In fact, it sounds quite relaxing," he says, almost wistfully.

"It's really not that great," I reply.

"I think it sounds—*fun*."

"*Fun* is not how I would describe it, but who am I to ruin the perfect picture of our tiny town?" I quip, causing him to give me a coy smile. "What about you, Ethan— What's your story?"

"What would you like to know?" he asks, taking a long sip of his wine.

59

"*Well*, you show up out of the blue—buy the biggest house in Iron Lake—you're surrounded in mystery, and personally I'd like to crack that wide open," I say brightly, placing my hand under my chin while batting my eyelashes comically at him. He chuckles and I notice his shoulders and body relax at my foolish behavior.

"I moved here from New York City about two weeks ago."

"*Wow.* The Big Apple, eh? I've always dreamed of going there," I say in awe. It's one of the top places on my list if I ever save up enough money to go."

He shrugs. "It is nice—but it can be very intense. I found myself craving silence after a while."

"Then you came to the right place. Iron Lake is known for its silence. Unless of course you count the town gossip as noise, then it can get pretty loud," I snort.

"I gathered that," he grins.

"*So*, why did you move here?"

"Very nosey," he teases.

"Product of that small-town gossip, I suppose. You were saying?" I look at him expectantly.

I see him release a small breath. "I moved on my own accord. My father did not approve of my decision very much, seeing as I had to leave my position at our

60

company—but I was no longer happy there."

"Your company?" I ask, full of curiosity toward this man—I want to know *everything*.

He looks hesitant for a moment but continues. "My family owns a large publishing house in New York City. We also dabble in real estate."

Ah—so that explains his money.

"Out of all the places you could go to escape, why here?" I ask.

"My family used to have a summer house in Northern Wisconsin. I enjoyed those summers very much when I was a child. I simply remembered it as relaxing and peaceful. When I decided I needed a break, I thought finding a place in the Midwest to live for a while would be the answer to my problems."

"You don't plan on staying permanently?" I question too quickly. My stomach clenches at the thought of him leaving. I scold myself internally for having such a reaction; I don't even *really* know him yet, and already I'm mourning his potential loss.

He half-smiles. "That depends—so far I am enjoying the scenery."

I flush, my face turning hot from not just his innuendo, but the glass of wine I've almost finished. I need to slow down or I'll be drunk before too long.

I hastily cover up my embarrassment by changing the subject. "How old are you, Ethan?" I think he's around my age, but by the way he talks you'd think he was from 18th century England.

"Twenty-eight," he answers, his tone serious.

I nod. 28 is a good age. I actually thought he looked younger. His features are all man, but he has a very boyish look in his eyes, especially when he gives that one-dimpled smile.

"Is that a bad thing?" he asks, his smile failing.

I immediately feel bad for being silent after he told me.

"Oh no! Actually, it's good you're twenty-eight. The men in this town generally range from fifty to ninety-five. You're in a rare age bracket," I reassure him.

"I noticed that." His face lights up again. "I forgot to look up the median age when I researched locations. It is not so bad though," he adds, leaning in closer. Now we're only about a foot apart. *How did we get so close?*

I find myself staring into his eyes again. Every time he sips his red wine the reflection makes his irises a dark amethyst. His eyes lock with mine, his left cheek showing off that cute dimple. I begin to lean farther forward—like there's a magnet between us—pulling us together. His eyes

62

narrow slightly, his breathing becoming short and tight. We're *very* close now, my eyes never leaving his until we're a whisper away from each other's lips. My body is anticipating a kiss as his warm breath washes over me— *entrancing me*—my gaze flutters to his mouth, my tongue reaching out to wet my parched lips. I feel my chest heaving up and down to match his. Every fiber in my being is screaming for me to press my lips to his, my hands itching to touch him. Just as our lips are about to meet, the loud blaring of his fire alarm sounds through the room, breaking us from our trance.

I jump back, almost spilling my wine everywhere. Ethan, on the other hand, looks like someone has smacked him hard across the face. He's confused and baffled and seems completely oblivious to the fact his smoke alarm is going off. I smell the familiar scent of burning food and notice smoke filling the air. I stare at him, waiting for him to respond, but he just sits on the couch with his eyes closed—his fists clenched to the point that they're white— taking deep and calming breaths.

"Um, Ethan?" I solicit, trying to snap him from whatever self-imposed drama he is in. His eyes fly open, practically black. It's slightly alarming.

"I think either your food or your house is on fire!" I

practically yell, the noise of the fire alarm starting to grate on my nerves.

He curses under his breath before jumping up and making his way to the kitchen. I follow him, silently wondering why his reaction is so strange. Upon entering the kitchen, we're met with thick gray smoke coming from the oven. Ethan grabs an oven mitt before going toward the offending smoke.

"I wouldn't do that if—" I try to stop him, but it's too late.

He opens the oven—black smoke pours out in thunderous clouds. Ethan starts to cough as I run to the nearest window, throwing it open. I then grab a cloth and start fanning the smoke detector, attempting to get the obnoxious beeping to stop.

When I look to Ethan, he's removed some sort of domed pan from the oven. Whatever was in there is surely burnt to a crisp. There's no way we're eating that. Finally, I'm able to stop the fire alarm and quiet once again fills the house. I set the towel down, and stand next to Ethan, who's still fanning some of the leftover smoke out of the window.

"I'm sorry your dinner got ruined," I say sympathetically. "You must have worked so hard on it."

Ethan sighs in defeat. I'm about to lay a comforting

hand on his shoulder when a look of excitement flashes through his eyes—like he's had an *a-ha!* moment. He turns his gaze back to the domed pot. The same look of intensity that sends flutters up my spine returns to his face but now it's aimed at the kitchenware instead of me.

"Ethan?" I ask, wondering what he's thinking.

He quickly turns to me. "We will not know if it is ruined until we look under the cover and assess the damage," he grins.

"Really, Ethan—*nothing* could have survived with that kind of smoke!" I exclaim, laughing at his optimism.

"Let us just see, shall we? You never know."

I roll my eyes but placate him anyway—watching as he lifts off the cover from the pan—bracing myself for more smoke to start pouring out, but it never does.

"See?" he says happily. "Looks great to me."

I peer into the dish, shock washing over my body. To my disbelief, inside is a perfect, tender-looking roast. Carrots and golden potatoes cooked to perfection frame the meat perfectly, like an image from a cookbook. It's impossible.

"But—but the smoke!" I exclaim.

"It must have been some spilled food or grease in the bottom of the oven that set on fire," he says, shrugging his shoulders.

"I don't understand—I mean—that's *impossible!* It was burning!" I repeat, looking at the perfectly cooked roast, then back up to Ethan's amused face watching me.

"It is obviously not impossible, seeing as the meat is not burned," he states.

My eyebrow pops up suspiciously at him, my lips forming into a tight frown. His explanation doesn't make sense. I huff in frustration, my grip on the counter tightening.

After a few seconds Ethan takes one of my fisted hands. He sweeps his thumb gently over my knuckles attempting to calm me.

"Come—I have set the dining room for us."

I agree dumbly and begin to relax at his touch. He then leads me into another large, beautifully modern room. There is a long dining room table that looks like it seats twelve comfortably. Two places are set—one at the head of the table and the other in the closest seat next to it. Before I can sit, Ethan pulls my chair for me. Once I'm comfortably seated, he pours me a fresh glass of wine.

He turns to leave. "I will be right back."

I study the delicate china placed before me. It looks old and really expensive. There's an ornate glass vase adorned with white roses between us, with a white votive candle display lit as well. The classical music finishes the romantic tone of the entire space. He really pulled out all the stops. I wonder if the book he checked out on romantic meals also gave decorating tips. I laugh quietly at the thought.

"What is so funny?" Ethan asks, returning with the plate of roast and vegetables.

"I was just wondering if *Romantic Cooking for the Romantic Fool* also gave you decorating advice," I tease.

"And if it did?" he asks, sitting down across from me.

"Then it did a good job."

He beams warmly at me before relaxing against the back of his chair.

"I hope you like roast."

"I do. I haven't had a real home-cooked meal in forever."

"I cannot promise it will be good. You saw what happened in the kitchen," he says anxiously.

"I did—but honestly it can't be much worse than my mom's cooking."

"I feel the same way. My mother's idea of a home-cooked meal is ordering from the restaurant down the street and pretending she cooked it."

I smile at this because it sounds exactly like my mom.

Ethan serves me a nice chunk of roast with a few potatoes and some vegetables, then serves himself.

"It really looks great, Ethan."

"Bon Appétit," he says in a perfect French accent that makes my lady parts twitch.

"*Ditto*," I say, trying not to cringe at my lameness. If I were to try and speak even the smallest bit of French back to him, I would sound like a complete idiot. Not that I don't already.

I bring my fork to the roast, admiring how it practically melts against my utensil. It is so perfectly cooked I am in awe. I tentatively bring it to my lips, hesitating before taking a bite. At the first taste, *I moan*. Not a small moan, but a very guttural moan. It is one of the best things I have *ever* tasted. My eyes close involuntarily as I savor the taste of the perfectly spiced meat. When I open them, I notice Ethan watching me, his eyes dark with desire. I swallow thickly, lowering my head in complete mortification. I can't believe I actually moaned like that. *OUT LOUD.*

"Sorry," I swallow. "Food and I have a *very* special relationship," I laugh awkwardly. *Did I just say that?* I grab my wine, taking several large gulps, trying to quell my embarrassment. When I lift my eyes back to his, he shifts uncomfortably in his seat before taking a big bite of the roast. After he savors it for a moment, he flashes a tilted grin at me.

"Not bad for my first try. I take it you are enjoying it?"

"Yes," I say, trying not to blush. "I can't believe it came out so well. Not only because it's your first time making it, but also because I would have thought the smoke ruined it."

"Just lucky I guess," he answers back quickly before changing the subject. "So, Sophia, tell me what there is to do in this town."

I swallow another bite of food. "You're lucky you came during the summer. There's boating and cruises, there's also lots of town picnics, bonfires, water shows and other random things—I mean if you like that sort of thing. Ana and I always joke that summer is the time for cute tourists and one-night stands." This time I do slap my hand over my mouth, wishing that I hadn't just told him that information. Not that I mind, but I just met the guy—I don't want him to think I'm easy.

Ethan surprises me by letting out a giant belly laugh.

"You astound me with your openness, Sophia. The people I am normally around are not so—*free.*"

"I don't know if it's a good trait to be honest. I have a filtering problem. Ana tells me I have word vomit disorder, especially when I'm nervous."

Ethan unleashes his deadly half-smile—leaning towards me—drawing me in with his freaky special power.

"Who is this Ana you keep referring to?"

"She's my best friend," I say, noticing my heart speeding up at his closeness.

"And why are you nervous?" he inquires, leaning even closer.

"I—*I don't know I*—you just make me nervous."

"Is that so?"

Ethan gracefully moves his chair closer so his body invades my personal space. We're so close that our arms are almost touching. I feel the energy we had on the couch earlier returning quickly and faster than before. The magnetic pull is back in full force. This time I hope there's no smoke alarm to stop us. His eyes pull me in—*the purple hue is just so bewitching*—I find myself wanting to drown in it.

"Your eyes are beautiful," he breathes, his lips just a whisper away now. "They are the most vibrant green I have ever seen—like emeralds."

"You're one to talk," I tell him softly.

Ethan brings his thumb up, brushing it gently across my lower lip.

"I would like to kiss you," he states so quietly I almost don't hear him. "May I?"

All I can do is bow my head. *Yes, please kiss me.*

Without another word his lips are on mine. My heart stops beating for a second, and I lose all sense of time and space. Most first kisses that I've experienced were awkward and wet. The guy would move one way and I would somehow end up moving the same way, causing our noses to bump or teeth to clatter together. Not this kiss—there isn't an ounce of awkwardness in it—Ethan's kiss is gentle and controlled. His lips taste of red wine and salt from dinner. *It's bliss.*

He brings his hand up to cup my cheek, pulling me deeper into the kiss. My arms seem to have a mind of their own, coming to wrap around his shoulders. I lose myself in the taste and masculine smell of him—like pine and expensive cologne. I'm pretty sure my brain has flatlined.

Ethan's movements become more heated and assertive. His tongue runs across my bottom lip—*begging entrance*—which I quickly grant. As his fingers tangle in my hair, he pulls me in deeper into his embrace. I realize I've ended up on his lap, our position too awkward to fit together on the dining room chair. When one of his hands glides to my torso, it feels like a trail of fire radiating down into my bones. I want more—*need more*. I release a throaty moan that flutters against his lips as his hand grips my waist.

Then, without warning, he swiftly pulls away, his warmth leaving my body. The loss causes me to quake. With the distraction of his kiss gone, my over-active mind begins to swirl with negative thoughts. This intense behavior is unlike me. I don't feel for guys like this. Sure, I've had boyfriends, but they were just that. Usually they were more boy and friend than anything else. Long ago I had decided that I am a loner, destined to be an old lady spinster. Hence the random one-night stands and lack of social life.

I begin to ask myself why I agreed to have dinner with him like it was the easiest thing in the world? And why am I now making out with him like he's the last man on earth? With Ethan everything suddenly feels different; this only adds to my list of everything that's gone wrong in the last few days.

During my internal spazz-fest I completely forget that I'm still sitting on his lap. I quickly stand up, sitting back on my own chair with my hands wringing nervously in front of me. I take him in, his eyes closed, hair now messy and cheeks flushed; he looks as frazzled as I feel. His fists are clenched at his sides, his knuckles white again. I remember the moment on the couch earlier when we had almost kissed the first time. Ethan had made the same expression— like he was mad at himself for doing something wrong. He's now oblivious to me, just like he was oblivious to the fire alarm going off. I wonder what he's thinking and if he's having similar thoughts to mine. Maybe he regrets inviting me over for dinner and kissing me.

"Sophia," he says sternly. I jump, not expecting him to speak so abruptly. I don't answer, not sure if it was a question or a statement. Not to mention I don't know what to say to him or why he sounds angry.

When he finally opens his eyes, his gaze is sharp, and his pupils black. I realize he isn't angry. In fact, he's far from angry. He looks hungry—*and it isn't for dinner.* The attraction in his eyes is evident.

He takes a deep breath to calm himself before speaking again.

"I—*that was*—I want you to know that I am not used to doing this sort of thing."

"Which would be what, exactly?" I ask.

"I do not go around cooking people dinner and then *attacking* them! Not that I do not want to kiss you, Sophia. Clearly, that was my intent—just not like *that.*"

I almost laugh. "If it makes you feel any better, I don't

normally go on dates and agree to people attacking me either—unless that was the intention."

My eyebrows lift suggestively as he lets out a shaky laugh, running a hand through his already disheveled hair.

"I hope you do not think less of me," he mutters, casting his eyes downward towards his half-eaten meal. He is clearly upset with himself.

"I don't think less of you, Ethan." At that he looks up to me, *hopeful*. "I actually thought you might think less of me. What I said earlier about one-night stands with hot tourists—though I'm not lying about it—I'm not a woman who only sleeps with men for a little fun—*not that there is anything wrong with that!*" I quickly say. "You know—I'm usually really boring and kind of strange. I don't even go out—just ask Ana! I have no clue what's come over me recently. These last few days have been off—"

Ethan stops my rambling by placing his hand over mine, squeezing lightly. "I think I have been going about this the wrong way. I like you, Sophia. Despite the fact we have just met, it is quite obvious that I feel drawn to you," he says, looking into my eyes with an emotion I can't read. "I do not understand it, and frankly, I just decided I do not need too. I enjoy spending time with you. If I did not screw tonight up too horribly, I am really hoping you might like to spend more time with me," he adds.

I'm relieved he feels the unusual pull between us too. Though I have doubts, and a lot of questions—not only regarding Ethan but all the abnormal events leading up to this date—I feel that pull toward him return—building in the pit of my stomach and spreading through my body. I know I can't stop it, so in a split-second I decide I want to continue whatever is going on between us. My mind is all over the damn place!

"I feel the same way," I eventually admit.

His face lights up. "Good! I mean great—that is great," he stumbles.

I smile back at him, not able to avoid his contagious grin, before standing up to leave. "I should get going. I have to be at the library by 7:00 a.m. tomorrow."

"Oh, of course," he says with evident disappointment. "I will walk you out."

I glance down at the half-eaten food on my plate. I can't help the flush of my cheeks upon realizing we didn't finish dinner.

"Do you want to take the rest home?" he asks.

I shake my head. Although it's tempting, I just want to get out of here before I do something I regret. Ethan comes to stand next to me, placing his hand on the small of my back. He flashes that dang dimple, gently ushering me toward the front door. When we reach the foyer, he takes my jacket from the coat closet, helping me into it with careful attention.

"I had a good time tonight," I face him, warmly looking up at those pretty eyes of his. He surprises me by reaching up and tucking a strand of brown hair behind my ear.

"As did I," he smiles.

"Goodnight," I utter, opening the door to leave. I walk out to the porch rather fast, but just as I'm about to take a step down the stairs, Ethan grabs my arm, swinging me around and placing a small but lingering kiss on my lips.

"Goodnight, Sophia. I will see you soon."

I open my mouth, attempting to say something back, but before I can he's gone. I stand there for a few moments dumbfounded, before touching my fingers to my still tingling lips.

CHAPTER 5

Monday morning I wake up completely out of sorts.

When I jolt out of my sleepy haze, I look at my alarm clock to find I slept through it. I fly out of bed in a panic, grab some clothes off my floor, and throw my hair up in an untidy ponytail before bolting out the door. I'm in a bad mood now and not even memories of my night with Ethan can change that. It's when I don't have time to stop for my mocha that I get *really* pissed! As I pull up to the library at exactly 7:00 a.m. I'm extremely surprised—at least I haven't completely lost my *always on time* mojo. I jump out of my car and dash to the door, coming to a sudden stop when I notice Ethan—*looking as hot as ever*—perched in front of the entrance.

"What are you doing here?" I blurt out in a rather hard tone.

"Good morning to you too, Sunshine," he smiles. He then hands me a coffee. "I thought you might need a morning pick-me-up."

I hesitantly take the coffee from his outstretched hand. I take a tentative sip, sighing when the rich chocolate slides past my lips. When I feel his eyes on me, I come out of my coffee-induced haze.

"How did you know my order?" I demand gently—realizing what just occurred was very weird and could be considered stalker-ish.

Ethan looks at me a little sheepishly. "I asked Joey what you usually order and he whipped that right up for me. He mentioned you had not been in yet and figured you were late again, so—here I am."

I study him, his face plastered with a genuine smile, and know that I'm being ridiculous—he isn't stalking me. "Sorry I gave you the third-degree. I'm not used to people doing something like this for me. Thank you, it was very thoughtful of you—Joey was right—I was running late and I really wished for this coffee. I'm afraid I'm a major grouch in the mornings without it."

Ethan seems to get lost in thought for a moment before smiling back with a hint of surprise—a little strange, but I brush it off.

"It is really no trouble. I have the same problem in the mornings but I go with a straight double shot of espresso or black coffee."

I raise my eyebrows at him. "Yet here you are, bright and early to greet me. Twice in less than a week, I might add."

He flushes. "What can I say, you make me want to be a morning person."

"Wowee! You don't hold back on the cheese, do you? You'll fit right in, in Wisconsin." I chuckle, before taking another sip of my delicious coffee.

"I suppose I achieved my goal then." He looks up at me through his long black lashes, rocking forward on his toes slightly. I find myself wanting to kiss him again but am able to resist.

"Thanks again for the coffee. I better get inside before Mary shows up," I motion towards the door behind him.

"Right. Before you go, I actually had something I wanted to ask you about."

"Okay, shoot."

He takes a step towards me, his nearness making my heart pound.

"I was wondering—since I am new to town and all—if you would be my tour guide?"

I can't help but smile—feeling like a girl being asked out for a second date by the popular guy. Surprising myself yet again, I don't hesitate to answer. "I'd love too, Ethan."

His grin broadens and his eyes light up. "Perfect. When are you free?"

"The only days I have off are Thursday or Sunday," I say, my disappointed tone more prominent than I would have liked. Four days seems like a long time to not see him. With that thought, I know for sure I've officially gone off the deep end.

He looks knowingly at me like he's thinking the same thing. He brings his hand up to tuck a strand of hair behind my ear just like last night, and my heart flutters when his finger grazes my ear.

"Thursday it is," he confirms.

"Great!" I say clumsily. "I think I'm going to work now before I say something stupid."

I walk around him to the door, glancing back over my shoulder. Ethan gazes at me, smiling happily to himself. I give him a wave before making my way into the library, the door ringing as I enter. Grateful I'm alone, I let out a squeal of excitement, embarrassing myself at my childish behavior. Even though this morning started off on the wrong foot, I end up grinning like a fool the rest of the day.

When I clock out later that night, I'm eager to get to my weekly dinner with Ana. I arrive promptly at 7:00 p.m., happy to finally not be rushing somewhere. We always meet at our favorite local spot, a fun little diner in downtown called *Nifty 50s*. I find Ana sitting at our usual table, sipping on cherry pop and texting.

"Hey!" I call out, sliding into the booth across from her.

"I already ordered for us," she says before looking up.

"Awesome. Except for today I think I want to add a chocolate milkshake."

"That time of the month, eh? Lady parts screaming for relief?" she quips.

I roll my eyes, stealing a drink of her soda. "No, I'm just in a good mood."

Ana looks at me questioningly, "This has to do with a boy, doesn't it?"

God she was good.

"Oh my god! It's Ethan isn't it?!" she squeals.

"SHHH!" I cry, looking around the diner. Every person here is staring at us. Thank God most are tourists.

"It is him! *I knew it*," she says in a loud whisper.

"*Wow*—you're *so* good at being subtle, Ana," I say sarcastically.

She ignores me, rambling on. "Tell me what happened! Did he send you flowers or something?"

"*Well*—Ikindofhadadatewithhimalready."

"Excuse me—*WHAT?*"

"I had a date with him already," I cringe.

"And you didn't tell me?" she pouts.

"I'm sorry! I didn't want you to make a big deal out of it."

"It is a big deal, Soph! I mean you went out on a date with *Mr. Hottie McHotterson!* That is a fucking, BIG. DEAL."

"Would you keep it down please?" I shout-whisper. "This town already knows enough about my personal business."

"Sorry. It's just, *wow.* I mean—*wowsers*—I can't believe this."

"I know—and *wowsers* is a good word to describe him."

"You have to tell me everything and I mean *everything*, Sophia!"

"The full name—now I know you're serious."

Ana just stares at me with her, *I'm waiting*, face.

I shake my head. "Fine. I'll tell you everything, but let's take our food to go. I don't want people hearing this."

"*Eep!* This must be really, really good if we have to leave!" she exclaims, bouncing in her seat like an over-sugared five-year-old.

After Ana and I get our food packed up, we walk over to Lakeshore Park. I make sure to find the most secluded bench possible. By the time we get situated, Ana can't contain her elation. Her face is so red; I think she might explode.

"I can't take it anymore," she bursts out. "You have to tell me all about it, and p.s. I'm still super peeved that you didn't tell me you were going on a date in the first place!"

"I know. I'm sorry, okay? It was all so sudden and if it went horribly wrong then I could have pretended like it never happened."

"It *obviously* went well."

"We're seeing each other again on Thursday."

"Are you serious?"

"I'm taking him sight-seeing."

"O.M.G.—*that's so*—I don't know, but it's something

alright. You need to tell me how the first date went. Where did he take you?"

"*His house*," I quickly mutter under my breath.

"YOU WERE AT THE COOPER MANSION?" she yells, the vein popping out of her forehead. At that moment I thank my lucky stars we're not near any people.

"He cooked me dinner—"

"*Well shit*, Soph, this was more than a date!"

"We might have kissed—" I flush.

"YOU KISSED HIM?"

"Do you always have to repeat what I'm telling you?"

"This scenario is just so unlike you. Normally in this case if it were just a sex thing, you'd tell me straight away. You're like—*seriously blushing*—this is new."

I turn redder. "I know—but you'll be happy to know that he was a perfect gentleman. Like I told you, he even cooked me dinner. I've never had a man do that for me before."

"He sounds way too good to be true. Handsome, young, rich, cute, a gentleman, *and* he cooks you a dinner? There has to be something wrong with him. Some dark secret he's hiding—maybe he's on the run from the law! Or *maybe* he's in witness protection!"

I snort. Sure, Ethan was mysterious and odd in ways,

but I didn't think he had some big, bad, dark secret.

"Your imagination gets the better of you sometimes, Ana."

"You have to admit it's weird, Soph. I mean the guy shows up out of nowhere and buys the most expensive house in town. Not to mention the Coopers just up and left it. They've lived here since the beginning of time—*then poof*—gone without a word to anyone. Then said guy meets you, asks you out, cooks for *you*—it's weird," she finishes with a patronizing tone.

I stare blankly at her after this bizarre turn in attitude. "*Geez, Ana*—tell me how you really feel. I didn't realize it's *weird* for men to ask me out. I thought you'd be happy for me. Besides, you're the one who's always telling me I need to be more adventurous."

She puffs out her chest. "I'm happy for you, I really am. I just think it's weird is all."

"Well, you made that point very clear," I snark.

I try to calm myself. She's clearly getting upset about something else, and deep down I know she has a point. My thoughts were just as all over the place as hers. I had been thinking similar ones. However, that didn't stop me from being annoyed that my best friend couldn't just be happy for me when I wanted her to. I doubt myself enough as it is.

"He's a nice guy, Ana. I'll admit the way he talks so formally is a little strange, and he is very rich, but that doesn't make him bad or untrustworthy. He's been really nice to me."

"But you don't even know him!"

I feel myself getting frustrated. "Seriously? So, it's okay for us to hook-up with random guys after barely getting to know them—*ones we'll never see again*—but the moment a decent guy comes to town—*one who lives here*—and I have *one* nice date with him—you think he's weird and untrustworthy? Why are you being like this?"

She doesn't look at me. Instead she begins to pull invisible lint off her shirt. After a minute of this, she glances up at me, her eyes glassy.

"It's nothing, okay? I just want what's best for you."

I press my lips together, willing myself to relax. "What's best for me is having my best friend trust me and my decisions."

Ana goes quiet again, her focus back to picking at her shirt. I wonder how this conversation ended up here. We never argue about anything important. I know Ethan came into my life out of the blue, but I *do* like him, and I plan on spending more time with him. Ana takes a deep, ragged breath before looking up at me with fresh tears in her blue eyes.

"Chris and I fought again," she murmurs.

Now everything makes sense—this is about Chris. I push my annoyance and anger away, trying to be a good friend for her.

"What happened?"

"The night of the bonfire he stood me up. He claimed he had someone important to meet and he wouldn't tell me who. When I saw him the next day I asked him if he was seeing someone else and of course he denied it. He promised he would take me out to make up for it, but then he canceled again, said he had an important meeting for work. I know we never labeled our relationship or anything but maybe he's cheating on me," she hiccups. I frown, patting her back sympathetically.

Chris has always been a loose cannon. When he moved here two years ago, Ana was immediately drawn to his boy next door looks and bad boy tendencies. He has nice moments and can be very charming, but most of the time he is hot and cold about *everything*. I don't like him much but I also don't think he'd cheat on Ana—at least I hope not.

"I'm sure he's not cheating on you," I repeat aloud.

"Who is he going to cheat with anyway?"

"April's been eyeing him up lately."

"April's bad news. She's been filling my mom's head with gossip and lies about Ethan and me. I wouldn't worry about her. Chris only has eyes for you. He was most likely telling the truth."

"You're probably right," she sighs.

I open the box in my lap, and take a hefty bite of my burger, not wanting to talk about Chris or Ethan anymore. Ana picks at her food while we watch the water silently roll onto shore. I'm just finishing my burger when I hear her take a deep breath and turn her eyes on me.

"I'm sorry I got on your case. I was just jealous—I'm a bad friend."

I put my hand on her shoulder, giving her a soft and knowing smile.

"You're not a bad friend. You were just upset. Forget about   it,   okay?" "Forgotten. And for the record, I approve of you and Ethan. You could do a lot worse," she laughs a little sadly.

"Thanks," I say, taking a sip of my now melted milkshake. I cringe at the warm liquid on my tongue, throwing it out in the trashcan beside the bench.

Once we've finished dinner, Ana and I decide to take a walk along the lake. We joke and laugh like we always do, making fun of random tourists with crazy shirts and ridiculous tan lines.

"Soph, I just had the greatest idea!" Ana says suddenly, jumping up and down.

I wince. When Ana has ideas, they either get me into trouble or end in something worse—like jail. Last summer we got locked up in the local precinct for indecent exposure and public intoxication. I warned her not to flash one of the cruise lines, but she insisted. Even though I was not guilty of flashing, I was drunk at the time. Guilt by association is a real thing.

"This can't be good," I warn.

"No, it's perfect! What would you say to a little double date?" she asks, her sapphire eyes wide and hopeful.

"You mean, Ethan and I with you and Chris?"

"Yeah! Why the hell not? I bet Ethan and Chris will get along great."

"You don't even know Ethan."

"This way I can get to know him! I have to give him

the best friend seal of approval and make sure he's treating you right."

I roll my eyes. "I don't think this is a good idea."

"Why not? I promise I won't embarrass you!"

"Ana—"

"*Pleeeassseeee, Sophie, please?*" she cries, giving me her best pouty face. I can't resist.

"Fine."

Ana jumps up and down, doing her weird victory dance, arms flailing every which way.

"This is going to be so amazing; I can't wait to tell Chris! We'll even go to the Olive Garden!"

I snort. "Wow—how high class of you."

Ana pushes me teasingly with her shoulder. I'm grinning goofily at the fact that Ana's idea of sophistication is a chain restaurant. It's the sweetest, small-town thing that could ever come out of her.

"*Ahhh!* This is going to be so great. I know just the dress I'm going to wear!"

She patters on endlessly about dresses and make-up, among other things, so I tune her out. I love Ana, but once she gets going, there's no stop button. She can talk for hours without any input from me. People always wonder how were such great friends when our personalities are so

90

different. The truth is, I like Ana because she's my opposite. When I met her, she was the only person who wasn't afraid to be herself. She didn't care if others hated her or found her annoying; she just did what she wanted.

I always thought Ana would do big things and live in a big city. Remembering back to when we were younger, the two of us would dream up grand ideas and schemes. We were going to be famous, rich, and marry Orlando Bloom. I was shocked when Ana decided to move back home as well, but it only solidified for me what I was sure of—I belong in Iron Lake.

"Did you hear me, Soph?" Ana asks, tugging on my arm.

"Sorry, what were you saying?"

"Chris just texted. He's done with his meeting or whatever earlier than he thought. Do you mind if I go hang out with him?"

I look at my watch and notice it's close to 9:00 p.m.

"Of course not, I should go home anyway. I've been late getting up twice now in less than a week. I need to get my sleep schedule back on track."

"You, late? Twice in basically the same week?" Ana feels my forehead jokingly.

I swat her hand away. "I know—I don't know what's

wrong with me lately. It's like my internal clock suddenly changed."

Thinking about all the weird occurrences in my life recently has me frowning again.

"Are you okay?" Ana squeezes my shoulder.

"I'm fine, really. It's just been a strange past couple of days."

"I can call Chris and cancel—"

"No, Ana, really. I'm fine! You go and have fun. I just need to catch up on some sleep."

"Okay—but if you need me, do you promise to call me?"

"Of course, now go. Don't keep that man of yours waiting," I smirk at her.

She smiles back, excitement washing over her face. She kisses my cheek before dashing off to her car.

"I'll see you Thursday!" she calls over her shoulder.

I wave back, considering going home to read, but decide to keep walking. It's dark—but I never worry about my safety in Iron Lake.

CHAPTER 6

I find myself strolling along a park path that I know pretty well—having walked it with Ana or my dad hundreds of times. The trail starts out easy, winding downhill and then slowly increasing upwards. I feel like a bit of a workout might do me some good to clear my head and sort out my thoughts.

The memory of my 5-year-old self staring at my magically-appearing, brand-new, Malibu Barbie keeps forcing its way back into my brain. My mom had been so disappointed in me for *stealing her* that she took all my toys away for weeks. I remember being mortified when we arrived at the department store we never visited to return it. That day, at the tender age of five, I promised myself that I would never wish for anything special and new again. My mom grilled into me that you had to earn what you wanted, you couldn't just take it. In my heart I knew I didn't steal that Barbie, but I was five. What could I do to prove I hadn't?

My dad never scolded me about the Barbie. In fact he never said a word, which angered my mom. He did, however, also instill in me that I had to earn what I wanted and that I needed to work hard. He always told me that people were dealt a certain hand of cards, and with that hand you had to play the game of life. I always took that to mean that I was destined for great things—like a high-powered job or big city living—but real-life and adulthood changed that dream for me.

Damn, I'm depressing. I see now that what happened with that Barbie might be more significant in my life than I thought. No matter how much I try to pretend it didn't happen, it did happen. Maybe I really did wish that Barbie out of thin air?

If that were true, if that Barbie did, in fact, appear after I wished for it, it would explain the books shelving themselves, and the pizza and ice cream appearing. Of course, I can logically explain what happened with the pizza and the ice cream, but I can't debunk the Barbie or the books. Things like that just don't happen—*I don't even believe in God*—much less magic. The only real-world explanation I can think of is that I have some sort of brain disorder that makes me see things or a brain tumor. Maybe

I'll start hearing voices soon, and I'll be diagnosed with schizophrenia. I shake my head. Sometimes I really let my imagination run wild—I blame Ana for that.

The more I think about it, the more irritated I become. If my dad is watching over me, he's laughing his ass off. I can almost hear him say, *Just take a sleeping pill and snooze it off, Soph!*

A cool breeze brushes against the back of my neck and shiver. My mind shifts to my twenty-fifth birthday creeping up. Almost another year older and now I'm battling the idea of my developing insanity. I feel my eyes sting as more memories of my dad come flooding forth. He died suddenly after my twenty-first birthday. He was only fifty-seven but managed to have a stroke.

It was then I understood that life could be over in a blink of an eye. I thought my dad was untouchable, and then he was gone. Though I like to tell people I only moved back because I missed our town and my mom, I also know that after he died, I needed to return home. His death taught me not to take life for granted, that I needed to enjoy every moment no matter how small. Now, going through all the strange things happening in the last week, I know I'm not enjoying my life. I'm just living through the days monotonously. *I'm not following that mantra at all.* I take a deep breath, deciding then and there I need to fix that.

Ethan coming into my life randomly has given me inspiration for change. Something about him has helped to push me forward from a place where I had been stagnated. Since our dinner Sunday, I've felt more alive than I have in years. Minus the fight with Ana and my weird mishaps, I realize I'm—*happy*.

When the night of our recent make-out comes to me, my lips burn and my cheeks heat. I wish he were here to kiss me again now. It's the loud and hard snap of a twig nearby that breaks me from my fantasy. My heart begins to beat rapidly, fear replacing the excitement I had just been feeling.

I spin around looking for someone, but don't see anything. I laugh fearfully at my reaction. It's probably just an animal—then I realize exactly how dark it is. I check my watch and see it's almost 10:00 p.m. The sound of the crickets and leaves rustling seems to amplify my building paranoia and my heart beats faster. When I get the sensation someone is watching me I start to walk faster. I stumble over loose tree roots and chunks of dirt as I try to hurry down the path toward the light of the parking lot.

I wish that instead of just daydreaming about Ethan I

had called him to come walk with me. When I hear more twigs crack, and the sound of footsteps and heavy breathing, I start jogging towards the parking lot. There's pepper spray in the car's glove box that my dad gave me before I went to college. I hope I don't have to use it.

I finally break through the woods and into the light. I turn to see if a person is following me, but there's no one there. I turn back just in time to run into a veritable wall. I let out a small yelp, falling directly on my ass *again* for the third time in the span of five days. I scramble to stand when the figure reaches out and grabs my arms. I almost scream before my brain registers the familiar feeling of warmth spreading through my body that only one person has been able to cause in my life so far.

"Ethan?" I state breathlessly, my body tense in apprehension.

"Sophia?" Ethan responds, his breath matching mine.

"What are you doing here?" I gasp, my eyes fully adjusting to the dim lamplight. He looks as though he just rolled out of bed. His eyes are half-asleep, but I can still see the confusion in them. My gaze wanders down his body, taking in his loose-fitting black t-shirt and red flannel pajama pants. The strangest thing of all is that he isn't wearing any shoes or socks. He's completely barefoot.

"Where are your shoes?" I ask him.

"What?" he asks, appearing confused.

"Your shoes?" I ask again. "Where are they? And why are you wearing your pajamas?"

He finally releases my arms, looking down at his attire and then around at the park area in bewilderment. When his gaze settles back on me, he notices I'm breathing hard and sweat is dripping down my forehead. I run a hand through my frizzy hair and wonder if I look as horrible as I feel. My heart is still beating wildly out of my chest, and my stomach is in knots.

"What are you doing out here?" he asks sternly, now awake and his eyes full of anger.

"I was out for a walk," I state rather plainly, feeling anger build at the sound of his tone.

"In the woods all alone? It is nearly ten o'clock! There could have been a psycho-maniac out there just waiting to pounce," he scolds.

"I didn't realize it was getting late, *dad*" I bite back, pretending as if I wasn't scared out of my mind moments ago. "Besides, I can handle myself just perfectly, thanks." I cross my arms over my chest.

"Is that why you came bolting out of the woods like a bat out of heck? You were about to scream for help before

98

you realized it was me," he bites, matching my stance. He crosses his arms over his chest, puffing it out so that he looks twice as large.

"How did you get here?" I ask him, trying to change the subject, but also curious.

"Well, I—," he stammers, perplexed. "I was trying to sleep and was not able to. I thought maybe the lake would calm me."

"Without shoes?" I scratch my head.

"I forgot them," he says almost too quickly.

"You forgot your shoes?"

"You heard me." He takes another step forward so that he towers over my still trembling form.

"That's a bit strange don't you think?" I ask, my voice wavering and my confidence slowly starting to break. Ethan, however, is unfazed by my attitude and questions.

All the adrenaline in my body is beginning to wear off and I'm becoming awfully clammy. Every bad emotion is starting to bubble up to the surface, and I'm trying really hard to hold back unnecessary tears. My breath becomes labored as I recount what happened in the woods. I thought I was being followed, and then I began to imagine being with Ethan and he suddenly appears—half-asleep—in his pajamas and barefoot. *My breath hitches.* Could this be the same thing that happened with the pizza and ice cream? Did the same thing just happen with Ethan?

I look up into his eyes, the sparse lighting making them look dark grey. He's studying me carefully, his face tense. Before I can stop it, my body betrays me, and I begin to shake violently.

"Sophia, are you sure you are okay?" he asks, his tone changing.

I try to answer, but nothing comes out. The way his voice is so tender—*so caring*—it's the final straw that breaks me. Tears collect in the corners of my eyes, and I curse myself for crumbling. Before I know what's happening, Ethan's arms are around me, his warm body pressing into mine, and hugging me close.

"It is okay, Sophia. You are safe now," he says softly, rubbing my back while I silently cry. I let the tears roll down my cheeks, releasing all the pent-up emotions from my body. I inhale Ethan's freshly-showered scent, letting the solid feel of him ground me.

When I begin to regain control, I pull away from him, immediately shy about my behavior. I don't cry, much less fall apart in front of people. I know that I'm not only crying over my scare in the woods but over all of the confusion and fear I had felt in the past week.

Ethan's features have turned to that of concern as he brings his thumb up to wipe the leftover tears from my flushed cheeks. I bet I look like garbage right now.

"What happened, Sophia—did someone hurt you?"

I shake my head, giving him a watery smile. "It's silly. Like I said before, I went for a walk and was lost in thought. I didn't realize how dark it had gotten and I just made myself paranoid is all. My mind was playing tricks on me and I freaked. Nothing ever happens in Iron Lake."

He looks like he wants to say more but decides against it. "Come on, I will walk you to your car."

I accept his outstretched palm and he begins to rub his thumb across my knuckles in a comforting motion. He keeps sneaking concerned looks at me, his body slightly tense. I feel horrible for probably scaring the crap out of him.

Once we get to my car, we stand there for a moment. He brings our joined hands up to my cheek, brushing a loose strand of hair away. When the silence is too uncomfortable for me, I break.

"I should go—"

Ethan studies my face for a few more seconds, his brow scrunching in thought. "Can I ask you something?"

I nod, waiting for him to say whatever it is that is

making him uncomfortable.

Taking his free hand, he rubs the back of his neck timidly. "Could you give me a ride home?"

My eyebrows shoot up. We both live a good five or so miles from the park. There's no way he walked all this way without shoes.

"You didn't drive here?"

He takes his other hand out of mine, his face turning a brighter red. He then runs both hands through his already messy hair, laughing awkwardly to himself.

"I sort of walked?" It comes out as a question rather than an answer. The way he looks unconvinced himself only raises more questions.

"Really? You walked over five miles after nine o'clock at night without shoes?" I point to his feet, which now that I'm looking at them seem awfully clean for having walked such a distance.

He kicks a rock on the ground with his big toe. "It is a long story—"

I eye him suspiciously. I have the urge to lecture him about the double-standard of me vs. him walking alone at night but I don't want to keep standing in the middle of the parking lot.

I exhale. "Right, well, I guess the least I can do is to

give you a ride after crying on you."

His eyes ease back up to meet mine. Their normal light violet color has returned, although the intensity is still there.

"Nonsense. You are allowed to have emotions, Sophia. I am just glad I was here," he smiles kindly.

I blush in spite of myself, turning to open the driver's side door rather harshly. I'm hoping to end the weird sexual tension between us, but when I look over to see him still staring, my body tenses with excitement.

"Are you going to stand there all night? Sleep is calling my name," I chirp before getting in the car and slamming the door.

That seems to wake him up. He makes his way over to the passenger side door and opens it, then slides into my old beater with grace that I feel only royalty could have.

Once his seatbelt is on, I turn the key starting good ol' NAC up. The engine squeals obnoxiously, and I flinch.

Ethan looks on in worry. "That did not sound good at all."

"It's fine," I assure him. "My starter likes to give me trouble sometimes, but a good two or three turns of the key and we'll be back in business."

Sure enough, on the third turn, NAC roars to life, humming happily.

"See? Third times the charm."

Ethan stares at me like I have a third head before turning away and muttering something about having a death wish. I choose to ignore him and pat my car's steering wheel happily.

The drive to his house is quiet besides the occasional sound of our simultaneous yawns. A few minutes later we pull up beside his Porsche, and I throw my car into park.

He turns to face me with a look of curiosity. "May I ask you something?"

"You know, you don't have to ask for permission every time you want to ask me something," I tease, but he ignores me, continuing on.

"When you thought someone was following you in the woods, what were you thinking about?"

My face immediately contorts in discomfort—I had been thinking of him—but I don't want him to know that! Not to mention his question is strange.

"*Umm*—besides the obvious thoughts a person would have while thinking someone was following them in the woods?" I laugh uncomfortably, my body shuddering at the memory. "I guess I was thinking about—God this is embarrassing—" I try to avoid answering. I don't want to look at him.

104

"You can tell me. I will not judge you, Sophia."

He brings his hand down to cover my own, giving it a gentle squeeze, and I can't help but squeeze it back.

"I was thinking about you. I was thinking about you and how much I wanted to feel safe," I say quickly, my face hot. I feel his eyes on me, burning a hole right through me. This only makes my skin hotter.

The car is silent for a few minutes before I feel my chin being turned by Ethan's finger.

"*Sophia*," he says gently, his voice thick with concern.

When I finally turn my gaze towards him, I see we're once again extremely close to one another.

"You have nothing to be ashamed of. I am only glad that I could be there for you," he smiles, his dimple appearing. I can't help but smile back.

"I do wish, however, that every time we run into each other it would not happen literally," he laughs. "I am afraid next time you might break your ass."

My eyes widen at the word *ass* passing through his lips. It's the first time I hear him use a curse word. No matter how mild it is, I have to admit it's kind of sexy, and a little funny.

"I'll have to invest in butt-pads," I joke.

He laughs deeply, which makes my toes tingle and my

arm hairs stand on end.

He starts unfastening his seatbelt and then opens his door. "I should go."

I nod. "Thanks again."

"Anytime, Sophia—and whenever you feel like you need me—simply think of me."

Before I can ask him what he means by that, he gets out of the car and closes the door. With one last look back and a wave, he dashes up the stairs and disappears into his house.

"What an odd man," I say to myself.

I release a long breath before throwing my car in reverse and making my way home in no time. I quickly go through my nightly routine and climb into bed, Laker curled firmly into my side. When my eyes close, and I begin to drift off, my dreams are restless—full of dark woods and endless eyes watching me. I feel myself waking up, and then falling back asleep again—never fully at rest. At the worst, when I'm half-awake— startled—it takes a few moments to calm myself down. My brain thinks of Ethan as I start to fall into dreams again. Just before I drift off, I feel a recognizable warmth spread throughout my body, and what feels like his strong arms comforting me. With no more discomfort, I'm asleep in an instant.

CHAPTER 7

Monday night's events put me on edge for the rest of the week.

When Ethan stops by the library early the next day to make sure I'm alright, I try to brush off his concern. I tell him that the night before felt like some really strange dream that I was trying to forget. He seems a little taken aback, but I assure him that I'm happy he was there.

The whole situation is confusing and odd. Like most things in the last week, I try to bypass the fact that I had thought of Ethan and then he appeared, half-asleep and not wearing shoes. He reassures me that I'm not crazy—that he has some weird sleep problems and he likes walking barefoot. He calls it *grounding*—whatever that is.

I'm still trying to wrap my head around it all. If I did indeed magically wish him to the park, he would have been freaked out beyond belief. I sure as hell would be if one moment I were sleeping, then the next I'm in the woods with a person screaming then promptly crying on me.

After last week I have officially become a *crabby-pants,* as Mary puts it. I go to work and then leave, heading straight to the comfort of my own bed every night. Even Laker has fallen into a bad mood, avoiding me at all costs when I walk through the door. I'm glad Ethan has given me some space, although I have to admit not seeing him since Tuesday morning is adding to my edge.

Now, it's Thursday—the day of sight-seeing and the dreaded double-date with Ana and Chris. I asked Ethan when he stopped by on Tuesday if it was okay. At first when I mentioned Chris, he seemed surprised and hesitant. When I questioned him, he immediately backed down and claimed that he'd love to meet my best friend and her *boyfriend.*

I exhale, attempting to ward off the icky feeling I've had since this morning. The strange dreams from Monday night keep plaguing my sleep. I even start to dream of being 5-years-old again, my mom yelling at me for stealing the Malibu Barbie. No matter what I dream, I always startle awake—sweating profusely—my heart beating a mile a minute. It's getting old.

Ethan's coming to pick me up around 9:00 a.m. He insists on taking me out to breakfast at this little place called *Ham n' Eggs* in the old downtown area. Apparently, he's wanted to eat there ever since he moved but doesn't like going to sit-down restaurants by himself. Even though I prefer to make him breakfast since I'm low on cash, I couldn't say no—he is abnormally excited about it. It reminded me of Ana when she sees a chocolate chip cookie—he is *that* excited. I am excited about it too. I also have a full agenda of sight-seeing and hiking planned—I hope he enjoys it.

I dress in a white tank with my most comfortable flannel over-shirt and a pair of old jeans finish off the look with my sturdy hiking boots. After I throw my hair into a high ponytail I'm ready right at 9:00 a.m. when Ethan promptly rings the doorbell. Laker starts barking, not used to someone using the bell. Ana or my mom are the only people to ever stop by and they usually let themselves in.

"Hush, Laker," I say, making my way to the door.

When I open it—to my surprise—Laker bounds out, tail

in full-on wag mode. He immediately takes to Ethan, jumping on him excitedly and wanting to be loved by him.

"Hey, boy!" Ethan coos in a sweet voice. He squats down to Laker's level, scratching him behind his ears and letting him lick his face.

I look on in shock, squeaking out, "His name's Laker."

I can't believe he isn't trying to bite off Ethan's hand. He doesn't like people he doesn't know. It makes it hard for me to take him walking on public trails because he growls at others and scares their dogs. The last man he liked was my dad.

Ethan stands back up to look at me. "He is a beautiful dog."

"Thanks," I smile while noticing his appearance. He looks like he just stepped out of a pricey outdoor magazine. He's wearing a short-sleeved, orange and red flannel shirt, along with perfect fitting dark wash jeans. His hair is exceptionally styled as usual. He looks like a model. I notice that he's also sporting a very expensive looking pair of Doc Martens. We *almost* match again. When I remember I'm blatantly surveying him, that annoying blush reappears on my cheeks.

He unleashes a dangerous smile. "Ready to go?"

"Yep!" I chirp awkwardly, quickly putting Laker in the

house and locking the door.

When I finish, we begin walking towards his car while he takes in the scenery around us.

"This place is very nice. You have a great view of the lake."

"I'm definitely lucky. You should see the sunset during the fall. I can guarantee you'll never see a better one."

He smiles thoughtfully and goes to open the car door for me. I see it's not his Porsche convertible he usually drives. This car is sleek and sexy looking—and brand new. I can't stop my mouth from dropping open.

"What kind of car is this?" I ask, running my hand along the smooth silver paint.

Ethan cracks a lopsided grin. "It is my new baby. A McLaren GT. Just got her in yesterday morning."

It's very ostentatious. The doors are flipped up like the Batmobile to reveal two-seats with sleek leather interior.

"It's nice."

His face screws up funny. "Nice? This car is more than *nice*."

I stifle a laugh, making a note of his reaction for the future. Seeing him riled up over me calling his car *nice* is amusing. I get in without another word, not daring to touch the fancy door. He stands there a moment, collecting himself before getting in—the doors automatically closing. I feel like I'm in some sci-fi movie. No words are spoken as he starts the machine with a simple push of a button. It roars to life, the engine obnoxiously loud.

"Listen to her purr. She is more than *nice,*" Ethan reiterates while closing his eyes to bask in the sound.

I can't help but chuckle at his expense. The look of pleasure on his face is comical. He opens his eyes and looks at me like I killed his puppy.

"This car is top of the line. I have been dreaming about getting one for a while now."

"How very pretentious of you," I joke.

His face falls a little, and I realize that it didn't come out in the playful way I intended. It is pretentious of him, but it's also endearing the way he talks about something he obviously enjoys.

I reach over and squeeze his thigh gently, noticing how he jumps slightly at my touch.

"I'm only playing with you. I think it's cute how much you love cars. I'm also not used to people having money to get what they want. I'm sorry."

He pauses for a second before his lips upturn slightly.

"I am cute now?" he teases.

I roll my eyes. "I would have said handsome but that

wouldn't have made sense."

He flashes his one dimple. "Well, for future reference, I do like that description much better."

I snort. "Noted."

With a final look in my direction, Ethan turns his attention back to the task at hand. In a few moments we're on the road, making our way toward old downtown. I sit back in the comfy seat, the sound of classical music streaming through his stereo relaxing me. I feel at ease for the first time since Monday. I know that being around Ethan also has something to do with it. I don't understand why simply being next to him calms me, but it does. I close my eyes and feel my lids become heavy. *Damn, this car is comfortable*—so comfortable that I could fall asleep.

I feel Ethan gently shake my shoulder, causing my eyes to pop open. When I look around, I notice we're parked outside of *Ham n' Eggs*. I guess I *did* fall asleep. Ethan looks at me with concern.

"Your car has the ability to put me to sleep very quickly. I may have to sell my house and invest in one of my own," I joke.

"You are tired," he states, taking his fingers and brushing at the dark circles under my eyes. "Are you sure you want to do this today? I could take you home."

"No!" I exclaim a little too quickly. "I mean no. I'm fine. Really—I just need to get some coffee in my system and I'll be good to go."

He studies me for a few more moments before nodding his head. We get out of the car and walk into the small diner where we are greeted by several of the older residents in town. This is their morning hangout.

"Sophie!" an older woman calls.

My eyes track to the voice and I brighten.

"Hey, Catherine!"

She comes over to hug me. Catherine is an elderly woman in her early seventies. I've known her since I was a little girl.

"You look wonderful, dear! A bit too skinny though," she critiques. "I'll make sure Bob whips you up some of your favorite double chocolate pancakes!"

My stomach grumbles. "Sounds great, I can't wait!"

Catherine's eyes wander to Ethan standing next to me. Her eyebrows shoot up as she does a full body scan with no shame. I wonder if that's what I look like when I do the same.

"And who's this strapping young gentleman here?" Catherine asks.

"This is Ethan. He just moved into the old Cooper

house."

Her eyebrows shoot up again and the few people in the diner all quiet down so they can hear our conversation. I look to Ethan, who is now standing rigid and uncomfortable. This is exactly why I hate going out to eat with men. Now everyone will be talking more than they already are.

"It's nice to meet you, Ethan. I'm Catherine, the owner of this lovely establishment."

"It is nice to meet you; I am excited to try your delicious food."

Catherine blushes and shows us to a far booth in the corner—the farthest one away from prying eyes and ears. I want to kiss her for understanding we want some sort of privacy.

"This is perfect, Catherine, thank you."

"No problem. Now, what can I get you both to drink?"

"Coffee," Ethan and I say at the same time, causing the three of us to laugh.

"Coming right up!"

When Catherine is out of earshot, Ethan has a goofy smile plastered on his face.

"What?" I ask him cautiously.

"This town—I knew it was small, but everywhere I go

people look at me and listen to my conversations. It is very—"

"Creepy?" He nods. "I told you—you have to be careful. Growing up here you learn everyone's names and everything that's going on with them. If you want to keep a secret, you have to keep it to yourself or you'll regret it later."

He hums. "Can you explain to me why living in the Cooper house piques everyone's interest?"

"It's just strange. Do you know anything about the Coopers?"

"No—I have never even met the Coopers. I just bought their house when it went up for sale."

"Interesting—*well*, the Cooper family settled in Iron Lake before my family came here. Dana and Greg Cooper were the ones who lived in your house the entire time I was growing up. They rarely came into town, usually just to get groceries and necessities. There were always stories going around that they were involved with drugs or the Italian mafia. That family was the constant center of scary stories in school and around campfires. Until dinner last Sunday I had never seen the house fully. I must admit it was nothing like I pictured."

"I had most of it remodeled before I moved in. It was

quite outdated."

"That explains how new it looked then."

He sits proudly. "Yes, I designed it myself." *Impressive.* "Back to the Coopers. The only information I received about them is that they wanted to sell the house quickly. I never met them—I only spoke with their realtor."

"Strange. All I know is that they just up and left. Nobody knew why or when even. Just that the house was empty for a few months."

"The house was empty for over a year. I just moved in when the remodeling was done."

"A year? Maybe our town actually sucks at gossip. I never saw any sort of construction equipment or trucks going by—much less a moving van."

"Hmmm, that is interesting," he says rather quickly before flipping a menu up to cover his face. "What is good here?"

I raise one eyebrow at him in curiosity, but he can't see me. *My stomach grumbles.* I decide to drop it and look over my menu—even though I know what I'm getting.

"I heard the Ham n' Eggs is good," I say cheekily.

He chuckles. "Maybe that is what I will try then."

"I always get the double chocolate chocolate-chip pancakes. I've been eating them since I was three."

"Sounds like a sugar coma waiting to happen."

"Exactly, but it's amazing. Best pancakes you will ever have."

His eyes light up with an idea. "How would you feel about splitting the Ham n' Egg's and those delicious pancakes?"

I don't know why, but I blush. "That actually sounds perfect."

Over the next hour we eat our food and drink multiple cups of coffee. I find that even though Ethan comes across as stuffy and regal, he has a wicked sense of humor. I know he has a kind heart, but I discover that if you feed him a crapload of sugar and a pot or two of coffee, he's a whole different person. He even *giggles*. It's oddly charming and very sweet. Seeing this side to him makes my heart flutter in odd ways.

I manage to quell my laughter and give him a dead-serious look. "What did one lesbian frog say to the other lesbian frog?"

He hesitates. "What?"

"They're right, we really do taste like chicken!"

118

He spits coffee from his mouth, choking on it. I can't help but laugh harder at his graceful facade falling to pieces. I hand him a napkin as I notice a light red tint covering his cheeks.

He wipes his mouth and gives me a funny look. "I *cannot believe* you just said that. It is vulgar—"

I give him a cocky look, taking another bite of pancake. As our laughter quells, he glances behind me, his smile faltering a little. I turn to look and notice quite a few people staring at us. When I make eye-contact with one old man his face transforms, giving both Ethan and I the major stink-eye. I turn back to Ethan only to find him trying to maintain his cool, but as soon as we look at each other we both break out into laughter once again.

When Catherine comes with our bill, Ethan snatches it up before I can touch it.

"*Hey!*" I exclaim, trying to make a grab for it.

"I invited you out, I am paying the bill."

"That's not logical at all."

"Deal with it," he concludes.

I want to say something else, but I don't know how to respond, so I let him pay. I make a mental note to get the check at our next meal. He may be wealthy, but I didn't want to take advantage of him.

We thank Catherine and leave with our stomachs full of food and coffee. While we walk to the car, Ethan makes a groaning noise, placing his hands over his flat stomach.

"That food was great—I am stuffed. Did I not tell you it would be fun to come here?" he teases.

I snicker and roll my eyes at him as I get in the car. Once I'm settled, I watch as a few older men across the street moon at Ethan's car like it's a lost Picasso painting—it's ridiculous. Ethan hops in and fastens his seatbelt before we make our way to the park nearby.

I rub my hands together excitedly. "Are you ready for some hiking?"

Ethan flexes his biceps, showing me how ready he is. I swallow at the way his muscles look under the fabric of his flannel t-shirt. I shake my head to clear out my hormone-induced thoughts.

I wave him toward the start of a trail, deciding to take him on one of the harder ones to see if he can really handle a true hike. He doesn't exactly scream outdoor adventure man, but he definitely looks strong.

In the beginning everything starts off fine. We walk

briskly and chat, telling each other more bad jokes. It isn't until the trail starts to go uphill that things begin to get funny—at least for me.

Thirty-minutes in, Ethan starts to lag behind. I can hear him taking huge gulps of air every few moments.

I look back at him. "Are you okay back there?"

He takes another breath and waves me off. If he's having trouble now, I can't wait until we get to the part where we have to do some easy climbing.

Another fifteen-minutes in Ethan suddenly grasps my shoulder. When I turn around he's doubled over—sweat pouring from his forehead. He's trying to catch his breath in between taking large drinks of water.

I wince and place my hand on his wet back. "Geez, Ethan! Are you sure you're okay?"

"I—just need—to catch—my breath—" he manages to wheeze out.

"Why don't we sit down for a minute."

I help him over to some rocks and watch him try to breathe deeply, his chest rising and falling in rapid succession. Maybe it wasn't such a good idea to bring him on such a hard trail.

"How—how much longer?" he wonders.

"Um, well—there's this really amazing look-out that I

121

was going to take you to."

"*How far?*"

I scratch the back of my head sheepishly, kicking at some dirt. "Well—"

"How far?" he asks again.

"Probably another hour or so—" I say quietly.

"*An hour!*"

I avert my eyes from his again as I think about the climbing yet to come. Ethan notices the guilty look on my face.

"What else are you not telling me?"

"We may or may not be doing a little climbing to get there," I wince.

Ethan, however, doesn't respond. He just takes a deep breath and gets up, suddenly continuing up the path. I watch him stomp determinedly away from me and I'm confused by his strange reaction. Eventually, I run to catch up with him, surprised he could go so fast after almost passing out a minute ago.

When he sees me, he looks at me questioningly but keeps walking. "How well do you know this path?"

"I've been climbing it since I was little."

He mutters something to himself that I can't hear. I study his face and see that he's concentrating extremely hard. His eyes are narrow, and his fists clench at his sides so his knuckles go white like the other day at dinner.

"Ethan?" He doesn't answer back. "Hello—Earth to Ethan?"

I'm about to poke his shoulder but since I haven't been paying attention to where I'm walking, I trip on a giant rock. I tumble down in a heap to the ground.

"Shit!" I yell. Unlike most of my falls, this one really hurt.

Ethan appears above me. "Are you all right?"

"Yeah, I'm fucking fine," I bite angrily. I wouldn't have been on the ground in the first place if he had been paying attention to me.

He offers his hand, but I ignore it. I stand up and brush myself off. I discover my flannel shirt now has a hole in it. *Just great.*

I look up to Ethan who is amused.

My face hardens. "What?"

"I thought you said we had an hour of climbing left until we got to the top."

"We do—"

He half-smiles at me before gesturing to our surroundings with his hand. I look up and my mouth drops open.

123

"How in the hell?"

"I guess it was shorter than you thought."

He pats my shoulder smugly as he walks to the edge of the cliff. I rub the back of my neck in confusion, looking around the area. I'm positive that we still had an hour left. I come up this path on a regular basis during the summer. *It doesn't make sense.* I quickly rule out any of the weird things that were happening to me lately because I never wished nor imagined myself suddenly being at the viewpoint.

"This view is amazing!" Ethan calls to me while looking out over the edge.

Maybe I had been so absorbed in my thoughts that we actually made it to the top faster than I thought? But that still doesn't explain the missing climb. I try to work out what happened as I come to stand next to him—he's right—the views are truly amazing. It's the whole reason I hike such a hard path to get here. I have never seen anything quite as beautiful as this view. You can see for miles and miles out over the Wisconsin landscape. The colors are so vibrant—especially in the fall. Ethan stares out in awe, his violet eyes alight with childlike wonder.

"Beautiful, isn't it?" I ask him.

He looks at me and grins wide, nodding his head. The

light wind rustles his damp hair. A little sweat and hard work look good on him. He looks sexier than I have ever seen him. The annoyance I feel towards him dissipates at the sight of his happiness, and I can't help but relax in the beauty around us. Maybe I just took a different path by accident...

Ethan clears his throat to gain my attention. "You know, your eyes match the green of the trees."

I flush. "I've always meant to ask you about your eye color, actually."

"Most people do. I realize that it is not every day you see a man with violet eyes."

"It makes you different. I like it." His features brighten at my praise. "How does that happen anyway? I didn't even know someone could have purple eyes."

"It is a rare occurrence. I often will say my eyes are gray or deep blue to avoid questions. Violet is never an option at the DMV," he wisecracks. *I laugh.* "It causes people to look twice when I meet them—but very helpful for negotiating. I think that is why my father wanted me to become a lawyer someday. I could have made a lot of money."

I give him a confused look. "I don't mean this in a bad way but—you already have a lot of money."

He lets out a throaty laugh.

"True, but it would have *added to our legacy*, and *left larger trust funds for future generations!*" he emphasizes in a mocking tone.

"If you don't mind me asking—I know you said you needed a break from your family's publishing house—but are you planning to do something new now that you're in Iron Lake?

Ethan noticeably stiffens. "As of now, no—I have a little business to take care of—but it is *personal...*"

"Oh." I have to admit—I'm surprised. He strikes me as a type-A personality.

Ethan chuckles nervously, rubbing his brow. "I understand that makes me sound like a rich boy who has never worked a day in his life, but I can assure you that is far from the truth."

"I don't think of you that way, Ethan," I assure him.

He looks relieved. "It is one of the reasons I left New York. I know I have a nice home here, and nice things—but it is not meant to be obnoxious. I am afraid I just do not know how to be any other way. I never wanted to be that condescending, entitled kid that got everything handed to him by mommy and daddy. I have worked for everything I have and continue to."

I grab his hand closest to mine and squeeze. "You don't

have to defend yourself to me. You do have nice things, and you do talk like you could be the next King of England," I smile cheekily at him. "But you've been nothing but down-to-earth and nice since I met you. I may tease you about your cars, but you're a good guy from what I can tell."

Ethan squeezes my hand back in thanks.

"Thank you, Sophia. Your opinion matters a lot to me."

"I'll never understand why," I tease. "I do have one problem though…"

"And what would that be?"

"You're too *flawless.*"

He lets out a barking laugh. "What does that even mean?"

Instead of answering him, I take the hand I've been hiding behind my back and throw a muddy dirt-clot directly between his eyes. The dirt hits spot-on with a plop before sliding down his face and to the ground. I double over—cackling at the sight of him. He stands—shocked—with what looks like poop smudged on his face.

"You should see your face," I wheeze out.

Before I know what's happening, I'm pinned to the ground by a pair of ridiculously sturdy hands.

"You are going to pay for that, *Sophia*," Ethan growls before grinding dirt into my face—a little bit even going into my mouth.

"Get off of me, you big oaf!" I sputter, trying to push him off—but he won't budge.

When I decide it's foolish to try to move him, I settle my gaze on his face. He's no longer laughing; instead his pupils are dilated and the hands gripping my arms are squeezing a little bit tighter. The smile fades from my features and my heartbeat starts to pick-up. Even though I'm sure we both look ridiculous with mud smeared all over our faces, there's nothing ridiculous about the situation we're in. Our chests heave against one another as our bodies become aware of the closeness. I don't know why I always react to him this way, but when he touches me, I feel like some sort of current is being sent through me. I'm giddy with excitement.

"Sophia, I—"

This time I don't let him talk or take charge. I hoist myself up on my elbows and press my lips to his firmly. At first, he tenses, not expecting the contact, but it slowly fades and soon he's kissing me back. We kiss for a while, becoming lost in one another. I'm not sure how long we lay on the ground—making out like teenagers—but once

128

we need to catch our breath, Ethan pulls back and rests his forehead against mine. We're quiet for a few moments before he finally speaks.

"I always end up doing things I do not expect when I am with you."

I give him a flirty smile. "Is that good or bad? Because from my position, I wouldn't say anything was bad."

He blushes at my forwardness, looking at me tenderly for a few moments.

"It is a good thing—a very unexpected good thing."

"Good."

I try to wipe the dirt away from his forehead, but he stops my efforts by leaning in and kissing me again. Eventually he parts, his dimple denting his left cheek. I place my finger on it, grinning back at him. When he stands, he puts his hand out for me to take it.

I survey my clothes. *Talk about rolling in the dirt.* As I try to pick off bits of brush from my hair and shirt, Ethan looks on with a funny expression.

"What?"

"Nothing," he shrugs.

I eye him suspiciously before motioning for him to follow me down the side trail.

"Don't worry. The trail down is easy as pie."

"Thank God. I am already not going to be able to walk for a week…"

"What happened to those guns?" I tease. "I didn't think this would be that hard for you."

"Yoga and lifting weights does not necessarily prepare one for the great outdoors," he laughs.

"Now that you're living here, we'll have to change that. Next on the list is hunting."

"You hunt?"

I snicker. "That was a joke. Do I come off like someone who hunts in my free time?"

He quirks an eyebrow. "You do have a love for flannel…"

I smack him on the arm playfully. "I must have missed the memo that flannel is limited to hunting attire only."

He beams. "Must have."

We reach Ethan's car over an hour later with no issue—the rest of the hike silent and relaxed. When he drops me back at my cabin soon after, he makes a move to get out of the car, but I stop him.

"I can walk myself to the door. You need the rest

anyway," I taunt.

"Ha-ha," he deadpans.

I roll my eyes at him playfully before getting out of the car and leaning down so I can meet his gaze.

"See you at 7?"

Unfortunately for us—we still have our double date tonight. Every part of me wants us to stay in and watch a movie instead. I really have no desire to be in the middle of Ana and Chris's drama. Today has been pretty amazing and I don't want to ruin it with their fighting.

"Of course. I will be here at seven o'clock sharp," he affirms.

"Great. I'll see you then."

I close the car door before walking away. Ethan revs the engine playfully before pulling out of the driveway and making his way down the street. I head into my cabin and close the door, scratching Laker behind the ears as he jumps up and down. I calm him, throwing a bone out for him before walking over to my closet to look inside. For once, I want to look perfect for a date. I stop suddenly and press my palm against my forehead, wondering if I have a fever.

What is wrong with me?

I sit on my bed and look at Laker who gives me a doggy grin.

"Am I falling for Ethan?" I ask him.

To which he responds with a bark.

CHAPTER 8

I have a nervous feeling in the pit of my stomach when 7:00 p.m. rolls around. I re-check my appearance in the mirror for probably the 10th or 15th time. I feel my forehead again to make sure I'm not sick—of course, it's normal.

I exhale a breath I've been holding, smoothing my hands over my upset stomach. Besides our first brief meeting at the bonfire and this morning at *Ham n' Egg's*, Ethan and I have never been in public before tonight. I feel like I have to impress the whole town, show them I'm worth a man like Ethan's attention. I know it's silly to feel this way—I'm never one to care what people think about me. This is different though—*he's different.*

I turn to the side, giving myself one last look. I'm wearing a dark and form-fitting burgundy lace dress that my mom purchased last year for my birthday. When I opened it, I looked at her like she was crazy. I don't wear dresses unless it's required; they are one of my least favorite things.

She claimed that someday I would need a fancy dress and that I would thank her. At the time, I knew it was her cover for saying that she was going to try to set me up on blind dates in the near future, and I needed to look nice. She never succeeded in getting me to date the men she chose, but now I'm glad she gave me the dress.

I have to admit the garment fits me live a glove. It hugs my minimal curves perfectly and hits just above the knee. It's modest enough that I feel comfortable, but sexy enough that I feel good in it. I finish my look with a pair of black ballet flats and some light make-up, my hair hanging down in natural waves. I can't wear the heels Ana gave me. I know I'd end up killing myself in them.

Overall, I'm happy with the way I look. Ana is going to have a heart attack when she sees me. The last time she saw me in a dress was at my father's funeral, and even then I fought my mother tooth and nail over it.

I stare into the eyes of my reflection. In just a week, so much has changed. I notice that I seem to stand a little taller and my smile reaches my eyes. Wanting to look good for my date tonight has something to do with this new feeling. The changes in me are good and I'm trying to accept them—not judge them. Same goes for all the strange things that happened in the past week. I'm putting them out of my thoughts for tonight. I just want to have fun and enjoy the company of my friends. I only hope that Ana and Chris don't make a fuss.

I grab my purse just as there's a knock on the door. I look at the clock and see that it's exactly 7:00 p.m. When I open the door, all the air in my lungs rushes out—Ethan is on the other side looking sharp as usual.

Gone are the Doc Martens and the jeans from earlier; he's wearing a perfectly-tailored, dark charcoal grey suit with oxfords. The deep blue button-up shirt makes his violet eyes a more pronounced, vibrant color. His hair is tousled like he tried to tame it, but it didn't work. I think I actually prefer the slightly sweaty look from the hike, but he still is more than gorgeous.

When I meet his eyes, his pupils are dilated. He looks at me like a lion ready to pounce on its prey. My heart flutters in my chest.

"Hi," I squeak out.

"You look positively breathtaking."

"Thanks," I blurt. "You don't look too bad yourself."

He offers his arm. "Are you ready to go?"

I nod and grab his arm as we walk toward his car.

When we arrive, I see that it's a different one. A sleek, black, fancy sports car.

I am in shock. "You have another car?"

He looks at me sheepishly. "It is my going out car."

"You have a going out car?" I reiterate.

"Yes."

"I think you have a car addiction," I tease.

"I suppose—but I prefer to call myself a collector—rather than an addict. I have a few restored beauties in a storage garage not far from here."

"Old cars, you mean?"

"I have a DeLorean and a '59 Ford Retractable. I have also been working on a '69 Mustang."

"You've been working on them?" I ask in shock.

"I take classic cars and re-build them. It is therapeutic," he states like it's something everyone can do.

"Is there anything you don't do?" I wonder out loud.

He smirks. "I cannot play ping-pong very well."

"Ha-ha. I see you're also a comedian."

He flashes his dimple at me before opening my door so I can climb in. Much like the last car, the seats are a smooth, dark grey leather, and the inside dashboard has all sorts of buttons and gadgets. I click in my seatbelt as he gets in, starting the engine smoothly.

"What kind of car is this one?" I ask running my hands over the soft interior.

"It is an Aston Martin DB11 AMR. Beautiful, is she not?"

"She is. You know, I bet if she were a real person you would be dating her instead of me," I cackle.

Ethan shakes his head at my attempted sense of humor before turning to me and grabbing hold of my hands.

"Even if the car was a person, she could never beat the way you look—especially tonight. That dress—it is like it was made for you."

"Thanks," I murmur—swallowing—suddenly it's very hot.

He lifts my chin, placing a chaste kiss on the corner of my mouth.

"You taste like watermelon," he observes, running his thumb along my jaw lightly.

"My lip balm—it's watermelon flavored."

"Good thing I enjoy watermelon then," he smirks, giving me another short kiss.

"Good thing," I laugh.

He settles back into his seat, turning on his usual classical music before we drive to meet Ana and Chris. I take my time during the drive to study the profile of his face in the soft evening light. I never thought a man in real life could be beautiful until I met him. People like him only exist in books and movies. I shake out of my thoughts, reminding myself that I decided moments ago to try and not judge myself tonight. I take a deep breath and let my mind go blank for the rest of the drive as Ethan reaches out to play with the fingers of my left hand.

When we pull into the parking lot of the Olive Garden, I can't help but roll my eyes at how ridiculous it is that we got all dressed up to go here—but whatever Ana wants, Ana gets. Besides, it's one of the *fancier* affordable places in town. There's a steakhouse up the road, but Ana and I don't want to spend eighty dollars each on dinner.

When we park, I quickly get out of the car, Ethan falling in step beside me as we approach the entrance.

"What exactly is this place?" He asks curiously.

"What?" I stop in my tracks. "You've never been to an Olive Garden?"

"No, I have not."

"That's crazy! It's a chain. I'm sure they have them in NYC."

"They do, but I have never been there."

"Wow. I guess it's not fancy enough for wealthy people," I tease him.

He gives me a look that tells me he's not going to answer that. "Is it any good?"

"I personally love it. I mean you can do no wrong with endless soup, salad and breadsticks. Not to mention I could eat their pasta all day long, too."

He raises an eyebrow. "Endless soup, salad, and breadsticks?"

"Yeah, you know—pay one price and get as much as you want? It's flipping fantastic," I snort, not caring about my decorum.

"So, it is a buffet type thing?" he asks, obviously amused.

"Not really. Come on, let's go in and you'll find out."

I tug him inside the doors where we are greeted by two giggling high-school-aged hostesses. I'm glad they aren't people from my actual high school class. The fewer people I know tonight, the better. The girls, however, are ogling Ethan like he's Justin Bieber or something.

One of them smiles widely, sucking in her stomach and arching her back very obviously. "Can we help you?"

"Yes, we are meeting a few people here tonight," Ethan says politely.

The two girls twirl their matching blonde hair around their fingers, blushing madly at the sound of Ethan's voice.

"What's the name?" one asks, her voice rather husky for a teenager.

"Ana," I state evenly.

The girls glare blankly at me—their eyes look to my hand gripping Ethan's bicep. Apparently, I'm now also becoming territorial. They're only teenagers for goodness sake. I really need to take a chill pill.

"Follow me," one of them finally says, but not before giving Ethan a very sexy grin. As she walks in front of us, the girl sways her hips way more than one normally would. I look at Ethan—he is unfazed by the whole thing. I suppose this isn't new to him.

Ana and Chris are seated at a booth in the far corner of the restaurant. It doesn't go unnoticed by Ethan or me that the entire room turns to stare at us when we enter. I recognize most of the faces but try to avert my eyes and pretend to be really interested in my feet as I walk. The last thing I want to do is talk to fifty people, and I imagine Ethan doesn't want to explain to everyone who he is or why he moved to Iron Lake over and over again either. I laugh when I think of him just setting up a microphone at the front of the room for *story time*.

He turns at my laugh. "What?"

"I was just thinking about something. I'll tell you later," I whisper.

When we get to the table, Ana jumps up excitedly.

"You're finally here!" she squeals while practically squeezing the life out of me. "You look smokin'!"

"Shush!" I hush, making a dramatic show with my eyes to tell her we have an audience.

"Oh, right. Sorry."

I take a breath. "Ana, this is Ethan. Ethan, this is my best friend, Ana."

Ethan gives his best one-dimpled smile, offering his hand to Ana. She completely ignores it, giving him what I can only call a giant bear hug. I hide a laugh at Ethan's surprised face. After the shock wears off, he gives her a gentle hug back, but with less enthusiasm.

"It is good to finally meet you, Ana. I have heard many great things about you," he smiles again, pulling away from the hug.

Ana blushes. I have to laugh because hardly anyone makes Ana blush, not even Chris. Her mind is so crude she's hard to embarrass, and all Ethan did was smile at her and give her a compliment.

"It's nice to meet you, too! Soph hasn't really said much about you, so I'm happy you're here so I can grill you."

Ethan looks entertained, while I flush.

"It's not like I've had time, Ana," I scold.

"I know, Ms. Introvert," she retorts.

I ignore her jab, turning my attention back to the table where Chris has been forgotten during Ana's antics. He's sipping his drink and staring at Ethan with a look of pure hatred in his icy blue irises. I immediately feel my stomach fall. Chris is in a bad mood. That means tonight is going to be very awful—I can feel it in my bones.

"Oh, sorry! Ethan, this is Chris, my *boyfriend*," Ana says, sliding into the seat next to him. *He's her boyfriend today*—at there's that.

Ethan makes eye-contact with Chris, his face immediately turning into stone. Chris's cold gaze never falters; if anything, he now looks as though he's ready to jump out of his seat and punch Ethan across the face. I place a hand on Ethan's shoulder, giving it a gentle squeeze. He doesn't seem to notice that I'm touching him, however. He just keeps his eyes locked with Chris's, his fists clenching at his sides.

Ana and I share a look. She just shrugs her shoulders before turning her attention back to the boys who haven't moved or even blinked.

"Do you two know each other?" I ask, trying to break the tension.

"No," Chris clips, not breaking his eye contact. "I'm Chris," he grinds out, extending his hand to Ethan.

142

Ethan glares at him for a moment longer, practically burning a hole through his head. Finally, he clears his throat and brings his hand to Chris's in an overly firm grip. I feel like I'm watching a game of *Mine Is Bigger Than Yours*.

"Ethan," he practically hisses before sitting down, the tension not leaving his body in the slightest.

When I sit down next to him, I take a long drink of my water to try and quell the anxiety in my stomach. The stress coming from our table is already so thick, I'm scared what the rest of the night will bring. At last, our waiter comes to take our drink orders, rescuing us from the awkward silence.

We order a bottle of wine and get our first round of salad and breadsticks. Ana attempts to make conversation, but it seems like she can't get Chris or Ethan's mood to let up. I have a feeling they know each other. I just can't figure out why they would lie about it, especially Ethan. Before we came into the restaurant, he was perfectly fine, and now he's a completely different person. When we get our wine, and each have a few hefty sips, I decide enough is enough.

"Chris—how have you been? I haven't seen you in a while."

I'm surprised when that seems to break Chris from his trance. He turns—his cold blue eyes smiling—a slow grin

143

spreading across his face. Then he casually combs his hand through his short blonde hair before he takes a breadstick and bites off the end—chewing it slowly while looking at me in a creepy kind of way. I jump slightly when I feel Ethan's hand on my thigh, squeezing it gently. I look to him and try to smile. He has a weird expression on his face, like he's trying to protect me or something.

"I've been okay I suppose," Chris answers, causing me to bring my attention away from Ethan. "Just working a lot. A new job prospect has come up and I've been looking into it," he boasts.

Ethan tightens his grip on my thigh without looking at me. Instead he's back to peering at Chris with a death glare.

Ana makes a hurt noise. "You have a new job prospect?"

All that runs through my mind then is—*shit, shit, shit!* This is how I hoped the date wasn't going to go. As soon as Ana's good mood is crushed, the night is going to go further south. *Fast.* I know there's no going back at this point.

"I told you about it, babe, don't you remember?" Chris coos sweetly.

"No, I don't," Ana retorts. I can tell by the tone of her voice she's ready to kill him.

144

"Ana," Ethan turns on his charm. "Tell me about yourself."

I place my hand over Ethan's, silently thanking him for the change of subject. If *anything* can change Ana's mood, it's talking about herself and the things she loves doing.

Ana takes a moment to collect herself before she smiles brightly. " *Well*—there isn't really much to tell to be honest. I'm sure Soph has told you all about me by now. I'm pretty boring."

I try not to scoff, she's such a liar. I'm about to scold her, but Ethan beats me too it.

"I am sure you are not boring by the way Sophia talks about you."

Ana turns her eyes to me and quirks an eyebrow. "What have you been telling him?"

"Nothing bad, I swear," I say playfully, trying to lighten the mood. "You're a very fun person. Why else would I be friends with you?"

"For my good looks, of course!"

Ethan laughs gently and urges her to continue.

"I live down the road from, Sophie—she is my best friend since forever—I work a boring job at the cruise line with Chris in the summer, then I nanny during the off-season. Nothing special."

"I will have to come to visit this cruise line. I keep hearing about it, but I have yet to experience one. Would you be able to help me fix that?"

"Definitely! I can get you a great discount—I mean, not that you *need it* or anything—"

"Ana!" I chide, feeling the urge to smack her upside the head.

Ethan grips my thigh again in reassurance before grinning at Ana with delight. "I have a question for you, *Ana*."

Ana's eyes go wide as she eats her salad. "Ask me anything."

"Do you have any embarrassing stories about, Sophia?" he smirks.

"Don't you dare, Ana!" I exclaim. "If you tell him one thing about me, I'll choke you with this breadstick."

"Oooh, I'm *so scared* of you," she says sarcastically, waving her arms around like an idiot.

"Ana," I warn.

"This one time we went out to the lake—"

"No! Don't you even fucking dare!" I squeal at her, almost jumping from my seat.

"Language, Soph," she admonishes.

"I swear, Ana—do not say another word."

146

Just as she's about to talk, Chris interrupts.

"Why don't you just leave her alone, babe," he says before sipping his drink like he can't be bothered.

The whole table lapses in an awkward silence once again. Even though I don't want Ana to tell that story about me, I don't want Chris to be an ass either. Luckily the waiter saves us yet again and comes with our food at just the right time. Ana looks like she's about to cry.

"Ana, would you come to the bathroom with me?" I ask her quickly.

She jumps up stiffly. "Yes."

I give Ethan a sympathetic look, sorry to be leaving him at the table with Chris. He sends me a half-smile before I follow Ana to the bathroom. Once we're inside, the dam breaks. I wrap my arms around her and let her cry.

"*Oh Ana*, it's okay," I soothe.

"I'm sorry—he's ruining the whole night. I don't know why he's acting like this."

"He's just being Chris. I don't know why you let him do this to you. He's an asshole."

Ana pulls away abruptly—wiping the tears harshly from her cheeks.

"Not all of us have perfect relationships with guys we just met, Sophia," she sneers.

I feel like I've just been slapped across the face. I'm hurt by the tone of her voice and at the fact she rarely ever calls me by my actual name.

I put my hands on my hips. "What's with the Jekyll and Hyde?"

"You come in here and flaunt your perfect guy in front of me. He came into your life a week ago and everything is just great for you! I've been dating Chris for almost two years and I can't even get him to tell me he loves me—how fair is that?"

"You're upset right now, Ana. I don't want to get mad at you for saying things you don't mean."

"I do mean it. *I don't understand*—even Chris has a thing for you. I've tried to ignore it—but I just can't anymore."

"What in the world are you talking about?"

"You know what I'm talking about—I'm not good enough for him. I'm just the second choice so he can be around you more."

I wrinkle my nose. *"Really*—you want to go there?"

"Just think about it—I know you like to pretend otherwise—but it's true."

"You know that's not true—Chris *hates me*. You're upset and you're making things up—this whole

148

conversation is ridiculous."

"It isn't ridiculous to me!"

I put my hands on Ana's shoulders.

"Ana, I'm just trying to understand. If you felt this way, why didn't you tell me? You're beautiful and smart and amazing—you deserve more than how that asshole treats you. I've been telling you that for years! I just want what's best for you."

Ana stares coldly at me. *Where is this coming from?* I never thought Chris showed any interest in me. Ana was wonderful, and she obviously cared for him. This whole conversation is nonsensical.

"Is there something you're not telling me—maybe the real reason why you're upset?" I challenge her.

"I told you!"

"Ana—this is crazy."

"I think maybe I should go," she says sadly, pulling away from me.

"We really need to talk about this!"

"Later, okay? Go have fun with your *boyfriend.*"

Ana storms out of the bathroom before I can stop her. I slam my hand on the counter, scaring old lady Henderson as she comes in to use the restroom.

"Everything alright, darling?" she asks me curiously.

"Yes, Mrs. Henderson," I say stoically.

"Is that boy you came in with the one who moved into the old Cooper house?" she tries to ask nonchalantly.

I want to scream. Even 80-year-old women want to know my business, and I'm not in the mood for it.

"His name's Ethan," I say as I walk out of the bathroom. I know that's probably not a wise choice. I basically admitted that I'm with him—even though I have no idea where our relationship stands—but I can't think about that now.

When I get close to our booth, Chris and Ethan are talking heatedly. Ethan looks like he's about to jump across the table again, while Chris just looks like a smug bastard. When I reach them, Chris stops whatever he was saying and glances up at me.

"You're back," he states, looking behind me for Ana.

"What were you two arguing about?" I ask.

"Stocks," Ethan says tightly.

I raise my eyebrows. "Stocks?"

"Ethan here was just telling me I take my stocks too seriously. That my endeavor is out of my league. I tried to tell him that I thought I was making the right choice—that eventually I'll win what I'm after," Chris finishes, looking at me in such a way that a tremor moves through me—I can't stop myself from visibly shuddering.

Ethan's gripping his wine glass so tight that I think it's going to break. It's time I break up this macho-man fest.

"Chris, Ana left. You should go after her—she was pretty upset."

Chris huffs in annoyance.

I frown. "Please, Chris? We got into an argument and she needs you right now."

He grunts before standing. "Right. I guess I should go then...It was good seeing you again, Sophie. *Always a pleasure*, Ethan."

Chris winks at me before walking out of the restaurant. I'm still standing as I watch him walk out of my sight. I'm completely perplexed by the whole situation. I look at Ethan who's stabbing at his salad furiously like he's trying to murder it. When I sit next to him I place my hand on his shoulder. He immediately stops, looking into my eyes with a mixture of anger, but also fear.

"Ethan—why was Chris acting so strange toward you? I thought you said you didn't know him previously."

"I just met him."

"It didn't seem like that to me. When he left, he said—*always a pleasure*—that's not something you say to someone you haven't met before."

"He is a strange man," he states. "You should stay away from him."

Ethan shoves a piece of ravioli in his mouth.

I sigh. "*C'mon, Ethan.* Tell me what's going on! I know there's something you're not telling me."

"This is really good," he mutters while taking another bite—*and then another.*

"Ethan! Would you concentrate for a moment?"

"*Hmmm,* the sauce is so rich."

I huff in frustration. "Ethan, I—"

Before I can finish my sentence, he shoves a piece of ravioli in my mouth. I place my hand over my lips to prevent the food from falling out. I chew slowly—in shock.

He smiles at me cheekily. "Good, right?"

"I can't believe you just shoved food in my mouth," I say after swallowing.

"I love when you talk, Sophia, but sometimes you just do not know when to shut your mouth."

"*Hey!* Don't be rude," I cry at him for insulting me. "I just have questions!"

"I already told you the answer, now eat the food. We have a lot of it." He gestures to Ana and Chris's untouched plates.

I grumble and pick up my fork. I don't feel like eating,

but there is a ton of food on the table. I nibble at my pasta as my eyes wander to Ethan while he eats. His eyes are closed as he savors each bite, his angular jaw flexing as he chews. I let him swallow before prodding him again.

"So—what were you and Chris really talking about when I came back from the bathroom?" I ask again.

"You are not going to give up, are you?"

"Nope."

He sighs in resignation; however, I see a small smile play at the corners of his mouth.

"You both looked as though you wanted to kill each other."

"He rubbed me the wrong way is all. I was talking to him about Ana."

I take a deep breath, twirling my pasta on my fork.

"Are you okay?" Ethan puts his hand over mine—stilling the movement I'm making with my fork.

I look up into his concerned eyes—forgetting for a moment about him and Chris.

"Ana and I fought—we usually never fight—this would be the second time in less than a week."

Ethan frowns. "Why was she angry with you?"

"She was just taking out her anger with Chris on me. It wasn't that big of a deal, but it still doesn't feel good to fight with your best friend."

He squeezes my hand. "Want to get out of here?"

I nod—ready to leave the prying eyes and ears of the restaurant. Ethan flags down the waitress and pays—much to my protest. It doesn't escape me that Chris left us with the entire bill, including his drinks prior to us arriving. I'm extremely annoyed, but also curious as to what is actually going on between Chris and Ethan. I think Ethan isn't telling me the whole truth about their relationship, but I also know my attempts at getting him to tell me are futile. Maybe I should keep pushing him, but I'm exhausted. I can mull it all over endlessly later when I'm alone. I'm sick of fighting with people, and I just want to enjoy the rest of my night with Ethan.

We walk out of the restaurant hand-in-hand with everyone watching us intently. I'm positive that our double-date tonight will be the talk of the town for the next year. Maybe if we're lucky enough a juicer piece of gossip will come along—I wish.

CHAPTER 9

I manage to make it into work a few minutes early the next morning—much to my relief.

Mary has left me several carts of books to put back, along with a note saying she won't be in today—I cock one eyebrow in question. She must have gone to her cabin in Door County—that's the only time Mary ever leaves. I wonder why she didn't tell me in advance, but I figure it fits in with all of the other things that are going against the grain lately. Maybe *weird* is my new normal—I just have to get used to it.

About halfway into shelving I hear the bell ring at the front desk. When I see Ana standing there, I immediately have the urge to walk the other direction. She turns towards me—her features contrite. I walk over hesitantly, my face tight.

"Hi," she whispers.

I ignore her, straightening a few books on the desk.

"How are you?" she asks again, but I still ignore her.

Ana puts her hand on my arm—stilling my movements. "Just hear me out, okay?"

I pull my arm from her grasp and cross them over my chest protectively. "I'm not sure I want to right now."

"C'mon, Soph. I'm your best friend."

I take a deep breath and sigh—I know I'm acting childish. "You have one minute to explain yourself. Then I have to get back to work."

She nods in agreement. "I know this is going to sound crazy—but I honestly have no idea why I went off on you the way I did. One minute I was having an okay time—minus Chris's foul mood of course—then the next I just had this surge of anger. I can't explain it, Soph—I was *so mad* at you. When I woke up this morning, I couldn't even remember why. It was almost like some strange force was making me be pissed at you."

"Making you—really, Ana?"

"*I know.* I know that it's a poor excuse for the way I treated you, and I feel so bad about it. You're my best friend and you didn't deserve what I said."

"You're right—I didn't. Ethan didn't deserve it either."

"I know. I'm sorry, okay? I just—I really don't know how to explain my actions."

156

I can see how hurt Ana really is. My fortress of anger starts to crumble, and I actually feel bad for her. She looks almost broken. When I think about what she said—about a force taking over her—I can't help but be reminded of all of the strange things happening around me lately. Maybe she's telling the truth. Maybe the things happening to me aren't only in my head, and it's now affecting Ana, too. It doesn't make sense, but I know I have to forgive her.

"Okay," I exhale.

"Really?"

"Yes."

"Does that mean I'm forgiven?"

"Somewhat," I state, not quite ready to completely let things go.

"I understand—you know I really am sorry, right?"

"I know," I smile gently at her. "Now I really need to get   back   to   work." "Okay—do you want to hang out on Saturday? We could have a girls' night with some pizza and a few beers."

"Yeah, sure. I could do that."

"Okay, great. *Oh!* We can talk about what we're going to do for your birthday party!"

"Ugh—let's not."

Ana shakes her head back and forth. "Too bad! It's

going to happen whether you like it or not—you might as well enjoy it. See you Saturday!" she chirps before running out the door.

There's really no stopping that girl. I don't want to celebrate with a bunch of people I don't really care about, much less a huge party where I'm the center of attention. I grab another cart of books beside me and get back to work.

All the quiet time in the library allows my thoughts to run rampant on an endless loop. Ana's confession about not being in control of her anger, the hike with Ethan, everything prior to it; nothing makes sense. *Nothing*.

I examine each moment in my head—putting together everything that started going haywire the day I met Ethan. It's odd that it all coincided with his arrival in my life. I feel silly, like I'm making it all up due to lack of sleep and paranoia—I've decided I need answers—but how do you get them if nobody would believe you? I try to imagine what a therapist would think if I told them I could make things happen just by wishing them—or that somehow, somebody or something is controlling my best friend's emotions.

With my brain a mess and barely any customers, the rest of the day drags by miserably. By 6:30 p.m., the library feels like solitary confinement. After I shut off the lights, I practically bust down the front doors, taking a breath of fresh air into my lungs in an attempt to calm myself. I lock the doors before going to my car, anxious to get home and relax with nothing and no one to disrupt me. I really hope my mom didn't decide to stop by to give me the latest gossip. However, since I've recently become the center of town gossip, I think it's weird she hasn't been bothering me more. Especially if she heard about last night's Olive Garden fiasco—which I'm sure she has by now.

The drive home is quick—I opt for silence instead of the usual oldies station I like to play. I think of Ethan...*again.* Every time I think of him, it's as if I'm obsessed with him. It both excites and terrifies me—I want more, yet I don't.

Life with Ethan is more fun, but it's also more complicated. Even though this past week's events feel like they've taken place over a year, I can't shake the nagging feeling that it's all just beginning, whatever it is—I twitch at the thought.

"What else could go wrong?" I ask myself out loud. *Great, now I'm talking to myself.* Needing a release—I scream as loud as I can right as I pull up to my cabin.

Feeling a bit better, I take a moment to collect myself before getting out of the car.

My hand is about to touch the doorknob when I abruptly get a full-body chill. I glance behind me, looking for the pair of eyes I think are watching me—of course, there aren't any. I fumble with my keys before unlocking the door. Laker comes to greet me, though he seems a little on edge too. I crouch down so I'm on his level, scratching his ears just the way he likes it.

"What's wrong boy—you feel it, too?" He whines in agreement. I stand and tell him to go to the yard to do his business. Looking around the perimeter of my property I don't see any signs of life—I must be more paranoid than I thought.

I wait for Laker to finish, standing just inside the door to my cabin. I look left—eyeing a framed picture of my dad and I hanging on the wall. It was taken shortly before he died at one of our last bonfires together. I smile sadly, touching the leather jacket he was wearing as if I could still feel it's worn material on the pads of my fingers—*we had laughed so much that day*.

My dad and I had an easy relationship. His death was something I did not expect to have to deal with in my young life. I thought he would live forever. He was so

160

healthy—healthier than I ever was! When I heard he had a stroke, I couldn't believe it. One minute we're sitting at his cabin drinking beers and the next he's gone. My mom tried to pretend like she wasn't that sad, but I saw it in her eyes. They divorced when I was 10, and neither of them talked about it much. They liked to say that they just fell out of love, but I knew it had something to do with my dad traveling all the time. He was a beer distribution manager—always off to different parts of the Midwest and sometimes to foreign places I had never heard of. He would consistently bring me back cool knick-knacks or postcards. When I turned 18, he started to bring me exotic beers. My mom hated it, but he would always say: *If you can go to war at eighteen, you can drink at eighteen!*

I remember when my mom would complain that his time away didn't add up. That beer distribution managers weren't supposed to travel as much as he did. One time she even thought he had a secret family somewhere—I would just roll my eyes at her. I didn't ever question my dad or what he did—he was just my dad, and I loved him for it. He gave me the best hugs and the worst advice. His cabin was the greatest part about my life here in Iron Lake. I could feel his presence every time I came home—it made me feel safe. This is why it irks me so much that all of a

161

sudden I feel like I'm not.

Laker barks, bringing me out of my memories. I'm still standing inside the door waiting for him to come in, but he's already in the kitchen expecting his dinner.

"Sorry boy. Mom is out of it today."

I close and lock the door before making my way to the kitchen to feed him and heat-up some leftover Olive Garden. Once I'm settled in front of the TV with my meal and Laker beside me, I feel somewhat more at ease.

I'm dozing off with Laker snuggled into my side when a noise jolts me awake.

Laker jumps into action, snarling and barking like a crazed wolf. I hear the gravel from my driveway crunch as footsteps make their way toward the front door. Laker continues to bark—looking so wolf-life it actually scares me. I've never seen him this way—it only feeds my sudden anxiety.

"*Hush*, Laker—I'm sure it's someone we know," I tell him—trying to convince myself of the same thing. When I hear the footsteps stop outside the door, I wonder if the gun my dad kept in one of the kitchen cabinets is loaded.

"Hey, Sophie!" a male voice yells from the other side, before knocking loudly. *Crap.* I know who it is.

"Chris?" I yell back.

"Yeah, it's me."

I approach Laker carefully and speak to him in a calming voice. "Laker, you know Chris. You're ok, boy." I run my hands along his fur in a gentle motion. It seems to help a little, but he's still growling under his breath, teeth bared. After a few more moments I finally open the door. My face goes hot, and the sound of my heart pounds in my ears.

"Hey," he smirks.

"What are you doing here? You scared the crap out of me!" I snap at him. Laker barks and growls at him loudly.

"Woah there, puppy! It's just me."

"He doesn't like being called *puppy.*"

"I can tell," he swallows thickly before looking back up at me with a bit of fear in his eyes.

"What do you want?"

"Can we talk?"

I pause. "Have you talked to Ana yet? She was really upset yesterday."

"I have, but I need to talk to you about Ethan."

I cross my arms over my chest. "Ethan—why?"

Chris tries to flash me a charming smile, but it only

gives me the creeps. Gooseflesh fans out over my arms and I seriously doubt my judgment in ever being friends with him or letting him date my best friend.

Laker growls again.

"Can we talk outside? Your dog is scaring me."

I glance back at Laker, who really does appear like he wants to kill Chris. My dog has better taste than I do. I scratch his ears quickly before standing to full height again— Chris watching my every move.

"Fine."

I follow him out until we're standing by my car. It doesn't escape me that his car is nowhere in sight.

"Did you walk here?" I ask suspiciously.

"Something like that," he smirks again.

Whatever game he's playing, I don't want any part of it. I just want him off my property and out of my space.

"Chris, I don't know why you want to talk about Ethan, but I really have nothing to say to you."

"*Wow*—" he ridicules. "I expected you to be nicer to me. I thought we were friends."

"I wouldn't exactly call us buddies," I cut. "I'll be honest and say I tolerate you because Ana loves you. Which I don't understand because you're nothing but an ass to her. *So really*—I don't have the time."

I watch his eyes turn a steely blue. His pupils dilate, and he clenches his fists at his sides, like he's concentrating too hard on something while trying to hold in anger. I realize that he looks similar to how Ethan looked on our hike right before we magically appeared at the top—or the first time we had dinner and the roast had burned—yet it somehow came out perfect. However, this is creepier—*way creepier.* It's more than just intense concentration, it's almost— *sinister.* Chris continues to stare at me, a sheen of sweat starting to form at his hairline.

"What the hell are you doing?" I ask—snapping my fingers in front of his face several times—he finally comes back to reality.

His square face transforms into a look of pure curiosity mixed with disappointment as he mutters something to himself under his breath.

"Seriously, what the hell is your problem?"

"Interesting," he says quietly. He scans my body up and down like he's checking me out. The smarmy look returns to his face as I attempt to cover myself from his gross looks.

"What's interesting—and why are you acting so weird?" I prod, my patience wearing thin.

"You," he states before taking a step closer.

"You're not making any sense," I utter, instinctively

taking a step away from him.

"I never thought it was possible—to meet someone like you of our kind."

Chris takes another step toward me—I take another step back—I am now pinned between him and my car.

"Our kind?" I manage to ask, trying to keep my breath even. I don't want the bastard to know I'm scared.

His face fills with surprise. "He hasn't told you yet?" *he laughs.* "Ethan has always been a coward."

Chris reaches out, brushing a stray lock of hair from my face. I shy away from his touch and put my hand up to his chest to push him away.

"You're not making any sense—and I still don't understand what Ethan has to do with any of this."

"Ethan has everything to do with this."

"I don't even know what *THIS* is!" I cry out in frustration. I push harder against his chest, but he doesn't budge. He only comes closer.

"You're special, Sophie—more special then I could have imagined."

He leans in closer, his disgusting, hot breath fanning over my skin. I shove him as hard as I can, pushing him back for a moment.

"Stay away from me before I do something drastic."

That only seems to inspire him—the look in his eyes turning to that of a mad man. The blue of his irises is now gone, replaced by the black of his pupils.

"Can't you feel the energy between us? You drive me crazy."

He gets close to me once again, I try to push him off, but he grabs my wrists—rendering me immobile.

"Chris, I'll say it one more time—get the hell off of me before I let Laker have a piece of you," I growl. Laker's snarling can be heard through the cabin door.

Chris laughs mockingly. "Don't you get it? I don't want to hurt you. I want you to let me show you what people like us can do—let me be your teacher," he practically purrs, squeezing my wrists a little harder.

"What the hell are you talking about?" I yell. "You're not making any God damn sense."

I struggle against his grip on me, thinking of ways to get out of his hold. I squeeze my eyes shut, wishing somebody would drive by, or that Ethan would perform an appearing act just as he had in the parking lot last week.

When Chris squeezes my wrists even tighter, his body now almost flush against mine, I debate kneeing him square in the groin. That would at least keep him off me long enough to get in the house to let Laker loose. It actually would be much easier if he would disappear like the books off the library cart had done—now that would be a perfect solution. *I wish.*

Two things happen simultaneously.

I blink, and Chris is *gone*—he literally disappears right before my eyes. Immediately after I hear my name being yelled—loudly.

My brain is foggy with adrenaline and bewilderment, like I'm in some sort of tunnel. I hear my name again, the voice getting closer. When Ethan's concerned face comes into my vision, I'm barely able to focus on him. The blood is roaring so loudly in my ears I think I might pass out. He grabs my shoulders firmly, shaking me.

"Sophia?"

I don't answer.

"Sophia, are you okay?" Ethan demands again, shaking me harder.

"I—Chris—he just—*poof!*" I finally manage to get out.

In one swift movement, Ethan's arms wrap firmly around me, holding me to his chest tightly. I breathe in his musky scent, the tension in my body draining out as the adrenaline begins to dissipate, and I start to shake.

He rubs soothing circles on my back. "What happened, Sophia?"

168

"I don't know…" I say into his chest. "I don't know."

He pulls me gently from his embrace, looking into my eyes worriedly.

"Are you all right?"

"Physically yes…*mentally*," I laugh wearily. "Not so sure."

He hugs me again, tighter this time.

With my heartbeat now mostly under control, Laker's barking fills my ears, effectively taking me out of my meltdown. I pull back from Ethan abruptly, hugging my arms around my torso. His eyes are puzzled, a frown marring his features.

"What is wrong?"

"You lied to me," I utter.

"What do you mean?" His frown deepens.

"Chris—he was babbling about me being special, and some weird stuff about *our kind*," I air quote. "He said that you haven't told me yet, and that you're weak. That you have everything to do with this—whatever *this* is," I sputter.

Ethan's mouth hangs open but no words come out.

I grab his biceps. "Can you please tell me what's going on? One-minute Chris is here, assaulting me, and then the next he disappears into thin air and you—*you* show up to save the day yet again? Please explain why you've been lying to me ever since we met!"

He exhales, his face falling into defeat. "You are right—there are things that you need to know…"

I scoff. "Well no shit, Sherlock—I'm freaking out here! Things keep happening and I can't explain any of them. For over a week I've been convinced I'm going crazy."

"You are not going crazy. *Trust me.*"

"You're seriously asking me to trust you? You know all this weird stuff started happening after *you* showed up," I cry. "I was normal—now I'm going to end up in a mental institution!"

Ethan takes a step toward me. "You are not crazy—but you are not normal either."

"Well that's good news," I roll my eyes.

"I will explain everything, all right? But not here. We need to go someplace private—*safe.*"

"Why should I trust you, huh? You could be just like Chris."

"I am not like, Chris," he says defiantly, his body tensing. "We may not have known each other a long time, Sophia, but you know me—you know I would never hurt you. You have to believe me when I say you can trust me. *Please*, I need you to trust me," he pleads.

I observe him for a long while—searching his eyes for the answers I need to know. In my gut I know I can trust him. I'm just angry that he hasn't been 100% honest with me about whatever's happening. Ethan would not hurt me intentionally—it's a little crazy to trust him—but what other choice do I have? I think I just made a man disappear!

"Fine," I concede.

He lets out a breath of relief and grabs my hand, squeezing it tightly.

"It is time, Sophia. It is time to know who you really are."

CHAPTER 10

Laker is going absolutely crazy by the time I get to him.

When I'm finally able to relax him, I quickly settle him in for the night before Ethan and I drive the short distance to his house in silence. Neither one of us knows what to say, and frankly I'm thinking about all the questions I need to ask him. I'm confused, angry, and hurt. I wonder if Chris did actually just disappear—and if he did, where did he disappear too? Those thoughts quickly escape me when I remember what was going down between Chris and me before Ethan showed up. I rub one of my sore wrists; I'm sure there will be a nice bruise tomorrow. All of a sudden, I don't really care where Chris has gone. *Good riddance.*

We pull into the driveway and Ethan leaps out of the car as soon as it's in park. He runs to my door just as my hand is on the handle and pulls me out aggressively.

"Where's the fire?" I mumble, pushing him off me. I'm done being manhandled.

When he tries to grab my hand again, I pull away. A grimace mars his face, but I don't respond, just gesture to him that I will follow. I know he wants to say something, but he thinks better of it. Trailing him to the door, I wait while he fumbles with his keys in a very un-Ethan-like way. Once we're inside, he locks several deadbolts, and sets a keypad.

"That wasn't there before," I state, pointing to the locks.

"It is a precaution. I will explain it all soon, but we are not safe here anymore."

"You keep saying ominous things. I swear I'm developing a stomach ulcer," I grimace while touching my stomach. It feels like an alien is inside me trying to get out.

"We will be fine, I promise—but we do not have time to waste."

He makes a motion with his head for me to follow—we arrive at a door that leads downstairs into the basement. When we reach the bottom, he flips on the lights, illuminating an area that is just as nice—if not nicer—than the rest of the house. It's like a separate living space, but without doors or windows. The walls are painted a light blue to keep the room from being too dark, and the furniture is a bright cream. More expensive-looking art fills the walls, lit by their own individual lights.

"You are probably wondering why I brought you down here," he begins. "But we need to stay away from windows and doors for the time being."

A weird strangled laugh escapes my mouth before I can stop it. "Ethan! Will you please get to the point?"

He grabs my hands and somewhat pushes me down on the couch next to him.

"First, I need you to tell me what happened back there. I saw Chris with you, holding you against the car. I was on my way to kick his butt and then like you said—*poof*—he was gone," Ethan muses, trying to hold in a pleased smile.

"How can you find this even remotely funny?"

"Because I hated that man."

"Then you do know him."

"Yes," he admits. "I do. I have known Chris for many years."

"*Years?*"

"As I said, I can explain it all—but what is more important right now is you. You need to know who you are."

I snort at that statement—he sounds ridiculous. My only response is to stand up and pace—my anxiety going through the roof.

174

"*Who I am?* I *know* who I am—I'm me, Sophie Black. A library assistant who doesn't take shit from people, and lives a simple, boring life. I'm a nobody. That's who I am."

Ethan stands up and blocks me from pacing further.

"You are far from a nobody, Sophia."

My eyes begin to clear with understanding.

"You've been lying to me about who you are, haven't you?"

Ethan pauses. "Not exactly…"

"Ugh!" I yell.

"Sophia—"

"Will you just tell me already," I bark, hot angry tears now slipping down my cheeks. I wipe at them furiously, not appreciating my body's reaction in the moment.

He takes his place back on the couch. "Sit."

When I don't, he pats the spot beside him, turning his blasted violet eyes on me in a pleading gesture.

I huff but sit anyway—as far away from him as I possibly can.

"Is your name even Ethan? Let me guess—you're actually a serial killer," I deadpan.

Ethan stares at me wide-eyed for a moment before he breaks into a huge burst of laughter.

"That is not very original," he half-smiles. "But my

name really is Ethan. Everything I told you about my life is true—I just left out a few details."

"A few *details*—is that how you sleep at night?"

"You do not understand."

"Well make me understand before I make you disappear like your pal, Chris," I say with conviction.

Sheer panic flashes through Ethan's features. He swallows and opens his mouth as if he's going to say something, but a very bizarre squeak comes out instead.

"I was kidding," I assure him.

He takes a huge breath before scooting forward to place a hand on my shoulder in relief. His eyes penetrate me as if they are looking into my soul.

"Please, do not joke about that—your gift is anything but funny."

I pull back from him. "Say that part again."

"You have a gift, Sophia."

*"Okayyyy…*like gifted in going crazy?!" I splutter.

He shakes his head. "No. I told you—you are not crazy. Your gift, it is special. Unique for our kind, even, but a gift nonetheless. You were born with this—it did not just happen out of the blue."

"Now you sound like the one who's crazy."

"I am being serious," he stresses. "You wanted me to

176

explain, and I am trying to explain. You are not making it easy."

He's right. I'm not being easy, but my mind can't grasp what he's saying. The snark is how I deal with the fear.

"You're right—go on," I encourage.

"Just let me finish before you interrupt me, all right?"

I nod, making a show of zipping my lips and throwing away the key. He takes a deep breath and after what feels like forever, finally speaks.

"You are a Wisher—we both are."

I almost laugh, but Ethan's finger is over my mouth to silence me before I can.

"We are both gifted, and so is Chris. That is why he said—*our kind*. It is how I know him. We were all born into this life—into W.I.S.H.—or The Society as we often call it.

At this point, I can't contain the nervous giggle that bubbles out of me.

He stares at me. "Why is that funny?"

I hold my eye-roll, but not my tongue. "I'm sorry, but I think you guys could have been more original with that one—*that can't be real!*"

"Sophia, this is no time for any sort of joke. This is serious—I am being serious," he says.

I swallow my sarcasm—one look at Ethan and I can tell he's being honest—I've really upset him.

"Okay, okay—I'm listening."

"Wishers are born with the power to wish things into existence. Many of us believe we are the creators of all—like gods if you will. Our people created earth, and all things in it," he gestures around to everything in the house.

"Excuse you? I'm pretty sure I'm only 24—hardly a *creator of all*—much less a god!"

Ethan shakes his head. "No. Our kind is old—you are very young—but Wishers have been here since the beginning of time."

"Is now when you tell me you're a thousand years old or something? Because that's just creepy, and I'd say you've hit your head."

Ethan glares at me. "I am speaking truthfully."

"You sound absolutely insane—you know that, right? I grew up with the story of Adam and Eve, God, Jesus, The Bible. Not some fairytale about Wishers who claim to be gods!"

"I am not saying that any of that is not true. In fact, Adam and Eve were the first Wishers."

I stand up, ready to leave. "Okay, Ethan. I'm sorry, but this is too much. I can't listen any longer."

He jumps up quickly, blocking the door so fast I barely see him do it.

"No! You cannot leave. I am very serious right now and I am begging you to listen to me."

"Ethan—"

A loud bang from upstairs interrupts my words—it sounds like a gunshot. My whole body jumps about a mile in the air, my hand flying to my heart as it begins to race.

"What the hell was that?" I cry, moving towards the door again.

"Are you crazy? Do not go that way!" he exclaims, grabbing my arm.

"Do you think it's Chris?"

Ethan shakes his head no, tugging me with him as we hear voices speak above us.

"We have to get her before she hurts another one of us," a woman's voice says.

A man's voice responds. "Still no word on where she sent Chris?"

"No—we can't pick up his location anywhere. As far as we know he's dead," the woman answers.

"I think they're in the basement," another man with a deeper voice adds. *"Remember to kill Ethan if needed—we need the Alpha,"* the woman orders.

"The Alpha?" I whisper harshly to Ethan. "What are they talking about?"

"I will explain when we are safe, but we need to get out of here."

"Can't we just will them away or something?"

"The proper word is wish not will," he corrects.

I roll my eyes. "Whatever! Can we *wish* them away?"

"It is too dangerous. You heard them say what happened to Chris. You do not know anything about your gifts yet, or what you are capable of. As well, I cannot wish them away like that."

"*Okay*...so how do we get out of here?"

"Follow me," he states, leading me to the back corner of the room. In front of us is a door.

"Was this here when we came down?" I ask.

"No—I wished it here. This is just a taste of what we can do."

As Ethan goes to opens the door, I hear someone trying to get into the basement. The handle is twisting furiously. It won't be long before whoever's chasing us is able to break down the door.

"Quickly," Ethan says, turning my attention back to him.

When the door opens, I see a long tunnel that looks like

it's made out of liquid silver. My heart is pounding, and my palms are sweating. I trip on air as we go through, my nerves getting the best of me. When I look behind us, I see the tunnel disappearing as we run.

"This is freaking crazy!" I say, not believing my eyes.

"Tell me about it. I lived a fairly boring life until you came along," he replies. I can hear the smirk in his voice as he says it—like his life could be boring.

Finally, we come to a set of stairs leading up. I chuckle to myself as I imagine there will be two white horses outside—waiting for us to ride away like in some movie—though a car would be easier and faster.

After climbing the stairs, Ethan opens a door that looks like a storm cellar hatch. We go through it and come out to a darkening sky on the other side. Once my eyes adjust to the lack of light, I see a white Mustang convertible sitting there—as if someone had planted it there for us.

"A Ford Mustang, Sophia? You could have wished us a faster car."

My eyes go wide. "What do you mean?"

"I had wished one of my cars here. My top-of-the-line car with bullet-proof windows and all the bells and whistles. You replaced it with this—*thing*."

"I did?" I think for a second, and realize I wanted two

horses waiting for us, but instead we got a brand-new Mustang convertible. *I wince.* "Sorry—I was thinking about riding away on horses and well—*this happened.*"

"Really?"

"Are we going to talk about the way my brain works right now? I would kind of like to live."

"Right," he says, coming back to himself. "Get in."

I seat myself quickly and buckle in—Ethan takes the wheel—keys already in the ignition.

My eyebrow quirks up in thought. "Does this make you my knight in shining armor saving me on a valiant white steed?"

Ethan barks out a laugh. "Your fantasy, not mine."

"Hey! Be nice," I huff.

"I do not know what I am going to do with you, Sophia," he says right before he punches the gas. I fly backward against my seatbelt, effectively cutting me off from a comeback.

The scenery flies by, but even in the darkness I'm able to tell we aren't too far from my house.

"Can we stop at my place so I can grab a few things? I need to get Laker—and what about my mom?" I say rather quickly, the panic setting in. It's the first time I think about her—is she a Wisher person? Are these people after her, too?

Ethan reads the panic in my voice, placing a hand over mine while keeping his eyes on the road.

"Your mother will be fine," he assures.

"What? How do you know?"

"I have sent for some people we can trust, they will make sure she is safe."

"What about Laker? He's all alone. What if they hurt him?"

"Laker will be fine, too. I took care of him."

"What do you mean?" I say anxiously.

"Please trust me, Sophia. He is safe with some very trustworthy friends of mine."

"*What?* I was with you the whole time. How did you do that?"

"Do not worry, Sophia. I know you have questions, but just be patient. Let us get to safety first."

"This is crazy! How do I know this isn't a cult or something?"

"You heard what those people said back there. You saw what I did with that hallway—and do not forget how you made Chris disappear, and this car appear out of nowhere—" he lists before I cut him off.

"Ok, fine. I get it—I'm a freak. Maybe I've finally lost it

living in this town my whole life—the monotony finally cracked me! I bet I'm sedated in a mental institution right now and this is a movie playing in my head."

"Stop being so dramatic," he mutters. "How many times must I tell you that you are not crazy?"

"Forgive me for trying to be realistic—it's all just a little hard to absorb. Not to mention we're on the run from some crazy people with guns, so I'm feeling a little stressed!"

"I know, Sophia. This was not how I wanted you to find out—I had a plan."

"You should have told me sooner."

"I know," he says softly. "Let us just focus on getting to safety."

Our moment is interrupted by a loud screeching of tires—I look behind us to see a black SUV approaching.

"Damn it," Ethan growls. "Hold on!"

He slams on the acceleration before I can react to his swearing—going as fast as the car will allow him. The smell of burning rubber invades my nostrils as I glance back again to see the SUV gaining on us. I start to think about what I can do to help. I know that Ethan mentioned I shouldn't be using my powers—gifts—whatever—yet—but now seems like the most appropriate time to use them. I almost ask

184

Ethan, but then I see the person in the passenger seat roll down the window and aim a very large gun at us. We're in big trouble.

"Shit!" I yell.

A loud *bang, bang, bang,* echoes as what looks like a man begins to shoot at us. A bullet ricochets off the bumper, another one just missing our back-left tire.

"Sophia, get down!" Ethan cries.

I should probably listen to him, but I don't. I'm going to try and use my gifts—I don't care what happens at this point. Maybe if I get shot I'll wake up from this dream and be at home with Laker instead. Ethan continues to try and get me to turn around but instead I focus on the SUV.

I take a calming breath—tuning out everything around me to the best of my ability. I start to imagine a rock. Not just any rock, but a giant, big-ass boulder falling from the sky and blocking their car. As I focus, I begin to feel a sort of buzz in my head, followed by a tingling sensation in my hands and feet. The sound of screeching tires and a large crunch brings my attention back to the SUV. Where the SUV had been, however, there is now a very large boulder in the middle of the road, the hood of the car barely visible underneath.

I let out a whoop of joy. "Oh my God, Ethan! Did you

fucking see that?"

I can't help but laugh and grin like an idiot. I turn around in my seat to face him, but his expression isn't one of excitement like I thought it would be—instead he looks mad.

"Please do not use your gifts," he scolds.

"That's what you want to say to me right now? I just saved our asses, thank you very little!"

"Sit down and buckle your seatbelt, will you?" he says.

I mutter a string of curse words to myself but buckle my seatbelt anyway—this is going to be a long ride.

CHAPTER 11

The car ride with Ethan is painfully silent.

Both of us are too stubborn for our own good, so we don't talk. When an airstrip eventually comes into view an hour later my gut churns—I finally break the tension.

"We're flying somewhere—are you even going to tell me where?"

He keeps his eyes on the road. "Massachusetts."

"Excuse me?"

"We are going to The Society's headquarters."

"You have a private jet, too?"

"It is actually not *my* private jet, it is The Society's."

"But let me guess, you also have your own private jet?"

"My family does."

"Of course," I mumble, not sure I'll ever get used to his wealth. "By the way, what do I tell my mom and Ana? They're going to freak and send the cops out looking for me."

"Tell them I took you on a surprise vacation," he answers easily.

"For real?"

"It is something I would do anyway. It is either something like that, or you tell them nothing—it is up to you."

"What if I just say you kidnapped me?"

"Sophia…" he admonishes.

"Got it—not in the joking mood," I say more to myself than to him.

I take my phone out, quickly tapping out a text to my mom. I tell her Ethan is taking me on vacation and I'm unsure when I'll be back. I figure I can avoid speaking to her for now. I know she'll be mad and have a million questions—to which I don't have any answers. When I go to text Ana, I remember my birthday.

"Crap," I mumble out loud.

"What is it?"

"I just remembered my birthday is next week—Ana is going to kill me. She wanted to do this whole big party."

"I do not think you will be back by then, Sophia."

"I will be back in time," I cross my hands over my chest.

"No, you will not," he reiterates.

188

"I can leave anytime I want—I'm not a prisoner."

"No, you are not—but if you want your family and friends to die, then yes, please, by all means, go home and celebrate your birthday with Ana. I am sure it will be your last."

"*Wowwwww*," I breathe out. "Thanks, Mr. Doom & Gloom."

My heart pounds rapidly in my chest, and I feel my cheeks get hot with anger, my eyes becoming watery.

"I didn't ask for this," I say loudly, the words coming out of me like fire.

Ethan goes tense. "We rarely ask for trials in our lives— we are dealt certain cards, and we must play them."

I quickly blink back my tears; the familiar words of my dad shake me. I shove the feelings down—angry that Ethan isn't being comforting in the slightest. I feel utterly alone.

It's funny—when I was a child I wished I had superpowers and beautiful men to come sweep me off my feet in private jets. Now, here I am—in a car with the guy I began to think could be the impossible man of my dreams—with some strange power at my fingertips, and everything I know and love is in jeopardy of being destroyed. It is anything but what my childhood-self had fantasized. This is unreal—*a stupid fantasy gone wrong.*

I look at Ethan. I can tell he is struggling to keep himself together; he wants to reach out to me, but he's stopping himself.

"We are here," he states, as we pull up to the private airstrip. A jet is being fueled with two men standing outside of it, waving at us as we drive up to them.

"Are they Wishers?"

"Yes, they work for The Society."

"I see."

He parks the car and wastes no time getting out. I follow suit, making sure I have my phone with me. When I glance back to the car, it's gone.

"Did you do that?"

"I did."

"Huh—that is oddly satisfying."

His eyes show a glimmer of excitement. "Just wait till you learn what you can do—it is an amazing feeling. It never gets old."

I calm a little at his tone—finally it seems like he's relaxing a bit. I can only hope that his mood is even better by the time we get on the jet and can actually talk. When we approach the jet, the two men are looking at us with partial smiles on their faces. One is older with graying hair, while the other is tall and young-looking.

190

"Ethan—it's good to see you in one piece," the gray-haired man says, coming to give him what I call a *man hug*.

"It is good to see you, too, Frank. I am sorry it took us longer than expected to get here."

"It's fine. We're glad you're both ok," Frank adds, turning his gaze on me.

"Frank, this is Sophia. Sophia, this is my friend and our pilot for the evening, Frank."

"Hi," I reach my hand out to shake his. "You can call me Sophie."

"It's great to finally meet you, Sophie. I never thought I'd see the day. You look so much—"

"We should really get going," Ethan cuts him off. "It will not be long until they catch up with us again."

"Right," Frank says awkwardly. "Sophie, this is Aaron. He'll be helping us out on our flight."

I look to the other man standing behind, Frank. He's in his late 20s most likely, with brown hair and brown eyes.

"Hi," I wave.

"Hi," he waves back. "It's a pleasure to meet you."

"I wish I could say the same," I tell him lightly.

Ethan nudges my ribs a little.

I bite my tongue. "Sorry, I didn't mean it that way. I just meant the situation. It's not very um…pleasurable."

Aaron laughs a little. "I know what you mean."

"Come on, we need to go," Ethan mutters. He grabs my hand and practically drags me up the stairs onto the jet. I feel the anxiety rolling off him in waves.

Upon entering, I can't help but gasp. I've never been on a plane or a jet, let alone a fancy one like this. It has leather seats and tons of space. There is a small kitchen area and a large TV is set up on one of the walls, facing a sitting area with a plush couch.

"Are all jets like this?" I wonder out loud.

Ethan chuckles. "This one is nicer than a regular jet."

"You know—I've never flown before."

"What?" all three men say at once.

"Yep. Road trips only. My dad took planes all the time for his work, but I never got around to it."

I notice the men share a look—like they know something I don't—but there's a lot I don't know, so I bury it for now and add it to my long list of questions. I walk around the space, letting my fingers touch the leather of the seats. Aaron and Frank go to ready the jet for take-off. Soon I hear the engine roar to life.

"Come on, let us sit," Ethan points to two of the large chairs.

I'm tempted to sit in the chair opposite his but know

that would be childish. We have a lot to talk about. I sit down and let out a small happy-sigh at how comfy the seat is—luxury doesn't feel like a good enough word to describe it.

Ethan sits down next to me. "I cannot believe this is your first time flying."

"Small-town girl. It's not that unusual where I'm from."

"Are you nervous?" he inquires.

"Not really. I mean—I'm kind of excited. I've heard about what it's like, I've seen it on TV and movies, but it will be interesting I'm sure."

"It is not scary."

"Compared to being manhandled, chased and shot at, I think this is going to be a piece of cake."

"*Touché.*"

Aaron comes in to tell us to buckle our seatbelts, that we'll be taking off in a few minutes. Once I'm fastened in, I look out the window. I can't see much since it's dark, but I feel an odd sense of *calm* wash over me. I notice Ethan's hand on my shoulder—I had been too lost in thoughts to feel it there before.

"Are you doing that?" I ask him.

"Doing what?"

"Two seconds ago, I felt on edge—now I feel

193

strangely... peaceful."

Ethan sighs. "I cannot get anything past you, can I?"

"How did you do that?"

"It is one of my gifts. I can help sway people's emotions. I do not know why I can do it, but I thought you needed it."

I'm stunned. "Ethan—first of all—that's just weird, and second—you can't just do that to people without asking! Something tells me that's not the first time you've done it either."

"It is not any weirder than being a Wisher already is—I can stop if you want. Actually, you can stop it yourself. You do not have to bend to my wish—you can overcome it. I cannot force people to do something they do not want to do."

"That doesn't make sense," I challenge.

"Why?"

"You said you can't make people do what they don't want to do."

"That is right," he reiterates.

"How could I have wished Chris away? It's not like he wanted to go anywhere!"

"You *are* too observant," he says, though I can tell he doesn't mean it as an insult.

"Can you please just tell me the truth now? We're no longer in immediate danger, and I'd really like to clear the air."

"I will tell you when we get up in the air, ok? Oh, and turn off your cell phone." Ethan pulls his out and turns it off.

I turn away from him, taking my phone from my pocket to finish my earlier text to Ana that I never sent. I tell her I'm boarding a jet with Ethan for a surprise vacation. I'll wait to break the news to her about my birthday—I know she'll be disappointed.

"Get ready, we are about to take-off," Ethan bounces.

I can't help but smile at his goofy behavior. "You're more excited than me. I'm sure you've done this a million times."

"I have, but I am excited for you. I remember the first time I took a jet when I was a boy—I loved it."

The jet starts moving faster down the runway. As it gains more and more momentum, I get butterflies in my stomach again, my body not used to the strange feeling. When we start lifting off the ground and the jet boggles a little, on reflex I reach out to grip the armrests. My left hand instead finds Ethan's, and he gently squeezes it in support. I take a deep calming breath, opening my eyes to see the lights of my small-town fading into the night sky as we go higher. Then, as soon as takeoff had started, it was over.

"Not so bad, right?" he asks, squeezing my hand again.

"No, not bad. I'm excited to see it in the daytime."

"We will have to fly over the Grand Canyon on a trip sometime in the future—it is beautiful."

I turn to look out of the window again. It isn't until I turn back toward the front that I realize we're still holding hands. I pull away and fold them in my lap, trying to ignore the disappointed look that flashes across his face.

"Ethan, there is a lot you need to tell me, but I need to know you're going to be completely honest with me about everything—including this last week."

Ethan turns serious, his eyes staring into mine with such intensity I almost have to look away.

"I will be, Sophia. Anything you want to ask me, I will do my best to answer."

"Alrighty then. But first, I want you to know I understand it hasn't been easy between us in the last few hours. We're obviously both stubborn and have quick tempers. I get that everything you've done so far has been what you thought you needed to do to protect me, but this last week has been confusing and scary."

"I am sincerely sorry for that," he says sadly.

"You must've known I was struggling. You had ample time to tell me the truth, yet you went out on dates with me, and said nothing. You appeared out of nowhere—*barefoot*—and I know you lied about how you got there. Looking back on it, I'm pretty sure I'm the one who wished you there...On top of that, you lied about knowing Chris, and now I know you've been using your emotion control thing on me. I just feel very betrayed. I like you Ethan, I do. I feel something when I'm around you, but now I don't even know if it's real. Have you been making me feel what you wanted so you could get close to me?"

"Sophia, no! How could you think that?" he cries.

"I don't know! It's not like I know what's real or not anymore!"

"I would never do that. Ever. I told you, I cannot make people do anything they do not want to do."

"But can't you see why I feel this way?" I stress.

"I do—I know everything is very confusing. I understand this is a lot to take in. You do not know how much I regret not telling you about who you are sooner."

"Then why didn't you?

"Because I wanted to gain your trust. I wanted you to feel comfortable around me. What I had to tell you was not exactly a normal thing to say to someone. I did not want you to think I was crazy."

"So instead you made me think I was crazy?"

"I know, and I cannot say sorry enough. I admit my plan was severely flawed. None of this would have happened if I would have told you right away."

"Well at least you're admitting it now," I exhale. Honestly, I'm sick of fighting.

Ethan tentatively reaches over and takes my hands, gently holding them in his and looking into my eyes. The warmth of his touch tingles throughout my body—that familiar sensation returning that I've felt every time he's touched me.

"Are you doing that?" I ask quickly.

"I swear I am not doing anything right now—I feel it too."

"You're not lying?"

"I am not lying—I promise you, Sophia. I am sorry I have been angry with you and snapping. I feel guilty about not telling you sooner, about lying to you. I just want you to know that everything that has happened between us is real. This feeling—it is not something I could even create. I came here to tell you about Wishers—to take you back to Massachusetts—I did not expect this to happen between

198

us," he murmurs, gripping my fingers. "I have been angry with you because I care for you, and sometimes you just push my buttons is all. We were being chased for goodness sake—I did not want you to die!"

"Are you finished?" I tease lightly.

He tries to hide a smile at my tone. "Do you want me to be finished?"

I chuckle breathily. "Ethan, I get it. I'm sorry—I was angry too. I was just so pissed, and I'm still pissed! You weren't making it easy for me, either. I'm also confused and sacred. This is not an everyday occurrence! I know there is a lot to learn and to know."

"I understand. It has been stressful, but we are safe now, and I will tell you everything I know—I swear it."

"Okay—I just want you to know I'm not totally over the lying yet. Give me time to process everything."

Ethan looks a little dejected but nods. "Take all the time you need."

"Thank you," I squeeze his hands in return. We have a lot more to work through, but with a clearer mind I'm able to see things from his perspective. I feel a connection to him I can't explain, and I know that if I give up on him now, I'll regret it. Just as he cares for me, I know I care for him—more than I want to admit.

I unbuckle my seatbelt and stand, Ethan looking on at me curiously. I walk the short distance over to the couch and pat the seat next to me just as he had earlier in the day. He doesn't ask questions; just simply gets up from his seat and comes over.

"Now," I say. "Tell me everything."

CHAPTER 12

"Now," I say. "Tell me everything."

I cross my legs underneath me, intently waiting for Ethan to begin.

"Honestly, Sophia. I do not know where to start."

"Okay—I'll just start asking and you can answer."

"All right, but just a warning that some questions will have to wait—I do not have all the answers. The Council will, though."

"The Council?"

"Yes—they are a group of Wishers elected by our peers to handle all matters past, present, and future within The Society. Every rule and law is created and enforced by them."

"Okay...why don't you explain everything to me how your parents explained it to you, then?"

"That is a good place to start," he gives me an assuring smile. "I had just turned five when I wished a giant banana split out of thin air right before dinner. It was the best moment of my life at the time—wishing for something and then suddenly getting it. After that occurred, my parents explained to me that I was different—told me that I was a Wisher."

I smile at the thought of a little Ethan, staring at a banana split bigger than his head.

"Both your parents are Wishers?" I ask him.

"My mother is. My father works for W.I.S.H. but does not have any gifts."

"I see. It isn't a lineage thing?"

"Not from what we can tell. Just because I am a Wisher does not mean my children will be. We do know that all humans are descendants of Adam and Eve, but that does not mean all humans are then automatically Wishers—it is not how heredity works."

"Adam and Eve? Really?"

"That is a question better suited for The Council."

I bite down on my tongue. "Then how many Wishers are there?"

"Again, we are not sure. It is not like we are born with trackers."

"How do you explain knowing about me?"

"*Sophia*—I am not sure now is the time for me to tell
202

you that. It may—"

"No! You don't get to do that, not when you know the answer," I demand, looking him hard in the eyes.

"You are not going to like it."

"Shocking," I deadpan. "Give it up, Ethan. How did you know?"

He takes a breath, almost as if to brace himself for my reaction.

"Your father—he knew you were special."

I feel like I've been punched in the gut. "My dad? But how would he—why would he...?"

I put my thoughts together—the puzzle pieces joining; Ethan cutting Frank off earlier when he was about to say I looked like someone—the men giving each other looks when I mentioned my dad flying a lot for work—Ethan using one of my dad's favorite mottos. *They all knew him.*

"My dad was—" I couldn't even say it.

Ethan nods curtly. "Yes, Robert was a Wisher."

I flop forward, resting my head in my hands. After a second, I feel Ethan begin to rub calming circles on my back.

"I am sorry I did not tell you sooner, but we already covered that I have been an idiot about this whole thing."

I don't answer, just welcome the comfort of his touch

for the moment.

"I can't believe this. Why wouldn't he say anything?"

"I think you will get the answers you seek in Massachusetts."

"Please don't tell me my mom is one, too!" I cry—sitting up rather suddenly—my head spinning.

"No, she is not. Your mom does not even know Wishers exist."

I brush a tear from my cheek, taking a shaky breath to compose myself.

"That explains a lot—do you know if anyone else in my family is a Wisher?"

"Robert—*your father*—his grandmother was a Wisher. She was on The Council for many years. Wishers have always talked about how much they adored her."

"My great-grandmother—really?" Ethan just nods.

I try to remember her—I think I only met her once or twice when I was young. I've seen pictures of her, but that was about it. I do remember my dad saying she was a very private woman, and when she died, they didn't want me to go to the funeral.

"Just when I thought things couldn't get worse," I mumble, feeling a migraine coming on.

"I know it is painful for the people you love not to tell

you the truth. From what I understand, Robert did not tell you because he wanted to keep you away from this life—he wanted to protect you."

"Look how well that worked out! What is it with men wanting to protect women all the time? Between you coming to town and not telling me about all this right away, and my dad not telling me anything about my *entire life*, I can very much say that this should be a lesson that keeping things from women to *protect them* is NOT a good idea. It just makes things worse and perpetuates *the women are helpless victims* stereotype," I blurt out.

Ethan blinks rapidly at me as if I slapped him across the face.

"That is a bit dramatic, is it not?"

"Don't try to minimize what I'm saying. I get it, you had good intentions, but think next time."

"Sophia, I am not trying to minimize it. I am just saying that he loved you and wanted to keep you alive. Can you at least try and understand where he is coming from? I also apologized several times for my errors. I do not know what more you want from me," he resigns, his jaw clenched.

"I just don't want to be treated like a porcelain doll—I can take care of myself," I challenge.

"I am not saying you cannot. I think you are very

capable, but I would also like to point out that several times over the last week—whenever you felt scared or in danger—you wished me to your side. You wanted me to be there—you wanted me to protect or comfort you. I want you to know there is nothing wrong with that. We all need help sometimes, we just have to let go of our egos and ask for it. Even I need help, Sophia. I cannot take on this life alone—nobody can, nor should they."

I'm only half-listening to him, as I'm still focused on what he said about me wishing him to my side.

"So," I clear my throat, my cheeks heating. "I really did wish you to my side all those times? In the woods—*oh shit!*" I cry in realization. "Were you in my house that one night...*you held me!*"

Ethan's skin flares red. "Well—*Yes.* It is not like you did not want me there—you wished for me."

"I was half-asleep!"

"I know, but you were terrified. I did not know what else to do."

"You could have left!"

"I did as soon as you fell asleep."

I grunt, laying my head against the back of the couch.

"Sophia, I was perfectly respectable. I did not do anything except provide the comfort you asked me for—

that is it."

"Why do I have the feeling every bit of information you're going to reveal to me is just going to make everything weirder?"

"It is the nature of this life, I suppose."

I sit back up. "At least now I know I wasn't crazy. It was weird how you kept showing up when I thought of you—I thought you were stalking me!"

Ethan laughs uncomfortably. "No, I was not—though you made it rather hard for me to get things done. You thought of me more often than you know."

"*What?*"

"More than once a day sometimes—I had to hide outside of the library bushes in hopes you would not see me."

I face-palm. "*Oh God.*"

Ethan grins a little. "I know you did not mean to wish me to you all the time, but that is why it is so important that you learn how to use your gifts before you wish anymore," he finishes by squeezing my shoulder.

My cheeks burn thinking about how often I thought of Ethan over the course of the last week. I'm embarrassed he knows how much he's been on my mind.

"Do you remember the first time you wished for

something and it came true?" Ethan asks curiously. I nod, grateful for the subject change.

"I do—though I convinced myself over the years it was all a dream," I say sadly before recounting the Malibu Barbie story to him. Ethan listens sympathetically, my anger building now that I know the truth. "I remember my parents arguing over it—but my dad never made me think he believed me when I told him it just appeared," I finish bitterly.

Ethan's expression is slightly troubled. "I cannot speak for Robert, and I do not know why exactly he chose to go about things the way he did, but there is still a lot you do not know. And—*he stops me from interrupting*—I am not saying what he did was right, but just wait to pass complete judgment on him before you know everything."

"Fine," I spit out. "Does this have to do with me being this Alpha thing?"

"It does."

"Tell me what that means."

"I am afraid you will have to wait for The Council to tell you."

"Ugh—*why are you such a tease!*" I say, trying to lighten the mood a bit. Everything is starting to feel too heavy.

His lips upturn. "I am sorry, but they know more about it than me. I want you to hear it from them. But I can tell you that Alphas are extremely rare amongst Wishers."

"How rare are we talking?" I prod.

Ethan thinks for a second. I can tell he isn't sure if he should say or not.

"How rare?" I press again.

"As far as I know, Sophia, you are the only Alpha."

My mouth drops open, the butterflies returning to my stomach.

"Me? The only Alpha?"

"Yes."

"I—I don't understand."

"You will. I promise," he assures, his hand coming to rest on mine again. "I probably should not have told you yet, but you make it very hard not to. However, I do not want you to have too many more surprises."

"Many more?" I swallow.

He sends me a look that tells me how sorry he is.

"I cannot imagine how scary this all must be for you. When I found out I was a Wisher I was terrified and thrilled all at the same time. But what you have—what you can do with your gifts—it is a whole different world."

My eyes widen. "That isn't comforting."

Ethan cringes. "Sorry."

"It's fine. You're trying and I appreciate it."

"I can tell you why your gifts have been acting up recently," he says, smiling so that I can almost see his dimple.

"That would be nice."

"It is your twenty-fifth birthday. Our gifts actualize completely on our twenty-fifth year. We do not know why that happens, but we can perform small wishes prior to that—banana splits, pizza, Barbies…." He smirks at me.

"Party tricks," I state.

"Exactly right. But at twenty-five, that is when our true gifts kick in. You can wish bigger things—rooms, houses, paintings, cars…money."

"For real?"

"For real," he repeats teasingly. "However, with most Wishers it is not just as simple as wishing something and that is it."

"What do you mean?" I wonder.

"The items have to come from somewhere, do they not?"

"But I thought we were the creators? *Gods…*"

Ethan smiles.

"What are you smiling at?"

"You said we."

"Oh—well I am one of you now, aren't I?"

"You always were, Sophia. You just did not know it yet."

It's a strange thought. Didn't I work in a library less than a day ago?

"I suppose that's true. But what did you mean before—about the items having to come from somewhere?"

"When a Wisher wishes for something, the item is not just made from nothing—it is taken from the place it was originally created."

"But that's stealing," I frown.

"In the plain sense of the word—yes. But there is more to it than that. It is not like one person had the item in their hand and then it is gone. It is taken from a place where it will technically go unnoticed."

"That seems impossible."

"I am not positive regarding the mechanics of it all, but I am sure you have heard of the concept of Karma."

"What goes around comes around."

"In its simplest form, yes. If I take, I must give back. Otherwise I lose everything."

"*Wow*—"

"I have tried to live the most honest life that I am

capable of living. I try not to use my gifts unless necessary, and when I do use them, I use them for things that will not cause any harm or major shifts in the Universe."

"Like banana splits," I joke.

He laughs. "Yes, like banana splits."

"Did you wish that original Warhol?"

He scoffs. "Of course not. I just told you—I try to live an honest life. I earned that the old-fashioned way, through hard work and long hours."

"But I'm curious—if I wished a million dollars, I could have a million dollars?"

"That is correct."

"This would have been *really* helpful during college," I think out loud.

Ethan looks at me with understanding. "It is easy to think that, but the risk is often greater than the reward. To take money, you have to eventually give it back one way or another. Your father—at least from what I knew of him— understood the risk of taking things he had not earned. He used his gifts when necessary and did what he felt was right. We all live by our own ethical and moral codes. He earned his money, he worked hard."

"Wait, I'm confused. If Wisher's created everything in existence from nothing—then you are saying two different

212

things—how could karma exist? How—" I hear Ethan sigh faintly as I start to put the pieces together. The muscles in back tighten and I sit up straight. "Hold on, does that mean—"

"I really should keep my mouth shut. You are figuring everything out with the little I am telling you," he mutters.

"Tell me," I urge.

"Yes, Alpha's are the only Wishers that have the ability to create things from non-existence, but that is all I can tell you. Again, I was trying to avoid it until The Council could explain, but your observational skills are destroying my plan."

"What can I say—*I listen.*"

He exhales. "I know you do."

"So, if I'm an Alpha, then that means I could technically wish for a million dollars and I'd have no consequences."

"I believe so, but again —"

"It's a question for The Council," I finish for him. "Have you ever met another Alpha?"

"I have never met anyone like you, Sophia," he says with reverence. "I cannot even begin to understand your gifts or what you are capable of. I would have never been able to wish a car, or a giant boulder from thin air before I turned twenty-five, and I definitely cannot wish people away to God knows where."

"*Shit—Chris!*" I had totally forgotten about him. "You really have no idea where I could have sent him?"

"He could be anywhere. You heard what his lackeys said back at my home. They have not been able to find him."

"You don't think I killed him, do you?"

"I honestly have no idea, Sophia. You could have sent him to another dimension—or another time."

"You mean like, with the dinosaurs or something?"

Ethan smirks, his eyes shining. "Let us hope not—for his sake."

I turn my eyes downward. "I feel a little bad that I did that, he is an ass, but I don't want to be a murderer!"

"You are not a murderer. I am sure he is fine—wherever he is."

I relax back on the couch, staring off in thought. I don't know for how long, but eventually I feel Ethan staring at me.

"What?" I ask, turning to him.

"It is scaring me that you are so calm about all of this."

"Trust me, Ethan—I'm freaking my shit."

"Freaking your shit?" he snorts.

I can't help but laugh. Not only because he snorted but

because hearing him say my phrase out of his proper mouth is weird.

"Sorry, you can take the girl out of Wisconsin, but you can't take the Wisconsin out of the girl."

"It is fine. You are keeping yourself awfully composed is all."

"What other choice do I have? In all honesty, I'm a little relieved. Now I know I'm not going crazy—at least not in the conventional way...and I understand my childhood a lot more now. It's strangely comforting."

"I am really very sorry."

"I know, but it's not your fault—if anything it's my dad's," I tell him. I reach out and grab his hand, squeezing it. A smile breaks out on his face, and I know he's happy I initiated the contact.

"Look, Sophia I—"

"You know," I interrupt him. "You don't have to call me by my full name all the time. You can call me Soph, or Sophie."

Ethan blinks a few times in surprise. "What is wrong with your name?"

"Nothing. It's just that usually my full name is used when I'm in trouble, or when I don't know someone that well. I prefer the others is all. I should have said something sooner, but I didn't want to be rude."

He raises an eyebrow at me in question. "It would not have been rude for you to correct me if that is what you wanted. I do like calling you Sophia, but if it makes you uncomfortable, I can call you Sophie."

I grin. "I'd like that."

He beams back at me and that proverbial heat rises through my body. I look into his eyes, studying him for a moment—he's exhausted. I reach up to gently rub my thumb over one of the bags under his eyes.

"You're tired," I state, lowering my hand.

"I have not had much sleep since we met. A certain someone kept wishing me to them at all times of the day."

I look at him sheepishly. "Sorry."

He brushes a lock of hair behind my ear. "It is okay, Sophia—I mean, *Sophie*."

I bob my head in approval. "Let's hope that now I'll be able to control that a little more."

"I am sure you will," he assures me.

I yawn, a big yawn that causes my eyes to water. "Sorry," I mutter. "I guess I'm tired too."

"I think we should both try for some sleep. The seats lean back into a bed. They are actually pretty comfortable."

"I still have more questions."

"I know," he grins. "But we only have another hour or so until we land. We should really try and get some rest."

I'm about to protest when I yawn again.

"Trust me, Sophie, you will have all of your questions answered when we meet with The Council."

We both settle back in our chairs after Ethan hands me a blanket and a pillow. He's right, the seats are extremely comfortable as beds. I feel myself fading quickly, the events of the day swirling in my head. I'm about to fall asleep when I feel a kiss on my forehead.

"Sweet dreams, Sophia," Ethan whispers.

"It's Sophie," I grumble.

I hear the distant sound of his laughter as I drift off.

CHAPTER 13

I don't know how long I've been asleep, but when I wake up, I'm no longer on the jet. I sit up quickly—a wave of dizziness washes over me—my heart batters in my ears. I hear a chuckle, bringing my attention to Ethan sitting across from me, looking tired and amused, his hair all mussed, and clothes wrinkled.

"Are we in a limo?" I ask, trying to get my bearings.

"I love how that is the first question you ask," he smirks.

I roll my eyes. "How did I get here?"

"I carried you."

"And I didn't wake up?" I ask in disbelief.

"Not even a little bit. I knew you were exhausted," he says before getting a wistful look in his eyes. "I remember when I first started using my gifts, I had to take long naps to recover. My mother told me I was dead to the world."

That must have been why I passed out. My head feels all

fuzzy, too, like I have a bad hangover. I rub my eyes, looking out of the black windows. It's still dark, so I can't see much. "We're going to headquarters now?" I ask, turning my head back to him.

"Yes. We will have time to rest and freshen up before your meeting. It is not even four in the morning yet. You will get to meet my mother as well," he finishes, his expression unreadable.

"Wow, we're at that step already?" I half-joke.

"I did not realize we were together in that way," he cuts. I stiffen at his tone, not sure what to make of it. He notices the way I react and immediately looks uncomfortable.

"I apologize—I do not know where that came from."

I blink. "It's okay, I think we just have a lot to figure out. But I don't know if this is the right time to start a relationship—" I trail off.

"You are probably right," he laments, absentmindedly playing with his watch.

My heart clenches, and I can't help but mirror his disappointment. I think carefully for a few minutes before speaking again. "Ethan?" He looks up at me, his eyes dark and brooding.

"I know it's bad timing, but—I wouldn't mind seeing

what happens from here."

His eyes light up. "Are you sure?"

"I may regret it," I tease. "But yes, I'm sure."

He skillfully climbs over to my side of the limo, sitting down next to me with more grace than I have in my whole body.

"I know I do not deserve to be given another chance with you, but if you are really serious, if you think you can trust me—then I would like to see where this goes between us. Bad timing and all," he adds with a lopsided grin.

"I think I can trust you. I mean, I do trust you, Ethan. I'm still here, aren't I?"

"You are," he says, smoothing hair behind my ear.

We're closer now. I feel his breath on my cheek, and my body starts to react to his. One of his hands comes to cup my cheek as I lean toward him. Just as our lips are about to connect, the limo stops and there's a sharp knock on the divider. I jump, my hand flying to my chest.

"I suppose we will have to save that for later," he exhales.

"It's probably for the best. I haven't brushed my teeth since yesterday," I mention.

Ethan laughs a bit, a husky laugh that makes my toes tingle. He brushes his thumb over my bottom lip before the

220

doors to the limo open abruptly. Ethan signals for me to get out of the car first. I step out and greet the dark-haired man who opened the door, giving him a slight smile—he smiles back. When I look past him, I can't help but stare, my jaw falling open in awe. In front of me is a massive modern glass building. It looks like a very, very, very big shark fin. The glass curves upwards into a point, seemingly going forever up into the sky. Lights illuminate the building from the front, turning it into a beacon of sorts—I've never seen anything like it.

"Holy crap," I whisper.

"Beautiful, is it not?" Ethan comments, coming to stand next to me.

"Is this your version of Hogwarts?"

"Hogwarts?" Ethan's eyebrows shoot up.

"*Oh lord.* Never-mind." I shake my head. *Where had he been the last twenty years?* "Is this where all the Wishers come to study?" I ask him.

"Sort of..."

"So, it is like Hogwarts," I say to myself, still staring at the building. "Well, what are we waiting for? Let's go."

"Someone is excited," he teases.

I think for a moment. He's right. "I am. I mean, this all makes magic real in a way."

"It is not really magic. That is a very…*human term*," he says with a hint of arrogance.

I scrunch my nose at him. "Oh, my God. If you knew who Harry Potter was, you'd know that this *is* like Harry Potter—and you're the rich asshole that nobody likes!"

Ethan blinks, shaking his head. "You are a very odd person sometimes, you know that? Come on," he grabs my hand and pulls me along.

I fight the urge to cross my arms and say *duh*, instead letting him lead me toward a large flight of stairs. When we get closer to the building, I see it has a unique green tint to it. Two large guards are standing in front of the doors, armed with guns and what I assume are bulletproof vests. When we pass them, I can tell they're trying very hard not to look at Ethan or I. Ethan must have noticed too, because he mumbles a hello to them as he pushes open one of the large glass doors.

Nothing could have prepared me for what's inside. Beautiful seems like too dull a word to describe it. When I look up, it goes on endlessly—I can't even see the ceiling. Glass elevators are climbing up and down the center of the building to their destinations. It's fairly empty since it's so early in the morning, but you could guess that a lot of people usually occupy this space by its size. What really grabs my attention, however, are the windows. Where there should have been landscape, there's a tranquil ocean scene. If you didn't know you were in a building, you'd think you were on a tropical island somewhere. Just as I start to walk towards one of the walls to touch it, it changes to a jungle.

"It changes scenery depending on what a person wishes to see," Ethan says. For a moment I had forgotten he was beside me.

"Does that mean you can't see what I see?" I ask.

"Right now, it is a rainstorm in a forest," he answers, closing his eyes for a moment. He's pretending he can feel the rain on his face. "What is it for you?"

"A jungle," I state.

"Interesting choice. Not something I would have picked for you."

"At first it was a beach, but then I thought of a jungle. I've always wanted to go to Costa Rica."

"I will have to take you someday. It is exquisite."

I blush a little at the thought before turning to the wall of windows again. I run my fingers along the glass, pretending I can touch the leaves of the trees.

"*Ethan!*" a woman's voice calls, slicing through the air like a chime. It sounds a little frantic and winded. We both

223

turn, Ethan looks delighted when he recognizes who it is. I know right away that it's his mom. When she comes into view, she's exactly how I would have imagined her to look. She's taller than most women, with light brown hair, and wearing black flared dress pants with an azure blouse that makes the gray of her eyes almost shine a clear blue. She looks older, with laugh lines covering the corners of her mouth and eyes in a delightful way. But right now, she looks like a mom who has been worried about her only son. When she reaches us, she flings her arms around Ethan, giving him a bearhug.

"I am fine, mother," he tells her quietly, appearing slightly embarrassed.

She pulls away and grabs his face. "Are you sure you're all right? I heard what happened."

"Like I said, I am fine. Not even a scratch, thanks to Sophia," he finishes, nodding over in my direction.

"Sophie," I interject. "Call me, Sophie."

His mom turns sharply towards me, her eyes going wide for a second before she smiles. She ignores my now outstretched hand as she throws her arms around me. I feel like I'm being strangled.

"Mother, you are going to suffocate her," Ethan laughs.

"Oh! I'm sorry," she blushes, pulling away abruptly.

"It's very nice to meet you, Sophie. It's wonderful to finally put a face to the name after so many years."

"It's nice to meet you, too." I take a second to study her face. Ethan really did take after her in looks and personality. They both have a certain energy around them that seems to draw you in. I realize she's examining me too, her eyes scanning my every feature with a wistful look.

"You look so much like him," she remarks quietly.

Him? I almost ask her who, but I think I know who it is. Ethan clears his throat and touches his mom's shoulder. When she feels the contact, her eyes flit to Ethan, and she shakes her head a bit before the smile returns to her face.

"Sorry. It's not every day a ghost of the past walks through your door."

"What do you mean?" I ask a bit awkwardly. She shares another glance with Ethan.

"Later, Sophia. Okay?" Ethan asks with an underlying pleading tone.

I make a move to say something else, but Ethan's mom interrupts me.

"I'm Alice, by the way. In case my son didn't already tell you, and you'll meet my husband George at some point."

"He didn't, but we've been a little busy," I say, annoyed

that my previous question wasn't answered.

"Yes, I'm sure you have," she grins a little. I eyeball Ethan, wondering if he told Alice about our relationship. It seems like he did by the heat of his cheeks.

"I'm sorry I lost myself when I saw you. Ethan texted me that you know about your father being a Wisher. Robert and I were great friends for many years. He talked about you all the time, always showing us pictures. Seeing you, especially in that jacket, takes me back to a simpler time," she says, again looking lost in her past memories.

Now her comments make sense. I look down at my worn leather jacket, having forgotten I was wearing it. "You know this jacket?" I ask, curiously.

"I helped him pick it out for you."

I feel my mouth go dry. "This is one of the last things he gave to me."

Alice turns bashful. I'm not sure what's going through her mind, but now I want to ask her a million more questions.

"Mother," Ethan interrupts. "I think that is enough for now. We have been through quite a lot, and I am sure Sophia would like to clean up and get more than an hour of rest."

"Sophie," I correct him with a smile. "And yes, Sophie

would like a shower," I mimic.

Alice lets out a breathy sound and Ethan looks as though he wants to roll his eyes at me. I guess my snark is really rubbing off on him.

"Alright then, I'll show you to your room. Ethan told us what kind of clothes you like, so hopefully you'll find something clean to wear."

I nudge Ethan with my shoulder. "You already know what kind of clothes I like, huh?"

"What can I say, *I pay attention*," he grins, flashing his dimple.

"Oh my," Alice observes. "You two have gotten to know each other quite well, haven't you?"

"Mother," Ethan whines like a puppy. It's cute, but I also share his embarrassment. This is not how I pictured my first meeting with Ethan's mom to go.

"Okay, got it. Zipping it," Alice jokes. "Come on, let's get you two settled," she finishes before taking off toward the elevators.

Ethan places his hand on the small of my back, directing me to follow Alice. Behind us, two extremely big security guards keep watch.

I study the complicated architecture of the building, trying to take my mind off of well—*everything*. There are hundreds of hallways, stairs, and elevators everywhere you turn. "How do you not get lost in here?" I wonder aloud.

Alice chuckles. "It's easy once you know where you're going."

"That was helpful, mother," Ethan states. I can't help but smile quietly at their mother-son exchange.

When we approach the doors of the elevators, they're just as ornate as the rest of the building. They're made of glass and utterly spotless. At the top I see W.I.S.H. spelled out in capital letters, an infinity symbol weaving around and between the letters flawlessly. I raise an eyebrow in curiosity at the periods between each letter. Ethan hadn't mentioned that wish stood for anything. I make a mental note to ask him what it means later. We all quickly pile into an elevator once the doors open, security guards included. My mouth falls open in shock when I see there are 160 floors.

"Here," Ethan says, handing me a piece of gum. "It will help when your ears start to pop."

"Thanks," I swallow. I'm not really afraid of heights but—*160 floors?*

"This is the second tallest building in the world—but only Wishers can see it from the outside. People without gifts need our wish to see it. Amazing, no?" he smiles.

I'm only able to nod weakly.

Ethan grabs my hand in assurance. I feel that calmness again, and I know what he's doing.

"Don't do that!" I say under my breath, nudging him in the side.

He looks at me apologetically. "Sorry, it was not for you per se. I was doing it for me and then it transferred to you."

I give him a— *seriously?*—look before pulling my hand from his gently. I don't want to get into it with him while we're stuck in a fish-bowl elevator with a bunch of people I don't know. Luckily, he doesn't say anything else, just looks down at his feet silently. My stomach drops at the crestfallen look on his face. Great, now I feel like an asshole again. I sigh quietly to myself as I chew my gum, my ears popping as we ascend higher and higher into the air.

In no time we arrive at the top floor, exiting the elevator as Alice leads us down a long hallway. The same reflective glass panels from the lobby line the walls. It's now covered in ice blue waters that look like the posters I've seen of Greece. I have the urge to jump through the wall and swim in it—it looks that authentic.

When we get to a pair of white French doors, Alice stops.

"Here we are! This is where you'll be staying while

you're here, Sophie. Best in the place if I do say so myself," she states. When I don't move, she pushes open the doors, gesturing me to walk inside. "Go on."

I hesitantly walk inside, Ethan behind me.

"Jeff, David, you will both stay outside this door," Alice orders. I turn to see her talking to the guards who had accompanied us. "No one gets in unless I tell you they have clearance," she finishes, her voice stern.

"Yes, Mrs. Moore," they both say in unison. I half expect them to salute her.

She enters the threshold before turning to close the doors. Just like Ethan's house, deadbolts litter the entire door. Suddenly I feel like a prisoner. I don't like it—I don't like it *at all*.

Alice locks the doors hastily before turning towards me with a soft smile. She must have noticed my change in energy because she puts a hand on my shoulder in a very motherly gesture. "It's just as a precaution, Sophie. You're free to go wherever you'd like. All of this is for your protection. I promise we're not going to hurt you."

I blink rapidly at her. My feet feel heavy, my stomach is going haywire. I don't really know what to say or do. How do I know for sure these people aren't going to hurt me, or at least try too? My gut told me I could trust Ethan despite his initial lies—but then there must have been a reason my dad never exposed me to this world. I have never wanted my dad alive more than I do in this moment. I wonder fleetingly if I can wish him back to life. A hand touches my shoulder and I jump.

"Sophia?" Ethan calls, his face full of concern.

"Are you okay?" Alice asks.

I press my palms against my eyes, breathing deeply. "Look, I'm exhausted and I smell. I think I'd like a little time alone," I say, leaving no room for question.

Alice nods. "That's fine. Someone will be back to get you at five o'clock tonight. Rest, eat, get cleaned up. You're safe here," she repeats, squeezing my arm once more.

I don't say anything, just nod my head in understanding.

Alice heads towards the dead-bolted doors. When she notices Ethan hasn't followed, she turns back around. "Come on, Ethan. Let's let her be."

Ethan stands, his gaze never leaving me. "I will be right there. I just want to ask Sophia something first."

I mentally groan. "I'm fine Ethan. I just need some space right now."

"But I—"

"Ethan," I state calmly. "We'll talk later. I need to call

my mom and Ana. My phone's been off for far too long. I know Ana is probably freaking out."

"You cannot—"

"I know. I won't tell them anything about whatever this is," I say making a gesture around the room.

"Tell them I took you to Hawaii," he repeats.

"You just have to make my life more difficult, don't you," I huff, half teasing.

"I am sorry."

"Ethan! I'm *teasing* you. For goodness sake, just go! I'll see you later."

He pauses for another moment to stare at me before finally giving in and following Alice out the door. As soon as it closes, I lock all the deadbolts as fast as I can. Leaning back against the surface, I take a breath before pushing myself away to walk into the room.

Room is not the correct word for it; penthouse is more fitting. It looks like one of those places you see in a *James Bond* or *Mission Impossible* movie. The walls are still made entirely of glass, and it's bigger than any apartment I had ever stayed in.

After I get over my initial shock, I realize it has a very homey feel to it. The decor looks like it had come directly out of my cabin or a store back home. Realization washes over me as to who decorated it. *Ethan*. He really did pay attention to *everything*, didn't he? It's unnerving, and a little endearing. I walk to one of the windows—if you could call it a window—and look out into the distance. It's still dusk outside so I can't see much, but I can't stop my hand from flying up to my chest at how high up we are. It's almost like I'm still on the jet. The little I can see below looks like tiny specks.

I explore the rest of the space, taking my shoes off as I go. There are several leather couches, chairs, and a large coffee table in front of a fireplace. There's a huge kitchen off to the left with a massive island made of granite and dark wood cabinets. The appliances look so top-of-the-line—I don't dare use them. The wood floors are dark and rustic-looking throughout.

I keep walking until I find a bedroom with a California King-sized bed. It's covered in a mint green comforter with blue accents and way too many pillows. The carpet that covers the bedroom floor is plush beneath my feet as I walk through its threshold to find a bathroom. I smile when I see the walls are covered with paintings and photographs of flowers and forest scenery. Ethan had to throw his tastes in as well.

I quickly find the connecting bathroom, only to be

blown away by what I see there. It's larger than my entire cabin. There's a huge glass shower that doubles as a steam room. In front of it is a massive jacuzzi tub that easily fits two people. There's also a double sink with a countertop that has way too much space in my opinion. I try to decide what to do first. I'm in complete sensory overload and feel like I need a year to process everything.

Eventually I decide to take a bath, wanting to take full advantage of the huge tub with jets, something I've only experienced once before on a random family vacation when I was 8. I start to fill the tub and begin a search for some candles and bath salts. After a few moments I stop my search, deciding to try out this *gift* of mine.

I hear Ethan's voice in my head telling me not to do it, but another voice—a louder voice—reminds me that I had wished a car and a boulder out of thin air only hours before. Surely a few candles and bath salts won't hurt anyone? I take a deep breath and concentrate on the tub. I visualize everything exactly how I want it: Candles lit around the edges, the scent of lavender wafting through the air, salts dissolving in the hot water right before my eyes…

I start to feel a warm sensation in my lower stomach, followed by a familiar tingling in my hands and head. Something shifts and I know before I open my eyes, I've done it. I smile when I confirm my suspicion. Right before me—where there had once been nothing—is an exact replica of the image in my head. I take a deep breath, smelling the lavender in the air and I giggle.

Party tricks. I grin to myself, thinking of Ethan's words earlier. I grab a fluffy towel and place my phone next to the tub. I debate if it's too early for a glass of wine. I quickly decide that after all I've been through, I can excuse myself and have a mimosa. Screw societal standards. People in Wisconsin drink as early as 8:00 a.m. on football game days anyway. I close my eyes again and concentrate. When I open them, a mimosa is sitting right where I want it to be.

"I could *so* get used to this," I sing, awfully proud of myself.

Excited for my bath, I strip quickly. I briefly look at the leather jacket my dad had given me now on the bathroom floor. I'm still baffled by what Alice had told me about it. *I huff.* Why did things have to be so complicated? I attempt to discard my thoughts—I am trying to relax for God sakes! I struggle to breathe easy and sink my body into the steaming water.

"Oh. My. God," I moan. The hot liquid feels like heaven against my tired muscles. I pick up my mimosa and sip it. It isn't too long before my stomach growls and I have a sudden craving for pizza. An excited noise escapes my lips as I close my eyes again. The warm feeling returns to my stomach, and I smile. *That's how I know it's going to work.*

Sure enough, it had. A slice of piping hot cheese pizza now sits next to me. I immediately inhale it, certain that it's the best pizza I've ever had.

I relax for a while before I pick up my phone to check the time. When it powers on, I realize it's only 5:00 a.m., I cackle at myself for eating pizza and drinking *that* early. Since I'm on the East Coast, it's only 4:00 a.m. in Wisconsin. Ana is probably fast asleep, but if I call her, I know she'll pick-up due to my special ringtone. I debate for a minute until I press her speed dial, deciding it's better to call her now in case I don't get a chance later—I could always leave a voicemail.

The phone rings twice before she picks up, her voice booming through the other end of the phone. "SOPHIA MARILYN BLACK! WHERE THE HELL ARE YOU?"

"Ooooh, I got the full name," I tease back.

"Damn straight you get the full name! You literally sent me the most blasé text in the middle of the night saying that Ethan is taking you on a surprise vacation. Then turned your phone off! I've practically been up all night waiting," she wails.

236

"I'm sorry," I cringe.

"That's all I get?"

"It was all so sudden!" I cry back.

"No shit!" she barks. "Chris disappeared too, by the way. Did he say anything to you?"

My stomach drops, and my hand flies to my forehead. Crap, I didn't think of her asking me about Chris.

"He didn't…I haven't heard from him since the Olive Garden," I lie, glad she can't see my face.

"Ugh—*whatever.* I'm sure he'll turn up at my door tonight groveling like he usually does."

"Probably—" I trail off. "Guess what I'm doing right now?" I grin, changing the subject.

"Whatever it is, I know I'm going to be jealous."

"You are, because I'm currently soaking in the biggest tub with jets and drinking a mimosa."

"Wait, where are you?"

"Hawaii."

"How are you awake—isn't it later there? It's past your bedtime!" she teases.

Shit. I forgot about the time zones. "Jet-lag—*duh.*" I quickly try to recover.

"You are such a liar!" she exclaims. "You had sex, didn't you? You had to call me and tell me how good it

237

was, *right?* Was he so big you had to take a bath afterward?"

I immediately blush at the thought, letting out a loud guttural laugh. "Oh my God, Ana! NO. That is not what happened."

"Fine, don't tell me," she complains.

I cower at the sad tone in her voice. "I swear I'm telling the truth. We haven't had sex yet. Ethan found out my birthday was coming up, he wanted to do something spontaneous. He took me on a private jet."

"Whaaa? That's insane!"

"I know. I never expected all of this, that's for sure."

"I'm happy for you, Soph…really. I'm jealous, but happy. Does Ethan have a brother?" she asks, hopeful.

I chuckle. "No—he doesn't."

"Figures. So, when are you coming back?"

"I'm not sure, but I might not be home for my birthday. *But I'm not sure yet!"* I rush out. I hope I can still make it.

"For serious?" she asks, the disappointment evident in her voice. "What about your job?"

Double shit. I didn't even think about Mary or the library.

"Well, I haven't told her yet. But I'm sure she'll be glad I'm finally getting some action."

Ana laughs. "You're probably right. She'll be proud that you're finally taking a vacation too, especially with the hottest rich guy in town."

I snicker. "Yeah. Look, Ana, I'm sorry I might not be home for my birthday. I know you were looking forward to celebrating with me, but we will celebrate when I get home, I promise."

She sighs. "Fine. I suppose that will have to do. But you better bring me back something amazing, not just an airport keychain."

"Okay, I'll bring you an airport shot glass."

"Ha! That's better."

I smirk. "I better go. I've gotta call my mom and smooth things over."

"You better! She called me a bunch of times."

"Sorry about that."

"It's fine. I didn't answer," she chirps. "I'll let you go. I'm going to try and catch a few hours of sleep. Have fun for me! And send pictures."

Of course, she wants pictures... "Ok. I'll talk to you soon. Love you."

"Love you, too! Byeeeeee!"

I hang up and take a deep breath, wiggling my toes in the cooling water. Ana is a good friend, and I'm not sure how I'm going to break this bizarre news to her. Can I even tell her? She's like family and from what I know, Ethan's dad isn't a Wisher, so I should be able to tell people outside of The Society. Even if they say no, I plan to tell her anyway. There's no way I can hide this from her.

I glance through my texts and missed calls. There're a few from Ana, of course, and a bunch from my mom. I'm surprised Mary didn't call me. I can't believe I totally forgot about my job! Hopefully one of our part-time helpers can cover for me.

Deciding I'd deal with it after I've slept, I slide down into the water a bit farther with an overdramatic noise. *It's now or never.* I hit the speed dial for my mom and wait. When it goes straight to voicemail, I frown. I know she's probably still sleeping, but I can't help but worry a bit. I am however slightly thankful for the break in trying to explain the fake Hawaii situation to her. I ramble out a basic voicemail and hope I can call her again later in the morning.

I set my phone to the side of the tub, my thoughts going to my dad and his relationship with my mom. I feel guilty knowing this colossal secret about my dad when she still doesn't have a clue. Everything in my childhood is clearer now, especially the issues between my parents. My dad lied to her about his life—*about me.* He lied about everything. No wonder they couldn't keep their marriage together. I feel sad for my mom. She never stood a chance with him.

With some fuss I eventually get out of the tub, taking a quick shower to wash my face and hair. When I'm done, I go in search of some comfy clothes. I spot what I assume to be the walk-in closet and head over to it—it's as large as my mom's living room. It shouldn't surprise me at this point—but it does anyway. There are so many clothes and items in it, it looks like I've lived here my whole life. I realize then that a lot of them *are* my clothes. Someone, aka Ethan, must have wished them here too. I search for my favorite sweatpants and t-shirt. When I finally find them amongst several new items I know I'll never need—like a ballgown—I change and walk back into the bedroom, feeling much more like a person again.

I close the door to the bedroom—extremely thankful the walls aren't made of glass. As soon as I climb under the sheets, I sigh at the touch of the silk against my clean skin. Exhaustion hits me, and I feel like I could sleep for a year. Right before I close my eyes, I see a button next to the bed with a note that says, *push me for sleep*—I push it. The lights dim and then go out entirely. Next, the few windows in the room automatically shade themselves, enveloping the room into total darkness.

This must be what heaven is like.

With that, I close my eyes, pushing out all thoughts of Wishers, Alphas and Ethan. I'll obsess about it when I wake up.

CHAPTER 14

A loud and obnoxious noise wakes me up.

My body feels like lead as I try to move it, my skull pounding rhythmically. I throw the blankets over my head, hoping the noise will go away. However, the sound gets louder until I finally register it as someone knocking.

"Sophia?" I hear Ethan call from the other side.

"It's Sophie," I grumble. He must have heard me because I hear a throaty laugh come from the other side of the door. "What do you want? I'm sleeping," I call back.

"It is time to get up. I figured you might want something to eat and a chance to get ready before The Council meeting. I also wanted to talk to you."

I curse a few choice words under my breath, rubbing my palms against my eyes in annoyance. I don't know how long I've been asleep, but my body wants to continue resting. I'm also enjoying avoiding whatever is going to happen at this meeting tonight.

"Sophie, are you all right?" Ethan's concerned voice rings once again.

"I'm fine, just give me a minute," I answer back.

Hemming and hawing the whole time like an old lady, I press the button next to me that turns on the lights and open the windows. I grab my phone to find it's already after 4:00 p.m. I slept for almost 11 hours. I gripe, knowing my sleep pattern is going to be off for days. I quickly make myself presentable and walk out to the living area 10-minutes later. Ethan is sitting on the couch dressed in dark wash jeans and a pale blue shirt. He's leaning slightly forward to fix himself a cup of coffee on the table before him. I see his back muscles moving against the fabric of his shirt as he works, and my stomach flutters automatically. Even if I'm annoyed with him, I can't stop the attraction I feel when he's near. I clear my throat and compose myself before walking over to him.

He has a fire going, which is amusing since it's most likely a warm summer day outside. There's a tray of fruit, cheese, bread, and nuts sitting in front of him, as well as my beloved coffee. He turns when he hears me clear my throat, flashing a one-dimpled smile in my direction. Damn it, I really can't stay peeved at him. There's just something about him that makes me want to trust him no matter what.

"Sleep well?" he asks.

"Yes, actually. I probably would have slept until tomorrow if you'd let me."

He smirks, "I figured. That is why I am here."

"And to talk," I state, knowing he's probably been chomping at the bit since he left earlier.

"Yes. Sit with me?" he gestures to the space beside him and I take a seat.

"Coffee?" he asks.

"Have you met me?" I tease.

He laughs as he pours me a cup. It's not a mocha from Java Joe's, but it'll have to do for now. I sip the dark liquid and my eyes flutter shut.

"Better?" He asks.

"Give it a few minutes to hit the nervous system," I smile.

He matches my grin while sipping his coffee. We sit in comfortable silence for a while until I feel like I can function properly again.

"I know you're dying to talk about earlier...."

He sets his coffee down on the table, looking pained but also determined.

"Look, Sophia—*Sophie*—I know this has all been really hard to take it. I ripped you away from your life and your home. I cannot even imagine what it must be like for you to learn about who you are and come to a strange place. I wanted to say sorry for my mother, too. She does not meet new people too often, much less someone like you."

"Me as in *someone you're seeing?* Or me as in *an Alpha who is the child of her dead friend?*" I wonder thinking about the leather jacket and my exchange with Alice when I first arrived.

Ethan cringes. "Both, I think. She feels bad about bringing up your father and the jacket. She can see how it was an inappropriate time to do that."

"It's okay. It just threw me is all."

"I know." His eyes once again bore into mine, like he's searching for something. "How are you doing with all this? I know when my mother and I left you were reacting to something," he finally asks. *I raise an eyebrow at him.* "Besides me," he finishes.

I think for a moment about how much I want to share. I can feel a weight on my shoulders holding me down, and I want to release it. I look into Ethan's peculiar colored eyes and all I see there is care. I smile gently at him and take his hand. He grins hopefully at me and squeezes back.

"What is it?" he asks lightly.

"When I saw the security guards and the deadbolts on

246

the door, it all just hit me, I guess. I don't know your mom—I just met her—yet I'm supposed to trust her with my life? A woman who knew my dad and helped pick out *my* leather jacket? It's the one thing besides my dad's cabin that keeps me connected to him and now it feels tainted. I don't mean that in a bad way," I say quickly. "I know she's your mom, and she most likely means well, but I just felt trapped. She knows more about me than me. *I also miss my dog!*" I cry in frustration.

Ethan tightens his hold on my hand to assure me. "I do not understand what you are going through completely, but if I was in your position, I think I would feel the same way. I know we had a rough start together, but you can trust me. You can trust my mother. She would never jeopardize your life—I would never let her," he claims, his voice confident.

He reaches over and tucks a piece of loose brown hair behind my ear. My body reacts by leaning closer to him and his warmth. I swear we're like magnets around each other. I palpitate involuntarily, looking at his lips.

"You're trying to distract me," I say in realization.

He hums. "Is it working?"

"Maybe," I lick my lips. Now is not the time for us to be kissing, but I really, really want too. A million thoughts run through my head but as he leans closer, my mind goes blank and all I can think of is him.

"Sophia," he whispers in a low voice.

"Sophie," I smile as I press against him. I feel his soft lips perk upward against mine before he deepens the kiss.

We kiss for a while until he finally breaks the kiss to rest his forehead against mine.

"You don't do things halfway, do you?" I tease.

"No, I do not," he boasts, kissing my lips one more time before reluctantly releasing me. "I suppose we should get ready and head over. We do not want to be late."

I agree and pull away, trying to gather my bearings. I grab my now cold coffee and take a sip, remembering I have a question to ask him.

"Hey Ethan, did you happen to think about my job? I need to call and tell Mary where I am. She was out of town yesterday and surprisingly hasn't called about the library."

"Mary knows you are here," he says.

"Really? How did you manage that one?"

"Well—" he pauses. "Mary is a Wisher, too."

"Shut the front door!" I say in shock.

Ethan chuckles. "She has been watching over you."

"You know, this really is—" I start, but Ethan cuts me off.

"Let me guess—*just like Harry Potter!*" he mimics in a

248

high-pitched voice.

I shove him a bit. "I do not sound like that!"

He pinches his lips together for a beat. "I would have told you earlier about Mary, but I did not think of it until you mentioned her."

"I can't believe it. Little old Mary. Did my dad send her?"

"Yes," Ethan says, looking at me like I was reading his mind.

"It was a lucky guess," I shrug.

"Mary was his mentor in many ways—she is part of The Council. She is very wise that one. I really like her," he muses.

"Now it makes sense why she encouraged me to go for you," I reflect.

"She thinks we make a *cute* couple. Her words, not mine," he surrenders, his eyes shining.

"Oh God," I bellow, throwing my head in my hands and taking a deep breath. "Every time you talk things get stranger."

"I am afraid it does not end here. We need to leave soon for the meeting," he says sympathetically.

"How much time do we have?"

He looks at his watch. "About twenty minutes."

"Great. Wait here, I have to change."

"Really? You do not want to meet The Council in your sweatpants?" he teases.

"Funny," I snicker.

"I have my moments," he quips. "Now go! We cannot be late."

"Oh, and creepy move by the way—putting my stuff in the closet."

"That was actually my mother."

"Wow—you made it creepier!" I gag.

"Go, Sophia!" he scolds.

"Sophie," I correct, before managing to dodge the pillow he playfully throws at my head in response. "Wait, should I go formal or casual?"

"Whatever you are most comfortable in. No need for anything fancy, but not shorts," he smirks at me.

"I wasn't going to wear shorts."

Ethan looks at me knowingly.

"Ok fine, I won't wear shorts," I huff, walking rather ungracefully towards the closet.

Eventually I settle on a pair of jeans, black converses, and a loose-fitting green blouse. I apply a little bit of make-up and throw my hair into a high ponytail. Within ten minutes I'm satisfied that I look presentable. I walk out to find Ethan admiring the art in the room, oblivious to my presence.

"Do you paint?" I ask. He jumps a little, coming out of whatever trance he was in.

A sullen look crosses his features. "A little. I am not very good though."

"Knowing you, you're trying to be modest."

He shakes his head. "Not this time."

"Can't you wish that sort of thing?"

"I suppose I could, but even if I did wish to have the tools to be the best artist in the world, I would not have truly earned it. Where is the fun in that?"

"I see your point. It's not fair."

"Exactly—but that does not stop some Wishers from doing it."

"I'm guessing those Wishers are frowned upon?"

"By some…."

It sounds to me like this place has more issues than I thought. I'm curious as to how I fit into the puzzle.

"Ready?" Ethan asks, holding out his hand.

"As ready as I'll ever be."

"You will be fine, Sophie. Trust me," he assures.

I beam at him and squeeze his hand. "You called me Sophie."

He smirks and gives me a chaste kiss.

"You can be trained," I kid.

"Be nice, or I'll call you Sophia again."

I snort before he gently pushes me toward the door.

CHAPTER 15

It's a short walk and an elevator ride with some *friendly-looking* guards before we arrive in front of two large doors flanked by four more stern guards. The entrance to The Council room looks like fluid silver—it reminds me of the tunnel Ethan created back in Iron Lake. Adorning the archway is the same W.I.S.H. emblem from the lobby elevators.

Ethan moves to stand in front of me, punching in numbers on a keypad near the entrance. The doors slide open automatically to reveal an immense room, much like the penthouse I was just in. The walls are all glass, but instead of warm natural light, the room is illuminated with harsh overhead lighting, giving it a sterile white glow. I must have been staring because Ethan places his hand on my lower back, guiding me into the room. As we enter, I notice several people seated at a lengthy plated table with white chairs. The front of the table is solid with a saying scrawled on it in beautiful loopy letters. When I get closer, I can see the quote clearly—*With Intention Springs Hope.* Realization lights my features—*now I know what W.I.S.H. stands for.*

Ethan and I come to a stop at the front of the table, my hands folded nervously in front of me. I subitize seven people sitting there staring at me, and one of them is Mary. She's grinning like a cat who's caught the canary, clearly enjoying herself. Adjacent to the group is a smaller table with three more chairs. Alice is currently occupying one of them.

"Come, Sophie, Ethan. Have a seat," Alice addresses us, pulling out one of the extra chairs for me.

Ethan gives me a lopsided grin, nudging me towards the chair. The nervous butterflies—*no, aliens*—intensify in my stomach. The eyes of each Council member boring into me doesn't help. I feel like I'm on trial.

As soon as I'm seated, I take them all in; along with Mary, there are three more women varying in age, as well as three older men. They're all in business casual clothes. I half expected them to be in ceremonial robes or something. I'm surprised they look so normal. Mary is still smirking at me like she knows what I'm thinking. I look at her, bug-eyed with my eyebrows raised, causing her to chuckle.

Eventually the woman seated in the middle stands and turns her gaze to me. She's beautiful. Her long wheat blonde hair and grey eyes seem to pierce right through me. She couldn't have been older than 30, but there's something about her that makes me feel very intimidated.

"Welcome Sophia," her bright, airy voice rings through the cold space. "I hope you found the room to your liking?"

"Uh, yes. It was fine, thanks," I answer, not sure what else to say to such a normal question in a weird circumstance.

"Good," she chirps. "My name is Isabel. You can call me Isa if you'd like. I'm sure we'll be spending a lot of time together."

"You can call me, Sophie," I say, seeing Ethan smile to himself from the corner of my eye.

"Well Sophie," she says, the corner of her mouth upturned. "I know you have a lot of questions, but I'm sure you'd like to know who we are, and why we brought you all the way to Massachusetts to speak with us."

"That would be nice," I say with a little sarcasm.

I hear Ethan stifle a laugh. Alice, on the other hand, doesn't seem as pleased with my answer; she looks a little mortified. I focus on Isa, composing myself as much as possible—my arms now crossed over my chest.

"I thought as much. Ethan has filled us in on everything that has happened over the last week," Isa states.

Immediately I blush. I really hope she didn't mean *everything*. Isa must have caught it because when I look back up, she's looking inquisitively between Ethan and me. I internally scold myself for obviously blowing our cover. Thankfully the other Council members, except Mary, seem to have missed that little moment. I clear my throat, wanting to change the topic.

"Yes, it's been an interesting week. But honestly, I would really like to get home to my dog," I say wistfully.

She looks at me sympathetically. "I understand. But what we're dealing with here might take some time. I'm sure Ethan's already told you that."

I nod stiffly, not trusting my voice to speak at that moment.

"Of course, you're free to leave at any time," she assures, "but I'm hoping that once you know the whole story, you'll understand why we need your help."

I hear the desperation in her voice. It almost sounds like she's pleading with me to listen. I'm not planning on leaving, at least not yet.

"I'm listening," I say, my voice stale. I drop my hands

to my lap and take a breath to relieve some of the tension in my body.

"Thank you, Sophie," she says, taking a seat in her chair. "As I said before, I'm Isa. I'm also the lead Council member. In many ways, I act as president of The Society. You've already met my mother and older brother," she says gesturing to Alice and Ethan.

"Excuse me?" I exclaim, my eyes practically falling out of my head.

"I had a feeling he didn't say anything," she utters, looking to Ethan. "Ethan, why didn't you tell her?"

"It did not come up, Isa," Ethan flushes, bringing his hand up to rub the back of his neck.

I stare wide-eyed at him, wanting him to look at me. When we spoke about his family he never talked about any siblings, much less a sister who led The Council. He avoids eye contact—obviously embarrassed. I turn back to Isa who is looking between the two of us curiously again.

"I'm sorry for my brother's lack of social skills and manners," Isa continues. "But you can trust me, Sophie. I may be young, but I know everything there is to know about The Society and Wishers. I've been excited to meet you since I first heard you existed. You can't imagine what you can do—or who you are. It's hard for any of us to wrap our minds around," she says in awe.

"I'm pretty sure I know that feeling," I clip, the words coming out harsher than I intended.

"Of course," she backtracks. "That was thoughtless of me. Let's get introductions over with, shall we?"

I don't say anything, just look on at the other six pairs of eyes gazing at me intently.

"The Council is made up of the seven of us," Isa continues. "All of us are elected by current Society members. I have two votes in the case of a tie, the rest have one. We don't campaign. We are simply elected on our merits and reputation amongst others. We can quit whenever we desire. Terms last as long as people choose to keep us here. I have been on The Council for two years now. Mary, with whom you are familiar, has been here the longest—over thirty years. I won't bother with everyone's names, you'll know them in time. I want to reiterate that we are here to help you, not to hurt you. The Council has been watching over you for some time—in case you didn't know that yet," Isa's mouth turns upward as she looks to Mary.

I make eye contact with her, the shit-eating grin still plastered on her weathered face. This woman is different from the Mary I know. She comes across wiser, stronger, and more fun. "Hi Mary," I finally say.

"Hello dear. It's good to see you here in one piece. I hope you can forgive me for not telling you the truth, but once we explain, I'm sure you'll understand my reasons. If you don't already," she says knowingly.

Mary is right. I'm not stupid. I now know she had reasons, and most likely those reasons had to do with my dad.

Isa inhales, bringing my attention back to her.

"You'll have time to catch up, I promise. But for now, I have a feeling you'd rather know about who you are."

"Isn't that why I'm here?" I glower.

Isa doesn't dare answer that. "Then let's begin."

CHAPTER 16

"Then let's begin."

I can feel the anxiety thundering off Ethan at Isa's words—but I refuse to look at him. I want to finally understand what's going on—and I don't want any more feelings or distractions getting in the way. The Council all look toward Isa like she's about to tell a bedtime story—it's odd.

"W.I.S.H. history is complicated and long-winded, but I'll stick to the basics," Isa begins. "Although the human forms we know now have only been on this planet for roughly 2,000 years, Wishers have been around for billions of years. The first of our kind were the first of any kind. We started off as energy, and that energy created Earth over 4.5 billion years ago. We're not exactly sure how we ourselves came to be, but from what we have gathered and studied over the last few hundred years, we know that Wishers were the first of humankind. We also know that a Wisher created these bodies for us to inhabit," she eyes me carefully.

I feel a spark of knowing in my stomach, and I understand where this is going. Between what Ethan told me on the jet, and what Isa is saying now, I can't ignore my truth any longer.

"Let me guess," I say, gathering all my strength. "I'm *the Wisher* who created humankind—this Alpha that Chris's thugs were after?"

Isa pauses heavily, "Yes—that's right."

The room is so quiet, all I can hear is Ethan's slightly labored breathing and the sound of my own heart rattling in my ears. I feel the heat rise in my body, and I start to sweat. Isa must have noticed because suddenly Ethan is shoving a glass of water at me.

"I understand it's a lot to absorb," Isa says cautiously.

I grip the glass of water, feeling the icy condensation slip over the pads of my fingers. I watch the water ripple from my shaking hands for a moment, letting my mind go blank. I'm not sure how long I sit there, but as I turn my gaze back to Isa, I feel Ethan place his hand on my shoulder in a comforting gesture. I shake it off—not allowing him to work his weird emotion changing gift on me.

"Do you want to stop?" Ethan whispers.

"No, I want to know the rest." I place my water back on the table. "What else, Isa?"

She gives me a look of admiration. "Ethan mentioned to me that you brought up the Biblical story of Adam and Eve. That story is correct in some ways—both Adam and Eve were Wishers. However, Eve was the original *Alpha-Wisher*. After she came to be, she wished for Adam—*a companion*," her eyebrows raise at me like she expects a reaction—but I have none.

She continues. "Over the years we've collected as much information from the Alphas that have lived throughout history as we could. We know that they have always been female—never male. It's unclear why Adam wasn't an Alpha, but we can only assume it's because Eve created him from her gifts. The skill of creating directly from energy didn't pass on to him. We also found that there is only one Alpha at a time. When one dies—another Alpha eventually emerges—though the timing is never immediate. The last recorded Alpha was in 1551, her name was Maria—*Maria Black*," Isa pauses, studying my face.

"We're related? I thought lineage didn't necessarily matter," I say, thinking about what Ethan had told me earlier.

"That's true, we haven't yet learned why some people

have been given the gift of Wishing and others have not. While most Wishers are descendants of either Eve or Adam, some are of both. You have to remember that Eve could create human life out of nothing, or through sex like the rest of us," Isa grins. "But—we did find that Alpha's always share a bloodline and carry the maiden name of Black."

I think through her words. "Then are Alphas born only from direct descendants of both Adam and Eve?" I venture.

"We believe so."

"I don't understand why there aren't more Alphas then."

"You're forgetting what I said about the Alphas. Eve was the original and only Alpha—while she lived there was no other. That is why we believe Eve's soul can only live on in one Wisher at a time." *She takes a breath.* "But there is also one other detail I haven't mentioned yet—Eve was immortal. Every Alpha that followed has lived to be over 200-years-old."

"Excuse me—what?"

"An Alpha's gifts are far beyond anything a normal Wisher can do. You can heal and not only create a human life, but *any* life. You can do anything at the snap of your fingers. Money, houses, cars, trips—you can do it all. God doesn't have an age—God just is."

"You're telling me that I'm not only immortal but that I'm *the* God?"

The room is silent.

"This is great, just great," I mutter to myself.

"In the way that many non-Wishers speak and think of God, yes, you are technically their God."

I can't help it—*I laugh.* A deep belly laugh that leaves me in uncontrollable tides.

"This is crazy!" I hiccup.

"I know it sounds unbelievable, but you can, and you will learn how to use your gifts. You'll see that you are who we say you are," Isa stresses.

I look around at everyone staring at me. They're all very serious about everything—which only makes me feel worse.

"I'm sorry," I whisper. "This is just—"

"We understand, dear," Mary chimes in. "Just let Isa finish and we'll let you process everything."

I laugh mockingly. "Process everything? You heard what she just told me, right? I'm fucking *immortal!*" I yell. "I wasn't planning on living past 90, much less forever. And I'm supposed to believe that I'm *God?* The big man in the sky is me? That's impossible and completely crazy," I rant. "I'm dreaming, aren't I?" I look to Ethan with wild eyes. "I'm in a coma—*that's it*—none of this is real."

264

I stand and start pacing. My breath is becoming short—anger and fear are coursing through my body like wildfire.

Ethan reaches for me again. "Sophia, please. You need to calm down. I just want to help you—we *all* want to help you," he begs.

"No," I scowl. "You all want to help yourselves! I was living a perfectly normal life before you came to my town, Ethan."

"That was all an illusion—you were living a lie. Chris was living right under your nose for years—we think he was planning to kill you. You could have died I had not come along," he argues.

My eyes widen and I let out a strangled laugh. "Great. Just great. I love that I'm just learning this now!"

"Sophia—" Ethan tries to interrupt.

"No. You don't get to talk," I clip. "So, the solution is what then? I'm God and you all get to use me for my gifts? That's what you want, isn't it? That's the whole reason you befriended and brought me here," I accuse. I feel like the truth has finally been revealed to me.

"Sophie, if you would just take a breath and hear us out, we're trying to explain everything to you. You're jumping to conclusions," Isa interrupts.

I pinch the bridge of my nose, trying to think happy

thoughts, but failing.

"Listen," I hiss. "There must have been a reason my dad wanted to keep me from this life—from here," I gesture around me. "He died before there was even a chance for me to talk to him about it. If Alice and Mary were so close to him and he was such a big part of this place, why wouldn't he tell me?"

"Sophia—" Ethan pains.

"No!" I yell.

"Sophie, please!" Isa cuts in. "Robert didn't want this life for you, he wanted you to be normal. When he discovered you were exhibiting gifts of an Alpha from birth, he wanted to keep you safe. You have to understand that the history of our Alphas are not happy ones. He knew that if Wishers found out you were born, that they would want to kill you. It has been over 400 years since Maria Black died. None of us knew if or when another Alpha would be born, but then Robert discovered you had gifts."

"What do you mean by that? Besides the Barbie incident—which I'm sure Ethan told you about—I don't have any recollection of being different."

"You wouldn't—you were too young when it happened," Isa explains. "When you were two, your mother left you alone with your father while she went out with a friend. When he took a phone call, you ran outside without him knowing. You went to the pier and fell in the water. When he found you, you had drowned. You were dead, Sophie. At least that's what he thought."

"What? But that's—that's impossible!"

"Robert couldn't find a pulse. He said you were blue—cold to the touch. Just as he was about to call 911—you started breathing—almost as if an unknown force imbued life back into you. That's when he knew you were the Alpha."

"That's a stretch, don't you think? My dad was afraid he killed me! He might have just thought I didn't have a pulse, but I actually had one."

"I would agree with you if you didn't exhibit other gifts that none of us have ever had nor experienced."

"You made Chris disappear," Ethan adds.

I shuffle my eyes towards him, then back to Isa.

"He's right," she confirms.

"I don't get it. You told me Alphas are immortal. If that's true—Eve would still be here—Maria and the other Alphas, myself included—wouldn't exist. Nobody would be able to kill me even if they tried!" I rave.

"Eve is immortal because she lives on in any new body she chooses to inhabit. Her soul cannot be destroyed, just like any soul cannot be destroyed for that matter. The difference is that Alphas can live as long as they can inhabit the same body—unlike myself who will die at a normal human age. I also cannot come back from the dead like an Alpha can. If I drown, I drown. My soul will move on and return with a new consciousness and a new body. Maria Black was killed by fire—there was no body left for her to inhabit. Her soul left and found a new body in her bloodline. Same goes for all the Alphas before her."

"If this is all true, and Alphas are so important, why did Eve take so long to come back?"

"First of all, I want to be clear that we're talking about you. Your soul is Eve, but you just have a different name. I can't answer your question because we don't know for sure. You could have come back several times before you inhabited this body, or you could have waited until the right time—when you felt you were most needed."

"But who would be killing me all the time? If the Alphas are the creators of all, then why kill them? Her? Me?" I ask, confused.

"Mary," Isa chimes. "I think you could answer this better. You've been around longer than most of us," she jokes a little.

"Thanks for that, dearie," Mary snickers. "She always

has to remind me of my age."

"Mary," I bark. "I don't have the patience for jokes. You know I'm pissed at you."

She cackles. "Of course, you are—I would be, too. But Robert asked me to look after you and your mom, so that's what I did. He was like a son to me, I couldn't say no to him. I'm sorry again for lying, but it was for the best," she states. Her tone is so matter-of-fact, I can't even question her reasoning.

"Then tell me," I order.

"Well dear, Eve—with her unique gifts—lived for thousands of years in her human form, creating life and this planet as we know it. She instilled goodness and light in her creations and was loved by many. Because of this, it was natural for other Wishers to feel less-than standing next to her—it was especially hard for Adam."

"Men. Aren't they always the problem?" I snark. I hear the women in the room chuckle to each other and I can't help but smirk. All of the men, Ethan included, fidget nervously.

"You have a point my dear," Mary clucks. "But Eve didn't know how Adam truly felt towards her—not until it was too late. One night, when Adam felt his jealousy too much to handle, he stabbed Eve in her sleep, but he didn't know she was immortal. When she came back to life, the pain and betrayal she felt ran deep, and she accidentally made Adam disappear. Just like what happened with Chris."

"Was she able to bring him back?"

"No."

"But then how did she end up dying?"

"Before Adam disappeared, he had already spread his hate. For the rest of Eve's existence, she struggled to maintain peace with those she had created. Specifically, the children she made with Adam and their descendants. For a long time, Wishers just spoke behind her back, thinking they could never kill her. They lived in fear of what happened to Adam happening to them. She tried to bring Adam back or give them things to please them, but nothing worked. At a loss, she offered herself over to them."

"She just gave herself over to the people who wanted her dead?" I say in disbelief.

"She thought it was the only way to make them happy and bring peace. Eventually they discovered that fire was the only way to rid Eve of her body."

A violent quiver descends through me and I feel an odd sensation. My hands go clammy, and my muscles seize, causing me to freeze. All at once my skin starts burning, like it's on fire. I want to scream, but I can't. The pain is worse than anything I have ever felt; it's blinding.

Everything goes black and I hear feminine voices fill my head. They almost sound like mine, but they're wiser, richer—like a resounding chime.

"Listen to us, Sophie. Do not be afraid—we're here with you."

Who are you?

"You know who we are," multiple voices sing. *"We are you, and you are us. What they say is the truth—your truth. You are the key. But you must be cautious. You must listen to your inner guide. There are some around you that do not care for you —that wish to harm you. You know who those people are—you just have to listen."*

I don't understand—why is this happening?

"You must see, you must listen, and you must learn. It is time for you to embrace your gifts. Embrace your personal power. You are the key. We are here with you always—all you need to do is listen," they promise.

The voices leave, and I'm left with silence. Without warning, images begin to play like movies before my eyes. It's almost as if I'm being downloaded with information. My body shakes like an earthquake is moving through it and then—*there's nothing.*

CHAPTER 17

My eyes flutter open and air burns in my lungs.

"Thank God you are awake!" Ethan's voice rings with relief.

I groan at the noise. My body aches and my head feels like it's split in two. I'm thankful the lights are dimmed, and no sunlight is making its way into the room. I squeeze my eyes shut and push my hands against my pounding temples.

"How long was I out?" I croak, taking a sip of the water Ethan thrusts towards me.

"For several hours. It is almost five o'clock in the morning."

"What?" I exclaim. "Have you been here the whole time?"

"Of course I have, Sophia. Regardless of how you feel about me and what happened in that room—I care about you. You scared the living daylights out of me," he says softly, reaching out to take my hand in his gently.

I stare at our hands together, remembering what happened before I woke up. The images from my blackout are becoming clear in my mind, and I know I can trust Ethan more than ever before. All doubts I had are erased, and I find my body wanting to move closer to his. My intuition—or inner guides—are validating that I have nothing to fear from him. He's only here to help me.

"Ethan," I say quietly. "I'm sorry."

He looks surprised. The soft light of the room makes his eyes a dark violet—his lips turn up in his single dimpled smile and he squeezes my hand in assurance.

"It is okay," he says gently.

"Hearing all that—it was a lot. Not to mention you didn't tell me you had a sister!"

"I apologize for that. I really did not mean anything by it—I did not think it mattered. Plus, you were already so overwhelmed by everything."

"That's hardly something I would've been concerned about. But you can tell me about your aversion to Isa later," I grin knowingly. Ethan flushes just as my stomach grumbles loudly.

He laughs quietly. "Let us get something to eat, shall we?"

I slowly get out of bed, accepting Ethan's hand as we

273

walk to the kitchen. The calm I feel has everything to do with my impromptu blackout session. Something is different inside me—*I'm different*. Ethan's still pretty tense. I can only assume he's curious regarding what happened to me—I'm curious too. I know what I heard and saw, but I wonder what went on while I was blacked out.

The suite is dark save for the fireplace and a few dimmed lights. I feel like I'm walking through a tunnel, my ears echoing softly. The world feels older, like a hundred years have passed instead of mere hours. In some ways, it has. Ethan lets go of my hand to turn the kitchen lights up before he begins to rummage through the fully stocked fridge.

"Are you cooking?" I ask.

"I thought you said you were hungry."

"I am, but remember the last time you tried to cook? Not to mention, it's early as hell. Why not wish whatever we want?"

He cocks an eyebrow at me, his five o'clock shadow prevalent now—*damn, that's sexy*. Abruptly I feel like kissing him. He must have sensed my hormones spike—don't ask me how—because his pupils dilate slightly and his breath hitches. *Crap*. I look away quickly, trying to sweep my mind from the gutter. When I glance back he's smiling at me, light shining from behind his eyes.

"We could wish something, but you are exhausted, and frankly I am too. A sandwich does not require heat. I am pretty sure I can handle it," he says confidently.

"Alright Master Chef, prepare away—but no mustard!" I shudder. *I hate mustard.*

"Got it," he laughs. "No mustard for the lady."

I smile in silence before sitting to watch him work. When he starts assembling the sandwiches, he makes them with such care and attention you'd think he's creating something precious. While he works—he makes a weird pout with his lips in concentration. It reminds me of a duck. He looks completely ridiculous, and before I can stop myself, I'm laughing.

"What?" he asks.

"It's nothing."

"You laughed at me—so it must be something."

I pause, considering my options. "You make this funny pout when you're concentrating. It's cute."

He scrunches up his face in a disgusted look.

"Ah yes, your aversion to being called *cute*," I jest. "Fine—you look like an idiot."

He scoffs playfully.

"You kind of look like a duck when you do it," I add.

"Seriously?" he asks.

"Dead serious," I answer, doing my best impression of it.

"I do not look like that," he argues.

"You do too. I'll take a picture of it next time," I taunt.

"You are trouble, Sophia Black."

"It's Sophie, you goof. And you're just figuring that out now?" I tease.

The corners of his mouth turn up before he places a sandwich in front of me. It looks delicious. My stomach growls obnoxiously again.

"Eat," Ethan orders as he pours me a fresh glass of water.

I dig into my food in a very ungraceful manner, not looking up from my plate until I hear Ethan stifle a laugh. I look over to him, a piece of turkey slipping out from my sandwich, hanging from my mouth. I must look like a rabid dog.

"Sorry," I swallow. "I'm really hungry."

"I noticed," he muses.

After we finish our sandwiches and clear the plates, I can tell

Ethan is exhausted. When I see him turn the coffee pot on, I stop him.

"What are you doing?"

"I want to know what happened and I definitely will not be able to stay awake without coffee."

"You're beat. Did you get any sleep at all yesterday?"

"I do not need much sleep," he says, trying not to yawn.

I roll my eyes. "I don't buy that bullshit for a second."

"Sophia, I know you want to boss me around right now, but please—what happened in that room was frightening. We thought we had lost you for a second."

"Immortal, remember?" I try to joke with him.

"It is really not funny," he answers sadly.

"*Oh, come on*—it's a little funny. At least I can joke about it now, right?"

He looks into my eyes, trying to understand what I'm saying. Eventually realization flickers across his face.

"Does that mean you accept who you are?"

"I don't know if I accept it—it's been a crazy few days and I still need time to process it all. But when I blacked out the Alphas showed me. They showed me my—I mean *our* history. Not everything, but at the rate they were going before I opened my eyes—I'll know everything soon," I divulge.

Ethan goes into shock, his jaw dropping open.

"Should we sit?" I ask, motioning him toward the living room.

He agrees, hastily pouring two mugs of coffee before handing one to me. I'm actually feeling quite energized now that I've eaten, but the warmth of the coffee feels comforting against my hands. We walk to the couch and I see the fire starting to die. I stare at it intently, wishing it to roar brighter. It flickers back to life with almost no effort from me. Ethan sucks in a surprised breath.

"Did you?" he asks.

"Who else?" I state, taking a sip of the coffee. It's bitter against my tongue and I grimace.

"Do you understand how to use your gifts now?" he asks.

"Yes—during the blackout the Alphas taught me. It's like a switch was flipped on and now all the lights are on up here," I tap my skull. "Now I just—*know*."

"Any explanation on how your gifts kicked in fully before twenty-five?"

"The only thing I can't do until I'm of age is create life and maybe the larger healing jobs. At least, that's what I think. Honestly, it's confusing and I don't want to try it.

What if I try to create a person and they end up inside out or something? And don't even think about cutting yourself and asking me to heal it! I won't do it," I chide playfully.

"You knew I would try that?"

"*Please!* You're a curious person, of course you're going to want to know if it works."

"You are correct, but we will have to test it at some point," he says with a far off look on his face.

"Not on you," I say rather quickly.

"Does that mean you still care for me?" he teases, his eyes dancing with flames.

"You know I do. No matter how frustrated I was or am with you, I know that you care about me, and you practically saved my life back in Iron Lake—so I guess I owe you."

"I think we are even. You remember that boulder?"

"*Ah yes*, my first intentional wish," I reminisce cheekily.

He grabs one of my hands and gazes at our interlocked fingers for a moment.

"What it is?" I ask.

"I know it has been a long night but I—I need to ask more about your blackout. If that is even what to call it."

"It's ok, we can talk about it," I assure him. "I think it

279

was triggered by the mention of Eve being burned alive." My body reacts violently to the memory. Goosebumps fan out over my arms and I tremble.

"Are you all right?" he asks, rubbing his thumbs over my knuckles.

"Despite popular belief, the feeling of being burned alive is not pleasant," I jest.

His jaw clenches. "You could feel it?"

"It's not something you forget after you experience it. And it wasn't just Eve being burned alive...it was every Alpha that came after her."

Ethan's grip on my hand tightens. "I am sorry you had to experience that."

"Strangely enough I'm glad I did. It helped me understand where I came from," I taper off, thinking of the memories they showed me. "It's true that Eve was the first creator and Alpha, but she was her own soul. Isa believed that I'm Eve—that's not exactly the case. I'm sure Eve and I share similar qualities, but we are not the same. Her soul— as well as every Alpha—is part of mine. It's almost as if our energies are intertwined."

"That is—*that is something...*" he says—stunned.

"Eve's soul makes every Alpha an immortal and the bloodline allows me to carry on her work. It's unclear why

I was chosen to inherit the gifts of my ancestors—it could have easily been anyone before or after me. It's not exactly what The Council thought, but they were right about, Maria Black. She was murdered before she recorded much history. Wishers were out to get her, and she didn't think they deserved to know about Alphas. Since I'm the first one to follow her, that would explain why our history is so fragmented."

"But you are trusting me with this information—*Why?*" Ethan asks curiously.

"Eve, the Alphas—they told me to follow my gut. I *know* that I can trust you despite everything that has happened between us. I can't explain why, and maybe I'm stupid, but I feel like you were meant to be by my side in this. Call me crazy if you want but—"

I'm cut off by his lips. It takes me a second to get my bearings, but then I'm a goner. He tastes bitter like coffee, and rye bread, but I can't bring myself to care. I grab his face, drawing him closer to me. He then pulls me by the waist so I'm in his lap.

Sure, we've kissed now several times, but this is by far the winner. My hands find his sandy hair, gripping it to try and bring him even closer to me. The moment my nails make contact with his scalp I hear him groan in the back of his throat. The sound makes my body tingle, and I want to hear it again and again—it makes me feel powerful. After a long while, the early morning sun starts to creep across the floor. I finally break away from him—breathless.

I'm now pressed against the back of the couch cushions, Ethan's body plastered to mine. He trails open mouth kisses down my neck before settling once again at my lips for a few light pecks.

"That was nice," I say between each kiss with a sly smile.

Ethan gives a hearty laugh before sitting up—nimbly taking me with him. "You are one of a kind, Sophia Black," he says, unleashing his full charm on me.

I grin so wide my cheeks hurt. "You know, you really *are* a walking, talking, cheesy romance novel."

He rolls his eyes, taking after me, and I can't help but like him more. In this moment he looks relaxed and happy, almost boyish and carefree. After meeting Alice, I have a feeling his life was pretty hard in terms of expectations and stress. It has aged him somewhat and given him that regal air I tease him about. Ethan is definitely unique and unlike any man I've ever met. He intrigues me and leaves me wanting more.

"What are you staring at?" he wonders.

"You," I say. "You just seem happy, and I was thinking about how much I like it on you."

He looks like he's about to kiss me again but instead he tucks a stray hair behind my ear.

"I guess you have that effect on me," he purrs, his violet eyes shimmering.

I actually giggle a little, a rarity for me, before squeezing his hand and making my way over to one of the glass wall panels.

"Look at this view," I say in awe. "The sunrise is beautiful."

"That is one of the things I love about Massachusetts—when we have time, I will take you to the Berkshires—you will adore it.

After a few moments, Ethan pulls me a bit closer. "Did anything else happen during your blackout?"

I stare out at the colorful sky. "Besides the whole being burned alive part, the Alphas downloaded me with information. Almost like I was a memory stick or something," I grin. "They showed me the basics of what I needed to know right now—how to use my gifts. There's still so much more to learn. I expect I'll be having more blackouts in the next few days. They also told me that I knew who I was, to trust that, but then they said something even more cryptic. I don't really know what it means…"

"What did they say?" he urges.

"That I was the key. Do you know what that means?"

"Are you sure they told you that?"

"Yes, several times actually."

"I knew it," he sighs with relief.

"Knew what?"

"You *are* the key, Sophia. The key to Wishers becoming united again. I have always known that—just as many Wishers here know that. However, there are many who believe that the Alpha will not be able to bring peace within The Society even if one existed. Isa never got to this part, but we have been in a type of civil war with each other for as long as I can remember. The Council has always tried to convince Wishers the Alpha is the key that will fix all of our problems."

"But why do some believe the Alpha is the key and others don't?"

"In their minds, the Alpha—Eve—was the one who caused the unrest in the first place."

"I'd say that was more Adam's fault," I grumble.

Ethan smirks. "I would have to agree with you. Though I cannot understand why he felt the way he did towards Eve—seeing as he had one of the most amazing beings in front of him," he says, his gaze intensifying on me.

"*Ahh-ha-ha*," I croak uncomfortably under his praise. Ethan only smirks—*bastard*.

"By the way, you know how weird this whole Adam and Eve thing is, right?" I say, gaining my bearings. "I mean technically Eve created Adam, then they slept together and had babies. I mean, props to Eve for creating her own damn man even if he was super flawed, but it's all kind of wrong."

"It is not like they were related genetically."

"Still, it all seems incestuous."

"But it is not—Eve created many humans who populated this planet. The chances of all of us being physically related is very slim—but I do not know for sure. Maybe this is something you should ask the Alphas about? I am sure they know more than I do," he states.

"I could," I say, my thoughts running wild now. "What about the fact that I'm supposed to live forever? Don't you find that weird? Or that I'm technically billions of years old? Well, not me but I've got a whole bunch of souls inside of me, which sounds *so weird* out loud."

He laughs at me under his breath. "You are forgetting I have known a lot of this information for a long time. I have always known about you being immortal and it did not affect me before, so why would it now?"

"I suppose—thanks for the warning by the way. Would have been nice to know."

He sighs tiredly. "It was not my place to tell you."

"So, it was your sister's place?"

"Do we have to talk about my sister right now?"

I see the stress on his tired face and decide to drop it. "Fine. Then tell me what was so scary about the blackout. I'm curious to know what happened after I dropped off."

He shudders. "It is something I personally do not care to experience again, but it sounds like I might have too."

"Most likely," I warn, grabbing his hand in comfort. "I'm sorry I scared you. I didn't mean too."

"I know, but it is not like you knew what was going to happen," he trails off, the memory of the event now clearly on this face. "You basically started screaming and yelling about fire and pleading for help. You kept demanding that you were sorry over and over again. Eventually you stopped and went quiet. Everyone in the room lost control. We could not find a pulse for a second."

"I died?" I ask in shock.

"I cannot say for certain, but it looked that way."

"I'm such a freak."

"You are not a freak. You are beautiful and gifted. Wishers owe you and the Alphas our lives. This planet.

286

Everything," he emphasizes.

I'm not sure what to say. It's clear he's very serious, and I feel unworthy of his compliments. "You know," I eventually say. "A few days ago, my biggest responsibility was working at the library and feeding my dog."

"I wish things could be easier for you," he says quietly.

"I know you do, Ethan," I murmur. "Look, I have a lot more to say but I think you need to sleep," I add, touching the circles under his eyes.

"You should sleep, too."

"I know. That's why I'm kicking you out," I grin.

Ethan laughs lightly and kisses my forehead before standing up and heading towards the door. When he gets about halfway, he stops and turns back toward me with an apprehensive look on his face.

"Sophia, I hope this is not too forward but—"

"Sophie," I remind playfully.

"*Sophie*," he corrects. "I well—*I want to*—well what I am trying to ask is—"

"You want to sleep with me?" I blurt out.

Ethan turns beet red and I have to bite my tongue to keep from snorting with laughter. That came out blunter than I planned. Probably because it's on my mind also.

"Well," he coughs. "I was not going to ask like that."

"And what if I say yes?" I sing, my confidence unshakable.

He blinks rapidly at me, clearly unsure of what to do.

"Are you serious?" he asks, his voice now huskier than it had been only a second ago.

"Ethan—have I ever gave you the impression I was shy?" He just shakes his head. "Sex is not something I'm afraid of. And to be honest, I feel different after the blackout—I can't explain it."

When Ethan doesn't say anything for a few moments, I wonder if I should have just kept my mouth shut. I'm clearly telling him that I want to be with him and it's obvious he feels the same. But I wonder if I'm moving too fast for him.

"If I'm being too forward and you're tired, we should just go to sleep. I'm sorry if I made you uncomfortable," I tell him.

His eyes are still wide and gazing. I think I broke him somehow.

"Umm, Ethan? Can you say something? I'm feeling a little rejected here."

In an instant, the energy shifts inside the room. Before I can say more his lips descend on mine. All prior thoughts go out the window as we once again become lost in each other. I open my mouth willingly to his, groaning as his hands come to my ass to wrap my legs around his waist. Soon I feel myself being lowered down, my back hitting the soft bed. He leaves my lips, his forearms resting on either side of my head.

"In case that was not clear enough—I could never reject you, Sophie," he breathes.

I trace my thumb under his tired eyes. "Are you sure? We can wait."

"I believe that should be my line," he teases.

"You know I've never been one for tradition," I joke back, placing my index finger in the dimple of his cheek.

"There is always time for sleep once I am done with you," he growls.

"Then what are you waiting for?" I challenge.

He smothers my lips with his, and I'm pushed back into the mattress, his body heavy on mine. *Challenge accepted.* I grin against his mouth, before gently taking his bottom lip between my teeth and biting down. A guttural moan escapes from the depths of him and I think I laugh, but I'm too wrapped up in him to know or care.

Ethan's scent is all around me as I grasp his sandy hair in desperation. Wanting to feel his mouth on my skin, I push his head down toward my neck—he complies. His tongue hits a sensitive spot just behind my ear and I gasp. When he feels my hands struggling to remove his shirt from his body he leans back on his knees, his hair mussed and cheeks apple red. He looks delicious and I feel my lower stomach clench in anticipation.

When his shirt sits in a pile on the floor, he moves back to hover over me again, but I stop him with a heated palm.

"The rest of it too," I say, my tone slightly commanding and thick with lust.

His lopsided grin lights up his face. "That hardly seems fair."

I can't stop my eyes from rolling, but I sit up and undress faster than I think I had in my entire life. I can feel Ethan's eyes on me, like he's studying one of his favorite Warhol paintings. Suddenly I feel slightly self-conscious, but I refuse to let him see that. The air of the room feels hot— *too hot*—now that I'm naked before him. His body is still half-covered and his chest heaving in time to my rapid heartbeat.

"I'm waiting," I manage to breath out. He finally breaks his gaze at my words and with fumbling hands he shucks his pants and briefs from his body with a grace I could never achieve.

"You are exquisite," he exhales.

290

I blush red at his cheesiness but manage to beckon him forward with one finger. As his skin touches mine—hard against soft—I yank him down and pin him underneath me. He lets out a surprised noise, but I quickly close my mouth over his in a long kiss.

Our tongues duel for dominance before I finally give in to his relenting lips. Before long, I feel his hands coming down my back, strong and comforting. I sigh, bringing our chests together so that my breasts rest against him, the stimulation adding to my already scalding skin. I want—*no need*—him to touch me before I explode.

I grab his hand and lead it where I feel him already thick between my legs. When his fingers make contact, I moan, leaning forward to gently nip his shoulder. Without my help, he brings his other hand to cup one of my breasts, brushing the hardened bud with his thumb—*I'm in paradise.*

"*Faster*," I breathe out, his fingers between us obeying my words. My hips begin to move in time with his motion and I can't help but feel myself beginning to come undone by his hands. At this moment he could do anything he wanted to me and I would let him—*gladly.*

My movements affect him as well—how could they not—his face straining to remain composed as I let myself

291

ride the high he is providing me. After a few moments, when I come down, my body is tingling sweetly. Ethan's face is glazed over and I can't tell what he's thinking. It doesn't take him long, however, to regain his bearings, his hard body returning to our initial position.

I let my hand wander till I'm touching his length—his eyes shut at the contact.

"Ethan," I murmur as my fingers close around him, giving a gentle squeeze. His eyes fly open, his pupils dilated and brow sweaty.

"Yes?" he asks, his voice almost non-existent.

"You are exquisite," I smirk, my eyes giving his solid form a once-over.

He chokes out a laugh, his forehead pushing into mine before he kisses my lips like I'm his last meal. I can't help but think this moment is perfect. I'd wanted this since I ran into him at the bonfire—but waiting till now made it even sweeter. When his mouth latches to my neck again, I guide him into me, my body moving and stretching to accommodate him.

Our breath hitches at the same time. The feeling of being connected in this way is overwhelming to say the least, and I can tell by the way his eyes search mine he feels it too. I urge him to move; the stillness is too much. I need to feel him—*all of him*. My hands clutch against his flexing shoulders and my nails bite at his skin. Arching my back, I let my hips thrust upward as he moves within me, deep and slow. His eyes connect with mine, his brow furrowed as if he is holding back. I reach my hands lower, pressing my palms into his ass, motivating him to do as he pleases.

His rhythm increases, and soon I can feel the familiar flames licking at my insides. I reach between my own legs this time, welcoming my release as Ethan buries his face below my chin, his strokes becoming harder and more diligent. His undoing comes quickly after my own. With it, a sound I'll never forget reverberates through the room before he falls on top of me—heavy and spent.

When it's all over, I'm boneless and buzzed.

Ethan's short breaths flitter across my heated skin as his head rests against my breasts. I let my body cool down, my fingers gently playing with his hair as I rest my eyes for a few seconds. Eventually, he rolls to the side, his lips gently press against my damp shoulder. I look over at him and I notice a small smile graces his features. I place my finger against his dimple, my mouth turning upwards into a grin.

"Again?" I ask.

Ethan can only laugh—but he happily obliges.

CHAPTER 18

My eyes crack open, crusted with sleep.

I raise a hand to rub them clear and I realize there's something very heavy on my stomach. I briefly wonder what time it is since the curtain panels are closed. Mine and Ethan's early morning activities come flittering into my mind. I smile as the delicious ache in my body registers in my brain. The heavy thing on my stomach turns out to be Ethan's arm. He must run hot because I'm sweating from the body heat radiating off him. He's softly snoring in my ear and I debate if I can get out from underneath without waking him. He needs the sleep.

I turn my head to find his sleeping face. It looks golden, illuminated by a few candles I had wished earlier that morning while we were going at it. My stomach flutters. I have to admit we're *very* compatible. More so than any man I have ever been with. He was generous and kind, but also not afraid to ask for what he wanted. I like discovering this new side of him. The men I have been with in the past never wanted to be vulnerable, but Ethan didn't seem to have much of a problem with it—especially in the bedroom.

I look at the clock and see it's 10:00 a.m. We didn't go to bed until at least 8. But I'm feeling quite energized and I definitely need a shower—I'm a sweaty mess.

I grab a pillow from behind my head to use it as a prop. Carefully I wiggle free from his arm, replacing myself with it. He stirs for a moment but then quickly falls back to sleep. Once I'm clear of him, I make my way to the bathroom, shutting the door as quietly as possible. Safely inside, I turn on the light before looking at myself in the mirror—I am very much a mess. I look tired but not in a bad way. Had I known Ethan was so passionate I would have pushed for this to happen sooner.

I take a long shower, relishing in the heat of the water against my sore muscles. After I'm done, I return to the bedroom to find Ethan still dead asleep. I grab a few things I need and slip out into the living room, deciding I'll wish some breakfast and a mocha for myself while I wait for Ethan to wake up.

Grateful for the time alone, I retrieve my cell phone and text Ana and my mom. Just as I expect, there are several messages from each of them waiting for me. My mom texted me a diamond ring emoji with a question mark. Of course, Ana is only interested in knowing how good the sex is. I choose to ignore my mom's message and send Ana a bunch of fireworks. Turning off my phone, I sit at the breakfast nook, my stomach crying in hunger.

I focus on the empty counter space in front of me and within a second there's a steaming plate of scrambled eggs, chocolate chip pancakes, bacon, and a mocha waiting for me.

"*This will never get old,*" I happily say to myself before digging in. I hum as the delicious eggs hit my taste buds. They're just the way I like them. I take my time with breakfast, enjoying the mid-morning sun on my back as I eat. After I clear my plate, I explore more of the suite before I come to a bookshelf filled with several different genres. I run my fingers gingerly over the spines before I find myself drawn to one. When I pull it out, it looks like a journal. It's very old and worn with various pages peeling from the spine.

Curious, I bring it with me to the couch and settle in. As I open it, I get a strange sense that I've seen this journal before. Just by touching it, my fingers tingle. That's when I see it—written in very neat cursive—a name I haven't heard but somehow know.

Bridget Black, Salem, Massachusetts, 1692

"*Bridget*," I whisper. I know her. I feel her intertwined with me in my soul—*another Alpha*. When I told Ethan that Maria Black was the last Alpha—I was wrong. There were more. A quiver of excitement washes over me as I hastily flip open the journal. The yellowed paper is filled with her dainty handwriting. You can tell by looking at the words that she was young. She must have been writing frantically because the loops and lines are smeared together in many places. Some words are barely finished. I take a calming breath as I begin to read—

Dear Sisters,

I am afraid. Afraid for my life and afraid for the lives of Wishers. The people with no gifts have gone insane with fear and hatred for us. I am afraid that I do not know how to repair it. I am not strong enough to change the way they think of me or the others in the village. Our creations have formed their own Alliance—one that spreads their malignant fear and hate like a foul disease. I know they are coming for me. I could wish myself from here, but this village...my

297

family, they are all I have ever known. I love them too much to leave them on their own.

My sisters, I can hear your words of wisdom ringing in my ears, but I am not ready to do this alone—I need help. But the Wishers who are on our side are afraid for their lives. Their own brothers and sisters are killing them! Their own family members are accusing them of dark magic and things that do not exist in this world. Family and friends without gifts have exposed those with them to the people who do not understand what we are. They have done this to prove their "Satan" exists. It is a peculiar thing to watch our creations fear something of their own inception. They have truly created their own evil or "hell" as they call it.

Now more than ever I understand why you surrendered yourself to your creations, my beautiful sisters. A life like this is no life at all. I know I am weak. I know I am not the Alpha you hoped for when you chose me, Eve. If only I knew the key to change our fate. To save us all. They have come for me now. I can hear them screaming for me not far from here. I am just going to let them take me. Maybe my sacrifice will end their suffering. Even if I chose to stay and fight, the Wishers against us will find me no matter where I go. I can only hope that the next Alpha is stronger than me. I am sorry. Goodbye my sisters. I will see you all very soon.

With all my love,

Bridget Black, age 17

When my tears hit my hand holding the journal, I realize I've been crying. I can feel her pain and confusion. It figures we were burned at the stake. Wishers being confused for witches makes total sense. I put Bridget's journal down and wipe the salty remnants from my eyes. There are more pages but they're all empty. It only reminds me that this girl had lived a short life—Isa was incorrect when she said all Alpha's had lived over 200 years—Bridget clearly hadn't.

I lean back against the couch and close my eyes, feeling a darkness begin to drift over me. It's similar to how I felt right before the first blackout, except this time there's no fire, no pain, just darkness.

When images start playing before my eyes, it isn't as rapid as it had been the first time. What's strange about this vision is that I'm not watching from my own perspective—I am Bridget. I see through her eyes as though I'm living her life. I can see and feel her mom, her dad, her younger brother—actually smell the crisp farm air and taste the fresh bread and butter she liked to make by hand with her brother. I see her friends and experience her excitement over the first time she wished for something. I feel the power of her gifts and her inner strength, but I also feel her weakness.

I live the time she found out she was an Alpha. I feel her fear and her anger, then her joy and her love for Eve's creations. Bridget was very sensitive and felt a lot more than I have ever allowed myself to feel. She was passionate, kind and gentle. As I experience the emotions swirling with each interchanging image, I understand that this is my lesson.

I don't know how long I'm out for, but it doesn't feel like very long. As soon as my eyes open, I wince at the sunlight and feel a slight throbbing in my head. Thankfully, it isn't nearly as bad as when I had woken up earlier that morning. I look again at the journal before gently holding it to my chest.

"Thank you, Bridget," I whisper with a smile.

"Who is Bridget?"

I jump, looking up to see Ethan standing in the bedroom doorway. He's shirtless, a pair of briefs slung low on his hips and a curious look on his face. His eyes are still hazy with sleep and his voice is scratchy. Him standing there like that gives me a certain enjoyable feeling.

I quickly wish the journal away, hoping Ethan won't notice. I want to keep Bridget's words for my eyes only. Luckily, he seems too drowsy to realize what I have done. I stand and kiss him briefly on the mouth. He wraps his hands around my waist to draw me in closer. I press myself into him and bring my arms around his neck. He kisses me again, taking his time before breaking apart a few minutes later.

"Good morning," he says in a low tone, kissing down my neck. His stubble scratches me and I shiver.

I bite back a moan. "Good morning—or technically afternoon."

"Is it really?" he asks, surprised.

"We did have an eventful morning," I tease, wiggling

my eyebrows.

He laughs before kissing my nose. "I am starving—did you eat?"

"Yeah, a little while ago. I didn't want to wake you."

"Did you sleep well?"

"I did. Very well, actually. I woke up a few hours ago but you were dead to the world."

"I guess I was more exhausted then I realized. Not to mention you wore me out," he says with a smart grin.

"What can I say," I straighten up, brushing a fake chip off my shoulder. "I'm pretty good at a few extracurricular activities."

Ethan flushes red and I can't help but laugh. After all we did, he blushes at that. He clears his throat and seems to calm himself before sitting down in the breakfast nook. I'm about to ask him if he's going to cook when a plate of eggs, toast, and a double espresso appears in front of him. He doesn't even look up as he begins to shovel food into his mouth.

"You weren't kidding about starving, were you. Remember to breathe." He snorts a bit as I come to lean against the counter, stealing a sip of his coffee.

"Tell me—where did this food all come from?" I gesture to his plate.

302

Ethan swallows and looks up. "I used the food that we had stocked in the fridge. Do not worry—I told you I do not take unless necessary."

"*Oh*," I say, satisfied with the answer, but also in awe of how specific his gifts are. The fact he could use what was in the cupboard and not just take form anywhere was impressive. I had learned a lot in my blackouts, but there was still so much I needed to understand about Wishers.

The sun shines on my face pleasantly as I sip a cup of tea, a random book in my lap. Ethan comes out of the bedroom freshly showered and dressed before he makes his way over to me.

"So—" he settles in. "Are you going to tell me who Bridget is?"

Damn. "I thought you forgot."

"You did not want to talk about it earlier, I thought I would give you time."

I hesitate for a moment, contemplating if I want to divulge every bit of information I'm getting about the Alphas. They're becoming special to me and I don't want to ruin it. But there's also a part of me that wants to share everything with Ethan—especially after what we had shared together just hours before.

Ethan places his hand on my knee. "You do not have to tell me if you do not want to. I know this all has been a lot to deal with, but if you want someone to talk to about it, you know you can always trust me—I would never betray you. Never."

I give him an affectionate look and place my hand over his. "I know that. I wasn't sure if I should keep this to myself but, I do trust you, and I think you should know."

He urges me on.

"Bridget was another Alpha—her life was a lesson about compassion and sacrifice. She helped me feel more at peace—I don't know how, but she did."

"Was it another blackout?"

"Sort of. This one wasn't painful though—more like a vision."

He looks relieved. "Glad to hear it. Though I do not recall hearing about Bridget Black."

"We were wrong when we thought Maria was the last Alpha. There have been several Alphas before and after her, I believe. I'm getting the sense not all of them want to be known—as if they are embarrassed they didn't survive long; others are very private."

304

Ethan's eyes bore into me, his gaze critical.

"Why are you looking at me like that?"

He brushes a lock of hair behind my ear. "You are right—there is something different about you—I noticed it after your first blackout, but now even more."

"Is that a bad thing?"

"No, it is just different. But a good different."

"I do feel different. I'm more confident in what I have to do now, in my gifts."

"I am delighted to hear that."

We sit for a while just holding hands and sipping coffee—I know we need to speak to The Council, but I want another moment with Ethan. I get now that I'm not going home anytime soon. Explaining that to my mom and Ana isn't going to be easy. I also want Laker with me, but in time I will go back to Wisconsin and be with them all again. But I can't leave until the Wishers are safe—not until Chris and his asshole friends who tried to kill us are stopped.

I sense Ethan studying me again. The longer he stares, the more I feel his gaze intensifying. I know what he's thinking about and I can't help the sly smile that breaks out on my face. Men are so predictable.

"You want to talk about this morning, don't you?"

"How did you know?" he reddens.

"Please, you want to talk about everything! Not to mention I can feel the heat from your gaze burning a hole through my shirt."

Ethan chuckles and looks away. He really is like an old English gentleman, though last night he could have fooled me with some of the things he did. *Great, now I'm blushing.*

He flashes his dimple at me, and I know he's caught me thinking about it, too. I feel that familiar thrum of hormones coursing through my body and I quickly pull my hand away.

I take a calming breath. "As much as I'd like to have a round three, I think we have other important things to take care of."

"Right," he grins sheepishly. "So, do you want to talk about it?"

"Ethan, what's there to talk about? You obviously know how I feel about you and I know how you feel about me. I think we can talk about the details of our relationship later."

"You are right—I apologize...I just—"

"I know you get nervous, but really Ethan, last night

was great. I think I told you several times how great before *and* after. How much more ego-stroking does one need?"

"As much as you want to give me," he says, wiggling his eyebrows before regaining his composure.

I shake my head but kiss his cheek to reassure him that I'm not upset.

"Back to business. I need to talk to Isa about everything. How do I get ahold of her? Does she have a special number or something? OR do you guys have like a bat signal?" I bounce.

"Really, Sophia?"

"Sophie... and what? I think that'd be cool," I muse.

Ethan gives me a lopsided smile before taking out his phone and texting Isa.

"Texting? Oh, come on! That's super boring for a secret society."

"I will make sure to lodge a formal complaint," he states in a professional voice.

I shove him playfully before he gets a ping on his phone.

"She will meet us in her suite in ten minutes," he says, taking a piece of my hair and beginning to play with it.

My eyes light up with excitement. "Can I wish us there?"

"It is so amazing to me that you can do that," he says with starry eyes. "You know that Alphas are the only ones who can wish themselves to other locations—and as you know—other people..." he grins.

My skin turns hot—*did he have to remind me of that?* "I do know. It's one of the things the Alphas showed me. I haven't tried it on purpose yet or wished myself anywhere—I want to feel what it's like."

"I can speak from personal experience that it is bizarre being in one place, then all of a sudden being in another."

I press my lips together. "Sorry about that again."

"It was actually quite astonishing—even though you did not know you were doing it at the time."

"So, can I wish us there? Please," I beg with puppy-dog eyes.

"If you want. Just—"

Instantly we're both standing in front of a suite door. Well, I'm standing—Ethan is planted on his butt on the floor—his expression stunned.

"Be careful," he trails off, finishing his prior thought.

"This is her suite?" I ask, not even flinching. I offer him my hand to help him up, which he takes.

"That was—"

"Cool? Amazing? Insane?" I exclaim. "I didn't even

notice we were moving, did you? It was like I blinked and we were here! Remind me to do that and send us to someplace tropical when this is all over, eh? Like maybe an actual trip to Hawaii? I wonder how many rounds we could go then," I wink at a still dumbfounded Ethan—I feel exhilarated.

"You are slightly insane, you know that?" he says wryly.

Before I can retort, the door opens, and Isa stands there with a wide smile.

"Sophie just transported us here by wishing," Ethan spits out.

Isa blinks—shocked. "Both of you?"

"Yep," I sing. "Are you going to let us in or are we having this conversation out here?"

"Has she gotten feistier since yesterday?" Isa snickers to Ethan as she lets us in.

I want to roll my eyes but hold back. Luckily, Ethan's smart enough to keep his mouth zipped. Once we're inside I notice both Ethan and I aren't wearing shoes. I'd been so excited to try out my teleporting gift—if you could call it that—we weren't prepared to leave.

I quickly wish shoes onto our feet, glancing at Ethan to see if he notices. Apparently, he does, because the now familiar look of shock plasters across his features.

"You did that?"

"Did what?" Isa asks.

"She just wished shoes on our feet."

"Wait. *On* your feet?" Isa asks.

"Yes, look at my feet. The shoes are on them," he says with annoyance.

"Wow. But how is that possible? You're not twenty-five yet. Nobody has trained you."

"It's a long story," I mutter. "But essentially the blackouts have been teaching me everything I need to know."

"Blackouts? As in more than one?"

"Yep—I sort of had another one an hour or so ago."

"I think we should sit down," Isa states, before leading us over to her sitting room.

Her suite is just like mine. The walls are glass, looking out onto the scenery of rural Massachusetts. The coloring is different though, much cooler and more masculine. She also has several pictures of her family lining the walls with a grand piano sitting in the corner.

Ethan and I sit down on a black leather couch, while Isa takes a seat directly in front of us on a matching chair.

"Is the rest of The Council coming?" I ask, curious as to their protocols for this type of thing.

"Not after what happened yesterday—I thought fewer people would be best. My mother wanted to stay, she was having lunch with me when Ethan texted, but I noticed yesterday she seemed to make you a little uncomfortable."

Isa's right. Alice does make me uncomfortable. I'm not sure if it's something about her, or just the fact that she knows more about my dad than I do. But how I feel about Alice isn't important right now.

"Look, Isa," I say, changing the subject. "I know this is going to come across as blunt and maybe a little rude, but things have changed. I know things now. Things that even you don't know, that nobody except the Alphas know. I understand why we're feared, I understand why no one except Alphas know about our true history. I'm not just asking you, but I'm telling you to leave it at that. I need you to respect this decision from me, and all the Alphas before me. Even if you want to torture me, as they have previous Alphas, I won't tell you. With that being said, I will disclose what you and The Council need to know, when you need to know it. Period."

When I finish my little speech, I have to admit that even I'm surprised by how harsh and confident I sound. I see that with every passing moment I'm becoming more confident in my path. I'm stepping into my own personal power. It's eye-opening.

Ethan stiffens beside me, waiting for Isa to react. I can't tell if she's shocked, proud, angry, or all of those things combined.

"Well," she finally says, a soft smile appearing on her face. "I have to admit I didn't expect that. I knew you were stubborn and feisty after meeting you yesterday, but this? I can tell you've changed after what you experienced. You do seem different," she trails off as she studies me.

"Ethan said the same thing, and I agree. I want you and The Council to know I admire what you've created here. I don't know much about it, and I still have a lot to learn when it comes to The Society, but I want to know it all. I also don't want you to think I'm trying to replace you— you know your people best."

"Our people," Ethan interjects. "It is *our people*, Sophie. You are one of us. You always have been. I know you have said *we* before, but you need to know that we have always thought of you as our Alpha."

I squeeze his hands to reassure him that I understand. I can tell he's repeating that more for himself than for me. It comforts him to think of us all as the same, as a team.

"My brother is right, as much as I don't like to admit when he is," Isa smirks. Ethan glares at her. "Should we get back to business?"

"Yes, we should. Sophie, I know you have a lot of questions that you didn't get answered yesterday."

"I do—mostly I'm confused with the terminology of Wishers, non-Wishers— also the start of The Society, and the Wishers working against the Alphas. That's not clear to me. I wasn't given a historical timeline in my blackouts," I half-joke.

"Yes, I can help with some of that, but Mary is really the historian."

"That's probably why she makes such a great librarian," I laugh.

"Your father came up with that job for her—it is perfect," Isa reminisces.

I smile sadly at the thought of my dad. I have a lot of questions about him too.

"Should we bat signal, Mary?" I joke, trying to get out of my own head.

"I will text her," Ethan chuckles, pulling out his phone. Isa looks at us like we're crazy, not understanding our inside joke.

"Until Mary gets here, I'd like to know more about you, Isa—I'm curious."

"Really?"

"Trust me, there is nothing that interesting," Ethan chimes in.

"Oh please, look who's talking," Isa throws back.

"If you don't want to tell me about yourself, you could tell me about the relationship between you two," I say looking back and forth at them.

"That's an even longer story," she counters.

"You are such a great storyteller Isa, why not start from the beginning," Ethan says with such sass I can't believe it came out of his mouth.

"Ethan!" I scold. "I know you are siblings, but you could be a little nicer."

He doesn't respond, just glares at Isa like he's telling her something telepathically.

"Forgive my brother," she sneers. "He's a little complicated sometimes."

Ethan looks like he's ready to pounce, so I place my hand on his knee to steady him. "Okay, sorry I brought that up. Whatever you two have going on you can work it out another time."

Thankfully before any more words can be said, the doorbell echoes throughout the room.

"Saved by the bell," I say in a flat tone.

Isa gets up to go get the door and I turn to Ethan who is

314

in full-on pout mode. I open my mouth to say something, but he cuts me off.

"Sophia, can you please just let it go? And I would appreciate it if in the future you had my back, just like I have had yours this whole time."

I pull my hand away from his knee like it burned me. I'm stunned at his outburst. Normally I'd say something back to him, but I can't find a smart retort in me. I mull over what he's said, and I start to feel guilty. He's right, I didn't have his back just then. I know he and his sister don't get along, yet I pushed him into a conversation he didn't want to have. I can feel Bridget's lesson starting to creep in my brain—it's time I start trying to exercise more compassion and empathy. I'm about to apologize but before I can, Mary comes into the room with Isa.

"Stand up so I can hug you, dear. We didn't get a chance to properly say hello."

I stand and hug her with a smile, shoving down my prior feelings. "I'm actually really glad you're here with me."

"I know dear, I am too. I'm very happy you know the truth now. You're so much like your dad. That was especially evident yesterday. He would have been proud of you and how you've been handling all this information."

She raises her hand to my cheek like a grandmother would, and I can't help but smile, my eyes slightly glassy.

"Thanks, Mary. I'd like to know your story, too—you're a mystery to me now!"

She cracks a smile, "You'll get to know that in time. Now let's sit and get on with it. These old bones can't stand too long these days," she jests.

After we're settled, I can tell by the way Mary is eyeing Ethan and me that she knows something is off. She weighs her options before speaking.

"Isa told me that you've had an eventful few hours, and you'd like some history of our little club here?" she asks, choosing not to comment on the tension in the room.

I swallow. "Yes, I do. I need to know what we're up against here."

"Well, much like Alpha history, little is known about us until W.I.S.H. was established in 1807 by Emma and William Moore," Mary states.

I look to Ethan and Isa. "Wait…so like, your —"

"Great-great-great-great-great grandparents, yes," Isa confirms.

My face colors in realization. It makes much more sense to me why Ethan's entire family is invested in The Society now.

"Emma found a need for order amongst our people. She was an extremely talented Wisher, and well respected by many. She married William, a non-Wisher. He was a very kind and smart man. And understanding of Emma's gifts. He was one of the first people to prove to Wishers that they could have open and honest relationships with Eve's creations, aka humans," Mary explains.

"But you're all human. I mean, technically we're all human, some just have gifts and others don't, right? It confuses me every time you people say that," I grumble.

Mary chuckles. "In many ways that's true, but most Wishers have felt that those with gifts are greater than human. So, to call us that would be an insult."

"But that says we're better than *humans*—which we're not."

"You see the problem that has plagued our Society forever, then. As you understand, Eve's creations betrayed her because they feared her power. Adam, though a Wisher, was jealous of Eve's special gifts. He used non-Wishers as pawns to instill fear amongst all Wishers and non-Wishers alike, but I'll touch more on that later. To get this right we'll focus on Emma and William first."

"Okay," I relent.

"After Emma married William, many Wishers then

317

believed that non-Wishers could accept them for who they truly were. Emma and William gathered as many Wishers as they could and proposed The Society of W.I.S.H. to them. They declared it a safe haven for both Wishers and non-Wishers. A place where together, they could try and make the world a better place—to keep peace with one another. William believed that Wishers and non-Wishers were equal and asked Wishers if they could accept this. Emma of course agreed, and with several other Wishers backing them, they decreed that all of Eve's creations were to be called humans. In technical terms, those with gifts were called Wishers, and ones without, non-Wishers. You with me so far, dear?" she asks before taking a sip of water.

"I think so," I say—my head spinning a little.

Mary nods and continues. "The original members of W.I.S.H. not only believed they could establish peace but that they could keep the secret of Wishers contained to a small number of non-Wishers. Since an Alpha didn't exist at the time to help, they thought what they were creating together was the best option. Once established, they sought out Wishers, asking them to join in their cause. But it wasn't as simple as they hoped. For many years Wishers lived in fear of persecution. After the Salem Witch Trials— among many other incidences—our kind was terrified.

Afraid of being killed or ostracized from their communities. Many hid their gifts or at least tried to until Emma came along asking them to join her. The Society also believed in the time of the Alpha. That one day, Eve would return and be strong enough to lead the world into peace—that did not go over well with Wishers who believed Adam was in the right for what he had done."

I must look angry because Mary gives me a knowing smile—as if she knows my exact thoughts.

"Everything happened so long before their time, dear. The people were scared of power—especially if one person had too much of it. But Emma and William were smart and able to create a way to ease that fear—*at least for a while.*"

"The Council," I say.

"Exactly—they established The Council with the help of other Wishers who lived in different areas of the world. They came together to make rules and ways of living for Wishers. Since this had never been done before, and the act of wishing had never been studied prior to The Society's establishment, they learned many things about our gifts. It didn't take long for them to figure out that whenever something was wished for, they were taking it from another source. You can only imagine what bad effects Wishers were having on the world without even knowing it. After this discovery, Wishers knew they needed more rules and regulations than they had planned. In the beginning, those who joined W.I.S.H. agreed to limit the use of their gifts. Systems of checks and balances were established that we still have in place today. Many of those systems were created by William and the non-Wishers that married into or joined The Society. This was how non-Wishers found their place amongst Wishers. They saw how they could work with Wishers to make the world better."

"With Intention Springs Hope," I say quietly.

"Exactly, dear. Emma knew that Wishers could use their gifts to elicit hope when there seemingly was none. She believed that Eve's original intention of creating humans was to bring life, love, and creativity to this world. Emma and William used W.I.S.H. and The Council to restore Wishers faith in the Alphas. Eventually, written history was discovered that Alphas had passed down through direct descendants of Adam and Eve. The more information that was found, the more Wishers started to come out of the woodwork asking to join W.I.S.H. After many years of hard work—our little club was booming. Things started to change in the world—better governments, economies, trades. Wishers and those associated with them finally felt like they had a place to come to and be themselves—a place where they belonged and felt safe. W.I.S.H. grew tremendously, creating several branches all around the world that still exist today," Mary says proudly.

I am genuinely impressed. "That all sounds amazing."

"It is...*it was*. But, unfortunately, you can't erase feelings, and you can't erase history. Eventually, Wishers that were direct descendants of Adam and Eve began to harbor an attitude of authority over other Wishers. Those families and their allies came together to discuss grievances they had against The Society. They believed that without an Alpha, they should have more power—be able to use their gifts as they pleased. They didn't understand nor care about the consequences of unbridled wishing. They only cared about having control. When they brought their upsets and demands to The Council, they were denied. Because of this, *The Alliance* was created—in secret—with hope to one day bring down W.I.S.H. and every one of its members."

The Alliance. Something about it sounds familiar, but I can't place it. "Mary, are you telling me that they created a secret society within a secret society?" I ask with a funny laugh.

Mary grins a little and nods.

I let out a breath. "Cleary The Alliance is no longer a

secret. Tell me what happened—how did you discover them?"

"I'm afraid it's not a happy story," Mary's voice wavers.

The energy in the room shifts and my shoulders tense. I glance quickly at the people surrounding me. Ethan's eyes are downcast and that's when I know for sure that they're hiding something from me. Eventually Isa looks to me.

"What is it?"

"Right before your father died, we found out The Alliance existed," Isa confesses, her voice on edge.

"*Okay*—what are you saying?" I ask, my back now straight.

Mary and Isa share a glance before Isa nods, giving Mary permission to proceed.

"Robert suspected for a long time that something was going on with the Wishers of direct descendent and their followers. He was one of our history analysts and had been studying and working for The Society since he was a teenager. He was friends with everyone. He knew how to talk to people and get them to open up to him. Chris's father was a close friend of his…" Mary admits.

My eyebrows raise. "Okay, but that's not what you don't want me to know."

"No, it's not."

"Out with it, Mary!" I say impatiently.

She exhales. "Robert uncovered The Alliance a few years after you were born. He came to me and told me what he discovered, asking me and a few others to keep his secret. He understood that those who knew the truth were at great risk—the fewer who knew, the better—"

"*Wait, wait, wait,*" I interject. "Are you saying that my dad died because he found out about The Alliance?"

Mary only bobs her head, her eyes solemn.

"He died of a stroke," I say in shock.

"I know that's what it looked like, dear, but we don't think that's what happened."

My head is spinning. I feel like I'm going to be sick.

"Who else knew?" I pause. "Who else did my dad tell besides you, Mary?" I demand even louder.

"I believe just Ethan's parents. Your father was very close to both of them—he trusted them with his life."

"Well apparently he was wrong to do so!" I yell. "He's dead because one of you told!" I stand up, my chest heaving. Mary quickly stands and tries to grasp my shoulders.

"Sophia Black, you need to be reasonable," she scolds.

"I just found out my dad was murdered by one of his friends and you want me to *be reasonable?*" I shoot back.

"We don't know who killed him. It wasn't Ethan's parents and it sure as heck wasn't me. I get it—you're angry and it's ok to be angry—I would be too," Mary sputters. "But we need to you calm down and listen. Trust me when I say we want to find out who killed him and bring them to justice just as much as you do, but in order to do that you need to be clear-headed. We all need to be, or we'll all end up like him."

I take a moment to close my eyes, trying to breathe through my anger and intense feelings of hate. It's not long before I hear voices begin to swirl throughout my mind like faint whispers.

Breathe Sophie, it's going to be all right.

You can do this, just follow your instincts.

You can trust them.

I press my hands against my temples and remember that I'm not going crazy. The Alphas speaking to me like this is going to take some getting used to.

I know—I say mentally back to them.

"Sophia?" Ethan asks with concern, placing a hand on my back. "Are you all right?"

"Yeah, *Sophie* is peachy," I snap, feeling his hand pull away quickly. Man, I'm really striking out with this compassion thing. *Sorry, Bridget.*

324

I take another deep breath before opening my eyes. The Alphas voices are still ringing in my head, but I'm able to put them in the back of my thoughts. I look toward Ethan and grab his hand, much to his surprise.

"I'm sorry, I'm trying my best," I lament.

His face softens at that and he squeezes my hand back. "I know, I am too. We all are."

I turn back to Mary and Isa who are both worried. Mary, however, looks sadder more than anything. It's obvious my dad's death affected her more than I knew.

"Sophie," Isa calls my attention to her. "If it helps, I can tell you it wasn't my parents. They loved Robert. For years they kept his secret, trying to formulate a plan with him to stop The Alliance. Before he died, he called my mother and told her that someone from The Alliance found out. He thinks Chris's father somehow intercepted one of their phone calls or had his cabin bugged."

"My dad was a smart man. You think he would have been more careful," I counter.

Isa presses her lips together in a tight line before speaking. "We all slip up, Sophie, but that's not what matters. What matters is that The Alliance found out he knew about them and they killed him because of it. But they didn't know you were the Alpha at the time. They only killed him so they could keep their secret. They knew they weren't strong enough to take over The Society just yet."

"How did they find out about me then?" I wonder.

Mary steps in. "After Robert died, we sent someone we trusted to go and collect items he'd left to us in the event of his death. Before we got there, The Alliance stole one of his journals. In it he'd written about his experience with you dying as a child and coming back to life. He wrote about how you displayed early signs of a Wisher and a very gifted one at that."

"If that's true, why didn't they try to get to me sooner?"

"My assumption has always been that The Alliance didn't want us to know they knew about you. Somehow, they found out about Robert telling me and Ethan's parents about their existence. Because of this, they wanted to kill us first. Their priority has always been their secrecy. If they stay off the radar, then they have the element of surprise. Finding out you didn't know you were a Wisher—let alone an Alpha—you wouldn't be a threat to them," Mary explains.

"I guess that makes sense—The Alliance obviously didn't succeed in killing you or Ethan's parents," I state.

"No, thankfully they didn't. We were smart and on our

toes after your father. However, after he died, all heck broke loose around here. The last few years have not been easy—for any of us."

"Has anyone else died?"

Isa looks to me. "A few. There are unfortunately always casualties in war."

"War seems like a harsh word," I note.

"But that's what it is," Isa counters. "After The Alliance killed Robert, it didn't take long for them to realize they couldn't hide any longer. Their failed attempts at killing Society members made them quite obvious. After that, Alliance members came out and made themselves clearly known to everyone. They tried to take over our offices here and succeeded for about a year or so. Eventually, we managed to push them out again, but that is a story for another time," she frowns, lost in a memory. "Now, for the last two years we've maintained control. But I won't lie, people are afraid of who they can trust. Anyone could be secretly in The Alliance. We do our best to keep tabs on everyone, to make sure if anyone suspects anything that they report it, but it's not an easy feat."

When I take in everyone's somber faces, I realize I haven't been fair to them. I'm only now understanding what it must have been like for them in the last few years.

Fighting all the time and never feeling safe. I also can't help but feel for the members of The Alliance; they were just as scared, if not more scared then The Society members. Now I feel worse about Chris—I still have no idea where I sent him or if he's even alive.

"It has been hell," Isa reiterates, breaking through my thoughts. "And I'm sure you can understand why we need to take further action. The last two years we've been fortunate to live in partial peace after many of The Alliance members were imprisoned for their crimes. For now, we've put more rules in place for Wishers and for a while we even believed many of The Alliance members were coming back to our side," Isa fades off.

"Until?" I encourage her.

"Until one day last year, Chris walked into the library with your friend Ana," Mary interjects. "He was living with us in Iron Lake for two years—dating your best friend right under our noses. *Little turd*," she grumbles.

My mind is reeling. "How in the hell did you not figure that one out for two years?" I exclaim.

"As we expected, Chris and his parents didn't come around to joining The Society. After we regained control they fled and moved the remaining Alliance members further underground. We hadn't seen nor heard anything from that family until Chris walked into the library. I still don't know how he evaded us all that time, seeing as he didn't even know I was sent to Iron Lake to look after you," Mary says.

"What happened the day he came to the library?" I ask.

"We both pretended not to know each other of course. Ana seemed oblivious to it all. I have to admit—I thought for sure I'd find you dead once I saw him there, but you weren't. We kept a close watch on you after that, but Chris never made a move. "

"They don't want me dead—they want me to join them," I state.

"That's what we assumed," Isa says, clearly putting pieces together in her mind. "But do you know that for sure?"

"Before I accidentally wished Chris away, he implied that he wanted me and my gifts—in more ways than one," I grimace, the feeling of wanting to vomit plaguing me. Ethan makes an uncomfortable noise beside me. I see the equal disgust written all over his face, as well as his anger. I continue, "When The Alliance was chasing us, I heard them say to kill Ethan and keep me alive. I don't think they had any idea what I could do with my gifts yet since I'm not 25."

"That seems to be working to our advantage so far," Ethan interjects. "However, you wishing that boulder in front of their car probably tipped them off."

"Unless they assumed it was you," I say. "Question—if they've infiltrated W.I.S.H. before, how do we know I'm safe now?"

"The Council would never betray you, nor will the people we have in place protecting you. I know you have noticed the guards." Mary says.

"I have, but what about my mom and Ana? Are you sure they're ok? You'd think they'd use them as leverage or something if they really wanted me," I say, the thoughts hijacking my nerves.

"I promise you," Ethan says confidently. "We have some of our best people out there watching them. If we feel we need to protect them, we will take measures." He places a hand on my shoulder.

"And my mom really doesn't know anything about this?" I ask, looking toward Mary. After all, she'd been close to my dad.

"No. Robert really loved your mother, but it was hard for her to be married to him without knowing who he really was. He was just trying to protect you both, but he wasn't good at striking a balance. Especially after he found

330

out about you being an Alpha. There was so little known about you, and so many questions about what you would grow up to be. He thought if you could be normal, if you could live without all these complications, you would have a better chance of living a long life."

"Yeah, but what was he planning on doing when I stopped aging? How do you explain that to your kid—much less her mom," I shoot back.

"I don't think he thought much about that, dear, especially with what was happening with The Alliance. He was more of a—*cross that bridge when you come to it*—kind of person—as you know." She smiles ruefully.

"Honestly, I don't!" I say, my voice rising. "Apparently, I didn't know my dad at all, and now he's dead so I never will." I push my face into my hands again, feeling a slight headache coming on.

"I think we should take a break," Isa says. "We can have some tea, and Mary and I will update The Council. We'll call you when we're ready to meet." She stands, up not giving me a chance to answer.

"*Great*," I deadpan. "I'm going back to my room."

Before anyone can say anything, I'm safely standing back in my suite. Wishing really is as simple as blinking. I wonder how long it'll take for Ethan to come knocking at my door. I figure I have five to ten minutes tops depending on how long he speaks with Isa and Mary. I take off my shoes and head for the couch, but before I even reach it there's a knock. I groan and head for the door.

"Did you run here, Ethan?" I yell as I throw it open. To my surprise however, it isn't Ethan.

CHAPTER 19

"Alice!" I exclaim. "I thought you'd be Ethan."

"I'm sorry to disappoint you," she says stiffly. "May I come in?"

I stare for a moment. The guards had obviously allowed her to the door, so she posed no threat, at least in their eyes. It's funny, when I met her the day before she was so kind and open. The woman in front of me is not the same one from before. I begin to wonder if yesterday was a show for Ethan. I feel like in some weird way she's threatened by me; not because I'm the Alpha but because Ethan and I are involved.

"Umm, sure. Like I mentioned, Ethan's not here."

"I wasn't sure if he would be or not. I was notified by Isa that there is to be a Council meeting and I assumed you'd come back here. I wanted to talk with you."

I note that it didn't take them any time at all to call a meeting. I literally just left the room less than a minute ago.

Apprehension is etched in Alice's features, and now I'm curious as to what made her jump at the chance to see me alone.

"Right. Um—do you want something to drink?" I ask, leading her into the kitchen. I grab a cup and fill it with water from the tap. I know I can just wish it, but I don't want to use my gifts in front of her. I'm not sure why, but something tells me flaunting my newfound gifts in front of her won't help our relationship.

"No, I'm fine. May I sit?" she asks.

"Yes," I gesture to the stools next to the kitchen island.

"Thank you." She sits with her back frozen and her mouth in a tight line. I study her while she straightens herself out. I can tell the stress of the last 24 hours has worn on her. The frown lines on her forehead and around the corners of her mouth seem more defined. When she looks at me, her gray eyes determined, I can't hold it in any longer.

"I don't mean to be rude but I'm just wondering why you came."

She blinks. "I wanted to stop by because I know I haven't been the warmest with you since I left the other day. At The Council meeting I barely said a word to you— not that there was much time. But I wanted to let you know I was a little more than shocked after I met you. It threw me more than I wanted to admit."

Ah, so this isn't about Ethan. "You're referring to your relationship with my dad?"

Alice shifts awkwardly, her cheeks turning a light pink.

"Yes, it's about Robert." She gathers herself. "Look, Sophie, I wasn't going to tell you…I wasn't going to tell anyone but before I say anything, I have to ask if you can keep a secret?"

My stomach flutters. This is taking a *way* different turn then I was expecting.

"I suppose it depends on what the secret is. If it could hurt people or it's important, I don't know if I can guarantee that. To be frank, Alice, I just met you, and I don't get the greatest of feelings around you."

She looks a little saddened by that—which surprises me.

"I suppose I deserve that," she exhales. "It's hard for me to see you and not think about him," she finishes while gazing at me almost lovingly. A chill quakes up my spine as the truth hits me like a ton of bricks. If I'm being honest with myself, I think I knew the whole time, but I didn't want to see it.

"Oh my god," I cough out.

Alice's gaze flickers to me—she sees the realization on

my face.

"I suppose I gave myself up, didn't I?" she hums.

"You and my dad were…?" the shock not letting me say the rest.

"Yes," she affirms.

"Do Ethan or Isa know?"

"Isa does, as well as my husband. After Robert died, I was so upset, I had to tell him. But my Ethan, as you know, is such a sensitive boy, he always has been. I didn't have the heart to tell him. I knew he wouldn't be happy with me. Trust me when I say I'm ashamed of it. I know Robert was ashamed of it too. He and my husband were so close—it was eating him up inside. We were going to tell George—come clean—we wanted to be together, but then…well you know what happened."

"Wow," I breathe. "When you told me you were with my dad when he got my leather jacket for me, I thought that was a little strange. But I didn't want to jump to conclusions—I didn't think it made sense."

"I just thought you should know. Robert would have told you eventually—I know he wanted too. He really didn't like keeping things from you."

I puff out air through my nose. "You realize that's crazy right? He was keeping things from me my whole life. I'm

336

the Alpha of a secret society of people. A society of people that supposedly created this planet and everything in it. You would think at some point he would have brought that up to me!"

"Sophie, I know you're angry. I get that it's hard to understand, but please listen to me. It was destroying him not to tell you. When you turned 25, he was going to tell you and give you a choice on what to do. Things were getting worse here and he knew you were the key to the fate of our kind—of this world. All he ever wanted for you was to be normal and as safe as possible for as long as possible."

"People keep saying that, but honestly, it's the dumbest thing I've ever heard. If that's all true he really wasn't the person I thought he was. First, he lies to me, then he lies to my mom, divorces her and goes and gets himself killed. *Oh*, and has an affair with my lover's mom," I rant.

My hand flies to my mouth, realizing what I had just said. Not that she didn't know Ethan and I had at least been together in some capacity. I stand and place my hands on my hips, my face red with anger. I see that Alice is embarrassed and I can also tell I shocked her by both my outburst and calling Ethan my lover. I actually think that word is weird, but he isn't exactly my boyfriend either. It was the best I could come up with that made sense in my rage—I blame Ana—*again*—for that one.

"Sophie, I'm sorry. I'm really sorry. I didn't want to tell you like this, but I knew you'd have questions after learning about what has been happening here. I know the most about Robert, he told me everything."

"That's very sweet, but it's the last thing I want to hear right now."

"But there are things Robert wanted you to know."

"I'm sure there is, but I don't want to know them right now. I would really like to stop The Alliance and eventually go home to my dog. That's what I'd really like. I don't want to know about my dad's lover or the secrets he told her. This may sound harsh, and I know you have a good reason to tell me, but I don't want the details. Also, Ethan needs to know this—he isn't as fragile and sensitive as you think."

"Tell me what?" Ethan's voice comes from the doorway.

Both our heads snap towards his voice. He's standing there with a look of mixed curiosity and anger. This man really has impeccable timing. I sincerely hope I didn't wish him here by accident in my rage-haze.

"Ethan!" Alice cries—panic evident in her voice.

"Tell me what?" he asks again. At this point I can tell he's at least heard some of our conversation.

"How much did you hear?" Alice beats me to the punch.

Ethan takes a few large strides until he's standing next to his mom, who turns and pleads with me to help her. I shake my head.

"I think you should tell him, Alice. It's not my business."

"But—"

"I'll be in my room," I say, placing a comforting hand on Ethan's shoulder. I kiss his cheek much to both our surprise, before walking towards the bedroom. Alice tries to call me back, but I keep walking. I close the door and sit on the bed, wondering what I should do next. It isn't long before I hear them yelling back and forth. Actually, it's mostly Ethan yelling and Alice trying to calm him down.

I lie back against the bed with my legs bent over the edge, attempting to tune out their anger so I can concentrate. I'm very upset about the information I just heard. My dad's becoming more complicated as the day goes on. I look at my leather jacket lying on the floor beside the bed. Knowing that Alice was my dad's lover, knowing that she probably picked it out more than my dad made it feel gross. I feel like my memory of him is discolored. I wonder if mom knew about Alice. If that was one of the reasons she thought he'd left her. My mom—though a little crazy—is a good person; my heart aches for her the more I learn about the past. I vow to myself that when things settle, I'll tell her everything. She has a right to know who her husband really was—who I really am.

I sigh dramatically, becoming more restless by the minute. My thoughts tumble to The Alliance. Now that I know about what they had done—what they were trying to do—I want to take care of them before things get more out of hand. I'm not sure how to move forward from here. I need to talk to Chris's parents—the leaders of this *Alliance*. I only hope they won't try to kill me on the spot after what I did to their son. I bite my fingernails; a nervous habit mom was always trying to get me to break. I only do it when I'm really anxious; I guess now is one of those times.

I hear Ethan's yelling from the other room growing louder. I start humming to myself to block it out. I place one hand on my heart and another on my stomach, trying to feel the energies I have swirling around inside me. That sounds weird no matter how true it is. I drift to thoughts of Bridget, her cursive handwriting twirling around in front of my eyelids, then to Maria and Eve.

Eve's energy is always the most dominant from what I can tell. I turn to the first blackout and think of all the things I have learned. I haven't had time to contemplate everything since it happened. I bring my hands in front of my face, studying them as if they're going to spark with magical powers. Eve had shown me what kind of power my gifts possessed, taught me that I can have anything I want in less than a second. She also showed me the downsides of what that kind of power can do to a person. I can feel her own personal struggle with her gifts, as well as her deep desire for peace. Eve loved her creations, especially Adam, despite what he did to her. The intense yearning she had for him makes my heart ache. I can feel the pull Eve had to Adam the same way I do when I look at Ethan; like an invisible cord is hauling me toward him. I exhale, feeling a weight come down on my shoulders at all that's expected of me—at what my life has become in such a short amount of time.

"From library assistant to world conqueror," I say out loud before making a very unladylike grunt as I cover my face with a pillow.

"I would hardly call you a conqueror," Ethan's voice says with amusement.

I quickly throw the pillow off my head before sitting up

to face him. He's trying to smile but I can tell by the look in his eyes how defeated he is.

"You scared me," I scold.

"Sorry. I knocked but you did not answer. I thought you might be asleep."

"Just thinking." I pat the space on the bed beside me for him to sit.

He gently sits down and grabs my hand, releasing a breath he's been holding. He clutches my fingers almost too tightly—as if he's trying to ground himself.

We sit in silence for a few moments, the only sound his steady deep breaths. After it seems like he's calmed himself down, I squeeze his hand back, getting him to look at me.

"Did your mom leave?" I ask carefully.

"Yes," he says, his voice thick with emotion. "She wants to talk with Isa."

"Ethan?" I ask, using my finger to turn his face to mine. His eyes are glassy, and I notice his lip quivering slightly.

"Hey," I say softly. "It's ok to be upset. What your mom did with my dad—it was wrong."

He takes another deep breath as he blinks a few times to try and compose himself. "Sorry, I—I just feel like a child. I am an adult. It should not matter to me what my parents do."

"A.) You have nothing to be sorry for and B.) It does matter. They are your parents and you expected them to be better than that. It's okay to be disappointed. It's okay to be angry and upset. I'm upset, too. My dad knew your mom was married but apparently that didn't matter to him much."

"What I find most disappointing is that it goes against everything my mother taught me about love and relationships. Not to mention, finding out both Isa and my father have known this information for many years, and they continued to keep it from me is very hurtful." He stops to rub his eyes. "There were many reasons why I left New York City, but at least now I know why the last several years were so uncomfortable. They were all keeping secrets from me."

"I think I can relate to that feeling. I know it sucks."

Ethan looks into my eyes apologetically, but with a tenderness I've never experienced from anyone before. It makes me a little uncomfortable. I'm not sure what to make of it. If I didn't know any better, I'd say it looks—*loving*.

"I apologize," he atones. "That was silly for me to say. I know you understand. Thank you for being here for me, Sophia. I feel very confused. I do not even want to look at my family right now."

I try to brush off the feelings stirring inside me and just smile at him before placing my finger in that dimple of his in an endearing way. "It's Sophie," I tease.

He leans over to gently kiss my lips. When he pulls back, he looks at me with that expression again. I feel butterflies exploding in my stomach.

Ethan brushes a lock of my hair behind my ear. "How are you doing with all of this? And please tell me the truth."

I shrug my shoulders. "I don't know. Finding out about Eve, my gifts, having to save the world and my dad having an affair with my lov—Well, my…" I struggle to find the right word as Ethan surveys me—amused.

"Your…" he asks hopefully.

I groan, throwing my head against his shoulder. "I don't know what to call you! We had sex. I called you my *lover* to your mom." I cringe.

He snorts. "Seriously?" I just nod, embarrassed. "*Lover*," he says in a creepy, low, romance novel type voice. "Come here, *loverrrr*," he purrs, grabbing me and hauling me onto his lap. I squeak in shock, playfully shoving at him as he tries to attack my neck with his lips.

"Hey!" I laugh. "Who said you could do that?"

"I am your *lover* now, I thought it came with the job description."

I pout. "You know—I'm still annoyed with you."

"Really? It does not seem like it," he says, kissing my neck again.

"Right, well. I am—*lover*," I taunt, the word feeling funny on my lips. I hate it.

"Can we just hit the reset button on today and go back to this morning?" he asks, wiggling his eyebrows.

"You're incorrigible!"

"It is not like I can help it. You are cute when you are angry."

"Ugh—don't belittle me."

"So, you can call me cute, but I cannot call you cute? I do not think it works like that," he says.

"Whatever, I'm the Alpha so I'm calling the shots," I say defiantly, running out of comebacks.

"Please do not tell me you are going to use that against me. I might have to end this right here and now," he grins.

"Like you could," I snark, feeling the way his body is reacting to me as we speak.

He leans in to place a chaste kiss on my lips. "I suppose you are right."

Instead of going further like I thought he would, he puts his forehead to mine, taking a deep breath. With my arms now around his neck, I hold him to me for a few seconds, just enjoying the soothing effect he's having on me.

"You're not doing your emotional mojo on me, are you?" I wonder.

"No," he says sincerely. "You wanted me to ask first."

"Just checking."

He kisses my nose and hugs me tight to him, his breath now hot against my neck. I place my hands in his hair, running my nails on his scalp in a comforting manner. I feel him relax; before I know it, his body starts shaking slightly—I realize he's crying. For a moment, I panic. It's not often a man cries in your arms. But I quickly collect myself, glad he's finally releasing whatever he's been holding in. I hug him even closer, feeling grateful that he feels safe to be vulnerable like this with me.

"Sophia," his voice cracks awhile later. At some point we had laid down, still wrapped in each other.

"*Sophie*," I tease, running my thumb over the dried tears on his cheeks.

He rolls his eyes and laughs a little. "I like Sophia better."

"I know you do, but I like Sophie better."

"Can we not agree that I can call you whatever I want?"

346

"Only if I can call you E."

"E? That is annoying."

"Well, it's annoying when you call me Sophia."

He rolls his eyes again.

"You know if you keep doing that, they'll get stuck that way," I say in a serious tone.

"Then yours would already be stuck, *Sophia.*"

"Sophie."

"Fine," he gives up. "Sophie."

He sticks his tongue out at me, and it's my turn to roll my eyes at him. He just grins, his dimple reappearing on his cheek. After he tucks a strand of hair behind my ear, he sends a silent thank you through his gaze. I squeeze his hand in return to let him know I understand.

"So...about what to call our relationship," he smiles goofily.

I smirk. "Lover isn't really going to work, is it?"

"Well, we *could*—but that implies this is just sex. Is that all this is?"

I whine. "You really know how to break a moment, don't you?"

"Sorry," he says sheepishly.

"I thought we discussed this. A lot is going on right now. I don't think we need a label."

"I know we discussed it but that was before we had sex," he trails off, most likely thinking about our time together.

"Right. But the circumstances have only gotten more complicated. Didn't you hear me before? I have to go out and rule the world now," I say with confidence.

"Yes, if you have to be that literal."

"Can we just not deal with whatever this is right now?" I say defiantly while laying my head against his heart. "If someone asks, we can tell them to shove it."

"You already told my mom we are lovers," he says while playing with my hair.

"Do you want to make an announcement then? Dear Wisher people, your long-lost Alpha and princey-boy Ethan are lovers!" I put on a booming voice.

"Let us not do that. And did you just say princey-boy and Wisher people?" he muses.

I mumble nonsensical words against his chest before looking up at him. "Ugh, fine! You win. I guess girlfriend is fine. But I'm warning you now, I'm not a very good one."

He kisses my forehead. "So far I think you have been a great one."

"Ha! That's because there's no label and no pressure. Now I'm going to ruin it."

348

"Is that what you are worried about? That you are going to ruin it because we defined it?"

"I don't do relationships. I do summer flings and one-night stands," I exclaim.

He flinches. "You know, you really do not have to tell me about your relationship history. I would prefer not to know." I shove him a bit before sitting up and out of his arms.

"I'm just letting you know the truth, okay? As you can see from how my Dad handles relationships, I haven't had the best role models. Not to mention I live in a town where there weren't exactly a lot of men around to pick from. I had tourists."

He scrunches up his nose a bit at the last part and I realize what he thought I meant by that. Is that really all he could think about?

"Just don't say I didn't warn you if something goes amuck," I tell him.

Ethan glares at me for a moment, a flicker of pain moving through his violet irises.

"See! I already screwed it up."

"You did not screw up," he says sadly. "I just think you are already trying to push me away because you are scared."

"That's not true." I cross my arms over my chest.

"Yes, it is. Sophie, I know you feel this strange connection between us. You already told me that. You know I feel it too. What we have shared in such a short amount of time is not something I am willing to give up on that easily."

"I don't think I said it in those exact words," I fuss.

"You really like to make things difficult."

"I never said I was an easy person to handle."

"I do not want you to be easy to handle, I want you to be *you*."

"I am being me. So either you deal with the whole package, or we just decide we had a few good nights together, and now it's over."

He grabs my hands and forces me to look at him. "This is not over. I am hurt that you are willing to give up on us that easily."

"I'm not giving up! I'm just trying to be realistic," I say sincerely, pulling my hands away.

He exhales. "We had a big morning and a very eventful day. I think it is best if we eat some dinner and get some rest. Let us not decide our entire future right now, especially after what we just learned about our families." His eyes practically beg with mine to let it go for now.

"Ok," I agree reluctantly. "But I don't know how

much longer I can sit here. I need to figure out what happened to Chris, and I have to deal with The Alliance. The longer we wait the worse it could get with them. Who knows what they're planning as we sit here wasting time."

"I understand what you are feeling but we have been dealing with them for several years now. If we had anything to worry about in the next few hours, we would know about it. Just try to relax for now. We will meet with The Council in the morning and then we can go from there. I know you are restless, but we need to have a plan, all right?"

"*Man*—you people sure know how to make a girl wait. I feel like I've been here for months just *waiting and waiting and waiting…*"

"I know, but have faith in me when I say we do not want to rush into this."

"You just want Chris to suffer longer, don't you?" I smirk, breaking the tension.

"*What?*" he grins. "Me? No of course not."

I shake my head at him before standing up off of the bed and heading to the kitchen. Ethan follows behind me and before long we're pulling ingredients out to cook dinner.

"I will cook us something, you sit," he orders while

handing me a bottle of red wine. Holding my tongue about bad cooking jokes, I do as I'm told. I silently cheer in delight when the taste of alcohol touches my lips—letting it quell my restlessness.

After a few minutes, I turn on some music in the background and Ethan starts to hum along. My mouth upturns thinking about how funny it is that we're already becoming domesticated. Two meals in a row together that he prepared, sleeping in the same bed, waking up in the morning side by side—I feel as if I live with him. But I'm not going to tell him that. It'll only enforce his need and want to call me his girlfriend at every moment.

Feeling a little uneasy about everything again, I plop ungracefully on the couch and light a fire with my gifts. Despite the Alpha's history with the burning flames, it somehow calms me. I watch the fire and sip my wine, the combination warming my cheeks. I feel myself begin to tire, even though it isn't that late yet. I'm about to close my eyes when Ethan's voice cuts through my haze, telling me that dinner is ready. I shake myself awake, erasing the sleep from my features before heading over to the table. I can't help the happy grin that comes over my face as I take in the dining room table. Several candles, a bottle of wine, and red roses litter its surface. Ethan really can't help himself when it comes to romance. I don't know if I like or despise it yet, but right now I think it's sweet.

"What's all this?" I ask.

He smiles slyly. "I thought we could have a little date, seeing as I am not sure what is going to happen after tonight. This could be our last chance to spend time together for a while—we might as well make the most of it. Sit," he commands in a gentle voice—he's taking this date *very seriously*.

Once I'm seated, he pours me more wine before going to the kitchen to retrieve the meal he's prepared: chicken, sautéed vegetables, and potatoes.

"It smells good."

"Thanks," he replies sheepishly before sitting down and pouring a fresh glass of wine for himself.

"I didn't know you had this in you without your gifts. I thought sandwiches are where your culinary skills ended," I tease.

"Eat," he scolds playfully. "Before it gets cold."

I obey, taking a few bites of food and chewing slowly.

"The verdict?" he wonders, his eyes on me curiously.

"Not bad—I don't think I'd enter you into a cooking competition, but it's good."

He scoffs. "Well, I am rather impressed with myself

actually. Maybe those cookbooks I checked out did me some good."

"Maybe," I grin back at him.

We continue to eat and drink, enjoying and teasing each other back and forth for a little bit. When we're almost finished, I decide now is as good a time as any to figure out his family dynamic. I know he doesn't want to talk about it, and it's selfish of me to push it, but my curiosity gets the best of me.

"Ethan, can I ask you something?"

CHAPTER 20

"Ethan, can I ask you something?"

He looks up from the last bites of his dinner with his eyebrows raised. "Of course."

"I know we weren't going to talk about this anymore tonight, but like you said, this could be the last time we have some space alone—"

"What is it?" he urges.

"I'm really curious about what happened between you and Isa. I know there's more to the story than just basic sibling rivalry." My eyes oversee his reaction carefully—his face falls—a sadness coming over him.

"You don't have to answer if you don't want to," I quickly backtrack, feeling guilty.

"It is fine. It is just not easy for me to talk about."

I reach across the table to grab his hand. "I know, and like I said you don't have too. I just find it very strange that you two aren't close given everything that's happened here in recent years. I'm just trying to understand you better, and Isa too."

"I am going to need more wine for this," he mutters, pouring himself another glass before topping off my own.

"If you tell me quickly it will be easier—like ripping off a band-aid," I grin at him.

Ethan sends me a suspicious look.

"I want you to tell me about the real you—not the mysterious man that showed up in my town. The man that you are; I want to know him," I urge gently.

He plays with my fingers a little. "You already know me. I told you why I came to Wisconsin, about my gifts. You have met my family—minus my father."

"I know, but I want you to tell me about your history. Take me back to before we met. Tell me about your family and what you did in New York City; more about why you had to get out so badly. I want to know it all."

"You are not going to let me off the hook, are you?"

"Like I said, if you really don't want to discuss it, you don't have to. But I will probably ask you *again, and again, and again* until you spill the beans. I think it's important for me to know you. Hell—you know pretty much everything about my life—I think it only seems fair."

"I suppose that is valid," he laughs despite himself.

I smile cheekily. "I know."

I take Ethan's hands and pull him over to my favorite spot on the couch in front of the fire, grabbing the bottle of wine. I feel his trepidation, but from the display in my bedroom earlier it seems as though Ethan doesn't have many people to confide in. I know I can be that person for him, just as he's becoming that person for me.

"Let's start with some basics," I say lightly. "I know a few things from our last conversation on the jet, but there's a lot more you're not telling me about your family, your childhood, adulthood—*Oh!*—and you have to explain the fact that your great, great, etc., etc., grandparents founded W.I.S.H. —I did *not* see that coming," I quip.

He sips his wine. "I forgot about that—it is quite interesting. As I told you, my father is a non-Wisher. Actually, for many generations there were no Wishers in the Moore family. This caused their memories to fade and their history to be buried and forgotten by the family. Because of that, my father was unaware of Wishers existence until he met my mother," he says. "When she found out his last name was Moore, she thought it was just a coincidence. I mean, what were the odds she would end up dating a descendant of the Moore-Wishers? To make things even more strange, it was actually your father that figured it out."

"Your dad really had no idea he was practically Wisher royalty?"

He shakes his head. "The Moore-Wisher line disappeared until I was born. My father's family was working-class before they started Moore Publishing back in 1920. But my father really made it what it is today. The Moore name has standing in the world because he worked hard for it, not because his family started W.I.S.H. He takes pride in his work and wants his family to do the same. It was important to him that we made our own way in the world—he does not want us to use our gifts to get ahead—we must earn what we want."

I nod in understanding since my dad was the same way—no wonder he and Ethan's dad were friends.

"Was your dad shocked when he learned about his heritage?" I ask tentatively.

"Yes, but he took it rather well. Maybe it is because Wishing is in his blood," he says dimly. "I think he was more shocked about having two children with gifts. Mother was thrilled when I developed my gifts, then when Isa developed hers, she was ecstatic. It is extremely rare to have two Wishers born of the same mother. My father did not take the news as well. From my perspective, he has always been a little jealous of us. But I understand why. It must be hard to be so different from your family. However, he put aside his feelings. Ultimately, he joined The Society because he believes in our mission. I think one of the reasons he has hardened over the years is because he dreamt that at least one of his children would follow in his footsteps to publishing. Me leaving Moore Publishing to help W.I.S.H. was the final nail in the coffin so to speak."

"That couldn't have been easy for him."

"It was not. I felt bad about quitting, but things started to unravel here at W.I.S.H. —especially after Robert died. That hit my father hard since they were such great friends. They spent a lot of time together right before he died, figuring out how to keep The Alliance from getting strong again—how to keep loyalties in check." Ethan smiles to himself. "They were hilarious together. I wish you could have seen it—they laughed a lot, told stupid jokes. Like college buddies do."

"It's making sense to me now why you're more hurt by the affair than I could understand."

He takes a shallow breath. "My father was always tough on my sister and me, but after Robert died, it was like he was a completely different person. I see now that his death was not the only reason my father changed. This is why I find the truth about the affair so humiliating. My family should have told me the truth. It would have helped me understand what was going on with my father. I think things could have been different somehow."

"I don't understand why Isa knew about the affair and you didn't."

Ethan laughs sharply. "Well, at first my mother pulled the whole—*you are my sensitive boy*—excuse, but I knew that was a lie. Eventually she relented and told me that Isa had heard through another Wisher that he saw Robert and my mother together, and not just as friends. Apparently, Isa did some snooping and found out that it was true, that they were having an affair. She confronted them and said she would go to my father and tell him herself if they did not come clean."

"But why did she never tell you?"

"My sister and I, as you might have guessed, have always struggled to get along. I was the first-born son, the golden boy. I was the child to end the drought of Wishers for the Moore bloodline. Then, I developed the ability to

360

manipulate certain emotions with my touch. Because it is rare to have gifts outside of Wishing alone, I was singled out by many to be special."

"*Oh my god!* Did they think you were the Alpha?" I exclaim.

He gives me a lopsided grin. "At first, but it did not make any sense. All the prior Alphas had been women. Why would it all of a sudden change to a man? Because of this, Isa was jealous of me her entire childhood. The day she Wished for a packet of Skittles and they appeared in front of her was the best day of her life. Her gift came a little later than usual, so we all thought that she was going to be a non-Wisher like my father. After that, she made it very clear to me that because I was the boy, and I was the oldest, I had to help my father. She did not want to work in publishing, and she was not going to set foot inside the office unless it was to have lunch with one of us. I felt that I had no choice but to work for my father after that. So, I went to college and I worked for him. At the time it was an easy choice because I believed that all Wishers needed to participate in society and contribute to our economy. That view has never changed and will never change. But eventually I knew my talents could be of better use to The Society. When everything crumbled at W.I.S.H. and our

361

lives were being threatened, Isa acted like I did not know anything about our kind. She tried to use the fact that I had spent most of my time studying and working in the city against me. She claimed that I did not understand what was happening between The Alliance and The Society."

I stop him. "I'm not sure your sister sounds like the prime candidate for The Council. How did she manage such a powerful position with such an attitude, and so young?"

"Isa is good at talking, smiling, and being nice to everyone. She would be a great politician," he smirks. "Do not get me wrong, she is a good person. She is very talented and smart too—her personality just leaves something to be desired."

I snicker in response.

Ethan quirks a smile. "She really likes you, you know. Even though she is jealous of you. She always hoped that when she turned 25, she would suddenly be the Alpha. But then we found out about you and it crushed her. I think being elected to The Council was her way of proving that she was good enough—that she was the best of our family."

"Sounds like she needs therapy," I joke.

"I am not doing a very good job of talking her up, am I?" he grins.

"No, not really," I laugh. "But I get it. You guys have sibling issues. It's understandable, especially with the kind of life you've had."

"You mean you understand why I am so screwed up?" He tries to tease, but underneath that statement he's full of insecurity and self-doubt.

"You're not screwed up. I know I shouldn't stroke your ego, but you're probably one of the sanest people I've ever met. Remember, you haven't met my mom yet, but you've met Ana. I love that girl, but oh man." I laugh.

He laughs quietly. "She is an interesting woman. But really Sophie, I am surprised you have not run away yet."

"If this is my path, if this is who I'm meant to be, then who am I to fight it?"

"I hope you realize that if you really do not want to do this, you do not have to. You can walk away, and no one will stop you. I would be sad to see you go, but I would understand."

I bring my hand up to his face and cup his cheek. "Too many people have been hurt because of this mess. Alphas have died so that I could be sitting here right now. If I've learned anything from the blackouts, it's that weakness is natural, fear is natural—but there's a reason I'm here. There's a reason I'm the Alpha and your sister's not. There's a reason everything is happening now and not a day sooner. I inhabited this body, in this time, not by accident or chance. Eve knew what she was doing when she created me. It's time for me to own who I am, what I can do; what we can all do together, both non-Wishers and Wishers. If we can't work together, we're all doomed. Not just The Society but *all* of us."

Ethan looks stunned for a moment as he processes all I've said. To be honest I'm not sure where all that came from. I've been doubting myself this whole time. But I guess I needed to hear I had a choice to ignite the fire within me. I don't want to let my sisters—my Alphas— down.

His face breaks out into a huge smile, one that I haven't seen before. He leans down to kiss me hard on the mouth.

"I cannot tell you how happy I am to hear you say that."

"Did you really think I would leave now? I told you how I felt earlier."

He beams. "I know. But that was before everything else happened. I just—I really do not want you to leave. I am pretty invested now."

I flush. "I know you are, but I need you to trust me. Trust that I'm invested, too."

"I do trust you."

"Good."

"I want to tell you something," Ethan asks quietly.

"Anything," I assure him.

"I left something out earlier, about the reason why I came to Wisconsin to find you. It was not as simple as me just being the best person for the job, because trust me, Isa thought there were other and more qualified candidates. Initially it was because of a dream I had..."

"A dream?" I ask.

"Yes—about you."

"What?"

He takes my hand hesitantly. "I will never forget that dream, it was so vivid—I saw myself standing with you by a lake. We were holding hands, and I felt a strange pull. It was quite overwhelming. I knew when I woke up, there was no other option but for me to go to Wisconsin and help you. Funny part was, I did not know what you looked like before the dream. When I told The Council about it and I described you to them they were shocked. When they showed me your picture I almost fell over. After that, they knew they had to let me go."

"Ethan, if this is true, why didn't you say something before?" I say, slightly hurt.

"I wanted to tell you, but what I felt in that dream—it was like you and I were… Honestly, I am still afraid to tell you," he almost whispers.

I hold in a breath, understanding where he's going with this. In truth I don't want him to say it. I know the feeling he's describing. It was there the moment he bumped into me at the bonfire—it was there during the blackouts—and it was there when we had sex. It was always there when he was involved. It wasn't just the magnetic pull we had discussed before, it was more than that.

My stomach flops nervously. I have never believed in soulmates before. My parents were divorced for goodness sake. I'm not the girl who believes in romance and fairy tales. But Ethan, he's different. Everything about being with him is different. I feel like I'm coming to terms with that even though the feelings scare me. I had learned from my mom to protect my heart, especially after hers had been crushed by my dad. I also have a theory that the track record of the Alpha's love lives didn't help either. Collectively, their experiences with men were not pleasant.

"Sophia?" Ethan asks me, no doubt uncomfortable in my silence.

"I know what you don't want to say," I breathe out. "And I don't want to say it either."

366

He nods in understanding and I'm grateful that he leaves it at that. We sit sipping wine for a while longer, our hands holding tightly to one another. Eventually my head begins to droop, and I rest it on his shoulder. His hand leaves mine and he wraps his arm around my shoulders so that my head falls to his chest. I hear his heart thrumming against my ear and the steady rhythm of his breath. The fire blazes on in front of us, the reflection of the flames dancing with the red and orange light of the sunset. This is one the most peaceful moments I've ever had in my short life. As I begin to drift off, I can't help but hope we have more of these nights in our future.

CHAPTER 21

"*Sophia!* Sophie, wake-up!" Ethan yells.

My heart races at the sudden jolt.

I let out a groan, my body heavy with sleep. "What?" I snip, feeling his arms pulling at me to get up. I try to shove him off as I clear the sleep from my mind.

"Sophia!" he yells anxiously, "You need to wake up, *NOW!*"

Finally, I'm able to break out of my tired haze. I sit up and blink the crust from my eyes to find Ethan obviously in distress. I'm awake then, the blanket he must have wrapped around me in sleep falling to the floor. It's pitch-black outside, and once again I have no clue what time it is.

"We have to go!" Ethan barks, roughly grabbing my arm and heading towards the door.

"What? Why?" I exclaim. "What's going on?"

"The Alliance, they are here," he curses.

"*What?* I thought you said we were safe here?"

"Well apparently not!" he snaps. "We need to go—now!"

Anger and fear bubble up inside of me. I know he's scared, but I don't want to be pushed around. I shove down my feelings and pull my arm out of his grasp. I quickly find my cell phone and leather jacket and make my way back over to him.

"Where are we going?" I demand.

"To get you to a safe house."

I stop. "No! Ethan, this is ridiculous. Why don't I just face them? Unless they throw a fireball at me by surprise, I can just wish myself away before I get hurt."

"Please," he begs tiredly. "Just because you cannot die, does not mean you cannot get hurt. I am not going to let you just turn yourself over to them. Are you crazy?"

"I never claimed to be sane," I say defiantly. "And it's not like I have many options here. I'm not going to run away scared forever. I need to try to talk to them."

"I do not think they are in much of a talking mood! Remember, they tried to shoot us a few days ago."

"Correction, they shot at you! They were trying to capture me," I goad.

"Really? We are going to get into this right now?" he chides.

"Sorry! It's how I deal with stress," I yell back anxiously.

"Well, we are leaving whether you like it or not," he asserts.

Before I can say anything back, he flings the door open to the hallway. We're immediately met by Isa and a group of guards. She's dressed all in black and has a gun holstered at her hip.

"Are the guns really necessary?" I cross my arms over my chest.

Isa looks at me almost amused. "Unfortunately, yes. They may not want to kill you right away, but they won't hesitate to kill the rest of us. I would suggest you take one."

"Seriously?"

"You know how to use a gun, right?"

"I'm from a small-town in Wisconsin, what kind of question is that?"

She smirks. "Listen Sophie, this isn't how I thought this would go down. Sadly we have a leak and The Alliance found out how to get in. It's only a matter of time before they make their way up here and start killing us all."

I stare back at her, unblinking. "You said that in an oddly calm manner. I feel like I should be worried."

Isa lets out a barking laugh. "Don't worry—we are

370

prepared for something like this to happen. Come on, we'll take you somewhere safe. Mary is already on her way there with the other Council members."

The image of Mary in a black catsuit holding a gun crosses my mind. I have to hold in my inappropriate laughter at the mental image. It's quite funny.

"Here," Isa holds out a gun.

I exhale in resignation, reaching out to take it. Just as I'm about to grab it, one of the guards standing to my left lunges at me. The gun flies from Isa's hands and skids across the floor. I manage to somehow keep my balance and not fall over with the weight of the guard crashing into me.

Before I can comprehend what's happening, all hell breaks loose. A loud bang resounds through the hallway and I let out an involuntary squeal. The sound's so close to my ears that I can't hear anything but a high-pitched ringing. I feel myself being grabbed but I'm not sure by who. When I start to be propelled down the hallway, I blindly try to fight whoever it is that's holding me.

I manage to elbow the person in the gut, and they release me for a second. When I turn to try and break their nose with my palm—like I've seen in the movies—I realize it's Ethan.

"Jesus that hurt," he grunts.

"*Ethan, what the hell?* Stop pushing me like that!" I whisper harshly.

Instead of listening he grabs my elbow and starts running down the hallway so I have no choice but to run beside him. I register Isa yelling at us to run faster before I hear several loud grunts and sounds of fighting. When more shots go off, I jump multiple times. I turn my head to look behind us and see a guard not far from us. He has his gun aimed and he's getting ready to shoot.

"Ethan!" I exclaim. But it's too late.

The gun fires and a bullet ricochets off the wall to my right, almost hitting me. I'm about to wish us somewhere when Ethan pulls a gun out of nowhere, aiming back at the guard. His gun fires loudly, and the guard falls to the ground with a strangled cry, clutching his leg.

"Fucking hell, Ethan! Where did you learn how to shoot like that?" I shout.

"*Not—now*," he pants, as we continue to run.

"*Ugh!*" is all I manage to get out as we sprint down another long hallway. I breathe a sigh of relief when I see the elevators up ahead. But just when I think we're in the clear, several more men and women dressed as guards now block our path.

"*Crap*," Ethan mutters under his breath, obvious panic

crossing his face. When I see a door to our right, I use my gifts to wish us inside and deadbolt the door behind us with multiple locks. When I look around the suite, I'm happy to find it's empty.

"Are you all right?" I ask him.

"I am fine," he answers, catching his breath. He starts to move around the suite. "Hello?" he calls out, his gun cocked. After he does a sweep of the rooms, he relaxes a little when he's satisfied that we're alone. It doesn't last long—soon the door of the suite starts shaking. The guards are trying to get in. I know it won't be long before they make their way in; they're Wishers after all.

"Ethan, where do you want us to go? If I don't wish us out of here soon, we're in for it."

"There is a safe house near Mount Everett. If we go there, Isa and the others will know where to find us."

I nod. "Ok."

Ethan grabs my hand and clutches it just as the door is wrenched open. The guards come barreling in, and before I can think, a gun goes off. I quickly concentrate and keep hold of Ethan's hand, wishing us to be in that cabin near Mount Everett. With a small rushing feeling and a blink of my eyes, we're surrounded by silence. I glance around to find we're now in a cabin similar to mine in Wisconsin.

The space is black, but I can see just enough to get around from the moonlight illuminating the area.

"I don't think I'll ever get used to that," I grin as I turn towards Ethan. The smile falls from my face, however, when I see that he's unusually pale and riddled with shock.

"Ethan? What's wrong?" My stomach drops.

"I...I...," he stutters as his knees give out. He falls to the ground and tugs me down with him, our hands still joined.

"Ethan!" I cry as I fall to my knees, thankfully not on top of him. I pry my hand from his and try to look him over. Even in the darkness I see blood soaking through his shirt.

My hands start to shake, and my mind is screaming for me to panic. I try to say something, but nothing comes out. With a deep breath, I collect myself enough to lift up his shirt to see the wound. I can't stop the gasp that escapes my mouth.

"Is it bad?" he wheezes, his body shaking as he tries to take breaths.

I nod so he can see me. "I need to get something to stop the bleeding, I'll be right back," I say quickly, jumping up. I'm too panicked to use my gifts.

It doesn't take me long to flip on some lights and grab a

few towels from the bathroom before returning to him. I place one towel under his head and then use another to put pressure on the wound. He lets out a heartbreaking sound of pain the moment I touch him.

"I'm sorry, I'm sorry," I rush out. "We need to get you to the hospital."

There's no way he's going to survive if we don't. The blood has already soaked through the towel and starts to get on my clothes. He is pale, and his lips are blue.

"No!" he manages to yell out. "Too dangerous."

"Well, you're crazy because I'm going to bring you to the hospital and you're going to get help, so you don't die!" I cry.

"Soph—I..."

"Nope!" I cut him off. "I know what you're doing. Don't make any stupid declarations of love or any bullshit like that," I snap. "You're not dying."

He tries to respond. When his eyes start to roll back in his head, I know it's too late to go to the hospital.

"Ethan," I cry, tears forming in my eyes. I can feel I'm losing him. The magnetism I feel when I'm near him is lessening and I begin to feel cold. I grab his face between my hands, blood smearing on his cheeks.

"Ethan!" I yell frantically. "Don't you fucking dare fall

asleep!"

"Soph…" he wheezes.

"That's right—stay here with me. You can do that, can't you?"

"Heal," he manages to say.

"But I'm not 25 yet!" I cry, clutching wildly at his face to get him to open his eyes again.

"T-try," he utters weakly, using what strength he has left to reach for my hand on his cheek.

"Ok, ok, I'll try," I say softly.

His arm drops down to the floor like dead weight; I immediately bring my hands directly over the gunshot wound. His body convulses beneath them as I push down as gently as I can on it. I know he doesn't have much longer left. If I don't heal him, he's going to die. I'm worried the healing powers won't work, or I might end up killing him.

I take a deep breath and close my eyes. I tune into myself like I had earlier that day and called out to the other Alphas. The voices begin to move forward to my mind. My body begins to tingle and the first voice I hear is Eve's—sharp and clear. Then it's as if all of space and time slows.

"Focus, Sophie," she sings. *"Give the light to him."*

I try with all my might to focus on the energy buzzing in my body and a warmth deep within me begins to grow.

Eve's voice continues to echo in my mind and before long, the warmth turns to a burning fire. It courses throughout my body and I let out a cry of agony. I don't think I'll ever get used to this feeling.

"Stay connected, don't break," Eve commands, her *voice stronger.*

It takes every ounce of willpower I have not to crumble, not to take my hands away from Ethan's body or pass out. The biting fire only blooms stronger, and hot, ripping pain sweeps through me—more intense than ever. A full-fledged scream escapes my lips as my fingers clench into Ethan's muscles. I vaguely hear him cry out and I almost let go. I want the pain to end; no, I need it to end.

"No, Sophie! Do not let go. You are almost there," Eve *pushes.*

Her voice is so strong it's like she's standing next to me. I do everything I can not to move. It's then I feel hands over the top of my own. For a moment I think they're Ethan's, but they're not. They're feminine, delicate and soft. I detect a presence to my right and when I manage to look over, there's a woman with no distinct skin color or features. She's made of lightness and air, glowing and unearthly. Calm washes over me and I feel at peace. The fire slowly leaves my body and I'm filled with soothing

377

warmth. When she finally turns to look at me, it's like she's staring right through me. Even though she has no distinct features, I swear she smiles. One of her hands comes up to my cheek in a nurturing action. I lean into the feeling that's there, allowing her energy to flow into me. I try to say something, but I can't find my words. It feels like anything I say won't be right.

With another rush of warmth, she's gone as quickly as she had come. A tear trails down my cheek at the overwhelming emotion of it all. When the light dissipates, it's like a part of me has left with her. Then I hear my name being called. It's distant, almost like I'm in a cave. Through my grogginess I feel solid hands on my cheeks, followed by kisses all over my face.

My eyes shift back into focus and I comprehend that it's Ethan. He's kneeling in front of me, his face covered in blood from when my hands had grasped his face. His features are still pale, but the color seems to be returning quickly. Tears are running down his face, too, and he's smiling with a mixture of pride and astonishment.

"Ethan?" I sob in disbelief.

He nods rapidly. "You did it, Sophia. You healed me."

"I did?" I ask, still not believing it.

"Well, either that or this is a dream!" he says happily

before kissing me on the lips rather hard. When he pulls back my face is still in his hands. I look him up and down, processing the fact that he's alive and breathing. He's covered in dark red, the shirt he's wearing completely soaked and tattered. I lift the fabric up to reveal more now-drying blood. I cautiously bring my fingers to where the bullet wound had been. Now there's just smooth tanned skin and muscle.

"This can't be real," I say in a hoarse whisper, my eyes never leaving the now-healed skin. I'm not sure how long I stare at it but after a while, Ethan's hands come to hold mine. I look up at him and he has a big stupid grin on his face.

"I knew you could do it. I knew it," he beams.

I can't help but feel happy at his excitement. "I'm glad you did because I didn't. But, Eve, I think she was here," I say, looking around the room like I expected her to still be there.

"Here?" he asks, glancing around.

"Not here, *here*—her energy or soul came to me to help heal you. Are you sure you didn't see her?"

"No, I did not. I was dying and there was a lot of pain. Then it was like I was in a warm bath. Then fire—it felt like I was on fire. The next thing I know I could feel this strange life force enter my body and I was awake. I do not even feel tired. In fact I feel like I could run a marathon," he bounces excitedly. His violet eyes are shining with so much life; I can't help but smile with him.

"I think I know why you felt those things," I say after a few moments. "I think I gave you part of my life force." I trail off in thought.

"What?" he gasps, his face riddled with concern.

"I don't know how to describe it. But after Eve left, I felt like a part of me had left with her. But now I think that part was given to you—to heal you."

"I—I do not know what to say. Are you okay?" he asks worriedly, cupping my cheek gently.

"I'm ok. A little tired but not bad actually," I reassure him.

"Are you sure? Do you think we screwed something up by healing me? Maybe you should have just let me die," he rattles off, clearly panicked.

"You're kidding me, right? Don't even think that!" I scold him. "You didn't deserve to die because of me. I wasn't going to let you—no matter what the cost," I stress, standing up in anger.

Ethan follows quickly so he's facing me, turning my chin up so I have to look at him. His eyes are full of sadness and something else I can't place. He's trying to hold himself together, but his facade is crumbling. We must look like quite a pair, standing there covered in his blood with even more blood at our feet.

"Ethan," I rasp out. "I'm fine. Can we please move on and just be grateful you're alive?"

"If that is what you want," he agrees.

"It is."

He wraps his arms around me, hugging me as close as he can. Our bodies meld together, and I relish the feeling of his heartbeat against mine. After a few moments I can't stand the rusty smell that fills my nostrils. I wrinkle my nose and pull away slightly.

"We should clean up. Then we need to figure out what to do. I hope Isa and the others are ok. And wasn't Mary supposed to be here?" I ask.

Ethan thinks. "I am sure Mary will be here soon. She cannot get to a place the way you can, and I would bet the others are fine. But if they are not, we will find out soon," he says.

"Do you have your phone?" I ask. "Can't we call them?"

"I lost it in the jumble of everything. Do you have yours?"

I shake my head. "But I can do this," I hold out my hand, wishing for my phone. Within a second it's in my hand. "Honestly, no matter how many times I've done that in the last few days, it never gets less cool. Check your pocket," I tell him. He reaches in quickly and pulls out his phone.

"You are good," he grins.

I wink playfully. "I know."

We both check our phones and find that nobody has tried to contact us yet, which is either a good sign or a very bad one.

When I check on Ethan, a sudden panic crosses over his face. He abruptly powers off his phone, throwing it to the ground and stomping on it.

"What the hell did you do that for?"

He reaches for my phone, but I yank it away from him.

"Turn your phone off! I just realized they could be tracking them."

I cringe. "Was that really necessary?" I wish my phone away to an unknown location and he smiles bashfully. "You could have just wished it away! No need to break things, you big oaf!"

"I panicked," he states.

I shake my head at him. "Seriously, you should go get

cleaned up. You have blood everywhere."

"You need to as well. You are a mess," he comments before grabbing my hand and leading me toward the small cabin bathroom.

The shower isn't that large, so I urge him to go first. There's no way we'd fit in there comfortably together. I can tell Ethan's not keen on letting me out of his sight, but eventually I get him to shower while I wash my hands and face in the sink. I watch the water run down the drain after it turns pink from his blood. I tremble, trying not to think of what would have happened had my healing gift not worked.

"You ok in there?" I call to Ethan after he's been in the shower awhile. I can't see him, but I hear him let out a breath he'd been holding.

"I am fine. It is hard to get all the blood off," he says shakily.

"Okay," I say back to him, wondering what he isn't telling me. I decide to not push it. He's been through enough tonight. I look at myself in the mirror once again. I have dark circles under my eyes and my hair's a mess with caked blood. I don't tell Ethan everything I'm feeling since I've healed him. My gifts aren't gone, but I definitely feel lighter, a little less burdened. I'm not sure if that's a good thing or not.

A little while later, after we've both cleaned up, Ethan looks healthy and rested—his hair still wet and mussed almost perfectly. He smiles gently and hands me a pair of clean clothes.

I raise an eyebrow at him. "Did you wish these here?"

"I did. I figured you were tired. While you were in the shower, I threw our clothes out. I think they were beyond saving," he says, scrunching his nose.

"You didn't throw out my jacket, did you?" I ask, my stomach dropping.

"Of course not. It is right over there, drying," he points to it.

I take a breath of relief and nod at him in thanks. Even though the leather jacket has been a source of conflict during the last few days, I don't want to part with it.

I drop my towel then and quickly change. Ethan flushes but doesn't turn away. I feel heat rise in my body as his eyes roam over me.

"You know, I'm not going to disappear if you blink," I tease while slipping the blue t-shirt he'd given me over my head.

He looks tongue-tied but eventually finds his words. "Sorry."

I chuckle. "Sure you are."

I walk over to him and get up on my toes to peck him on the lips in reassurance. When I look down, I'm reminded that the living area is still covered in his blood. Not wanting to look at it for another moment, I wish it away, not caring if it makes me more tired in that moment.

Ethan lets out a low whistle. "Wishing is like breathing for you now."

I shrug. "It just feels natural after the last few days. By the way, I noticed earlier how you and Isa implied it was weird that I actually put shoes on our feet. That's odd compared to other Wishers gifts?"

"In some ways, yes. Most Wishers could wish for shoes, but they would have to put them on their feet themselves— or with what you just did with the floor. They could have wished for cleaning products, but they would have had to do the manual labor themselves. We do have more advanced Wishers who could do something similar, but it's rare—very rare. It seems you do not really have to do anything except wish it. It is remarkable."

"Hmmm—*interesting.*" The more I learn, the more I

can see why so many people fear Alphas. We could literally do anything we want, and nobody could stop us unless we wanted them to.

Ethan looks at his watch and frowns. "I am getting concerned. Mary should have been here by now, or Isa should have sent someone."

"What time is it?"

"Just after three in the morning."

I rub my eyes tiredly. "I think I need to turn myself over to them." Immediately Ethan stiffens.

"No," he answers flatly.

"Ethan," I plead. "Will you just hear me out?"

"No," he says again, starting to move about the room. There's a laptop on the desk that I'm sure wasn't here before. He moves over to it and boots it up with his back turned.

"Ethan," I say again. "Just listen to me!"

He stays turned away with his shoulders tense. I let out a shaky breath and walk over to him, slamming the laptop closed with my hand.

"Ethan," I demand. "Look at me."

He hesitates for a moment before looking up, palpable anger in his eyes. I sit on the desk and grab his face between my hands.

386

"Just listen."

"I do not like what you are going to say," he asserts.

I roll my eyes. "So, you're going to act like a child and pretend you can't hear me? What's next, you plug your ears and say—*la-la-la?*'"

"No," he grumbles unhappily. "But I warn you, I am not going to agree to whatever it is you are going to say, but go ahead. You seem determined to tell me anyway."

I let go of his face and cross my arms over my chest, "You need to understand, Ethan. This isn't about me. This isn't about The Alliance or The Society. This is about people and this fucking planet! It's not just us that's affected by what's going on here. It's going to be everyone. Hell, everyone is already screwed up by all this fear and selfishness—all the violence! You almost died less than an hour ago—Mary and Isa could be dead—or your mom! My dad already died because of me, and others are dying or have died because of me. I'm not running anymore. It's not right!" I yell, my chest heaving and face hot.

Ethan's face softens. Immediately he brings me into his arms. I don't return the hug but keep my face buried in his chest. He smells like cheap soap, and his shirt is starchy against my face.

"This is not your fault," he speaks against my hair.

"From what you have learned you know this is not new. All the fighting, the violence, it has been happening since the beginning of time. How could you think you had a hand in it?

"You don't understand, Ethan," I say gently, pushing him away. His eyes are sad, but I try not to let them break me. "I'm speaking the truth, nothing more. This is why the Alphas did what they did. Why they gave themselves up and let themselves burn. Many of them lost hope."

"But you are different, Sophie... you have hope. Please do not tell me I am wrong."

I give him a watery smile. He really believes in me no matter what—I can feel it.

"If there's one thing I now know, it's that there's always hope," I say confidently. "Especially after what I just did," I run my hand over his healed stomach. I feel his muscles twitch beneath the pads of my fingers and I can't help but beam. "You know, despite the fact that Eve gave herself over to Adam's followers, I believe she sacrificed herself with hope."

He quirks an eyebrow. "What do you mean?"

"I think Eve knew that she would be whole again in a new body. Eve had hope that when she returned, her new vessel would allow her to begin where she left off. She hoped that her creations would figure out what they did was wrong and learn a lesson—that they would understand her sacrifice and learn from their fear. But each time she came back it wasn't the right time. They still hadn't learned. In fact, their fears had grown worse. It makes me wonder if there will ever be a right time. Hell, maybe everyone is wrong and I'm not the key. But we won't know unless I try to make things right. I have to go and face them."

Ethan looks at me, determined. "Then I am coming with you."

I shake my head vigorously. "No."

"That is hardly fair."

"Ethan, it's me they want. They'll just shoot you again!" I say breathlessly.

"I do not think they will," he states.

"Of course, they will!"

"Even if they do, I do not think it will matter," he says cryptically.

I look into his deep violet iris's and see that he's completely serious. Something is coming from within him that I haven't seen before. It causes me to twitch.

"What are you keeping from me now?" I ask carefully.

"Sophia—Sophie, there is something you should know," he says quietly.

"Now what?" I ask, slightly annoyed.

He ignores my reaction. "I—I think something happened when you healed me," he finally says, his eyes downcast. *I urge him on.* "It is hard for me to grasp, but once you healed me you said a part of you—well, you said it felt like a part of you had left you somehow."

"Yes, that's what I said," I reiterate.

Ethan stares me in the eyes and grabs my hands.

"Hold on," he says.

Before I can ask him why I feel a rushing sensation. When I adjust and gain my bearings, I see we're no longer in the cabin near Mount Everett anymore.

We're standing in the middle of my cabin in Iron Lake.

CHAPTER 22

I'm in shock.

When my brain catches up with what I see, my stomach cannonballs. For a second, I wonder if I had accidentally wished Ethan and me to my cabin, but I know I didn't. The tightening of Ethan's hands on mine brings me back to reality. I look up at him to find he looks almost sheepish, but proud and amazed at the same time.

"You did that?" I ask, dumbfounded.

"I did," he affirms.

"But it doesn't make sense—I didn't…"

"I know," he says while watching me intently.

I let out a big breath, my lips flapping. "*Well crap*. This changes things."

"You can say that again," he murmurs.

I blink at him rapidly, my mind reeling. "You think it's because I healed you?"

"That is the only thing that could explain it."

I'm baffled. "How did you know you could wish us here?"

"I was not sure if I was right in my thinking, but the more I went over it, the more I believe you did not just heal me, you brought me back from death." His eyes glaze over in wonderment.

I stare at him, unsure of what to do or say. When I try to talk, a squeak comes out.

Ethan brushes his fingers down the side of my cheek. "I was in the shower when I realized it. I had calmed down enough to think about what had just happened. My body felt almost like it had been re-born. Not a sore muscle or injury in me. That is when I knew I had died. You brought me back to life—you did not just heal my wounds."

"This is ludicrous!"

"No—it is not. You said that you felt as if a part of you was gone after you healed me. In the moment, I could not help but be upset and confused by thinking I might have weakened you somehow. That is why I did not say anything immediately. I knew you were traumatized by everything even though you would never admit it. You always try to be so nonchalant about everything —"

"Ethan—" I try to interrupt, but he stops me by holding up his hand.

"Just let me finish, all right?" I nod reluctantly and he continues. "Then I was able to put the pieces together. The fact you felt like you were not whole anymore, how I felt like a new person—stronger than ever! When I looked inside myself, I somehow understood that I was not the same anymore. I tested my developing theory. I wished for a new cell phone—one that does not even exist on the market. I created it for myself out of nothing. I knew then that somehow I had taken a piece of your gifts," he finishes with a gulping breath.

"I—I wish you would have told me right away. Don't you think I should have known this information immediately?" I exclaim, unsure of what else to do.

"I am sorry for that, but we have established several times that I do not always do the best thing, especially when it comes to you. I am too invested in your well-being," he states.

I bit my tongue. "*Apparently so.*" I rub my temples gently. I feel a headache coming on. Ethan rubs my back as I try to process everything he's just told me.

"Are you all right?" he asks after a while.

"I will be," I utter. "I wonder if this happened because I tried healing you too soon. Maybe I did something wrong."

"Possibly," Ethan says thoughtfully. "Or maybe this was

supposed to happen."

I exhale a shaky breath. He's right—it could have been Eve's plan all along. Maybe Ethan was meant to share in this with me. It might explain his dream and how we were brought together, how we feel drawn to one another. I am conflicted about it all. I don't care about sharing my gifts with him; in fact, it's almost a relief to know he's in this with me now in more ways than one. I'm more worried that if The Alliance finds out, they'll kill him. We don't know if he's immortal now like me and I sure as hell don't want to try and figure that out.

Ethan's still rubbing my back. I look deeply into the unique eyes that have now become so familiar to me. I move to grab his hand and bring it to rest over my heart so he can feel it beating. For a second, he looks at me, confused, but after a moment his face softens. Before he can say anything, I lean forward and kiss him. It's not chaste or slow: in fact, quite the opposite. I'm not sure what comes over me, but maybe it's the need to feel connected, or because I realize I had actually lost him.

Ethan brings his palms to my face to deepen the kiss and I feel that we're connected in a way that we could never have been before. We share a part of each other that's beyond human or Wisher. *We share a soul.* Now, together in this way, I feel whole again, and I know nothing will ever be the same. I pull away rapidly, shock settling over me.

"What?" he asks, searching my eyes carefully.

"I think you're right. This—this was supposed to happen from the beginning."

"You do?" he asks.

"That pull we feel when we're around each other is there for a reason. It was meant to bring us together because—the key is not just me, Ethan. I was never meant to do this alone. You were always meant to do it with me. That's what makes me different from all of the other Alphas," I say, becoming more confident as it all becomes clearer.

"How can you be sure?" he presses.

"I don't know why I know, but I know I'm right. I'm not going to question it. The more I think about it, the more it makes sense. Even your relationship with your family, how you moved to Wisconsin, the way I feel when I'm around you. Even during my blackouts and visions the Alphas encouraged me to trust you. I think it was Eve's plan from the beginning, we just had to execute it."

Ethan lets out a heavy breath. "This is a lot to take in."

"Tell me about it," I huff.

"Are you okay with this?" he coaxes, brushing some hair behind my ear.

"I wasn't sure at first, not because I don't want to share it with you, but because it makes you a target. But I'm glad to be sharing this with you and not with Isa or Chris."

Ethan gags a bit in jest. "Can we not bring him up?"

"*Jealous?*

"Never. You are mine now," he smiles, that dimple I love appearing.

I scrunch up my nose. "Please don't ever call me yours again. If anything, you're mine, seeing as I shared part of myself with you, in more ways than one," I quip.

He flushes a bit. "I do not mind being called yours."

"*You are so cheesy.* Maybe I don't want to share with you after all. I wonder if Eve will let me take it back?" I tease, looking up to the heavens in a pleading motion.

Ethan takes me by the waist and pulls me so I'm plastered against him. "Nope. No take backsies," he says smugly.

I laugh—a hearty laugh that resonates all the way in my toes. "You're such a weirdo. How am I finding this out now that I'm stuck with you?"

"I had to keep the bad parts hidden so you could not run away," he jokes.

"Good to know. I'm scared to see what else is revealed," I sing. I kiss his nose quickly before pulling back from him. "Now, as much as I like teasing you, we need to figure a few things out. We know you have some of my gifts, but do you have all of them?" I ask Ethan.

"You mean, do I know if I am immortal now?"

"Yes, but you know I'm not willing to test it."

"I am not going to ask you to kill me after you just saved me."

"Ok good, and don't think of doing it yourself either."

"Do not worry, no plans of doing that. I have far too much to live for," he says softly.

"Promise?"

He kisses me. "I promise."

I hug him close again, enjoying the sensation of completion and ease. I need to feel his aliveness for a moment before we head back into our crazy reality.

Eventually Ethan breaks our cocoon. "We need to get a hold of Isa. They should know what is going on, and we need to make sure they are safe."

I squeeze him tighter. "I'm sure they're okay. But we should come up with a plan."

"That is a good idea," he affirms.

"And I don't think we should tell them about what's

happened with you, Ethan. I think that's our secret weapon in a way. Do you agree?" I ask him.

"I did not think of that, but it is smart."

I step away from Ethan and walk towards the kitchen to grab us some water. As I fill up the glasses from the tap, I look around my home. Though it hasn't been long since I left, I missed it. It's as if I've been gone forever, even though it's only been a few days.

When I come back into the living area, Ethan's sitting at the kitchen table with his computer.

"What are you doing?" I set one of the glasses near him.

"I am tracking Isa."

"You can do that?"

"Yes, we have heavily protected security systems in place for situations like this. I can see where all members of The Council are at any moment, just in case we need to go and find them."

"That's handy...but wait! Can't they hack your computer?" I panic, ready to wish it away.

"I have a VPN blocker, among other precautions. Do not worry."

"Okay..." I say skeptically.

"After we took W.I.S.H. back from The Alliance, we made sure to have ways to find each other should we not be able to use a phone."

"Why don't we just wish them here?" I ask.

He contemplates that for a moment. "I suppose we could, but I think we should go to them. We do not know who could be on The Alliance's side. The system does not tell me if someone is a traitor."

"Fair point."

Ethan turns his attention back to the computer and after a few minutes he pulls up a screen with a map. It has several dots on it that look like heat signatures.

"Is that them?"

"This is Isa," he says, pointing to one of the dots. "They are all at headquarters still."

"Can you tell if she's hurt?" I ask, cautiously.

"I am not able to tell that, but I can tell she is alive."

I take a breath of relief, looking at the other dots. I notice Mary's there as well, surrounded by several other dots with names.

"Those are the other Council members?"

"Yes. It looks like they are all there. Including my mother and my father."

"Your dad?"

"Yes. I thought he was in the city today," he trails off.

"This could mean anything, right?"

"It could. I wish it would tell us if Alliance members are in the room as well. This just gives me the locations of people with trackers. We do not have trackers on everyone. At least not in this system."

"What about the security cameras? Could we get a view of the room they're in?"

Ethan looks shocked for a moment. "I cannot believe I did not think of that."

I smirk. "That's what I'm here for."

"You are a genius," he says giddily.

I chuckle. Ethan goes to work, typing away and doing whatever it is he's doing. A few minutes later he's accessed the security cameras to The Council room, which I inappropriately want to call the throne room—but I keep my mouth shut.

When the cameras are up it's apparent that our fears are warranted. The Council members I recognize from earlier are there, but there are many others I don't know. It looks like they are being held at gunpoint. Several guards are standing around the perimeter of the room, also with guns.

"That doesn't look good," I say, stating the obvious.

"No. It does not," he echoes.

"Can you get closer so we can see if Isa and Mary are there?"

Ethan looks for few moments, zooming in on different areas of the room.

"There is my father," he says, pointing to an older man. His dad's hair is graying and his face stern. He looks like an older version of Ethan, but much stuffier. He's wearing a tailored dark blue suit that makes him stand out among the rest of the people in the room. Ethan switches to another angle and I gasp. Isa is on the floor, her face white. Mary is next to her, holding her hand. Alice is on the other side of her, talking to Isa, and stroking her forehead.

"Shit," I say under my breath, grabbing Ethan's shoulder in support.

"She is alive, that is what matters," he swallows.

"She might not be for much longer if we don't get her help," I say.

Ethan stands. "We need to go to them."

"I know, but first you need to tell me who these people are. Do you recognize any of them?"

"Yes, this blonde woman here is Chris's mother," he says, pointing to a very pretty and stuffy-looking woman standing near Isa with a gun.

"No way! She looks so young."

"Botox."

I stifle a laugh.

"We are going to have to be very cautious of her. She is obviously not very happy about what you did to Chris," Ethan comments.

"Clearly, but that isn't an excuse to shoot people!" I cry.

"Unfortunately, she does not even need a reason. She has wanted this for years. What happened to Chris will only give her an excuse to make another move."

"What's her name?"

"Camilla Davis. Her husband is Albert. He is the tall man standing next to her."

I nod, noticing he looks just as young as Camilla.

"Does Chris have any siblings?" I ask him.

"No, an only child."

"Figures."

"Any chance you could bring him back? It might make bargaining a little easier," he wonders.

"Maybe? I have no idea where I sent him—but I also haven't tried to bring him back."

"Right."

"You know, you could also try, now that you have part of my gifts," I tell him.

His eyebrows fly up. "I could, I guess, but I really would like to leave him wherever he is. *Forever.*"

"I know you would—but maybe we should try."

"Hopefully he is alive so we can use him. Then when this is all over, we will lock him up forever."

I groan. "We're wasting time! Your sister is hurt. Who knows what Chris's parents are going to order The Alliance to do if we wait much longer. They have to know that we would come back eventually. Especially when Mary and Isa never showed up to meet us."

"All right. Wish him back," he says, now holding a gun in his hands and cocking it at the ready.

"Is that really necessary?"

"It is. I do not know what is going to come back. We have to be prepared for anything."

"Okay fine. Ready?"

"Ready."

I take a deep breath, Ethan giving me a nod of encouragement. I close my eyes, thinking of Chris, wishing him back. When I open my eyes, nothing has changed. I try again, asking the Alphas to help me, calling on them like I had when I was healing Ethan. I feel a little dizzy, like something is trying to help, but I can tell before I open my eyes that it still isn't working.

"Nothing," I vocalize to Ethan, rubbing my temples a little.

"Maybe if we try together?"

"Powers combined?" I joke.

"Worth a shot," he says before tucking his gun inside the waist of his pants. He grabs my hands in his.

"Is the hand-holding necessary?" I cackle. "We aren't witches."

"Powers combined," he reiterates with a playful shrug.

I roll my eyes. "Okay, on three we'll think of Chris together. Try to focus on bringing him here in front of us."

"Got it," he says, squeezing my hands.

"One, two, three!"

We both squeeze our eyes shut, but after a few moments we hear nothing. I open my eyes to find Ethan staring at me.

"Nothing," he says.

"I don't know what else to try."

"Eve was never able to bring back Adam..."

"And she never figured out where he went. I'm guessing that's what happened to Chris," I sigh. "I really do feel bad. I never meant to hurt him."

"I know, but it is not your fault."

"It really is," I mumble. "But let's not argue about that now. We have to get to your sister and the others."

"Except we do not have Chris, and now we know we

cannot get him back."

"We have to go without him and hope they will listen to us regardless."

"And if they do not?

"I put them all in chains and we go from there," I state.

"If The Alliance was able to infiltrate W.I.S.H. like they did tonight, that means there are a lot more members than we originally thought. Look at all the guards they have on their side. Who knows how many people they have all over the world supporting them."

"Then what do you suggest we do?" I huff.

"I honestly do not know."

"I want you to stay here," I hurriedly say.

"What? Why?" Ethan startles.

"They don't know you share my gifts. If something happens to me, you can zap yourself in and come to the rescue. We can get Isa and everyone out. That's our main priority right now. Then we figure the rest out later."

"No," he snaps.

"Ethan," I say tiredly. "I know you want to protect me, but I think this is the best option. If you don't agree I'll trap you here somehow and you won't even be able to come and rescue me if I need it."

He sighs. "This is what you really want? To walk in

there and hope they decide not to burn you to death or worse?"

"What's worse than burning me to death?" I almost laugh at that silly statement.

"Torture."

I shudder. "*Okay*—didn't think of that. Thanks for putting that in my head."

"Now you understand why I am not happy about this plan."

"I know you're not, but you brought me here to begin with. You came to Wisconsin to tell me who I was and bring me to Massachusetts. What did you expect was going to happen when everything came to a head? My dad tried to protect me my entire life, and now you are doing the same thing. You know what I'm capable of. Hell, you're capable of it now too. I'm going to do this no matter how you feel."

"I know," he says in resignation.

"Then why are you fighting me? We're losing time."

"You are right. Go."

"You realize I'd go even if you said no."

He smiles. "I know."

"Just so we're clear on that," I punctuate.

I pull back from him, taking a moment to ground

myself. I close my eyes and inhale—silently asking the Alphas for their strength and guidance. I feel them within me, like energy solidifying into a singular unit—we're one Alpha in this moment. As I'm about to wish myself to The Council room, I feel lips on mine. I smile against them, wrapping my arms around Ethan's neck, his hands going around my waist to grip me tightly.

A few moments go by before I pull back from him with my hands on either side of his face. I place one more kiss on his lips and grin. "Watch from the computer. I'll wish you there if I need help."

"Or I will do it myself," he grins.

"I know, just don't jump the gun. I don't want them to know you can do what I can do. We don't know if you're immortal, and I really don't want you to die again."

"All right, I won't."

"Promise?"

"I promise."

"Good." I step away from him.

"Be safe."

"You, too," I tell him. Then I'm gone.

CHAPTER 23

In the blink of an eye I'm standing outside The Council room.

Two male guards stand before the large silver doors with their hands on their guns. It takes them a hot second to realize that someone has materialized before them, but by the time they've noticed I've already bound their hands with my gifts—their guns seamlessly turning into boxes around their hands. I smile with satisfaction as they just stare at me, wide-eyed.

"Can I go in or do I have to knock you out as well?" I say smugly.

"Are you the Alpha?" One of them stutters. I hear the fear in his voice.

"And if I say yes?"

They both look at each other, before turning back to me in disbelief.

"You're just a little girl," the other sneers.

"Well this *little girl* just bested you both. Now enough small talk, I need to save the day here," I deadpan.

"I thought you'd be scarier," says the first one.

"Look, I really don't have time to deal with this."

I think about what I can do to make the announcement of my gifts more prominent for when I need a little dramatic flair. Then it occurs to me—I snap my fingers for effect, wishing them both asleep. Instantly both guards fall to the floor in a messy heap, one right on top of the other.

"That did the trick," I say to myself before stepping over their bodies. I take a deep breath. *Ok, Alphas. It's showtime.*

I wish the doors open and am immediately assaulted by a woman's voice yelling. It's soon followed by a man yelling back to her. Then silence. I glance around the room to see it filled with more people than I had seen through the security camera. The guards all throw their attention towards me, their guns coming to aim directly at me in trained precision. I feel every eyeball on me, and I hear every breath.

I turn my gaze to Camilla, Chris's mom. She's staring at me with shock, awe, and a whole lot of rage. We stare each other down for a few moments. She can't believe that I'm actually here. When I can't handle it anymore, I break the silence.

"I think you're looking for me?" I say, trying to sound confident.

"Sophia Black," she says icily.

"The one and only—but please, call me *Sophie.*"

"Sophie, you shouldn't be here!" I hear a voice say weakly off to my side. I don't dare glance over. I know it's Isa.

"Isa, are you okay?" I ask, keeping my eyes trained on Camilla.

"I'll live," she wheezes.

Camilla smirks at that, her eyes unblinking. She's beautiful, but oh boy, is she scary.

"I have to admit, I wasn't sure you were going to show," she clips before walking towards me.

"Surprise!" I say, cheekily.

"You have your father's sense of humor," she says vacantly.

"Do I?" I ask.

"Though he's not here to joke now, is he?" she half-smiles. I almost jump across the room and punch her.

"I see Chris takes after you," I sneer back. If she wants to play dirty, we're going to play dirty.

"Don't talk about my son!" she yells, her shrill voice

410

echoing. The man who Ethan pointed out as Chris's father, Albert, steps forward, placing a hand on his wife's shoulder. She breaks her eye contact with me and tries to regain her composure. Albert looks at me, his eyes bitter and icy. It was like Chris had come back to haunt me; they look so similar.

"I'm sorry if I upset you, but seeing as The Alliance murdered my dad, maybe we're even now," I sling, the comment out of my mouth before I can stop it.

"You admit it then. You killed my son," Albert states before Camilla can retort.

I hesitate. "I don't know. It's only a guess. I don't know where I've sent him, and I tried to bring him back, but it didn't work."

"You little —"

"Camilla, calm down," Albert barks, effectively stopping her comment. I'm surprised at his tone with her.

"Al, how can you —"

"Just hold on," he cuts her off again before leaving her side to step closer to me.

As he stands before me, I look beyond him to scan the room. The guards are still waiting for orders to shoot me and Isa is now propped up on Alice's legs, her face pale and sweaty. Mary looks calm, like there's a smile on her face for

411

some reason. She nods at me, urging me forward toward Albert with her eyes. The other Council members look scared, or indifferent, I can't really tell. Then there's Ethan's dad. He sticks out among the others in that blue suit, standing on the other side of the room from Isa and Alice. I think it's odd that he's not consoling his family, but I don't have time to question it. I can only guess they're being kept apart for a reason.

I look back into Albert's steely blue eyes, his expression unreadable.

"My name is Albert," he says, surprising me by extending his hand towards mine.

This guy wants to shake my hand? I look at it, then back up at his face.

"Really?" I ask in disbelief, echoing my thoughts to him.

"I know what you must think—but let me tell you I don't entirely agree with my wife or my son's actions."

"Albert!" Camilla exclaims.

I raise an eyebrow at him. This just got interesting.

"Camilla," he says sternly. "Let me talk to her—I won't ask again."

I watch as Camilla deflates. It seems like Chris really takes after his father. I already don't like Camilla, but I also don't like assholes. Albert turns back to me, composing himself with a forced smile.

"Now, *Sophie*, I know you don't agree with our methods, and I know what you've heard about The Alliance from our own kind, but I'd like time to explain to you our point of view. You are the Alpha after all—I don't want to hurt you. Neither do any of the other Wishers in this room."

I gesture to all the guards with guns. "You could have fooled me."

"Men put your guns down," Albert orders. They hesitate but eventually do as he orders.

"Do you really think that proves anything to me? Your group shot Isa. You tried to kill Ethan, and God knows who else. Not to mention you attempted to kidnap me only a few days ago. Tell me how what you just said makes any sense," I say with disbelief.

"I know what it looks like, but we had no choice."

"Really? Because I'm pretty sure you always have a choice."

"We just want to talk to you," he says calmly.

"Normally when people want to talk to someone, they call them or invite them out for coffee. They don't send their son to spy on them for years, assault them, and then

try to kidnap them."

"Chris was a loose cannon. I love my son, but you're right. We shouldn't have sent him. That was a mistake," Albert concedes.

I hear Camilla let a hiss out under her breath at his words. Albert ignores it, trying to keep his wits about him.

"And what about all this bullshit?" I say, gesturing around the room. "What's your excuse?"

"You sure have a mouth on you, don't you?" he says in a way that makes me want to knee him in the crotch.

"If you're trying to get in my good graces, you're not doing a great job," I snarl through my teeth.

He smirks before looking me up and down like he's trying to figure me out.

"You're not what I expected," he says after a few seconds.

"Did you expect someone more compliant? Because that's not me, nor will it ever be."

"I'm gathering that," he mumbles.

I stop myself from rolling my eyes. "Look, Al," I say casually. "I know we just met each other, but I'd like to think that we could work together here."

"Never," Camilla's voice bites through the air.

Albert gives her a disapproving look. Camilla stiffens

414

and bites her lip.

He looks back at me. "What do you suggest?"

I take a deep breath, making myself as tall as possible before placing my hands on my hips. I probably don't look menacing, but I feel all the power inside me, and I don't feel scared. Not in the slightest.

"First, I want you to let me heal Isa or at least get her medical attention. Then we can sit down and have a nice adult conversation. No guns. No funny business."

His face looks surprised. "You can heal her?"

"Alpha, remember?"

"But you're not twenty-five," Albert says.

"Technicality," I shrug.

"How is that possible?" he demands.

"It doesn't matter now," I say impatiently. "Either you let me help her, or I put you all in chains."

"You think that would hold us?" he sneers.

"Maybe not forever, but long enough to figure out what to do with you," I say calmly.

"You'd just dispose of us then?" he asks. "How does that make you any better than the way we've chosen to handle this situation?

"I'm not evil, and I don't want anyone to die. What happened to Chris was an accident. I didn't even know I had gifts at the time, much less that I was even capable of making someone disappear. If I could bring him back I would. I tried; *I really did.* I don't want death and violence; I want to work together."

"Charming," Camilla snickers. "Did this little Council over here tell you to say that?"

I roll my eyes again. Annoyance flashes across Albert's face at her voice, but Camilla ignores him this time. She comes to stand in front of him, very close to me now.

"Did they?" she asks again.

"No, they didn't. I know more about the Alphas and what's best for Wishers than you ever will. Don't think you know better than me," I practically growl.

"Please, you know nothing! You're a child. Not to mention you just discovered who you are. How could you possibly know what we know? How could you understand what we've been through?"

"I don't have to justify myself to you, Camilla. I don't need to. I'm the Alpha, and if you know anything about the Alphas at all, you would know not to question how or why I know things."

"So, they came to you then? The other Alphas?" a new male voice chimes in. Everyone turns to Ethan's dad. Then, what he just said hits me like a ton of bricks.

416

"How would you know about that?" I ask him, cautiously.

He seems to fumble a little. I glance at Isa, Alice, and Mary, who are all looking at him like he'd grown another head. Albert and Camilla don't look surprised as much as they look angry.

He takes a moment to gather himself and stands a little taller.

"*Well*—I knew your father."

"I know that, but how would my dad know? Nobody should have known that except for me and who I told in the last 24-hours."

"I guess you don't know everything then, do you?" Camilla interrupts smugly.

"George," Alice says to her husband, her voice shaky and timid. "How would you know that?"

"George. I think it's time," Albert says in a stern tone.

"Time for what?" Isa asks desperately. "Dad? What is he saying?"

Shit! Now I wish Ethan had come, or that those damn security cameras had sound.

"Seems like your Georgie-boy here is as dirty as Albert and Camilla," I say in realization to Isa and Alice. "You're on their side, aren't you?" I ask George. His grey eyes turn to look at me. If I didn't know any better, I'd say he looks almost remorseful.

"Dad…?" Isa asks again, weak and hopeful.

"George," Alice pleads.

"I'm sorry," he says finally, not needing to say anymore.

Albert smiles pompously as George walks to stand next to him and Camilla.

Alice leaves Isa to stand next to me, determined. George makes eye contact with her but doesn't say a word. For a moment, I think she might hit him across the face, but instead she starts to cry silently.

"How could you?" Alice hiccups.

"I hope you realize how rich that is coming from you, *darling*," George sneers.

Hurt colors Alice's face. "What do you mean?"

He laughs condescendingly. "You had an affair with my *best* friend. If anyone knows anything about keeping secrets it's you, Alice." His voice drips with spite. "After what happened you expected me to simply go on with my life, doing whatever you said, and helping your kind while I got shit out of it," he scoffs.

"I thought we worked through this!" she cries.

He laughs again. "Obviously not, *darling*. Admit it, you never cared about my feelings. You married me for my

418

money and the Moore name, not because you loved me."

"George!" she grabs his arm suddenly. "You know that's not true!"

He yanks it away. "But isn't it? You had an affair with Robert and lied to me about it for years. I worked side by side with you both, and I thought I was helping. I thought I was doing good."

"You were! I told you I was sorry for what happened," she cries louder.

"It was never good enough, Alice."

"So you joined The Alliance to get back at me?" she balks.

"You give yourself too much credit, my dear. I joined them because it was the right thing to do. Because they care about what happens to this world, unlike you and your selfish society."

"I can't believe you would go against your own family! After everything we've been through, you chose to believe their lies because your feelings got hurt?" she yells.

"Please!" he mocks. "Isa's hated me since the moment she found out she was a Wisher. My own son refused to follow in my footsteps. Then you, *my dear wife*, cheated on me with my supposed friend. As far as I'm concerned, I have no family," he booms.

"Father?" a male voice rings through The Council room.

Everyone turns directly behind me and my stomach drops at the sight of him. I should have known he couldn't stay away, but I guess I got my wish.

"Ethan?" George echoes, his voice losing a little of its bravado. "How did you get in here?"

He looks to me desperately as I see him try to think of what to say.

"I wished him here," I say, covering quickly. "He deserves to know who his dad truly is."

"You are working for them?" Ethan asks, the hurt evident in his voice. He stands next to Alice and me, his body wooden and eyes wide.

"I'm sorry, son. I didn't want you to find out this way," George says, trying to keep his tone neutral.

"Right. Well, it seems I sorely misjudged my own father's character," he jeers.

"Tell me, Ethan. Did you know about your mother's treachery against me?"

Ethan looks down. "Not until recently."

"I didn't think so," George says. "Your mother and sister always did like to keep things from you."

Ethan stiffens at that, looking toward Isa who's still

being tended to by Mary. She looks up at him, regretful. After a second, Ethan turns back to George, his face unreadable once more.

"Why did you not tell me, *George?*" he asks. It isn't lost on anyone that he hasn't called him father this time. George doesn't flinch over it.

"I thought you would think less of me," George answers easily.

"That is ridiculous. Why would I think less of you?"

"Because I am your father. Because I am the man of the household. I taught you how to be a man of character, how to keep a house and home in line. How to manage money and your women. Yet, I could not even manage my own," George says with disdain.

"Misogyny much?" I cut in. "Does it run in the water here or something?"

Everyone in the room looks at me like I've grown another head. Ethan, however, is apologetic. I feel sorry for him that he was raised by such a prick.

George blinks at me angrily before turning his attention back to Ethan.

"I am disappointed in you, Ethan. You were supposed to have my back. You were supposed to take over for me like any worthy son should. You failed me. You cared more about your club and this Alpha," he taunts, turning to glare at me.

I shiver under his gaze. It's undeniable to see what kind of man George truly is; it's sad and, quite frankly, disgusting. I have never been happier to know that Ethan is nothing like him, besides maybe his tendency to be over-protective.

"I am sorry I am such a disappointment," Ethan interrupts my thoughts. "But you know that I want the same things you want. I, too, want this world to be a better place and this *Alpha* is the answer to that. She always has been, and she always will be," he finishes with certainty.

George studies Ethan before turning his attention to me. I can tell he wants to say something more, but Albert steps forward.

"I am sorry to interrupt this family moment, but we have more pressing matters to attend to," he says with sarcasm.

I exhale. "I hate to admit it, but you're right."

Ethan nods curtly but keeps his fists clenched at his sides. I see them turning white from how hard he's squeezing.

"Well," I say after a few seconds. "Even though Georgie-boy here has betrayed his family and is an all-around asshole, I still want to heal his daughter. Then I want to talk." I see George flinch and glare at me. He must not like his nickname, I think to myself with a smirk.

"Very well then," Albert agrees, gesturing to Isa.

"Sophia," Ethan says, grabbing my hand. "Are you sure?"

I pull my hand from his, noticing George watching us closely. I don't want him to get any ideas about Ethan and me.

"I'm sure Ethan, it will all be fine," I assure him.

I know he's worried that I'll give another part of my soul to Isa, but I have a feeling the only reason Ethan had that side-effect was because he had been dead, and because he was meant to have it.

I walk toward Isa and sit down beside her, opposite Mary.

"It's good to see you, dear," Mary says with exhaustion.

"You too, Mary. I'm glad you're okay."

She nods at me, looking down at Isa who's obviously in pain.

"Isa, I'm sorry this happened to you. I can help," I tell her.

"Thank you, I—" she says weakly.

"Shhh, let's just get through this and we'll talk later."

"I think it's broken too," she says, looking down at her leg.

I glance up quickly to see that pretty much every person in the room has gathered around to watch. Ethan looks on worriedly, while George, Albert, and Camilla are difficult to read. Alice sits next to Isa and grabs her free hand. She's barely keeping it together after finding out the truth about George.

"Okay, so you should feel some warmth," I tell Isa. "I've only done it once so I'm not sure if it will be the same for you."

"Are you sure you can do this, dear?" Mary asks.

"Yes, I can do it," I reassure them all.

"Stop wasting time and just do it," Camilla snaps.

I grit my teeth. "Are you ready, Isa?" She nods sharply. "Brace yourself," I whisper.

CHAPTER 24

"Are you ready, Isa?" She nods sharply. "Brace yourself," I whisper.

I look at the shot wound on Isa's thigh. It's clear of any fabric, obviously having been ripped open by someone trying to stop the bleeding. I place my hands over the area, hoping I'm right in assuming nothing like last time is going to happen.

I close my eyes and focus the best I can with everyone watching me. I feel the now familiar tingling come to my hands. Before long, it feels like hot fire spreading through my arms and out of my fingers into her leg. I hear Isa gasp, then a scream echoes from her lips throughout the room, followed by a loud snap. I feel hands trying to pull me off of her, and hear some yelling in the background, but I hold firm. Then it's done. I open my eyes and look to Isa who's breathing a little heavy, but seems fine—the color already returning to her cheeks.

"Are you okay?" I ask breathlessly.

She nods despite her obvious shock. I examine where the wound had been and sure enough, it's healed. Now it's just blood and torn clothes. I sigh in relief, glad that went smoother than the last time.

"Help me stand her up," I say, turning my attention toward Ethan. The room is deathly quiet. I feel everyone's eyes on me; it's unnerving. Ethan helps with Isa and once she's standing on her own, I pat her on the back.

"You should be all right now. How do you feel?"

"I-I think I'm ok. Whatever you did hurt like hell, but I feel just as I did before, if not better."

"Good," I say, looking down at my hands, now covered in Moore blood for a second time that night. I quickly wish my skin and clothes clean without a second thought.

"It's really that easy for you?" Albert asks with interest, eventually breaking the tense silence of the room.

"It is." I raise my shoulders, unsure of what else to say.

"Interesting," George mumbles.

"*And useful,*" Albert adds.

"Of course it's useful, Albert," Camilla belittles. "But you can't think that's any reason to—"

"Camilla, please. If you can't keep your thoughts to yourself, you need to leave," Albert hushes her.

426

It was too late, I know what she wanted to say. Ethan stands protectively next to me, anger emanating from his body. Albert eyes Ethan warily before looking at George like he knows something we don't. I know they've figured out we're together. I need to try and change the subject before it can be voiced or used against us.

I clear my throat. "I get that you don't like me, Albert, and I know that you're afraid of what I can do. But let's be clear on this—I don't want to hurt anyone. I just want to find a way for all of us to work together. We all have different views, but that doesn't mean we can't find some common ground."

"Do you really think you can solve everything by holding hands and singing Kumbaya?" Albert laughs. "Your father had a similar outlook and look where that got him," he says in a threatening tone.

I clench my jaw. "I won't begin to pretend I know exactly what we're going to do, or how we're going to do it, but what do you plan to do? Rule the world with an iron fist? Use me to heal, create, and do your bidding like a pet? Think again," I growl.

"I'm sure we can come to an agreement on how to use your gifts, *Sophie*," he leers.

I roll my eyes and snap my fingers dramatically. In an

instant, Albert, George, and Camilla are all tied up, their legs and hands bound with rope and mouths taped shut. They drop to the floor with a thud like bags of flour.

A thin grin forms on Ethan's lips. "Did you really have to snap your fingers?"

"I tried it out on some guards earlier. It's effective, don't you think?" I grin back at him.

"Um, guys," Isa's weary voice cuts through our little ego-fest.

When we turn around, all the guards have their guns pointed directly at us. I know I should have been worried, but I wasn't in the slightest. I want to laugh at their stupidity. Do they think their guns would do them any good? I mean, I don't want to get shot, but I can't die either. If they were smart, they would have shot immediately, not waited. I snap my fingers again, effectively turning their guns into toys. I giggle a little at the look of shock on their faces. After a few seconds they lower them to the ground, a few of them holding up their hands in surrender.

"You're having way too much fun with this, dear," Mary scolds playfully, but I can tell she's trying not to laugh.

"I don't mean for it to be fun. They were just pissing me off," I say, looking at Albert, George, and Camilla on

428

the ground, faces red as they struggle against their many layers of binding.

"So much for talking to them," Ethan mumbles.

"I guess my plan was a bad one, but I really did try. If only they would listen," I say loud enough for all three of them to hear. They just grunt in response.

Albert's struggling against his gag the most. He obviously has something he wants to say. I snap my fingers again, the tape disappearing from his mouth.

"What do you want?" I say in a frustrated tone, my hands gripping my hips.

"You made your point," he utters.

"Really? That's all it took? How stupid do you think I am?" I trill. "You've all tried my patience—honestly I'm over it."

"I'm sorry," he says with false truth. "We can work together."

I raise an eyebrow at him. "Right, and I'm Santa Claus." I snort.

"You could be," Ethan says smartly.

I pinch my lips together. "Anyway, I think I'm done trying to be nice. It seems you all had other plans for me that weren't very kind," I say sarcastically. "I think we all need to take time to figure some things out and cool off."

"What are you going to do then, keep us locked up? You know we'll get out eventually and then what? No matter what happens we'll keep coming for you, until you either agree to work with us, or we kill you. It will never end," he scowls.

"You can think that," I state confidently before snapping my fingers again. His mouth is again covered with tape, and I'm happy for the silence.

"Really? The snapping?" Ethan asks.

"Just go with it," I wave him off.

The room is still mostly silent, the guards at an obvious loss. I can tell they don't know what to do next. They're all avoiding eye contact with me, obviously scared about what I could do to them. Even though they would try to kill me without a second thought, I feel bad for making them fear me.

The Council members are now standing in a group. Isa and Mary at the front of them, Alice to the side. It's clear Alice is still trying to keep herself together. Despite her relationship with my dad, I feel for her situation. I wouldn't wish her misogynistic traitor of a husband on anyone.

"Sophia?" Ethan asks, placing his hand on my shoulder. "What do you want to do?"

"I —" I pause. *Fudge.* I really didn't think this far

ahead. I rub my temples, realizing I could really use a hot bath and some sleep to clear my head.

"I think we should take care of these guards," Isa says then, saving me from further embarrassment. At her words I see them all stiffen. I try to give them a reassuring smile, but it doesn't work.

"I don't want to hurt any of you," I say, projecting my voice so that it reverberates against the walls of the room. "*I promise* that I won't hurt any of you," I rephrase. "But The Society needs your loyalty," I continue, not sure where I'm going with this. "You've seen what I can do. You've seen what can be done. I don't want your fear, I just want your help. We all want your help. If you don't want to join us, you can leave. I won't stop you," I say truthfully.

"Sophie —" Isa tries to interrupt me.

"No, Isa. This is their choice," I tell her before turning back to the guards who are now watching me intently. "I'm not going to try and get any of you on my side. Believe me when I say I won't ever force any of you. That choice has to come from you and you alone."

One of the guards steps forward, looking a little frightened, but also determined.

"They promised us money and power, that we'd matter in the world," he says, standing at attention.

I nod at him. "Can I ask you your name?"

He looks a little stunned but answers anyway. "My name is Jackson."

"Jackson," I repeat. "how old are you?"

"35."

"And your family, are they Wishers?"

"My dad is, yes."

"Is he here?"

"No, he works a normal job in Boston. Lives with my mom and my younger sister."

"Does he know you're here? That you're a part of The Alliance?"

"Yes, he knows."

"I'm guessing he belongs to the group as well?"

Jackson bobs his head hesitantly but keeps his eyes locked with mine. He's still afraid I'm going to zap him into oblivion.

"I'm not going to hurt you or your family. I promise. No matter what they told you I would do or could do. I'm not going to do that."

"How do we know we can trust you?" he asks, his voice gaining a little more bravado.

"Sonny," Mary's voice cuts in. "If she meant any harm, she would've sent you and your leaders here to wherever

432

she sent Chris's patootie. That should have been your first clue."

I stifle a laugh. "Thanks, Mary."

"Anytime, dear," she smiles.

I look back at Jackson. "Though I don't necessarily agree with Mary's veiled threat, she's right. I haven't done that, and I won't. Jackson, are you in charge of these men and women?"

"Yes," he answers.

"What will it take for all of you to believe me? To fight with us instead of against us?" I ask him honestly.

Jackson looks towards the trio on the floor, who have now gone completely silent. Albert's glaring at the young guard, trying to threaten him with his eyes.

Jackson's gaze flickers back to mine. "We need to know that our families and friends will be protected from Alliance members. That you will work with us for what we want and deserve. We've hidden our gifts from the world for hundreds of years. A lot of us even hide them from friends and family who are non-Wishers. You can't understand what's it like to live such a lie. We won't do that anymore; it has to end."

"I do understand. But you know that we can't just do that all at once, right? We'd throw the world into chaos.

Wishers would be killed by non-Wishers in fear. History would repeat itself all over again."

"But with you, we won't have to hide anymore," Jackson says hesitantly. "You're a god."

That word. It's always going haunt me. I don't like it, but I realize as everyone in the room looks to me, that's what I am to them. It's what the Alphas have always been to them. Alphas were feared because Wishers and non-Wishers alike didn't understand them and were never given a chance too. Making Alphas gods made them easier to fear and to worship.

I take a deep breath and look Jackson in the eyes. "I can't promise the change you want right away, but I can promise change. I can't do this without your help. I need all of you to help me. We're in this together," I say, addressing the entire room.

Jackson seems hesitant, but then he steps forward. Ethan goes to stand between us but I stop him with my arm. When Jackson is within arm's reach, he puts a hand forward to shake mine. I smile before reaching out to grasp his hand.

"Thank you, Jackson."

"I hope you can keep your word," he says, gripping my hand tighter.

"I will try my best to be what you all need me to be," I

say honestly. "Now, I want you to tell everyone you know what happened here. I want you to bring them to me and we'll have a meeting. I'll speak to The Council and figure out all the details. But no weapons, no fighting, no killing. Do you understand?"

"Yes," he agrees.

"I realize we don't know each other, but we're going to have to learn to trust."

"I understand," he says.

"Are there more of you in the building?"

"Yes. We're stationed throughout. We've taken other Wishers into custody that wouldn't agree to join us."

"Has anyone else been killed?"

"Not that I know of."

"Injuries?"

"A few gunshot wounds, but nothing fatal."

"Thank you, Jackson."

He nods curtly. "You'll really help us?"

"That's the plan," I tell him.

"Thank you," he says before stepping back into line with the other guards.

"The rest of you," I say to the others. "If you don't want to help us, as I said, you can walk out of here right now. I'll even wish you wherever you'd like to go."

A few voices spread through the crowd.

"You can really do that?" a female guard says from within the line, her expression curious.

"I can."

A few more murmurs echo against the walls, but after a minute there's silence.

"Any takers?" I ask.

When nobody says anything, I smile. At least something's going right. It's almost too easy...

"Council?" I ask, not really sure how else to address the group before me. "Can you take these people and get them rooms to stay in while we figure out this mess?" I ask, pointing to the three tied up.

"Do you really—" Isa tries to interject.

"I really. Please, help them find rooms."

Isa gives a few instructions to The Council members behind her and soon they're leading the hesitant guards out.

"Thank you," Jackson says to me again. "I hope we can end all of this infighting and violence. We don't need any more death."

"I agree with you. And thank you for listening," I say truthfully. I turn to Mary as he leaves. "Mary, will you supervise?"

"Of course, dear," she says, squeezing my hand gently.

436

"Call me if you need any help."

"I'm sure we'll be fine."

Once she's gone with the rest, only Ethan, Isa, and Alice stay behind.

"What do we do with them?" Ethan asks, his eyes on his dad.

I sigh. "I'm not sure. They'll get out of those restraints eventually if we just leave them," I trail off. Before I really give it any thought, I snap my fingers again so they're free of all their bindings. I want to talk to them now that most everyone is gone with no barriers. They all stand up, dusting themselves off and grumbling angrily.

"You bitch," Camilla screeches, stalking up to me. I snap my fingers again and her hands are restrained right before she tries to slap me.

"Don't even try it," I snap at her. She huffs, fighting against her bound hands.

"You'll never win, you know," she snarls.

"This isn't a game! I don't know why it's so hard for you to understand that."

"You don't fool me," she says dryly.

"I'm not trying to fool you."

"You think you can just walk in here and destroy everything we've built just by flashing around your gifts and

437

your kindness act? It won't work."

"Camilla, I don't know what else to tell you, except that you're wrong about me."

"You're together, aren't you?" A male voice cuts in.

Camilla stops talking, and everyone faces George, who's looking between Ethan and me knowingly.

"Well, aren't you?" George asks again.

My nerves kick in a little, but I try to keep myself calm. "I don't know what you mean."

"Don't play cute, you're in love with my son," he snips.

I don't flinch. I had hoped George wouldn't voice his observation. I should have kept those gags on.

"I saw it, too," Albert chimes in. "Your son is just like you, George. *Soft*. Can't even go babysit a girl without falling in love with her."

George pivots to Albert, obvious anger in his eyes. Ethan is clenching his fists again, trying to hold himself back.

Albert laughs mechanically. "This makes things a little more interesting."

"I don't see how my love life is relevant," I finally say.

"It makes you weak, that's what," Albert sneers.

"You would think that, Albert. But I beg to differ. However, I'm not arguing about this. We have bigger fish to fry here."

"Yes, like your stupidity," he snarls.

Ugh, this man annoys me. I want to erase his mouth from his face. That would make things a lot simpler. Maybe I could try that next...

"Albert," I say tiredly. "How many times do I have to tell you people that I don't want to fight with you. Please don't give me a reason to wish you wherever I sent your son. I'd rather not!" I know I wouldn't do that to him, but I had to make him scared of me somehow.

Thankfully, the warning seems to shut him up a bit. When I glance at George, I can tell he's out of his element by how unsure he looks. I wonder if he never really meant to get involved in this whole thing.

"George?" I ask him, my mind going to his earlier comment. "How did you know that the Alphas can communicate with me?"

"Wouldn't you like to know," he says pompously.

A sickening crunch resounds, and instantly George crumples to the ground. It all happens so fast that even if I had wanted to stop it I couldn't. Ethan has lunged at George, hitting him square across the jaw. George spits out blood on to the floor.

"Ethan!" Alice cries. For a second she thinks about

going to George, but Isa stops her.

"He deserves it," Ethan yells to Alice. "You," he bites at George. "You deserve more than just a punch to the face. Now tell us what you know, *father*, or I will knock some of your teeth out next," Ethan threatens.

"I've always loved a good family drama," Albert sneers, sarcasm dripping from his words.

"I thought you were on George's side? Or did childhood trauma lead to your own loyalty issues?" I throw back at him.

"That lovely mouth of yours needs to close around something other than your teeth, my dear," he degrades.

Despite my dream of kneeing Albert in the groin, I quickly wish his mouth shut again, along with another round of hand bindings.

I look down at George who's still on the floor nursing his jaw.

"Now tell me what you know, George," I demand. "Or I'll sick Ethan on you."

His eyes bat to Ethan—he looks menacing to say the least.

George takes a shaky breath. "When Robert and I were working together, I found out you were the Alpha. I knew he was protecting you, but eventually he trusted me to keep his secret and told me himself. In order to fully protect you, Robert wanted to know everything he could about the Alphas. He knew I had the resources and money to search the world for whatever we could find on Wishers. Especially because of my ancestry. Nobody knew we were working together on this; we kept it a secret from everyone. Eventually we discovered a journal owned by a very old Wisher in Iraq. Her name was Zahra. She said it has been in her family forever and claimed that it belonged to Eve."

"Where's the journal now?" I ask eagerly.

"I burned it."

I let out a sad wail. *"Excuse me?"*

"Robert asked me to burn it. He didn't want it in the hands of the wrong people. It's been gone for years."

"What did it say?" I demand.

"Honestly, I don't know. I never read it. Your father just told me a few things about what he'd learned. That's how I knew."

"Don't lie to me."

"I'm not lying. I have no reason to. You've made it clear who's in charge now," he says, his voice cold.

I rub my hands on my face, feeling a loss form deep within me. The fact that my dad allegedly had a journal from Eve and destroyed it was devastating. I hope that maybe he'd kept a copy somewhere, or at least notes. I can't believe he'd be that stupid.

"Was it you who betrayed him?" Alice's voice slices through the air.

Then it all comes together like a puzzle, and I can't help the gasp that escapes my lips.

"Of course it was," George states clearly.

My eyes go wide, and my mouth falls open. I had wanted to believe that he at least had some remorse for stabbing his family in the back, but that isn't the case at all.

"Did you kill him?" I croak. The room is so quiet, my question hangs in the air like dead weight.

"Yes," he finally answers. "It was easy. Everyone here thought it was just a stroke, but if they paid attention, people would have realized it was poison."

I try not to react. I don't want him to see how his words affect me. My dad, regardless of his mistakes, didn't deserve to die that way. Especially at the hands of his friend.

"I can't believe you," Alice cries, fresh tears forming in her eyes.

Isa, who has been silent for a while, stands next to me. She's trying to hold herself together, her eyes more steely than usual.

"Dad," she says cautiously, her voice weak. George's eyes lock on Isa, and for a moment I think I see his cold gaze falter.

"Did you mean what you said earlier? About me?"

He stares at her for a long moment, but I'm not sure if it's for dramatic effect or out of contemplation that he takes his time to answer.

"Isabel," he finally answers. "You were my princess. I wanted to give you the world. But the moment you chose W.I.S.H. over me, was the moment you weren't mine anymore."

"Right," she says, her eyes glassy. She holds back the tears and composes herself. I have to give her credit. Isa's good at shoving emotions down. I don't think I could have done that.

As I go to step in front of Isa to look George in the eye, an all too familiar sound shoots through the room. Several screams rip into the air. When my brain catches up to the fact that it's a gunshot, I immediately look to see if Ethan's been shot again. The look of shock on his face is clear, but he's unhurt. A breath of relief rushes out of my body. Ethan lunges forward toward George who's now on the floor with blood pooling around him. My head flips back to Isa when she lets out a painful cry of anguish. Alice soon follows, running over to her husband who is now dying on the floor.

When I see Alice isn't the source of the gunshot, I quickly turn toward Albert and Camilla. Albert is holding the smoking gun with a pleased smirk on his face. How could I have been so stupid to unbind him! When we were distracted by the Moore family soap opera, he took advantage of the situation.

Albert grins wildly at me before aiming his firearm at Ethan's head. Without a second thought, I leap in front of Albert just as the gun goes off. The pain in my chest is immediate and explosive. I cry out in a voice that doesn't even sound like my own as I fall to the ground in a helpless heap. It's strange, the pain feels all-consuming yet numbing at the same time. I gulp painful breaths of air as I try to reconcile what I did. It doesn't take long for Ethan's face to come into my view. He's shouting at me, but everything sounds hollow and far away. When the pain begins to lessen, and my ears start to clear, the room is in complete chaos. I hope that someone got to Albert before he shot another person. I know I'll be fine, even if I die. I'll come back.

Ethan's hands grip my cheeks, and his voice invades my brain.

444

"Sophia!" he cries, "Sophia, why did you do that?"

I give him the best smile I can muster through my pain. "Didn't know if you'd die for good this time. I couldn't...I couldn't risk it," I grimace.

Ethan shakes his head in disbelief. "You are insane, you know that?"

"I know." I cough violently, blood coming up. I wince.

"Shhh, rest now," Ethan says calmly, stroking my hair in a very loving gesture. "Everything is going to be fine. I will be here when you wake up."

And then, for the third time—everything goes dark.

CHAPTER 25

I'm lying on something soft and prickly.

I take a deep breath in and the smell of dirt and fresh-cut grass fills my nostrils. My face is hot, and as I open my eyes the sun shines so bright, I have to close them again to avoid being blinded.

"Open your eyes, Sophie," a delicate female voice encourages.

"Too bright," I groan.

"They'll adjust," the voice laughs.

I feel soft hands lifting me effortlessly from the ground to stand me on my feet. I bring my fingers to my eyes, rubbing them until I feel like I can open them without being blinded. When I finally manage to see, a person is standing in front of me with a gentle smile on their face.

"Eve," I state knowingly.

"Hello, Sophie."

I still feel the hands who helped me stand, now keeping

me upright. I turn to them only to see two more ethereal-beings there supporting me.

"This is Maria, and I think you know Bridget," Eve says.

I nod out of pure reaction because I'm completely entranced by them. They're individually beautiful but oddly similar-looking despite their differences. Both women are young and bright-eyed, each with dark brown hair and eyes. They have curvy feminine figures and a glow about them that's unexplainable. Maria has dark ebony skin, whereas Bridget is pale and slightly freckled. Though they're soft and beautiful, their features are also sharp. It's hard to explain, but I understand why they were feared by those on earth. They are strong.

"Hi," I manage to say, not sure if I should hug them or wave awkwardly. They bob their heads in sync, smiling at me knowingly.

"You're probably wondering where you are," Eve says then.

I turn so I'm once again looking into her eyes. Her voice is like a melody still lingering in the air. Looking at her is like looking at an angel or something unfathomable. She's the light I had seen when I healed Ethan, but now a fully recognized being. Her hair is dark like the other

Alphas but very long, reaching past her waist. Her skin is a glowing olive color; she reminds me of Cleopatra or a Greek goddess. She is a woman, but also utterly undefinable. She has a fluid energy that seems to shine light through her being.

"Yes," I eventually answer her.

Eve purses her lips. "This is what some call The Garden of Eden."

I inhale sharply as I look around at our surroundings. I see why it's been called paradise. It's stunning. Lush, green, and peaceful. The air even smells floral due to the different species of flowers covering the earth. The sky is a vibrant sunset, full of pinks, purples, and reds, with a bright yellow and orange sun low in the sky. There's a light breeze that flows around us, keeping the air the perfect temperature. I detect little white dandelion seeds floating in the wind—*it's perfect*.

"It's real," I exhale.

Eve hums. "Well, this is paradise to you, but paradise to you is not a paradise to others."

"You mean it's not real?" I ask, confused.

"Some may call it the in-between. This is where your mind chose to take you. It would be different for others."

"Oh, so I'm like, dead?"

Maria and Bridget giggle lightly from behind me. Eve summons them to come stand next to her. They look like something you'd see in a movie about heaven. All standing in a divine beautiful row with soft, amused looks blanketing their features.

"You aren't dead, Sophie. Just in limbo for a bit while you're healing," Eve clarifies.

"I *was* shot then?"

"Yes."

"And I didn't die?"

"No. Ethan healed you."

I stutter a little. "He can do that now?"

"Yes. Much to his surprise. You would have healed eventually on your own, but now he can speed up the process for you," she says with a knowing smile.

"Is that why he died? So that I could give him a piece of my soul and he could help me?"

Eve reaches out and grabs my hand, sending a warmth through my fingers. I feel lighter then, like air.

"I think you have figured it out, but Ethan is your other half. He's pure in heart and soul. That man wanted to help you so badly. He understood how important you are to the world from the beginning. He's always believed in you, even before he knew you existed. We knew he could be of great help to you, but ultimately it was your choice to share your gifts with him; even if it was subconsciously," Eve admits.

My forehead screws up in thought. "What do you mean?"

Bridget steps forward and places a hand on my shoulder. "Sophie, we knew you could choose this path to share your gifts with Ethan, but it was you who ultimately wanted to share your burden with someone else. We didn't force this in any way. It was never written in stone."

"What? I don't think it's a burden!"

Bridget squeezes my shoulder. "But you do, sweet girl. It's nothing to be ashamed of. It's only natural to feel that way. You read my journal; you saw my life. You know I felt that way too," she assures me.

"But I didn't mean to dump this on him. I—can I take it back? He should have had a choice."

Maria comes forward then, her voice strong. "But he did choose it. He may not remember it, but he did. Though this wasn't meant to happen, we all hoped it would eventually. If there is one thing each Alpha has learned in their time on earth, it's that you can't save the world alone. Ethan is kind, empathetic, and sensitive, but also strong. In many ways, he's what Adam should have been, what Adam still could be," she finishes with a somber look at Eve.

Then it all came together. "Adam—you mean…"

Eve nods sharply. "In many ways, you created Ethan to help you. He's yours now."

I scoff. "He's not some animal that I can own!"

The Alphas laugh—it sounds like a symphony.

"I forget how sensitive you are to phrases like that. Your world is much different than ours," Eve says rather wistfully. "Ethan wanted this, just as much as you wanted it. He's your partner now. He will help you with all trials yet to come."

I grumble. "Why can't this be less complicated? Can't you just snap your fingers and everything starts over?" I ask Eve.

"We could do that, but then we'd never learn. We would all be doomed to just repeat ourselves again."

"Then what if I brought you all back with me? Could I do that?"

Eve nods. "You could try, but I won't allow it. You have us when you need us," she says, gently tapping my head. "You can call to us for help any time you wish, but I think you're doing just fine on your own."

I bark out a laugh. After what happened back in The Council room, I disagree. George is dead, Chris is gone; his parents are murderers and backstabbers. And don't forget the hoard of people either afraid of me or that view me as a god waiting for my next move. How is that *fine?*

Eve places a hand on my shoulder in assurance as if she can read my mind.

"This is a burden we all bear, Sophie. You are not responsible for anyone's actions but your own."

"I just don't understand, Eve," I say, searching her golden eyes. "If you created them, why can't we just fix it all?"

"It's true that I created earth, humanity and life as you know it. When I created humans, both Wishers and non-Wishers, I thought them to be perfect. I planned for them to be unflawed. But even I can make mistakes. You see, when I chose to have a companion, I created Adam. He completed me in a way I did not expect. Unfortunately, I saw him as my creation. I didn't think of him as a person with thoughts and fears. I did not see his flaws, just like I could not see mine. When I created more life, these errors were duplicated because I was blinded by my own naivety and wants. It was silly of me to think I could create perfection when I'm not perfect myself. I could not control them. I know that now," she says regretfully. "But—"

"But you love them too much to destroy them, you

452

always have," I say.

"Yes. Same old story, I suppose," she smiles rather sadly. "What happened with Adam is something I'll never be able to get over. But we can't keep dwelling on the past with regret. All we can do is learn and move forward. Wishers and non-Wishers all want the same thing. Now it's up to you and Ethan to right the wrongs. Do what the Alphas and I have not been able to do."

"You make it sound easy."

"I wish it could be easy for you. But if anyone can do it, it's you."

"Why me?" I say rather pathetically.

"You have us too, silly," Bridget giggles effervescently. "You have our wisdom and our light."

"And now you have Ethan," Maria adds a little suggestively. "He will help you more than you will ever know, you just have to let him."

"They are right—you know this," Eve says confidently. "Trust in yourself, Sophie. Trust in what you know and what you don't know. Ask for help and we will be there to guide you."

"Aren't there more of us?" I wonder, thinking I should have seen more than three of them.

"Yes," Eve gleams. "You'll meet many more Alphas in

due time, but for now, it's time for you to go back to reality—as one might say in your world," she finishes playfully.

I feel my chest tighten; I don't want to leave.

"You can't stay, Sophie. It's not your time," Eve responds.

I sigh. "I know."

"We'll be here, sweet girl," Bridget smiles before squeezing my hand.

"Goodbye for now, Sophie," Maria says gently.

"Remember you are the key," they chorus.

I try to say something else but can't. Instead my whole being is riddled with pain. Then once again, I'm falling into my darkness.

CHAPTER 26

In what seems like seconds, I'm jolting upright, air entering my lungs so fast that my whole chest burns. My eyes dart around the room frantically trying to place where I am and who's touching me. I hear words in my ear as I cough violently, trying to catch my breath.

"Breathe, Sophia, breathe."

"I'm…trying…" I wheeze, recognizing Ethan's voice

He laughs with relief in my ear. "I am glad that nearly dying does not change your spirit."

"Like anything ever could," I tease moments later, finally regaining my breath.

My eyes drink in our location. We're back in my bedroom suite at headquarters. Ethan is seated next to me, and the lights are partially out so it's not too bright, for which I'm thankful.

He hands me a glass of water, which I happily gulp down, letting it soothe my still-burning throat. After I finish it and set the glass on the bedside table, I turn to Ethan, studying him in the waning light. He's obviously exhausted. His hair is mussed from running his fingers through it in worry. I can tell he's bursting to talk, but all I want to do is hug him.

I launch myself at him, wrapping my arms tightly around his body. He mumbles something that I can't hear, before embracing me, one of his hands coming to gently cradle the back of my head to bring me closer. I bury my face in his neck so I'm able to breathe in his musky scent. He doesn't smell of cheap soap and spice any longer, now he smells like the Ethan I've come to know. I clutch him tighter, just grateful for him.

Once I have my fill, I start to plant kisses on the sensitive skin of his neck. I feel him squirm a little bit as I trail my kisses from his neck to cheek. After I plant them all over his face, I lean back, holding his cheeks beneath my dry hands. He's smiling a goofy grin, clearly confused but happy about my behavior. Just as he's about to try and talk again, I lean in and plant a kiss on his lips. I feel him chuckle, but before long he's kissing me back with equal enthusiasm.

Not liking our position, I push him sideways on the bed so that he's laying down, before crawling on top of him.

Our kiss breaks at the movement, causing our noses to collide clumsily. We laugh together before he pecks my now swollen mouth one more time. He gazes at me, his eyes dilated, and skin flushed.

He reaches up to brush a stray hair behind my ear. "I think that is how you should greet me every time you wake up," he teases.

I grin. "If you're lucky."

I lean in to lock lips again for a few more moments before he rolls me over so he's now on top. When I go to the hem of his shirt to lift it over his head, he grabs my hands.

"No?" I ask, quirking my eyebrow.

He gives me a lopsided smile. "Only you, Sophia."

"Sophie," I correct. He just rolls his eyes at me. *Yep—I definitely wore off on him.*

"*Sophie*. Do you not want to know what happened?"

"I already know," I tell him, my hands going to his shirt again.

He stops them once more. "You do?"

He really is the first man I've met who would rather talk than have sex.

"Yep! I talked to the Alphas and they told me what you did," I say with a smile.

"Really?" he says in wonder, still hovering over me.

I try to pull him back down, but instead he hoists me up so we're now in a sitting position. I guess I'm not getting any at the moment. I run my hands through my hair and cringe, discovering it's quite greasy.

"How long was I out for?"

"A few days."

"Excuse me?" I exclaim. "But how?"

"I guess you needed it. You scared the crap out of everyone though. I knew you were going to be fine, that we just had to wait for you to be ready to wake up," he says softly.

"That's bananas. It felt like only minutes where I was. I can't believe it was a few days!"

"Where did you go?" he prods, his eyes curious.

"Apparently a place that is an in-between of sorts, my paradise if you will. It was beautiful," I reminisce peacefully.

He plays with a piece of my hair for a moment. "Eve was there?"

I nod. "Eve, Maria and Bridget. They told me you healed me."

"I did. I was not sure if it would work, but I had to try. You know you should have just let that bastard shoot me," he huffs.

458

"And what, kill you?"

"You know that cannot happen," he says stubbornly.

"Well, I didn't know that then. I know that now. How do you know?" I prod.

"Eve told me."

"Eve told you?" I gasp.

"When I healed you, she came to me. I guess it was not really her, it was more like a ghost of her. That is the best way I can describe it. She explained to me very simply how I was like you now, at least in many ways."

I take a deep breath, looking into his eyes to see if I can read his thoughts. He doesn't look scared or fearful. He looks…*content.*

"I'm sorry," I mutter.

His face contorts, looking confused, "Why?"

"You have to live forever or die by fire. It's not exactly something most people would want."

"Sophie…"

I grab his hands. "I know what you're going to say. The Alphas told me you chose it, but I healed you and I feel like I didn't give you a choice. Now you're stuck here, fighting this with me, and I—I didn't want that for you."

I pull away from him suddenly and stand up, not wanting to deal with my conflicting emotions at the moment. I glance at the clock to find its mid-morning. Before I get far, however, Ethan's up and grabbing me around the waist. When I try to push him off half-heartedly, he holds steady.

"I am not letting you put this on yourself," he says, forcing my chin up to look at him, but I keep my eyes down. "Look at me, Sophie, please," he pleads.

At the tone of his voice, I can't help but look into his eyes. I'm surprised to find him smiling widely, that damn dimple more prominent than it has been in days.

"You are stupid sometimes, you know that?" he blurts out.

"Excuse me?" I scoff, not sure how to react.

He chuckles. "Now I am only going to say this once, so please get it through that stubborn skull of yours. I know it is soon, and I know it is crazy, and I know you probably do not want to hear it, but—I love you." He pauses for a brief moment, the words suspended in the air. He inhales. "I wanted to say it when I was dying, and you stopped me, but I am saying it now. I understand that people generally do not fall in love with each other in less than two weeks, but I think we both know this relationship is more than slightly out of the ordinary."

I can't help the very unattractive sound that escapes my

460

lips. "You can say that again."

His lips upturn, the grip on my waist tightening. "But I do love you, and I did choose this. When Eve asked me if this was the life I wanted, I did not even have to think about it. You know how much I love Wishers; how much I love humanity. And you know how much I believe in the power of our gifts, and what they can do for the world. This is my chance, not only to help you but to actually do something with my life...to prove my worth," he says honestly.

I sigh in defeat. "You already are worthy, Ethan," I assure him. "But you know people are going to come after you now? Everyone is going to have a lot of questions."

"I know, but all that does not matter. I hope you can understand that I had to say yes. I did not do it just for you. I did it for me, too."

I mull over what he's saying for a few moments, looking at him with curiosity.

"I don't understand, Ethan. Are you just remembering that Eve gave you a choice? You didn't mention it before."

"She brought it to my attention when I was healing you is all. Honestly, I know a lot of things now that I did not know before, but I am not going to question it. I have never seen things more clearly in my life. This was supposed

461

to happen. I do not want to fight it. We have more important things to battle than our destiny."

I groan. "Destiny, huh?"

"Why do I get the feeling you knew all this information already? Do you think I secretly regret my choice? Because I do not." he says stubbornly.

I place my hands on my hips. "You think you have me all figured out, don't you?"

He nods. "We do share a soul now, you realize."

"Oh god," I say, throwing my head back dramatically. "This is *sooo* cheesy, and *sooo* weird."

"It is only weird if you make it weird," he counters.

"Ethan," I balk. "Just because we share this now, doesn't mean you have to love me."

Hurt flashes across his eyes, and I immediately feel a little embarrassed at how self-conscious that sounds.

"I want to pretend you never even said that," he says flatly.

"I'm sorry, okay? I'm not used to things moving so fast."

He exhales. "I know, but this is different, and you know it. How could you think that?"

"I'm scared. Am I not allowed to be scared in all of this?"

462

He brushes his thumb across my cheek in a loving gesture, causing a pleasant feeling to course through me.

"You are. I am scared too, you know. However, when I remember I have you, I am not as scared anymore."

I laugh and push him with my shoulder.

"So cheesy."

"I was trying to be serious," he says through a puppy-pout.

"I know."

I take a deep breath and bring my hand to his cheek. He kisses my palm before looking into my eyes. I tremble at the depth of emotion that I find there.

"You really love me, don't you?"

"I keep trying to tell you," he grins.

"Would it be rude if I said thank you?" I tease.

He chuckles. "Not exactly what a guy wants to hear, but if you are not ready to say it yet, you do not have too."

"Just say it, Sophie," I hear a collective voice chime in my head and I almost roll my eyes at them. The Alphas are obviously on Ethan's side.

I let out a breath and make a choice. "I suppose I'll just have to say it—I love you, too."

Ethan gives me a funny look. "You suppose, or you know?"

"I love you," I finally breathe out, the tension easing from my body. I meant it that time.

"Was that really so hard?" he questions, a big toothy grin now plastered on his face.

I bring my hand up to place my finger in his dimple. "Just shut up and kiss me before I either slap you or leave."

When his demanding lips collide with mine, I smile against them. I could get used to this.

CHAPTER 27

I could kiss Ethan forever...

Sadly, forever only lasts a few minutes when he pulls away abruptly.

"Oh! I almost forgot!" he cries before snapping his fingers. In his hands appears a piece of chocolate cake with a candle. "Happy Birthday, Sophie," he says warmly.

"That's today?"

He nods. "I told you that you were out for a few days."

"Nice snapping, by the way," I smirk.

"Dramatic effect, right?" he adds playfully.

I laugh with him before looking at the single candle burning, then back up to Ethan's smiling face.

"Make a wish," he smirks.

I laugh hard in realization. "It all makes sense now why people do that!"

He gives me his—*really, Sophia?*—look before telling me, "Just do it, Sophie. Blow out the candle."

"Alright, alright," I snicker.

I glance back at the candle, then to Ethan's face again as he smiles down at me lovingly. I know exactly what I want.

I squeeze my eyes shut and blow out the candle. When I open my eyes, we're standing back in my cabin in Iron Lake. Before I know it, I'm being charged by a furry black and white blur. I fall to my knees as I let Laker attack me with doggy kisses. I chuckle, his excited barking and whining ringing throughout the cabin.

"Hey, boy! I missed you, too," I cry, tears filling my eyes.

I peek at Ethan as I try to defend myself from all the slobber. He's watching me happily, still holding the piece of chocolate cake.

"I should have known this is what you would wish for," he smiles.

"Where else would I go?" I shrug.

He puts the cake down on the counter before coming to sit next to me. Laker doesn't hesitate before jumping on him with gusto. Surprised, Ethan falls backward, giving Laker full access to his face. Ethan tries to fend him off but fails miserably.

"A little help?" he cries with laughter.

"Not a chance," I smile wide.

After a few more slobbery kisses, I rescue Ethan. At least Laker likes him, that's the most important thing.

Ethan stands, brushing off his clothes and wiping at his face. "Bathroom is right there," I say, pointing to my right.

Ethan nods and disappears into the washroom. I go and quickly wash my face in the kitchen sink before giving Laker a treat and another bear hug. I stroll out to the porch and sit on my swing, looking out at the lake. There's a light summer breeze, and I couldn't be happier that I'm finally home. Laker lies at my feet, content to have me back as the birds sing their familiar song. It's heaven.

When I hear Ethan exit the bathroom, I call out for him to join me. A few seconds later he's beside me, our legs touching. I join our hands, studying our fingers now puzzled together.

"It really is beautiful here," he exhales.

"I know. Too bad we can't stay longer," I whisper sadly.

"I am sorry. I wish we could."

"It's not your fault, it's not anyone's…"

"You will be able to come back to sleep here, you know? And to see your family and Ana if you want. But we have a lot to deal with back in Massachusetts."

"I know," I sigh. "Speaking of, what happened after I

got shot?"

He tightens his grip on my hand. "I was wondering when you were going to ask."

"I was trying to avoid it for as long as possible. I figured if it were urgent, you would have stopped me from kissing you," I quip playfully.

"True. Though, I am sure people are wondering if you are all right. You really scared everyone."

"I'm sure you did too. I take it they all know about you?"

"Unfortunately. Albert and Camilla witnessed it. There was really no way to prevent that. But they are in lockdown now, under surveillance constantly. I wanted to make them disappear like their dreadful son, but I knew you would be upset if I did that."

"I know that idea is tempting," I say. What about your mom and sister?

"They are in shock. Not just about my new-found gifts, but about my—"

"Oh my God, Ethan!" I yell, cutting him off. "I'm such an idiot! I'm so sorry, I can't believe I didn't say anything!"

I feel incredibly stupid. The man has just lost his father and the first thing I do is try and suck his face off.

"It is really okay, Sophie," he assures me. "A lot has

happened. He was shot right before you were, then you were unconscious and healing for the last three days."

"No, it's not ok."

I notice the sadness he's been trying to hide appear in his eyes. I'm at a loss for words.

"Are you okay?" I ask, even though I know it's a stupid question.

He shrugs. "He was not the man I thought he was. He was never perfect, but I did not think he was evil. After everything that has happened, I honestly do not even know if I feel sad about it. What kind of person does that make me?" His voice falters.

"You're not bad, Ethan," I say, brushing away a small tear that escapes from his eye. "You obviously feel something."

He clears his throat and looks out at the lake longingly. I see him holding it all in, but I don't want to push.

"What about headquarters? Is everything good with Jackson and the guards?" I ask to change the subject.

"Everything is great there actually. We were able to attend to all the injuries. Luckily nobody else was seriously hurt. I healed a few gashes and black eyes, but otherwise things are getting back on track."

"You healed them, too?"

"I felt partially responsible. Plus, if they were on The Alliance's side, it helped sway them in our favor. You know, show them what our gifts can do for them. That we are not scary."

"It's nice, you know," I murmur as I play with his fingers.

"What?"

"That it's we now instead of just me. It feels —"

"Easier?" he guesses.

"In a way."

"It may not seem like it, but things are going to get better. I am here to help you now, and so are my mother and sister—and Mary of course."

"What does your family think about everything?"

"We talked a little, but mostly I was with you the whole time, or trying to sort out all the guards and figure out who the members of The Alliance are. But everything is going to take time."

"Jackson has been helpful?"

"He has. He and several of the guards have been a great help in compiling a database of Alliance members. Now we just need to find a way to talk to all of them and convince them to leave The Alliance behind."

"Oh, just that?" I say sarcastically.

He grins. "We also need to decide what we want to do with Albert and Camilla."

I throw my head back and grumble. "Let's worry about that tomorrow, it is my birthday after all."

"That it is. Do you feel any different? Normally this is the day in a Wisher's life that is most celebrated."

"Not really...Just tired. Does that count?"

Ethan laughs. "Tired? You slept for almost three days."

"Not that kind of tired," I say plainly.

"I know what you mean."

A cool breeze blows by, and I can't help the chills that run up my spine. I shiver and lean farther into Ethan's side. He wraps his arm around me, hugging me to him tightly. I watch as the trees sway back and forth in the breeze, an easy silence enveloping us. Eventually Laker jumps up on the swing, squeezing in next to me before falling asleep.

I can't stop the events of the last couple of weeks from invading my mind. I try to relax and let it all fall away, but my brain won't let me. I vibrate again, this time for a reason unknown. The feeling that something is coming overtakes me, and my stomach sinks.

"Are you ok?" Ethan asks when he feels the change in my energy.

"Yeah..."

I feel him studying me but I don't look at him. The breeze picks up for just a moment and then stops, like when a tornado is coming. Laker stirs at my side, his head perking up, suddenly alert and at the ready.

"What is it, boy?" I ask him, scratching behind his ears.

Goosebumps break out on my arms, and Laker jumps off the bench, barking like he's seen or heard something in the woods.

"Sophie?" Ethan asks anxiously.

"Shhh," I say, putting a finger to my lips.

My stomach churns as the lake turns deadly silent. Everything is still. The only sounds present are Laker's barking, and my heart drumming in my ears. I stand and look out at the woods. Ethan comes up next to me to look off in the direction both Laker and I are now staring.

"Someone's here," I whisper to Ethan, although I see in his eyes he already knew.

He reaches for my hand. When I feel a gun appear in my palm, I look over to Ethan, who already has his game-face on. A gun in his hand as well.

"Be ready," he says quietly.

I quickly grab Laker by the collar and push him into the house. The last thing I want is for him to go lunging at whoever's coming. I don't want him to get shot or hurt either.

I return to Ethan, and we wait. When the sound of footsteps meets our ears, I tense. As they grow closer, twigs snap, and the brush moves erratically. Ethan's gun is cocked, ready to fire at whoever is making their way toward us.

My breath catches as the top of a head comes into view, and I point my gun, mimicking Ethan's stance.

"I love you," Ethan murmurs.

"I love you, too," I whisper back with a sad smile.

A man comes forward, dirty and dazed, staggering to the front yard before dropping to the ground a few yards from the porch. He's on his hands and knees gasping for air like he's drowning. When it's clear he doesn't have a weapon, I start to walk toward him, my heart hammering.

"Be careful," Ethan orders, following close behind me.

I stand in front of the worn man, his face turned toward the ground as he tries to catch his breath.

"Who are you?" I demand very clearly.

When he doesn't answer, I get closer to him, trying to see his face.

"She asked you a question," Ethan says from my side. "Who are you?"

The man finally raises his head and I gasp, dropping my gun to the ground and falling to my knees. It can't be…

"Dad?" I cry.

"Hi, Sophie."

ACKNOWLEDGMENTS

Where in the world do I even begin? To everyone who made this book possible—I love you more than my words can express.

To my family—Randy, Linda, and Tanya—I am here because you believed in me. Because you still believe in me. When my life was the hardest, you never gave up on me. Instead you cheered me on and bought me groceries and coffee. I will be forever grateful that you support my dreams and never tell me to stop.

To M.J., you are the best friend a woman could ask for. You encouraged me and held my hand through this process. Your advice and wisdom were invaluable to me, and I'll forever kiss the ground you walk on (ha-ha). But in all seriousness, thank you. From the bottom of my heart—I love you. And to Pete, thank you for letting M.J. spend hours with me on this book, and for giving me your loving thoughts and energy. I felt it every step of the way.

To Naomi, thank you for working hours and hours on my beautiful book cover. I changed my mind a million times, but you made it happen. Thank you for being a kind and generous friend, you are one-of-a-kind!

I need to thank my friends Sally, Cristina, and Adrienne. You were there with me when I went back to write this book, and you've stayed with me—cheering me on for over two years! Without your phone calls and your beta-reads, I would not be here today. All I can say is—we made it!

To my high school friends, Lanae, Katelyn, Katie, April, David, and Tyler… I love you. Your support since we were 15 is something I cherish more than you will ever know. April—you really made this book shine—you are my angel. I also can't forget my Cali squad: Valerie, Mike, Kara, Erica, Rachael, Linda, Katy, and every friend who's had to listen to me go on about this book for the last couple of years. You are amazingly supportive!

To my editor and beta readers, Gabriella Tutino, Lena, Lisa, Kelsey, Adrienne, Sally, Randy, Linda, Tanya, M.J., and Mark, thank you for your hard work and feedback. *W.I.S.H. Revelations* would not be what it is today without your immense help. As well, thank you to the writer's community on Instagram and Twitter. You all are so sweet and supportive—I hope this book made you smile.

To Desiree, Mia, Gianna, and Paulie—thank you for allowing me into your life and home. Without this safe space, my words would have never been put to paper.

Lastly, I'd like to thank coffee. This book was written by your smooth taste of encouragement.

Thank you, thank you, thank you, to each and every person that was involved in this process. I really love you all so much.

Now go turn your wishes in to reality!

Xo,

Kayla

p.s. I love you, Grandma & Grandpa White!

Printed in Great Britain
by Amazon